I0590547

The Nightfall Rising First Gomer Wars (Book 1)

By Michael S. Pauley

Executive Press Ltd
Edmonton AB T6A 0H7
Canada
343-554-1210

Paperback ISBN: 979-8-9987482-1-9
Ebook ISBN: 979-8-9987482-2-6

DEDICATION

This book is for my lovely bride, Elise, who is my muse, confidant, researcher, editor, agent, and chief science advisor. There is no question in my mind, her scientific or "egghead" skills and knowledge were critical to the completion of this tome, and they will continue to be just as critical to the others that will follow in the future. I have assured her that if there were any flaws in the science, they would be my errors. If on the other hand, you feel that the science is "spot on", then I would humbly acknowledge her expertise in the area.

My work is also for my wonderful daughter, Jennifer, who, like Elise, added more to the book than she will ever be able to fathom. Her skills at keeping the real world at bay, keeping me organized, and keeping me moving forward were invaluable. The number of times she was able to buy me a few minutes was vital in my being able to finish this work. She often jokes that she is CDO, because she must have the OCD in alphabetical order. Well, if that is her curse, for me it was a blessing. I cannot thank her enough!

You may find as you read this book that two characters stand out as being critical to the main character's sanity. Just as Leah and Chris keep General Patrick "out of the weeds", my spirit guides, Elise, and Jennifer, have done the same for me. To them, as with all things in my life, this original work and the "second edition" are both dedicated.

Michael S. Pauley,
Lexington, South Carolina
June 15, 2013 and
February 23, 2021

TABLE OF CONTENTS

SECTION 1   THE GOMERS INVADE:
THEY OWN THE NIGHT

SECTION 2   THE AMERICAN CAMPAIGN

SECTION 3   BUILDING A GLOBAL FORCE

SECTION 4   TAKING BACK THE
NIGHT: THE GLOBAL CAMPAIGN

APPENDICES

SECTION 1

THE GOMERS INVADE:

THEY OWN THE NIGHT

Chapter I.

It began as a mere pin prick of light in a part of the sky that is normally reserved for the deep infinite darkness of space. With each succeeding evening, this pin prick gradually grew in intensity until it equaled the glow of a distant star. At first, it drew absolutely no attention from anyone, to include the banks of telescopes and satellites that look outward into the heavens searching for the objects that could well have the earth in its sights. Instead, it would be an older retired astronomer who would finally point out this new anomaly. As the old man gazed through his backyard telescope, he noticed that not only was the light growing in intensity, it appeared to be wavering on its track. Assuming he had discovered a new phenomenon worthy of reporting, he contacted several of his old friends at NASA. Shocked and amazed, they directed all their resources towards this new object that was now clearly hurtling towards us. Unfortunately, their efforts would be too little and far too late for us to avoid the inevitable events that would change our lives and the lives of our children, for generations to come.

When the news broke, it was just another little blurb, something hidden in the SciTech portions of various news outlets on the internet. For most, it was just another newly discovered anomaly in our skies which, while interesting, was not something so unheard of to spark any foreboding or even significant interest. As a society, we were far too busy following our social media, the endless reality TV shows, and the 24/7 news cycles about politics or the various wars and conflicts that always seem to circle our globe. It seemed that very few of us were interested enough to peer into the dark void or even show any curiosity about what was coming. This oddly shaped light with the wobbling track was just one more light in the night sky. How could it compete with whether a star in Hollywood wore a certain bathing suit as she frolicked nearly naked on the beaches of the Riviera, or with the latest marriage or divorce of yet another celebrity? No, we knew we were the masters of our universe and, therefore, life was simple and devoid of any threat beyond what we already knew about. As with most things, we were dead wrong.

The first real sign of trouble came when the light appeared to grow significantly in size to the few of us who chose to be observers. I can recall standing out on my back deck, sipping a scotch, and gazing into the sky, wondering at the power of the universe. Being somewhat curious, I was looking into the portion of the sky mentioned in an online article, with the hope of being able to see this marvel of science. As I looked up, I would watch the light and ponder what it could mean. I noticed that the intensity of the light seemed to change, and there was just a slightly ominous cast to it. For some reason, that to this day I cannot explain, my observations triggered a small feeling of concern or sense of foreboding. Assuming it was just paranoia, I made it a point to start watching this thing every evening. That first night, it was just the size of a small star at a great distance, but then I noticed that over the next several days, it seemed to be growing. Each night, the star would appear to grow in size, and I would stand on my deck, sipping my scotch, and just marvel at the show. I could swear this thing almost "winked" at me in the dark sky.

That last evening, as the world slipped from its blissful ignorance into stark terror, I specifically recall that the light was so eerie looking that I hollered for my bride to come "look at this damn thing". It was much larger in the sky and had a rather odd color to it. While reflected light is one thing, this object seemed to be emitting its own unnatural color. As we both watched, it appeared to change direction, as if it were being manipulated by some unknown force, and then it returned to the original course. We both looked at each other to confirm what we had just witnessed. Looking back on it, we were completely mesmerized by what we were seeing, so much so that I hardly noticed the incessant ringing of my cell phone.

I guess here it would be a good place to digress a little to mention our respective backgrounds. My lovely wife, Leah, is an accomplished schoolteacher. Extremely academic, she is one of those special people who can excel at anything she wishes to pursue. Her skills in her "primary" field of the English language are easily eclipsed by her even greater skills in both math and science. Skills that, over the course of the next few years, would serve us well and probably do a great deal to save our lives. In fact, it was her love of the sciences that led to our standing outside on this cool early spring evening observing the newly found astral phenomenon. My professional standing was more of a mixed bag. I had retired once from military service and was attempting to pursue my second career as an attorney. This new career lasted only for a short time before a return to the old career was mandated by world events. In what would be two more wars and several new conflicts, I was now over ten years older and still tied to the military as a Reserve Officer. I was far more fortunate than most in my new field of "Military Intelligence" because my progression led me ultimately to the temporary rank of Lieutenant General. I was quite resigned to the fact that this rank was more honorary than meaningful, and frankly, it was significantly more than I ever wanted or needed. I was in command of very little but, instead, I was simply a face to put out to our allies to either negotiate a better deal or to gather intelligence through the "back door". Most of these efforts were focused primarily on several of my old friends in other nations, most of whom I had served as a young special operator several decades ago in the darker corners of our globe.

So, on that fine March evening, I was standing there on the deck with that glass of good scotch, just another old man who had grown extremely weary from watching his fellow man constantly engage in ludicrous acts for idiotic reasons. Simply put, I was an old soldier that would always be ready to run towards the sound of gunfire, but who now could only run at a pace that would cause a younger man to laugh. On that fateful evening, you would have found a General without an Army, at the twilight of his career, watching the opening salvo in what would be the worst single military defeat in recorded history. Sadly, none of us knew or understood what was about to happen, but we all could see that what was coming was not something normal or expected. Oh, sure, we had all seen the television specials in popular culture about near-earth events, asteroids, meteors, and the trails of comets. Usually, these specials, and the discussions that went with them, were all designed to scare people into being more aware of the universe around us, and mainly to raise money to fund the projects that would detect and stop these events from ending our existence. Sadly, none of these television specials were focused on what was coming.

Of course, we also saw movies about space aliens and alien predators that have pervaded our culture for decades. What we did not see were specials and movies about what to do if this was not just a natural event or was, in fact, something quite alien in nature. In those days, before that spring evening, those who spoke of aliens or UFOs were often the subject of laughter or derision. Unfortunately, today there is no more laughter about such things. Not anymore. Now, these statements are simply acknowledged with just a nod of the head or the passing comment of "no kidding!" On this fine evening, we just did not see that the worst was coming, like a runaway freight train, or that there would be very little that we could do to stop it.

As I looked at my wife, she finally broke eye contact, and simply said, "Honey, your phone!" She looked back upwards into the night sky, and I dutifully answered the phone, while still casting my gaze back at the odd light. It had grown now, and I noticed that it was growing to the size of a very small rock. The voice on the other end of the phone line was, well, in a word, panicked. The disbelief and the tone of the caller immediately made me look away from the sky and focus on the conversation. "Sir, we've got a problem!" The duty officer was slightly out of breath and, you could tell, quite scared. I asked him what was going on and his response sent an instantaneous chill up my spine.

"Sir, the Chairman has activated the COG plan, and you are to get your family prepared to move within the next four hours, less if you can swing it." I responded with disbelief. "The Continuity of Government Plan? Really?" The duty officer said, "Yes, sir," and then continued, "Sir, we are sending you a car, driver, and a force protection level IV security detail. Just pack light. Space is at a premium." Then, almost as an afterthought, he said, "OH, and the Chairman said for you to immediately deactivate your locator on the phone and keep your personal weapon handy. I'm also to tell you that you are to be prepared to assume command of NORTHCOM once we can get you evacuated to their headquarters." He then added a sobering comment, "Sir, we aren't sure of any details, but it looks as though there is something VERY weird going on in Washington. We've already lost track of most of our key personnel, and the Chairman is going nuts trying to raise anyone at the Pentagon or anywhere else in Washington. It is like they just disappeared off the planet!"

Naturally, I had a ton of questions but could only squeak out the response that I could be ready within the hour, and to keep me updated with any changes. As I raced into the house, my wife was asking me, "What is going on?" I gave her the same speech I was given, and she scampered to grab our "go to hell bag". Something my bride has always made sure we maintained around the house was a pre-packed bag for just about any emergency. Whether it was a hurried response to a death in the family or a hurricane evacuation, my bride had it covered in one of her several "go to hell bags". I finished throwing on a field uniform and tossed a few of my extra uniforms into my kit bag. Then I grabbed my web gear and began my weapons check. I chose several of my old standby favorites for personal protection, and then I took the time to check, load, and give my bride her pistol, just in case. Her pistol was the one I was issued when I was first promoted to Brigadier General and, frankly, I hated it. She, on the other hand, liked the 9mm, while I preferred the more traditional and hard-hitting Model 1911A1, classic.45 automatic.

In the meantime, my wife had changed clothes and was now decked out in blue jeans, a warm sweatshirt, and boots with her weapon already strapped to her leg. I looked at her and asked if she was "headed to the OK corral". Her reply was anything but glib.

"No, smart ass, from what you've said, something not only isn't right, but right now my woman's intuition is off the charts." When she said this, and almost as an afterthought, I found my old 12 Gauge shotgun, checked it, and then tossed it into my kit bag. My only thought was that "you never know when a scatter gun will make a difference". Again, I still do not know what triggered that thought but, as it turned out, it was a good choice that would probably save us less than 12 hours.

During this entire time, as we were getting ourselves together, millions of Americans, to include us, tried to listen to the news to discover what was happening. I think what drove the severity of the situation home to me was that the news went from a clear signal describing small but odd events, to simply no longer transmitting anything that you could watch or really hear. It was obvious, even to someone that only followed the entertainment news, that something was wrong. Even the local channels were completely ghost, with lots of static and just enough sound to convey the clear message that something unexpected was happening around the country and that the impact was huge. When I checked my cell phone again, it was completely useless.

Then, suddenly, the power went out. It was a complete failure too, not just the house lights and electrical things that were plugged into a wall, but a failure that included anything that required a battery. It had even taken out the regular phone lines. I listened as my wife muttered, "Well, doesn't that suck! Hey, Mike, come take a look at this?"

At this point, I was no longer curious about the power or the phone. There was little question that these things were the clear sign of an electro-magnetic pulse failure for any item that required electricity to function. Whether this was global or local, I had no way of knowing. What I did realize was that our leaving with a driver or the arrival of a security team just became very unlikely and that, if we were to survive, it would be on us to make it happen.

When my wife called me, I stepped back out on the deck and instinctively looked up. The light in the sky was now about the size of a small moon, and it was no longer wavering. Emitting from it were various other solid streaks of light that, at first, appeared to be like falling stars, but were moving much more slowly and far too deliberately to be "falling". I recognized immediately that they were moving like aircraft and that the odds of them being friendly were just about nil. I told my wife, "Grab your other weapon, grab your bag, and let's get the hell off this deck." Without a second's hesitation, she did exactly what I was doing, which was to put on my web gear, chamber a round in my

M-4 carbine, and grab my kit bag. The only difference was that she was doing the same thing with my old 9 mm and, at the same time, snatching her infamous "go-to-hell bag". Without any further hesitation, we were both down the back deck stairs, across the yard, and into the woods beyond in less than 2 minutes. Once we were well under cover, we took up a vantage point near a drainage culvert that was within sight of the house and road, but still well inside the wood line. It was there that we took up our initial positions and waited. We did not have to wait long.

Fortunately, I had previously identified this section of woods as a good hiding spot if the need ever arose to move quickly, but I had no idea that those few minutes spent looking around several years ago would now be so critical. Within a few minutes of assuming our positions, we noticed that the sky was now completely black. We could no longer see the stars or the moon, but we could both sense that there was some sort of movement right over our house. Something was there and even though we could not make out the size or shape exactly, it was above our home and not moving. A small shaft of light began to sweep over the house and then began a sweep that moved ever outward. Immediately thinking of our own infrared capabilities, I whispered to my wife, "Get back into that culvert and lie down as low as you can go in the standing water." What was obvious to me was that something or someone was now searching for us, and while it was not a good solution, it was the only one we had at that moment. When we got settled in the cold water, we were each facing the opposite end of the culvert with our weapons ready. After what seemed like hours but was probably only minutes, we heard rustling right outside where we were hiding. The movement was hardly perceptible, at least at first, but then it became more regular and was clearly headed towards our hiding place.

Peering into the darkness, I was about to release the safety on my weapon when a small cat appeared at the entrance of our cold, damp hiding place. Taking a deep breath and slowly relaxing to stave off the shivering, it was quite apparent that we were not the only ones that wanted to seek shelter from whatever was hovering over our house. The cat was looking inside and seemed to make the decision that it was going to climb into the culvert with us. Then before it could climb in, the small light appeared and the cat suddenly just disappeared, almost like it had evaporated or disintegrated. Sensing rather than seeing it, we both knew there was most certainly something outside that was observing or inspecting the concrete tube in which we were hiding. I removed the safety and took aim at the approximate center of mass that comprised the opening of our concrete tube. When I did, I nudged my bride and pointed to the end of our concrete culvert. Leah also quietly assumed the same position, ready, aiming outwards in her direction. There was little doubt that if we were to die in place, we were each going to do our level best to take a few of them with us. We both took aim and waited for any sign of movement or even a little sound that would let us know that we were being observed. Again, the minutes drug into what seemed to be hours, and we waited and shivered in the cold. I could feel Leah's warmth against me and feel her breathing, otherwise, there was nothing but the cold permeating all around us.

After what seemed like hours of misery, I noticed the beginning of some natural light outside our culvert. It was not much, but it did seem natural, and then I realized that I was seeing moonlight. I leaned into my bride and made a signal to her that I was moving to the end of the tube where I could maybe see what was going on outside. She nodded, and I began to slowly crawl forward. As I neared the end of our hiding place, I could see more natural light and some shadows from the trees. I hoped that this meant that the sky over our house might now be clear. At the very least, moonlight was now appearing, which had not been present before, in what otherwise was a perfectly clear night. Taking care not to reveal my position, I began the slow, deliberate process of doing a survey of the more immediate area and then expanding my observation to encompass more of the terrain outwards from our location. Finally, after satisfying myself that we were at least clear as far as the house, I slowly left the culvert and took a position to better observe the area. Nothing was visible and nothing appeared to be disturbed. The sky was again clear, and the only movement around us was from the light cool breeze that was now sweeping through our portion of the woods.

After waiting and listening, I finally emerged further from our hiding place to get a look around us. I took my binoculars and did a full 360-degree sweep of the area. Again, nothing unusual or out of place was around us at all. There was more waiting and listening, and I again swept the area just to make sure that there was still nothing unusual or out of the ordinary. Eventually, I ducked back into the culvert and made sure that my wife knew it was me. Still not wishing to take any further chances, we waited until dawn before leaving our apparent safe zone. Finally, with the first streaks of dawn, we both moved out to examine the area and to visually confirm what we already knew. We were alone. In fact, we were so alone that nothing stirred around us. There were no neighborhood dogs or cats to greet us, no barking in the distance or any human sounds that could be attributed to our suburb at that time of the day. This silence was frightening and extremely disconcerting. It took far longer than normal, but we eventually heard a single bird begin its morning song. We then noticed some other animals emerging from their hiding places, but we still did not move from our own until we saw a family of squirrels begin leaving the trees and chattering at us in the morning light.

We approached our house very quietly, cautiously and, when I pushed through the door into our living room, it was exactly like when I was a young soldier trying to use stealth in entering a house in a foreign war zone. Inside the living room everything appeared relatively untouched, and the only signs of life were where we had hurriedly evacuated the house the evening before. We still had no electricity and the phones were completely inoperative but otherwise, it looked normal. The only real good news was that the water system was still working and my wife began to load up on what I was sure would become a very precious commodity in the coming days. As she was getting the water bottles filled, I was checking the status of the cell phones when I heard it. It was a small sound that took me a second to register. It was the same faint but frightening click that I had heard before when someone stepped on a land mine or triggered a trip wire. I signaled my wife to "freeze" as I slowly pulled the old trench gun out. I pulled the slide back as quietly as possible, chambering a round, and then started to move towards the sound upstairs. It was then that I first saw our enemy. He was going through some of my cabinets in my home office, and why he had not heard us before was something I filed away for future reference. As he looked up, I took in his appearance but before I could fully process it, he raised his weapon towards me, and I immediately fired.

The sound of the shotgun in my office was truly deafening and the impact on the intruder was even more devastating. He appeared to literally explode, with his head disappearing in an instant and the rest crumbling like a pile of dust to the floor. What was left was not enough to really examine, but whatever the hell it was did leave us two important pieces of information. The first was that it could be killed, and the second was that its weapon was now in my possession. I grabbed what I could and we left the house for the last time at almost a dead run. The only thing I knew for sure was that, despite being surprised, his friends would no doubt be back to check on him or to pick him up. I surely did not want to be there when that happened, so speed was now going to be of the essence.

Taking our supplies, which were now supplemented with warmer dry clothes and all the water and food we could carry, we headed to another location that was several miles from where we lived and well away from our original culvert. It was not necessarily an unpleasant trip since the further away from the house we traveled the deeper into the woods we were, and the more normal things seemed to us. The animals were acting normal here and there were even birds floating in the morning air. We moved quietly, but with some speed. The last thing we wanted was to be anywhere near where the house was located. When we did take breaks, we huddled close together, and Leah would whisper questions about "Where are our babies?", "Do you think they're okay?", "What about out grandson?" Each time, all I could do was shrug and hug her closer to me. I did not have any answers, and like her, I was wracked with the same concerns.

Eventually, we found another very well-concealed location and were able to build up and hide our supply cache of food and water. As I began to look around our new "home", I was confident that this series of large rocks and crevices located within a quarter mile of the Interstate Highway and near the high transmission power lines would offer both overhead cover and concealment. It had the added plus of being a point where we could observe anyone who might approach our position over land or in the air. It was here that we waited and enjoyed our first food in about 12 hours. After a semi-decent meal, we then settled down to take stock of what we would do next and what we would do to try and locate our children who were scattered to the four winds when the attack came. I was also trying to process why our home had been specifically targeted and just exactly what this alien weapon I was carrying. I just hoped it did not have a form of locator on it, which is why I was almost tempted to dump it. Instead, with that locator in mind, I set it in a location that would allow me to use it as bait for anyone who might be looking specifically to find it.

The more I pondered the selection of our home, the more it became clear to me that there was no similar activity around any of our neighbors' houses. While there did not seem to be any sign of life at our neighbors' homes, there also was nothing to indicate that someone had specifically hovered over their houses either. I was seriously pondering these things and trying to put it all together in my mind when I apparently fell asleep fast. I have no idea how long

I slept, but when my bride woke me, it was still daylight. Shaking the cobwebs from my mind, I heard my wife whisper, "There are people moving around down the hill from us, and it appears to me that they are coming our way."

As I peered over the rocks, I got my binoculars back from my bride and took a closer look. I did not see them at first, but then I noticed a small movement that looked to me like an infantry squad, moving as though they expected contact from the enemy at any moment. There were several men maneuvering just inside the tree line that was the boundary along the power line right of way and it was clear that all of them were armed and wearing military uniforms. It was then that I realized that this was probably the security team that was dispatched to pick us up and they were now moving on foot to access our home from the woodland approach to the house. I was impressed that they had continued the mission despite it becoming more than difficult. It was then that I came to the realization that they would not have continued the mission unless we were all standing knee deep in a bucket full of excrement.

Weighing all of this in my mind, I decided that it would be safe to reveal our position to these guys. Still, I did hedge my best. I had my wife cover me, and I then attempted to get their attention without them shooting at me. I began by making distinctly human noises (okay, I sang "Take Me Out to the Ball Game"), and then I stood up with my arms in the air and waved them down. When one of them approached me, I offered the coded sign to which he responded with the appropriate countersign. With my bride covering my every move, I met with the officer in charge of the details, while the security team took up positions around our new hiding place. It was only then that I was given a real feeling for the full enormity of the events overtaking us, and believe me, they were unquestionably a hell of a lot bigger than I had originally been told the night before on the phone.

As he approached, the officer in charge snapped off a perfect parade ground salute and said, "Sir, Captain Simmons and security team with 12 souls, reporting. What are your orders, Sir?" As odd as it seemed, my reflexes dictated that I return his salute, and then I ordered him to finish deploying his men to cover the perimeter. Once he set out the security around our position, I waved him over to brief me on what he knew and to tell me about his previous orders. As I looked at this young man, I noticed from his uniform that he was airborne qualified and assigned to Third Army. Unfortunately, with the new uniform changes, I had no information regarding his branch or specialty. For all I knew, he could be a supply officer with very little knowledge about basic combat skills. The only thing I learned from his uniform was that he must have been dispatched from the Third Army Headquarters on the previous evening and that he was not wearing a combat service patch that would represent any actual combat experience.

As young Captain Simmons who only recently took charge of the security detail, related their story, you could almost smell the relief pouring from his body. Now that he was able to finally spit out the information he was given to pass on to me, he seemed to personally calm down. For me, his words were chilling, because the message being conveyed was huge. For one thing, it was very apparent that we were being attacked and that our enemies' attack plan was extremely well thought out. This young Captain then went almost teary eyed when he said, "Sir, all of the key guys in Washington have disappeared! The Joint Chiefs, NORTHCOM, and the Commander of the XVIII Airborne Corps, along with their complete staffs, were just wiped out, or at the very least, taken prisoner at their duty stations or in their quarters. From what I heard before leaving Shaw Air Force Base, only the dispersed and highly classified personnel or locations were spared from their initial assaults." He then looked me in the eye and said, "Hell, I had no idea there was a Lieutenant General living out here in the middle of nowhere, at least until my General said, 'Here is where you go, now get his ass, and get him here!' Sir, my General is convinced that even you spooks will be swept up in short order, and he was really concerned about you."

I had to laugh at his use of the term 'spook' since I hadn't been called that in about 20 years. My guess was that Lieutenant General Marks, an old acquaintance, who was now the Third Army Commander, probably used that term. Ergo, the term was now quite stuck in this young Captain's head. I could only conclude from hearing his earlier comments that the rounding up of the leadership was critical to the enemy, and if we were not careful, it was going to be only a matter of time before we got swept up too. When I looked at the Captain again, he had sort of blanched a little and then said, "Sir, that isn't all. Apparently, the civilian leadership was also hit hard. Even though Congress was not in session, most of them have disappeared, along with most of the cabinet. The Secretary of Defense is missing, but at least the President is safe and in an undisclosed location. I know that he is still able to communicate with other hardened facilities because it was his direct order to General Marks that we come get you."

I asked about my old friend, Marty Blanchard, who was the current Chairman of the Joint Chiefs, and the Captain responded, "He is fine and with the President, but that was like 12 hours ago. Right now, I am as in the dark as you, sir." Throughout all of this, Captain Simmons was very mechanical in his delivery, but he went on to explain, "Just prior to the global EMP burst, the President and some of his staff were taken to the hardened command facilities." He went on to elaborate that most of the Defense staff had the same warning as I had, which was not much. It was his belief that while NASA was communicating with our senior leadership in DOD, the irony was that my immediate boss with the CIA was not too concerned about the threat. It was his complete disbelief in all things "other worldly" that ultimately would lead to quite a few wasted deaths at the top of the leadership chain, to include his own. Fortunately, the Chairman of the Joint Chiefs was not quite so "unconcerned or disbelieving". It was his pulling the "COG fire alarm" that saved us, and it came none too soon for my wife and me.

Fortunately, the Chairman's alarm also came just in time for most of my family to seek refuge or at least to shelter in place for the time being. Captain Simmons related to me that our youngest daughter, Holly, who was in class when the alarm sounded, was collected by an FBI detail even before DOD could manage to start the process of recovering us. According to the Captain, "She was swept to a safe haven, and was out of harm's way somewhere in the mountains." I cannot imagine what her coming into the house would have done during our visit of the night before, but the thought of it still sends cold shivers down my spine. There was no question that this bit of news finally gave both my wife and me a huge sense of relief, at least for the moment.

I kept pumping the Captain about what else he knew, and it was the final piece of information that really made my stomach churn. I was no longer concerned about the honorary nature of my rank, or about my being an old soldier. Now, the shock of reality seeped in with a vengeance. The lowly retired former Lieutenant Colonel that they dusted off for their convenience to talk to allies and to make nice was about to take a giant leap into the abyss. It would seem that aside from the Chairman of the Joint Chiefs and the Third Army Commander, I was now the only surviving senior leader left in the entire United States Army. Oh, from what I understood, there were a handful of Major Generals floating around in the Pacific and maybe one or two in Europe, but of the Army's leadership in the grade of Lieutenant General and above, we were now down to three. The three were the Chairman, General Marks, and me. It seems that our enemy not only knew when and where to strike, but they also had a comprehensive listing of what and who to hit.

After disgorging his messages to me, the young man almost appeared to deflate. Then, almost as an afterthought, he looked me in the eye and said, "Sir, my orders are to get you the hell out of here because you are now the new Chief of Staff of the Army! The new Chairman of the Joint Chiefs, you know that Air Force guy from Mount Thunder, said get the reserve guy and put his ass to work! Right now, the old Chairman is the new Acting Secretary of Defense! So, and these are the new Secretary's exact words, sir, 'tag, you're it!'" Once I felt I had all I could get from the Captain about the overall situation, we then discussed the more local issues.

Aside from the Global Tactical Situation being highly fluid, the Captain and I began to share a little more local significant information. I made him aware of our incident at the house and the weapon that I had recovered. We then discussed his team trying to get to us for evacuation. It seems that they were already on the way to retrieve us even before I received the call to evacuate. They were traveling in a three-vehicle convoy, and they were fully prepared tactically for combat. They were about 12 miles away from us when the convoy was frozen with the EMP burst that disabled every other vehicle on the road around them. Having a clue as to what was happening, they deployed on both sides of the highway along the trees and then began to move by "leapfrogging" one group, and then another, along the highway in the general direction of my house. In classic military language, this is known as "bounding overwatch", which is a formation that is often used to cover each other as a small unit moves towards any contact with an enemy.

Captain Simmons then explained that as they moved forward up the road, they noticed an object moving slowly along the highway and just like the one at our house, it began hovering and using the thin beam of light to examine anything found along the road. What chilled every soldier, now positioned around my wife and myself, was what they saw as this object projected the thin light beam on a passenger car stranded on the road. It seems that as the light passed over the car, the people who were seated inside the vehicle simply disappeared. The Captain just stared straight ahead when he told me this, and he said, with a great deal of awe in his voice, "It was as if they just friggin' evaporated! One minute there was a family in the car and the next, nothing... Simply nothing! No Mom, no Dad, no kids, and even the family dog just disappeared right before our eyes! It was all I could do to keep my men from shooting at the damn thing."

The Captain's answer to my final question about their journey to rescue us caused me to think long and hard about our next move. I asked if the Captain could recall when the last time was he saw anything flying or searching in the sky. His response was very interesting. According to him, nobody on his team had seen anything flying or moving in the sky since sunrise. One of his young soldiers was very specific about it. "Sir, I was watching the damn thing as it went down the road, and I noticed that it stopped just as the sky in the east was starting to get those streaks of sunlight. When the sky started to get that kind of blue look with the little red tinge going along the horizon, then whatever the hell it is, just hauled ass straight up. Oh, and I mean straight up, too, with no hesitation. It was like a rocket or missile moving out. It was fast, too, like a real bat out of hell!" As he said this, I looked at my watch, which unfortunately was now completely useless. Looking at the position of the sun, I guessed that, if we were going to move from our location, it would have to be real soon, since it looked as though sunset would be within the next couple of hours.

I asked the Captain if he had a plan to extract us or if he knew of a nearby "safe haven" with a communications node. His response was less than inspiring, which made me realize that whether I was Chief of Staff or not, right now, my Army consisted of myself, my wife, and 12 very young and very scared troopers. Given how little time we had left before sundown and how little distance we would be able to cover over the next two hours, I gave the simple order to "dig in and dig deep". Using the rock cover and terrain, that is precisely what we did, but not before we set the captured weapon out at a considerable and observable distance away, to make sure that it would not lead the bad guys to our holes. I wanted that thing to go with us, if it was possible, since I had a feeling that it might help us find the answer on how to kill these things. At the same time, I did not want to find out the hard way that it was going to lead them to us. At this point, we were guessing, and only time would tell us if that guess was right or not.

Chapter II.

After telling the Captain that we would dig in for the night, I took a walk around what would be our "night" perimeter. It was a quick assessment of both the soldiers and the terrain, with the latter being almost perfect against a normal worldly enemy. The young soldiers, on the other hand, were a far larger unknown quantity. I was correct in my earlier examination for the Captain. He did not have any combat experience, but at least he had Infantry training. It seems that, up until last night's panic started, he had been my old acquaintance's Junior Aide. The rest of the soldiers were mixed bags. Several were combat veterans from either Iraq or Afghanistan, while some were extremely new and obviously green. The Sergeant was the normal leader of the security detail which, as it turned out, was the "night shift" that normally accompanied General Marks to provide him protection whenever he left his headquarters or quarters at night. From what I remember about Marks; he was someone who needed protection, and most likely from his own people. Later when circumstances permitted, I walked our little perimeter, just like I had as a young officer, and did my best to learn a little about each of these men. My goal was to see things around us through their eyes, and to maybe help keep them calm. After all, if the General isn't afraid, then maybe we don't have to be, either. It was not an easy thing to hide my own fear, but I made a real effort.

As for the terrain, I felt like we occupied excellent ground to defend, assuming we were attacked by other men. The only thing that truly left me uncomfortable was the unknown about our enemy. We had a lot to learn about our new enemies, and all I could do was hope we weren't about to get caught by the learning curve. The rock formation that my wife and I used earlier became our observation post. It was elevated, covered, and offered a complete field of view over the entire open area associated with the power lines and their right of way. The Captain put two of his troopers there and they began to dig in at an angle to put themselves primarily under the natural cover of the rocks and still be able to see into the open. Approximately 20 yards away was the tree line with a heavy stand of pine trees that were probably planted as a boundary when the power lines were first erected some 50 or 60 years ago. These trees were not your typical Carolina Pines, either. Instead, they were wide-bottomed, heavily rooted, and growing out of the rocky ground adjacent to the right of way. It was here that we set up our base of fire at the highest point and then dug in the rest of the team on either side of that base.

Not wanting to make our children orphans in one fell swoop, I had the Captain put the Sergeant with my wife at the furthest hole with the best escape route into a deep cut creek bed. I then settled in with the Captain, and we dug as deeply as we could before the sun set on us. As our last official act of the evening before sundown, we passed around some of our limited supply of MREs to share in each hole for the night, checked that everyone had sufficient ammunition, and then we waited. On my last check of the perimeter, I felt confident that a normal enemy would have a hard time dislodging us, assuming they ever found us.

It was several hours after sundown that we heard the initial signal from our observation post that something was moving in the right of way. It was barely perceptible, but it was movement, and it appeared to be around 50 feet off the ground. We passed the word along to everyone in their positions, and we continued to wait and watch. The object did not go towards where we hid the alien weapon, which was my first indication that perhaps the thing was not sending out a signal, at least in the dormant state. As it moved towards us, the hovering object began to emit that light we had seen the night before, the same light that the Captain described moving down the highway. It did not come near us at first, but it did begin a slow methodical sweep along the right of way. As it neared the rocks around our observation post, the object stopped moving forward, and instead, began to hover over that spot. As the light swept around the rocks, it became quite clear to us that it was homing in on our two forward troopers.

The object was hovering back over the rocks, and its altitude began to descend just a few feet, when one of the troopers opened fire to the object. As a result of his panic, we learned a valuable lesson. Small arms fire only "pissed it off", because the initial thin beam of light was then immediately broadened and became four or five times more intense. Instead of things evaporating, there was a thunderclap and the entire position was completely obliterated. I took the chance and told everyone to hold their fire and stay low in their positions. What I did not want to happen was to start a firefight that we would clearly lose. The earlier shots had simply bounced off the object but the fact that we could hear the ping of the bullets ricocheting off what sounded like a heavier metal gave us at least a little comfort in discovering that there was no "shield" or some other energy-based protection. Perhaps a LAW or M-47 DRAGON, or some other heavier anti-tank weapon could kill it but there sure was not anything we had with us that would do the job. Nope, for now, discretion was most definitely the better part of valor.

Once the smoke and dust cleared from the initial blast, the object returned to the same sweeper pattern of a few moments earlier. It swept the tree line in front of us but then came no closer. After a few minutes, it maneuvered back into the center of the right of way and continued moving in the direction of my house. Once the enemy was clear from our vicinity, several of the troopers went out to check on their friends. Unfortunately, they found nothing to indicate that a human had ever been near that spot. We did detect the object one more time that night, but it was no longer searching with the beam of light. Instead, it was moving at a lot more speed back in the direction of the highway. About an hour or so later, we heard another extremely loud explosion to our east and while it didn't sound quite the same, we could only guess that some other soul must have incurred its wrath. For the rest of the night, we took turns on watch and held our position. One thing was for sure, from here on, we would move only in daylight and would dig in and opt for concealment in natural cover at night instead of trying to hide in any type of open area or normal man-made structure.

At dawn, we began moving, but prior to completely leaving the area, I wanted a closer look at the impact site where we had our observation post. While the Captain and one of his troopers retrieved our capture prize, myself and my bride did a survey of the damage from the object's weapon. What was most impressive is that the uneven ground, the holes dug by the soldiers, and the rocks were all completely gone. The ground beneath was completely leveled, with absolutely no debris or indication that anything other than a huge dirt depression ever existed in this spot. It was no longer the high ground, in fact, standing at the bottom of this new crater you could barely see over the rim. As I was standing next to the crater, it hit me that it was only good fortune that put my wife and me in the woods. My initial thought had been for us to stay within those rocks for the night, and if we had been swept by the object, I'm almost positive that one of us would have fired at the thing, too. I decided not to dwell on that or on the loss of the two young men. We had bigger problems, and there was no time to deal with our mental issues about the dead, at least not if we wanted to help the living.

Once the weapon was retrieved and our security team had assembled their equipment, we set out in the direction of the interstate highway. It took us less than an hour to reach the fence and once through, we stayed along the near side of the roadway along the trees. We were all vigilant in watching both our path and the sky, but you could not help noticing all the empty cars. As we neared the urban area, the sun was almost overhead of us, and we were running out of trees as a source of cover. The deeper we moved into the city, the more bizarre and odd things we would encounter. One thing that stuck in my mind was the crater pattern around what used to be the city's main police station. It was striking how, in one case, a police car looked as though it had been cut with an arc welder in a circular pattern. Only the rear portion of the car remained, as it nudged against the rim of what was now a deep but level depression in the parking lot. From this, we could only surmise that one or two police officers were firing on the object and incurred the same response as our two young troopers from the night before.

I had originally thought that it might be possible to clear through the city in one day, but it was not really an option, and we certainly couldn't avoid it completely. Time was not on our side, and there was also the need to find a secure hardened communications node that made me head towards the Federal courthouse, and the Department of Justice hardened communications lines. While not directly tied to the Department of Defense, there was a way to manipulate the telephonic security access codes in a pinch. I thought, too, what the hell, if there was ever a time to break a rule, then this was it. Besides, it wasn't like a Federal Judge was all that scary to me anymore. With this destination in mind, we cut towards the city through the neighborhood adjacent to where my oldest daughter, Christine, lived. As we neared her house, there was no outward sign that anything was out of the ordinary. We even detected signs of life, although it was a highly subdued and secluded life. Curtains would drop or you could hear the occasional door shut, but otherwise, it was obvious that the people here were staying hidden inside their homes out of terror.

We approached my oldest daughter's home with a great deal of caution, but we did move with speed. Leah was beside herself and decided that our idea of speed just wasn't fast enough, so she just went up and started pounding on the door. While I was cringing at what we would find, the door swung open and there stood Christine, holding our young grandson. Once she saw us, there was a small cry and a lot of hugging. "DAD! LEAH! Thank GOD, you're here! Look, Michael, your grandparents are here!" The more she cried, the more Leah cried, and the more my grandson bounced up and down. At three years of age, he was without doubt a handful, and I knew that adding them to the mix was going to make the trip tougher for all of us, especially if we had to cut and run in a real hurry.

Still, not wishing to step on the moment, I had to bring the reunion to a fairly quick halt. I asked, "How long to grab your gear? Let's get out of here!" Her reply was simple, "I can't leave, John isn't home yet!

"Leave a note, and let's go!"

"But he is still at work!" Then I asked the very hard question, which finally forced her to start grabbing things for her and her son. "How long has he been at work?" When I asked it, she just stared a moment, and her hopes faded. She looked at her son, looked at me, and then with huge tears in her eyes, she turned around and started throwing their things in a bag. We both knew that the odds were probably stacked against John ever coming home, and there were better odds that there were a lot of other people who worked in the city. Still, if he did, there would be a note to let him know that she was moving to safety and where she was hopefully headed. I even countersigned the note with her, just in case it would do him any good later. Right now, it was starting to be a game of speed and cover, and the longer we waited, the harder it was going to be in getting where we needed to be before darkness set in on us.

After a little more pushing and shoving, and some help from the security team, we finally reached the courthouse around mid-afternoon. It was extremely odd seeing the place completely abandoned, or at least we thought so initially. After one of our troopers shot at the locked main door windows, it was starting to dawn on me that the place was probably a fortress, since all his bullets did bounce around without breaking anything except our nerves. Fortunately, the noise attracted at least the "semi-right" attention. As luck would have it, an older Deputy United States Marshal took the time to open an upper window and give us some return fire. On the one hand, we were glad to know that not everyone was dead, but on the other, if he had been a halfway decent shot, we could have had a real problem on our hands. As it worked out, we were able to finally identify ourselves, and after some lengthy negotiations, he let us into the building.

It took a while to fight our way through the codes and other associated problems with the hardened and secure phone lines, but on the third try, I was able to raise the National Military Communications Center. They were glad to hear from us but, clearly, they had their hands full. After more code swapping, I heard my old friend, the Chairman, get on the line. He confirmed that he was now the new Secretary of Defense and that I was now the Chief of Staff of the Army. He then told me that was the good news. The bad news was that the Army was not even a shadow of its former self. We had been hit fast, hard, and with real vengeance. We gave him our location, and he promised to get us some help, but it also turned out that it could be at least another day or two before anything could get to us. I then passed on what we had learned about the enemy, and then asked if they had any lessons that would help us over the next 24 hours. The conversation that followed was another one of those "holy crap" moments for me.

"Well, General, the situation is this. The only thing that will fly now is so damned old that we don't know what will kill you first, the bad guys or the equipment. The night belongs to them and although nobody knows why yet, they hate daylight. So, stay inside, stay low, and if possible, stay away from places where people normally stay for shelter. Trees and even sewers are holding quite a bit of our population. Hell, half of your Army is hiding in the sewers and subway systems at night and then trying to relocate and take care of civilians during the day."

When I related the experience of our two troopers shooting at the object, he explained that "Well, it isn't just the bullets that bounce off. None of our basic anti-tank stuff works that well. Even a Hellfire missile has only very limited impact, unless it is on one of the little ones." I thought, 'Little ones?!' "What do you mean little ones?" The Secretary replied to me, "Mike, it is just this simple, what attacked your house was a little one. The thing is about 75 feet long and shaped a lot like the older F-117, stealth fighter jet. What carries the little ones can best be described as the size of a new nuclear aircraft carrier, with a full air wing of the little ones on board. That light in the sky? It is about the size of a small moon, and there appear to be one or two new of the bigger types being launched on a nightly basis from that beast. Mike, I think we're probably well and truly screwed, but if you have one of their weapons, then, whatever happens, that damn thing needs to get here ASAP!"

With that, I put our Captain on the line with the Secretary's new Director of Operations to see what could be done to get us the "hell out of Dodge" After a while, the young Captain reported to me, "Sir, I don't believe it, but they are sending a flight of three UH-1 helicopters out first thing after daylight, and they should be here around mid-day tomorrow. The operations guy said that the expected ETA to our location here at the local park will be around noon tomorrow." I had to smile, since I'd logged a countless number of hours in the old UH-1 Huey, and we'd joke then that the Huey would be used to pick up the last Black Hawk pilot when he dropped his ride off at the boneyard. Now here we were, being picked up by the old "beastie" that I had flown all those years before. I saw it as a little justice and couldn't help but feel just a tad proud of the old girl. My only hope was that the things came armed, but then I remembered the craters, and just hoped that they would come with a full load of fuel and a lot more speed.

As we were about to pull out of the courthouse, to a safer location in the woods adjacent to our extraction point, the older Deputy U. S. Marshal made it clear that he did not want to be left behind. He also noted that there were three more Deputy Marshals downstairs holding several prisoners. All I could do was think that this was a bucket of worms we did not need at the moment. The discussion was long and arduous, with the net result that the Marshals were now sworn into the United States Army, and at least two of the prisoners (one for check offenses and the other for wire fraud), both with prior military service, were sworn in as well. The rest were more violent offenders, and we sent them in the general direction of the local sewer system with instructions to stay low and feel free to shoot at the enemy instead of the populace for a change.

As I looked over my "force", we were now all the way up to 16 men, not counting the two former prisoners, my wife, daughter, grandson, and me. We did manage to pick up a few weapons we did not have before. For example, we all now carried shotguns, in conjunction with our other weapons and plenty of extra ammunition "just in case". Finally, we raided the vending machines for sandwiches and other food to hold us until we were extracted. One other thing of value that we retrieved was perhaps my favorite item. We located two old-fashioned "thumpers" or as they are known in official parlance, the M-79 grenade launcher. The M-79 grenade launcher is capable of firing the 40mm grenade, or in this case, "flash bangs" and "tear gas" grenades. While I had no idea what we would use them for, it struck me that it was a good idea to bring them with us. Besides, my new 'older' soldiers knew exactly how to use them, and it made all of us old guys feel better having them around.

As the sun was going down, we were all well settled in our new vantage point in the woods surrounding the open area adjacent to the city park. There were no real signs of life, although we did hear talking in the distance near the city center. There were survivors, and they were out and about scrounging for food. None of them came near us, and we did our best to remain out of sight and hopefully out of mind. The last thing we wanted was to create a situation that would keep us from getting the alien weapon to someone who could make sense of it. I briefed the older men, and then the Captain gave a run down on what to do in case of an object getting near us. Nobody wanted to be a hero, so everyone agreed that getting low in the woods was something they could live without any problem. Knowing how frail things are in life, I tossed my earlier caution to the winds and bunked down with my bride for the night. For some reason, having her near me was the most comforting thing, and as the night wore on, her breathing in her sleep was very reassuring. I think I just needed her near me. There were no near misses this night. We did see the objects in the distance, but they were working the buildings and streets more towards the east of the city. At one point, I am pretty sure we observed one of the large objects because the moon was completely blocked for several minutes off to our south. As we watched it traverse where the moon was supposed to be in the sky, it took almost a full minute before the moonlight returned. I think this sent a cold shiver down all our spines.

After the events of the previous two nights, when the sun came up, you could sense the relief from everyone in our little perimeter. We didn't lose anyone and, if anything, the look on everyone's faces seemed to be almost hopeful. As the sun rose, we maintained our positions, making sure that the Landing Zone or LZ was clear of obstruction, and then we remained out of sight. There wasn't a single soul to be seen or heard and, for once, this wasn't as troubling as before. My personal concern was that a group of civilians might impede our extraction or might exceed our ability to get that enemy weapon back to a safe area where it could be examined.

As I sat by the open area, one of the former prisoners came up to me. I looked at this bedraggled soul and asked him what he wanted. His reply was not expected at all, "Sir, I just wondered if you knew my dad, Sergeant Major Greene?" I took a closer look, and sure enough, this kid looked like a hairy version of a very dear old friend, Daniel Greene. I remember thinking about how Daniel had saved our asses several times, and how he was eventually killed in a fire fight in a particularly nasty place near the coast of Africa. I looked at this young man and told him that, not only did I remember him, but he was an old friend. Then I remembered something else. "Say, aren't you his son that joined the Army? Yeah, that's right; you're the son that was following his old man's footsteps? He was pretty proud of you when you graduated from West Point and were commissioned.

"Yes, sir, I'm the one, and loved every minute of it, right up until that unfortunate event in Portland a few years back." I looked at him and it came to me, "Wasn't that the training accident in a Federal Building, the one that wound up starting a fire that basically burned out half the building?" There was a small look away, and then he said, "Yes, sir, that was my team, and I was responsible." I was most impressed that he didn't make any excuses nor did he point out that it was a rookie on his team that screwed it up. It all came together in my mind, and I realized that this was the kid that was the Delta team leader, who had more Special Operations skills than you could imagine, and who had lost his wife, kids, and military career all in a few months after being promoted to Major.

Looking at him up and down, I knew that, while he might have been a prisoner, he was not just some no-talent clown. I motioned him to sit down, and we talked. He got me up to date with his family, and we talked about why he was in jail in the first place. It seemed that, having nothing else going on, he decided to try using his skills to obtain things from the internet to help with his survival. He was good enough to get by with it for about two years, but not good enough to keep from eventually being caught in a sting. Still, I knew his skill set was even better than his dad's who, for my money, had been perhaps the best Delta operator that ever lived. After a few minutes of chatting, I made a command decision. I asked him first about the other prisoner and was told that he was an old Special Forces Sergeant, who is down on his luck, but they are both ready to go and both still have skills.

I stood up and looked at him, "Major Greene, effective immediately, I'm restoring you to active duty at your former rank. Up that street for about two or three blocks you will find a pawn shop, a hunting goods store, and a military surplus shop. Our ride should be here around midday. So, go find something akin to a uniform, gather whatever you think is useful to us, and then get your ass back here before our ride comes. OH, and take my shotgun, you might need it." With that, he saluted me, grabbed the freshly re-enlisted Sergeant, and hauled their ass up the hill. When the Captain approached me, he asked how I could trust them, and I explained, "Son, there goes one of the best officers that ever carried a weapon. Don't worry, the Major will be back, trust me." When I said Major, Captain Simmons and at least two of the Deputy Marshals simply stared at me. When I explained that Major Greene was a former team leader with the 1st Special Forces Operational Detachment - Delta, and that he had seen more combat than they could even imagine, their collective jaws dropped to the ground. There was no question that the Deputy Marshals were reassessing their view of at least two of their former prisoners.

Looking at the sun, I could tell that we had at least three more hours before mid-day, so I requisitioned two of the Captain's men, along with two of the Deputy Marshals. Leaving the Captain and his remaining team, along with the other two Marshals, to guard the alien weapon and my family, my four-man detachment and I headed for the tallest building we could find. It was my intent to survey the area, since what we did not know about the bad guys would fill volumes. It was my hope that I might observe something useful. Along the way, we did encounter some people as they scurried from one hidden location to another, but they wanted no part of us. Not a soul asked us anything, stopped us, nor wanted anything to do with us. They were too intent on finding a new hiding place or food, and, while some looked at us with curiosity, they largely wanted nothing to do with what they saw as probable enemy targets.

When I got to the roof of what was a bank building less than two days before, I got my binoculars out and began a slow sweep around the city. There were definite pockets of massive devastation, mainly around the local Army Post, Fort Jackson, the South Carolina State House, and the other State Government buildings, but otherwise, it appeared to be untouched ground. Largely devoid of life or movement, most of Columbia just appeared as a ghost town. The University of South Carolina buildings were a mixed bag. Some of the main campus buildings were completely gone, while others near the "horseshoe" were left completely untouched. Similarly, the airport off in the distance seemed untouched, with the glaring exception of the runways and the control tower. There, the control tower and ATC facilities were gone, and each of the runways had large craters centered at each intersection between the runways and the taxi ways, as well as down the center line at regular intervals. The local flight facility for the Army and National Guard personnel, like the control tower, were all completely gone. Scanning the sky, we did not see anything out of the ordinary. There were normal passing clouds and a rain shower off in the distance to the south. After I satisfied myself that we had scanned the area sufficiently, we headed down and back to our anticipated departure point.

As we returned to our perimeter, I was pleasantly surprised by Major Greene, who was now in a more or less complete Army Combat Uniform and bearing me a gift. As they were raiding the local pawn shop, they discovered that the classic "wind up" watches, just like "wind up" clocks, were all still operational. Much to my delight, Major Greene had liberated several of them and had passed them out to most of the security details. He even brought back a "wind up" woman's watch, which he presented to Leah with a huge smile. The other items on his "shopping list" included rations, water, and canned milk for my grandson. He then reported that his reconnaissance turned up very few people, but that he did have a conversation or two with some of the locals.

It seems that the heart of the city was hit on the first night and that it was almost like what you would expect with a Neutron Bomb exploding overhead. The light beams passed over the restaurants and bars, the movie theaters, and any other likely location for nightlife, with the result that the building was still there but nothing living remained inside. As a matter of follow up, Major Greene had even checked a walk-in freezer at a bar near the pawn shop, just to see if that might have offered some shelter. Unfortunately, he reported, "Sir, that was some of the nastiest stuff I've ever seen. Not only nothing living, but everything else was beyond rotten. It was almost like it had been there for weeks and not just a couple of days." As for the people, it was apparent to all of us that nobody wanted to be near us. I guess it was assumed that wherever we were going or whatever we were doing, things could only end badly.

Fortunately, even when we heard the distant beating of the rotor blades, nobody seemed the least bit curious about stepping into the open. As the lead aircraft flared in for a landing, I shoved my wife on board with the alien weapon in charge. As the other 6 newly minted soldiers joined her, the first helicopter departed low and fast out of the city headed north. I took comfort in knowing that Major Greene was with her. Within minutes, the rest of us were on the last two birds and clear of the city within minutes. These ancient aircraft, with their extremely limited speed, were still like stallions when they picked us up. When I related to our pilot that the airport was intact and might be a source of fuel, the entire flight wheeled into what used to be the airport traffic pattern. As we air taxied up to the fuel trucks, several of the flight crew headed towards the trucks, parked by the old FBO or Fixed Base Operator, and prepared to use their hand pumps to refuel the aircraft. Meanwhile, my original security detail fanned out to provide covering fire if necessary. The fuel stop started off quite uneventfully, but then it rapidly turned into something else entirely.

As our flight crew was pumping fuel, there was some movement off in the direction of what used to be the terminal. One of the Marshals noticed it first, and we kept a close watch on it. As I scanned through my binoculars, it dawned on me that I had seen something like that once before. That "person" moving along the fence and hiding in the shadows was no person. That thing was precisely what was hiding in my office at the house and going through my filing cabinets! I knew it could be killed, but could it be captured? I grabbed Major Greene, two troopers from the perimeter, and the old "Green Beret", a Sergeant named Gamble. In turn, having immediately grasped what I was doing, Sergeant Gamble grabbed a thumper with a couple of the flash bang grenades. Then the race was on to get into position to protect the refueling operation, the aircraft, and hopefully, catch one of these "things".

After several minutes, Major Greene gave me the 'high sign' that he and the two troopers were in position. Looking at Sergeant Gamble, I used a quick hand signal to show that I wanted the first one somewhat behind the Gomer to cut off his line of escape, and the second one to keep him penned against the building. Sergeant Gamble lifted the thumper and waited on me to tell him to fire. As we watched, the target moved forward and started to raise his arms, like that thing in my office. It was clear that he had the same kind of weapon, and it was aimed at the nearest aircraft on the tarmac. I told Sergeant Gamble to fire, and he lifted the first shot over and behind our target. The 'bang' went off behind the target, and I first thought that Gamble had made a mistake and accidentally hit it. We all looked in disbelief as the alien literally just blew apart. Just as before, this thing collapsed into a pile of dust, with only a few items lying around the pile as it fell to the ground. I signaled Major Greene, who moved out and collected the new weapon and several other items lying on the ground. Still concerned about locators, we decided to take the chance, and we collected all we could that was surrounding the pile of dust which was now starting to dissipate with the breeze.

We didn't waste any more time, and soon we got the signal that the aircraft were all ready to leave. We scrambled back into the Hueys and were never so glad to be headed out of anywhere in our lives. Fortunately, within a few hours, we were coming in for landing in what seemed like a small field cut out of the woods in the foothills of the Appalachian Mountains. It took me only a moment to recognize the old Ranger Camp near Dahlonega, Georgia. I never once before in my life thought of this place as home but, this time, I was thrilled to see it. As we flared in for landing, I could see my grandson grinning and bouncing in his mother's arms in the aircraft next to us, and it hit me that at least somebody was having fun. There was no question that to a three-year-old boy this kind of excitement was priceless. I just hoped that it would be a memory for him in his old age since at this point I could only ponder a future without our new enemies.

Instantly landing, two fuel trucks popped out of the trees and refueled each of the aircraft. Shortly after taking on the fuel, the birds were manhandled back inside the tree line, and we headed to a makeshift bunker that was also set into the tree line. Naturally, these Rangers learned quickly, and what I saw between cadre and students showed me that we hadn't given up either. With a quick headcount, I saw a Battalion of solid fighting men and my security team fit in quite nicely with them. Somehow, even though nobody was actually living in the older camp itself, an ice-cold beer was magically placed in my hand, along with a cigar and a new set of "four stars" to stick on my uniform. As I was taking this all in, the camp commander, a Lieutenant Colonel, was on his feet toasting my health and congratulating me as the new "Chief of Staff". He opined that he was proud that the new "Chief" was a Ranger, and said it was about damn time they had a real Ranger to lead the way. I just hope I did not humiliate myself because before I could even light the cigar, I was sound asleep. My bride and Major Greene took care of me, since I think they must have explained that this was the first real sleep I had in over 48 hours. When I awoke several hours later, they got me a hot meal and made it clear that I was more than welcome to stay.

Naturally, to repay their kindness, I did something that probably would have ticked off a unit commander in normal times. I stole some of his people. The Colonel understood, but I made it known that I needed to swap him several old soldiers, who needed training, for at least two of his Sergeants, preferably one with communications experience and one who could work with improvised explosives. The deal was made, and I left him most of our newest members of the Army to get a little refresher, or in one case, basic combat training. I knew where I was going, and they would probably not learn a thing there. Soldiers with specialty expertise, on the other hand, would be at a real premium. Right now, what I needed were men who were not only trained but who could exercise initiative. If anyone could teach that lesson, it was my old friends in the Rangers, so I felt like my new guys were in good hands. The two new guys I refused to give up were Major

Greene and Sergeant Gamble. Now, these guys were my kind of soldiers, and I had already made up my mind that Major Greene was going to be my new senior Aide.

When the sun came up, the aircraft were pushed out of the woods and our journey continued up the very spine of the Appalachian Mountains. We stopped twice for fuel, but these stops were quick and offered little more than a chance to take a bathroom break and grab an MRE for the family. As we flared for our final landing of the day, the sun was nearing the horizon, and the choreography of securing the aircraft was even more efficient than at the Ranger camp. They were down, fueled, and inside the mountain in less time than I had ever thought possible. The New York City Ballet had nothing on these guys, as theirs was an efficiency born from desperation and a realization that to take longer, could only lead to death or worse.

As we stepped just inside the cave entrance, I was greeted by a newly promoted Major General, who welcomed me to the 'New Pentagon' with all the comforts of your average cave. He announced himself as the Director for my new Army Staff and stated that he was very proud that a week ago, he was just a Colonel in the West Virginia National Guard. I think when Major Greene and Captain Simmons were introduced as my Aides, they were both surprised, but it took about a nanosecond for Captain Simmons to assume the role. He quickly got my wife and daughter, along with my grandson, moving towards what would be our new quarters for the duration. Major Greene, on the other hand, was more pragmatic in his movements. He looked at the new "rookie" General and simply said, "Sir, where are your science

guys? We have some seriously important stuff to give them!"
With that, Major Greene was off to the races carrying the recently
retrieved alien equipment and the two weapons.

When I took a last look around before heading deeper
into the cave, I was almost floored by the notion that I was now
standing near the top of a mountain that was less than two miles
from my old boyhood home in West Virginia. Off in the distance,
I could even see the town I grew up in and as I peered off into
the failing light, I could also see one of the "large ones" as it was
moving along with the darkness. With that, we stepped deeper
into the entrance to our new home and set about assessing the
state of the Army and the extent of the damage. All I could think
was, "Jesus Christ, what a mess. An old 'has been', more or less
honorary, Lieutenant General, is now a full General, and in Charge
of the whole friggin' US Army, with a former Colonel from the
National Guard as the Director of his Army Staff? No wonder the
new Secretary of Defense thinks we're well and for truly screwed!"
With that thought uppermost in my mind, I stepped away from the
entrance of our new home and told my new Director of the Army
Staff, "Take me to my headquarters so I can find out the latest on
just what the hell is going on."

Chapter III.

I was taken into a makeshift room that had been carved into the side of the mountain. It was the size of a small commercial theater and was fully equipped with electrical power, which was something I had not seen in a while. There were concrete walls, paneling, and other amenities that demonstrated clearly that this was a facility which had been a long time in the making. I guess it really was the "New Pentagon" and it came complete with hot and cold running staff guys. My first official act was to get my new Director of the Army Staff to round up my Vice Chief of Staff and to get me access to the secure communications node to speak with the new Secretary of Defense or "SecDef".

When I picked up the handset to speak with the SecDef, it was almost like he was in the next room. This was so different from the last few days that it was a comfort just to hear my friend's voice. This time I could catch all the inflection, to go along with the words. "Marty, uh, excuse me, Mr. Secretary, I am reporting in from my headquarters to see if you have any orders, instructions or other directions from the President."

"Mike, damned glad you're there. Are you alone?"

"Sure, Marty, but I'm not sure for how much longer. I've asked to have my Vice Chief sent in and, honestly, I have no idea who the hell that might be... I literally got here about 5 minutes ago."

"Okay, well, here is the unvarnished truth. The 'Boss' is in seclusion. He got here and immediately started huddling with only his closest advisor; you know that little weasel, Martinson, and then with his family. The only time we see him is during a meal or if we can sneak past his little guard dog to tell him something. Honestly, Mike, I have never heard or even read of such defeatism, at least not since Bataan, in World War II!"

"Damn, is it really that bad? I mean, since I arrived here everybody has been pretty upbeat with me. I can tell you that nobody here seems defeated. Hell, Marty, I personally killed one of the sonuvabitches, and yesterday we took out another one at the airport in Columbia while the flight crews were refueling. I can personally attest that, while their equipment may be tough, they aren't. We've collected more of their gear and, even as we speak, my Aide is searching out the tech guys and engineers to find out how it works!"

"REALLY? You've actually killed two of them? I'll pass that on to the Boss since he needs something to cheer him up. I think he sees you as his new General Marshal, MacArthur, and Patton all rolled into one."

"Well, some other good news is that we met with a Battalion of fired up and highly motivated Rangers in the mountains of north Georgia. If you want to cheer up the Boss, just tell him that those boys have extremely high morale and are anything but feeling defeated."

"I'll be sure to pass that on, Mike, but seriously, he is counting on you to do things that none of the rest of us could. Somebody briefed him on your past, your record, and besides, you're the only one I have ever known to tell a sitting President, 'With all due respect, sir, you are both misguided and full of shit!' So, do you think you can handle that kind of pressure?"

"Christ, Marty, what is the worst that can happen? If we're already screwed, then I can't make it worse now, can I? Besides, I can always blame the guy in charge or just fall on my sword! Oh, and that reminds me. You remember our old buddy back in the day, Daniel Greene?"

"Sure, he was killed some years ago, why?"

"Well, I have reinstated his kid to the Army, and he is now that Aide I mentioned that is running down my local brainiac eggheads. He is currently a Major, but I want to promote him and give him a special job. Do you have any objections?"

"Not if you think you can use him. In fact, you have a free hand. It is your Army now, and you can do whatever you want, promote whoever you want, and do whatever you have to do to put a winning team together. This should be easy, especially since the Boss isn't playing anymore. Right now, I've got my hands full with General Bozeman over at Thunder Mountain, who took my old spot. That guy is half nuts and has been playing with his missiles for too long. Then there is Admiral Morton. He isn't much better, but at least he has done a good job of hiding the submarines from the bad guys. Oh, and your Vice, well, he was my ace in the hole if we hadn't finally pulled you in. You remember General Marks at Third Army?"

"Sure, he sent the extraction team that got me here! Is he my new Vice?"

"Actually no, he was killed shortly after he sent the security team to get you. In fact, everyone and everything at Shaw was destroyed, so your security team was saved just by being on that mission to retrieve your sorry behind. Nope, I was going to ask if you remembered the guy he hated even more than he hated you."

"Oh, you have got to be kidding me! You mean Jerry Larkin?"

"Yep, one and the same. I remember hearing a story once about some guy punching Marks out on the ramp at Pope Air Force Base. Now, I never had any real official notice of the incident but, if someone did do it, then it is one point in his favor! I also seem to recall that you defended him by saying you'd have done it, or worse, if Jerry hadn't beat you to it. Something about 'what damn fool flies into bandit country with the complete roster and plan for an operation then doesn't destroy everything before leaving the badlands when his aircraft breaks down?' Now, have I got that story just about, right?"

"Geez, Marty, there is no need to revisit old history. Especially since Marks is gone, but unofficially I'd have to say that, yeah, you're pretty close. So, why not give Jerry this job, he should be senior enough and wasn't he still in the Regular Army?

You must admit, too, that punching Marks at the time was a pretty gutsy thing to do. Sounds like leadership material to me!"

"Actually, no, you have him by date of rank by at least a few months, and besides, Jerry is the finest administrator I've ever known, but honestly, he is not as calculating in his aggressiveness. As for gutsy, defending him, and then getting ugly with Marks later means that you're a helluva lot smarter and meaner. You at least know when to pick your battles. Now go check in with your staff, make whatever changes you need to make, and get a handle on what you have at your disposal. Once you get settled, report back to me with a SitRep."

"Yes, sir, Mr. Secretary, I'm on it." With that, the line went dead, and I turned to face my old friend, and now the new Vice Chief of Staff, Lieutenant General Jerry Larkin.

Jerry Larkin was a definite contrast to me. He was way too husky to be a decent paratrooper and certainly too tall to fly the MH-6 'little bird', yet he did both with great skill as a young man. In fact, he'd been flying in a "little bird" on an operation in Africa when the then-Captain Marks had gone down with an engine malfunction in his UH-60 Blackhawk. Unfortunately, Marks left a complete plan and operation order for the bad guys to find and didn't take any steps to destroy the aircraft. What made it particularly awful was that my team of special operators and I were later ambushed because of his stupidity. I lost three guys that day, to include Daniel Greene, Sr., and I would have killed Marks had I been given just half the chance. Instead, Jerry got to him first, and the rest is history. I never figured out who looked after Marks over the rest of his career, but I wouldn't have made him a Lieutenant, much less a damn General. This was all the way in the past, and now here we stood. The fact that Marks sent the team to get me out was just the first of many ironic moments that would arise for me in this war. Regardless, now the two most senior officers left in the United States Army, which was now at war, were Jerry Larkin and me. How funny is fate!

Jerry was grinning like a 'shit-eating possum' as he stepped up and said, "Hey, Sir, how the hell are you? Was that Daniel Greene's kid that just went hauling down the tunnel with all that alien crap?" I explained that it was and then brought my old friend up to date with my 'Reader's Digest' version of our recent travels. When I finished, I asked Jerry if he had a smoke, a cup of coffee, and a place where the staff could finally tell me what the hell was going on. Again, with a HUGE grin, Jerry said, "Okay then, come on, 'Mighty Mouse', you're in for a real education." I hadn't heard that moniker in a very long time, but it was like coming home. Here we were, "Green Giant" and "Mighty Mouse", together again, like a very annoying boy band from the 1980s. The only difference now was that we owned the store, and we were not about to give up without using all our toys to inflict some damage. Now came the hard part, determining the how and with what?

The standard military briefing has a time-honored format, and this one generally was to be no exception. When I entered the room, everyone leaped to their feet, with the requisite calls to "Attention!" Key members of the staff took their places off to the side, while less senior staff personnel were arrayed around the room, trying to look official yet unobtrusive. My Vice Chief of Staff and I were taken to the two best seats in the house, while the Director of the Army Staff waited for us to be seated so he could start the briefing. I always loathed this process but had to admit that it offered two things to everyone gathered in the room. The first was that it was a routine that they knew and therefore made them more comfortable and less likely to panic under the stress of a situation. The second was that it facilitated a structure that was more about organization than about personalities. As I walked forward to my seat, I assessed my new staff. Primarily, I was searching their faces for anyone familiar and to gauge their morale. I did not see anyone panicking, and I did not see anyone who looked either defeated or scared. Instead, I saw a look of grim determination on everyone present, and this was excellent. This meant that I should not have to fire anyone on the first day, at least that was my hope, but as it turns out, I was wrong.

As I proceeded with, "Carry on," the Director of the Staff advised everyone to "Take Seats!" With this, he introduced himself as General Carter, and then, going around the room, he introduced the Staff. At my request, as each officer was introduced, General Carter advised me of where a particular staff member came from, along with their former and current function. This was a little off script, but since I was the "new boss", it was important that we all know one another from the start. My new operations officer or G-3 in Army parlance, was a former Brigade Commander with the 82nd Airborne Division, Colonel Rhymes. The intelligence officer, or G-2, was a Lieutenant Colonel Whitney, out of what was left of the XVIII Airborne Corps headquarters, also from Fort Bragg, North Carolina. The logistics guru or G-4 was a grumpy-looking Brigadier General by the name of Clark, who, up until 48 hours before, had been a Deputy Adjutant General in the National Guard for the State of Virginia.

Finally, I was introduced to both the G-1, personnel officer, Major General Gregg, and G-5 Planning officer, Major General Davis. The latter two officers were both professionals and maybe the only senior survivors out of the Pentagon. They were also originally part of the Chairman's Joint Staff, which meant that they had experience at the highest command levels. They had just arrived at our facility within the last 13 hours but given my past roles with the Joint Staff, at least I knew them by reputation. It was pure good fortune that both gentlemen had been on leave together on a hunting trip when the bottom fell out. Since they were both new arrivals, their deputies would be doing their portion of the briefing since, like me, they did not have a real clue about the current situation.

Colonel Rhymes began the briefing by telling me the overall global situation about the bad guys, and then our guys, which was also a little different than the accepted format for an official briefing. The tone of his voice was strained, but he was able to paint me a somewhat limited view of what had happened since the attack started. "General, the first attacks appear to have struck the Japanese first. Within an hour, our Eighth Army and the 2nd Infantry Division were hit in Korea. As would be the pattern throughout their initial assault, the first strikes were aimed at the leadership. Individual quarters were raided, and those who could not be 'snatched' from their quarters were hit when they attempted to rally their troops. General Tuckman went down fighting but, unfortunately, we lost half of Seoul in the process. There is no further information about the events in the Korean theater except it is believed that we MAY have had some success against one or two of their smaller craft."

As Colonel Rhymes worked his way around the globe, it was not a pretty picture. The forces we had in the Middle East appeared to be mostly intact, but their leadership was gutted, with the troops mostly holding up in places like the caves of Tora Bora. We also had some forces around the Golan Heights between Syria and Israel, hiding with the surviving elements of the Israeli Defense Force, and a few more hiding with the remaining elements of the Egyptian Army at or near the Mitla Pass in the Sinai. Similarly, United States Army Europe and most of our NATO Allies were left reeling with little or no leadership available. The Germans were holding up in Bavaria, along with some of our smaller independent units who were with them, while both the French and Spanish surviving forces, along with the remnants of our Seventh Army, were now hiding out in the Pyrenees Mountains. The Apennines Mountains in Italy were the new home of the 173rd Airborne Brigade, but it was currently under the command of a Lieutenant Colonel.

Colonel Rhymes then launched into what I would have to call the local news. "Sir, as for CONUS [Continental United States], we have roughly four 'half strength' divisions. The 82nd Airborne, minus the two brigades in the Middle East, managed to get their two remaining brigades here. In fact, the force around you is mostly our, excuse me, their two brigades. The 101st Airborne, minus one brigade that was in the Middle East, is in or around the mountains in Kentucky. They are being commanded by Colonel Harmon, who is the senior officer present. We have the 1st Armored Division, which is largely together, but stuck in the hills between Fort Irwin, California, and Fort Hood, Texas. The III Corps staff were almost completely wiped out. We also have two brigades of the 3rd Infantry Division that bailed into the swamps and woods around Fort Stewart in Georgia. Otherwise, we have several independent units of varying sizes, and a few National Guard Units that weren't gutted, but largely you are looking at your major combat forces. Unless there are questions, I'll be followed by Colonel Whitney."

"Thank you, Colonel; I do have a question or two. You said this all started in Japan and then, for us, in Korea. What about our Naval and Marine forces in Japan or further out in the Pacific, say in Guam? I also would like to know the status of the THAAD missile unit we just sent to Guam, thanks to the tensions with the North Koreans? Now, you briefed Korea first, but what the hell happened and why was there a delay of at least 13 hours before folks here got the word? Finally, I noticed that you gave me a fairly decent headcount of major active-duty infantry units, what I also need to know is how many tubes of artillery, tanks, aircraft, and other Reserve or National Guard units we have left, their locations, and their operational status for ammunition, fuel, food and supplies." As I was speaking, I noticed several of Colonel Rhymes' staff members began scurrying out of the room to get answers. I then looked at Colonel Rhymes and said, "Colonel, I realize you don't have all this information off the top of your head, so I want you to get with your staff, and get back to me within an hour after the conclusion of this briefing." I turned then to my G-2, Lieutenant Colonel Whitney, and said, "You may begin."

I hadn't meant to shake him up, but Colonel Rhymes had almost blanched from my questions. I knew exactly why, too. He fell over his head and did not feel comfortable briefing on this kind of level. He was used to getting briefings about the immediate tactical situation, so the more global look was beyond his training, and having to brief it was even more beyond what he was used to doing. I would have to watch him to make sure he shifted his mind set; otherwise, I'd have to find someone who could see and process the bigger picture. I also made a mental note that perhaps the Staff Director wasn't up to it either, especially since I now had some new talent that had just walked through the door. Clearly a shift was going to have to take place.

As Lieutenant Colonel Whitney stepped up to the podium, I was immediately impressed. Colonel Whitney was an assistant G-2 for a Corps Commander, which meant he understood his role completely. His briefing was relatively short, but directly on point. "Sir, I'm Colonel Whitney, and the enemy situation appears to be as follows. Their method of attack is to follow the twilight line around the globe. Within a 30-minute window after sundown, until approximately 30 minutes before dawn, their smaller objects have roamed the countryside taking out various targets. They appear to be keying on targets in the following order: 1. Key leadership personnel, both military and civilian; 2. Energy Infrastructure; 3. General population; and then what we would call, 4. Targets of opportunity. They have not attacked food sources, fields where crops are grown, or any of our significant fuel sources. There is also a real aversion to flying over woods, or at least attacking anything under heavy tree cover, and they have not yet attacked anything in the mountains."

Colonel Whitney then shifted at the podium and turned directly towards me as he said, "As for individual capability, it is my understanding that you are the source of most of that information, but for the benefit of the rest of the staff, the enemy appears to be rather fragile when away from the cover of their ships. A shotgun and a flash bang brought down the only two ever encountered outside their craft. Equipment was recovered from both encounters, and we have several people looking at these items. I don't have any further information regarding those items at this time, but I can provide you with a more detailed report at your convenience as it comes available.

Turning away, the young Lieutenant Colonel laid out the enemy fleet as he knew it, "Finally, Sir, we have identified three types of conveyances or ships. The largest is about a quarter size of the Moon and appears to be "hiding" just behind our moon, thereby keeping out of any direct sunlight; the middle-sized ones appear to be approximately 5000 feet long, and they normally operate with approximately 10 miles spacing in echelons of three. Our total count, which at this point is mostly an estimate, is roughly 500 of these ships, with at least 1 to 2 new ones appearing regularly from behind the moon every couple of nights. The smaller ones, which are about 75 feet long, seem to operate from the larger 5000-foot craft. These ships are too numerous for us to have an accurate count, but assuming they are like a standard naval air wing on an aircraft carrier, we can guess that there are at least 30,000 to 50,000 of them. It is clear to us, sir, that they are growing in strength every day. If there are no questions, I'll be followed by our G-4, General Clark.

I told Colonel Whitney that I had no questions for the moment, but I would be eagerly waiting to hear whatever he had on the weapons when he got the information. When Whitney turned to leave, I then said, "On second thought, Colonel, I do have a quick question for you."

"Yes, sir?"

"Colonel, do you have a team examining the weapon and, if so, who is in charge?"

"Sir, I've got a professor from Virginia Tech, who we picked up a few days ago, but he tells me that he knows of at least three other professors and/or Doctors of Physics that need to be brought in as well. Unfortunately, I've been told that we don't have the time or assets to search these people out."

"Colonel, who told you that nonsense?"

"Sir, Colonel Rhymes and General Carter."

"Thank you, Colonel, please come see me after this briefing is over." With that, he returned to his seat, and the stocky little Brigadier General strode up chomping a cigar. As he stomped his way to the front of the room, I already knew that my staff was going to have to take on a whole new look. I thought I had the answer, but I was going to see what was next.

"General, I'm Brigadier General Clark, and I'm your director of logistics. Right now, we have enough supplies, such as food, ammunition, gasoline, and clothing stockpiled in this mountain to last the current population about 6 months. After that, we're screwed up, unless you authorize me to scavenge the landscape. Some of my boys have an idea that we can maybe even start growing some food, at least something that can grow with a little less direct sunlight in the woods. The POL situation, you know... Gas, oil, and lubricants, well, there is a lot stockpiled and just waiting for us, assuming we can get someone to let us go get it. Ammo also isn't a problem, since we have tons of it cached around for everything from the 5.56 for the M-16, all the way up to 155 mm howitzer rounds. Hell, I've got an unmarked depot for that crap within about 70 miles of here! Now then, rolling stock and prime movers, we've got HUMMVs, HEMMETS, the old quarter tons, and a lot of even older stuff like the five tons and deuce and a half truck, in very large numbers. The batteries have now been recharged, and we're able to put a bunch on the road, assuming someone authorizes me to get outside this Friggin' Mountain! So, unless you got a question, this here other General is next!" The more General Clark spoke, the obvious that he wasn't a happy camper. His tone kept getting louder and more strident throughout his briefing.

As General Clark finally started to walk away, I stopped him in his tracks. "General Clark, I have a huge question for you! Just who is sitting on you and keeping you from getting what you need?" Without uttering a word in reply, he immediately and sharply pointed directly at General Carter, who shrank about three sizes under General Clark's solid glare. Yes, there is now no doubt, someone is fired, but how to do it without making a stink in an already teetering staff. With that, I looked at General Davis, the G-5, as he stepped up to the podium. He had a slight smile on his face, and it was quite apparent that he no longer wanted his deputy to brief me. It was equally apparent that he was truly a professional who was about to make a point.

Without skipping a beat, he looked directly at me and my Vice Chief of Staff, General Larkin, and said, "Sir, planning is at the earliest stages, and right now we are struggling to put together just the basics of survival. I think part of what we need to examine is the utilization of our civil population. Right now, the civilian population is terrified and dispersed. We have little to brief, given the turmoil involved, but it would be our recommendation to get our civilians mobilized as much as possible. At best, we can try to get out a presence to try and calm people and educate them as to the need to grow food and stay under wooded cover at night. We will also need to recreate or recharge the infrastructure to the point that they aren't working and living like mediaeval peasants. As of right now, we have no plan and, more to the point, there have been absolutely no efforts made to get people back on their feet under the new paradigm. Even if there ever was a plan, *I can assure you that it has been shot to hell through inaction.* With that, I will turn this portion of the briefing over to General Gregg."

Before General Gregg could stand up, I stood up and faced the room. "Gentlemen, I've heard enough! General Carter, I want you and the primary staff to stay, otherwise I want everyone else out of here right now! Jerry, tell them to stand by, and I will

call them in when I'm ready! Otherwise, they are to carry on."
With that, you would have thought I had tossed a live grenade in
the middle of the floor. To quote Jerry, "There was nothing but
'assholes and elbows' headed for the exit." As the dust settled, I
looked at Jerry and then at the staff, and I began my speech.

"Effective immediately, I am making the following
personnel changes at the staff level. General Gregg, who is the
more senior by date of rank, you or General Davis?"

"Sir, General Davis has me by about a year."

"Thank you, General Gregg. As with my new G-1, you are
hereby directed to do the following: I want you to move General
Carter to a new position. He is to be my G-9, civil affairs officer.
Since he is a local boy, he needs to think seriously about how he
is going to work with his friends and neighbors to get them going
again. He is then going to have to expand his thinking outside
the mountain. If you have a problem with it, General Carter, you
can always revert to your previous grade and return to your unit.
General Davis, you are now the director of my staff. You should
know me by reputation, and I suspect that you should have a clue
as to what I expect. Screw it up, and you will be looking for
work, too! Colonel Rhymes, you are to return to your Brigade. I
think we'll both be more comfortable there and I can tell you'll be
a whole lot happier back with your men. The good news is that
I've got another job in mind for you in the not-so-distant future,
and you will like it a lot more than trying to read my mind here
on staff. I will assure you that my replacing you has absolutely
nothing to do with you personally nor will it impact your career as

an officer. General Clark, you, sir, are immediately promoted to Major General, and your job will be to start putting your plan into action. Get with General Davis to get what rolling stock you need to make it happen. In other words, General Clark, you've got your authorization! Finally, Colonel Whitney, you are now promoted to Brigadier General. Pin on the star and start thinking about who you need on board to get our technology program going. I want the best and brightest guys you can find. Again, General Davis, this is a priority, so make sure Whitney gets the resources he needs to round these people up. Any questions so far?"

As I looked around the room, I was met with complete silence, so I continued with, "We also do not have enough experienced personnel to go around, so I want to combine the G-3, operations position, with the G-5 planning and G-7, information operations positions. General Gregg, start scouring our pool of manpower and get me someone that can handle the job. As for the G-6, Command and Control, Communications, and computer operations, I think that can be covered by General Whitney as the G-2, at least for the short term. General Gregg, before we switch over to offensive operations, I'll want this position filled as well, but, for now, let's just get the search going. Finally, back on the subject of planning, while the new G-3 will be officially holding that head, I want it very clear that Generals Larkin and Davis should be intimately involved with that process. Right now, General Davis, until we can get a new G-3 in here, you'll be doing that job. Now, are there any questions about those changes?"

Again, there was complete silence in the room. There were a few grins and shocked looks, but it was a shakeup that needed to happen. I wasn't going to let the overly cautious or incompetent drag us down any lower than we already were. After letting this all sink into their psyche, I then dropped a few carrots among the rest of them. "General Gregg, here is what I want you to do for me. One, I want you to promote Lieutenant General Larkin here to General, per the normal TDA. My key staff should also have the rank that the TDA requires, which means you and General Davis should have that third star. As for the colonels in the room, let's make that transition slightly less shocking and give them at least one, preferably two stars. Then I want you to make the TDA/TOE slot promotions across the board in our troop units. If the TOE or TDA calls for a but a Captain is doing the job, then assuming he is doing it with a modicum of competence, promote him. If a Private is doing a great job as an acting Sergeant, then promote him to Sergeant. We have NO room for slackers right now, so bust the duds and promote the hard workers. Got it?"

"Yes, sir!"

"Oh, and General Gregg…"

"Sir?"

"I'm working on an idea, so I need your strength numbers immediately. I need to know what we have, where we have it, and how it is structured. I think I have an idea on how we can make what is left of something we can work with. I know there is an Army Regulation or Department of the Army Pamphlet or some other publication for such things, but right now I'm thinking that flushing the book might be the way to go. Once we can get reorganized and equipped for an offensive, then we need to make sure we have a team that can hit them effectively and efficiently." After pausing to make sure my words had sunk in, I then added, "General Davis, I'm going to give you two hours to work with your staff and to get everyone acquainted with these changes. At the conclusion of those two hours, I want every key staff member here for MY briefing. Oh, and General Davis, I want you to set up a briefing here for two hours after the staff briefing. I want to talk to all the local Brigade and Battalion Commanders, and any other Brigade and our Division commanders that can listen via wire. If it isn't possible to hook anyone in, then I'll want it transcribed so that my message can get out as a later transmission to all commanders regardless of where they are in the field. Are there any questions?"

General Davis nodded, saluted, and began to gather his people. I looked at Jerry and we retreated to my office for a little chat. As we moved through the corridor, I was struck by the obvious fact that personnel issues were going to be our biggest problem in the short term. We had too many rookies being asked to run things that were way beyond their comprehension and pay grade. The real problem would be that we had to start with the basics, and the need to overcome the natural human resistance to serious change. We entered my 'office' and Jerry couldn't wait to launch into the discussion.

"Thanks for the star, Mighty Mouse, but GOD ALMIGHTY! You just dropped a dog turd into the punch bowl at the ladies' afternoon tea party!"

"How about that, but I may not be done quite yet. What the hell were you thinking putting Carter in charge of the staff?"

"Geez, Mouse, it wasn't my fault. When I got here, he was the welcoming committee, and since he was pushing paper around with some efficiency, I left him there until someone better came along. Lucky for you, Davis and Gregg finally crawled out of the woods."

"Actually, THAT fact was lucky for YOU! Okay, Jerry, you get a pass on that one but keep an eye on Carter. I think he may not be a solid leader, and I'm concerned that he might be just another blow hard politician type hiding behind an empty uniform. He also strikes me as being overly happy that we are all standing on the brink of extinction. With that in mind, I need you to ride herd on two main projects. The first is that the plan put forward by General Clark, the idea of growing food and developing a plan to sustain us longer than 6 months has a lot of appeal. After all, right now, going on the offensive might take us a little longer than 6 months to make happen. The other is helping Whitney round up the brains, eggheads, and science guys to make this whole thing come together. Right now, we must know how the aliens make their stuff work, how they think and, more importantly, what are their weaknesses."

"Okay, Mouse, I'm on it, and I'll even help keep an eye on Carter. You raised a good point about making him start with his own neighbors and friends. Then again, it is probably more about neighbors, since I doubt seriously he has that many friends."

"Well, I know that the civil affairs position seldom sneaks onto an Army Staff that isn't deployed outside the United States, but with the bad guys wearing our underwear with us, it seemed like a good idea. Especially, as General Davis pointed out, we have a huge population that is just wandering the woods with little food, and no idea of how to protect themselves. I also want to give Carter a second chance to succeed. After all, he might be a great officer, just not a staff director."

"Got it, and for the record, I still think it was a good idea to put him in the job."

"Thanks, but sucking up just doesn't become you! Now, let Gregg in. I've got an idea that is going to probably make him more than a little unhappy!"

With that, Jerry hopped up, opened the door, and then after spotting him in the corridor, motioned for General Gregg to come into the office. As General Gregg entered, Jerry sat back down, waving General Gregg to the other seat. Once everyone was semi-settled, I began, "General? I've got a reorganization idea that is more than a little outside the box. Right now, we do not have a single Division or brigade for that matter, that is up to any real effective strength. The leadership having been scattered or killed has left us with lots of holes, so from an organizational standpoint, I want you to begin the process of converting us back to a much older system."

The silence and look from General Gregg were palpable. I continued, "General Gregg, I want to go back to the Triangle

Division and Regimental system from World War II. From the numbers we have left and what we can scrounge, it is my thought that we can make cohesive units out of the smaller remnants much easier by stepping back in time and getting lean. What do you think?"

General Gregg then did what most good staff officers do when faced with a left field question. He replied, "Sir, on the surface, it sounds like a good idea, but can I have a few hours to think it through and properly staff it?"

"Sure, but hours are all we have right now. In the meantime, I've got another plan that I want kicked into play immediately after we're done here."

"Okay, sir, what is it?"

"My senior Aide is the young scruffy Major Greene, and I want him to be assigned nominally in the G-2 section. Not as a staff guy, but as a mobile reconnaissance commander in the field. We need intelligence gathering the old-fashioned way, and he is the man that I want heading it up. His skills are perfect, and he has seen the bad guys up close, like I have. I want you to cut orders promoting him to Colonel, and I want him to have approximately 500 men assigned to him. Now his buddy, Sergeant Gamble, I want him to be the Sergeant Major of that outfit, so get his orders done, too. As for the troops, cull the herd, and find anyone with experience doing recon or special operations work. If anyone from Delta or anyone from our Special Forces Groups is still around, then assign them to Greene's new unit. Maybe we can even steal him some out of that pool of Marines that were hanging around the entrance earlier."

"Yes, sir, we have an almost full-strength brigade of Marines, so I'm sure we can get a few of them, and I've also got a few dozen retired Rangers, about 25 or so retired Green Berets, and at least another dozen former operators from Delta. They heard the fire bell and the old horses are gathering here. I am kind of amazed at how many of these jokers have wandered into the cave in the last two days, and every one of them is looking for work."

"Great, reinstate all of them that are fit, equip them, and then turn them over to Colonel Greene. Oh, and he'll report directly to me through General Whitney."

"Is there anything else, sir?"

"Not right now, but once you work through the Regimental Organization, let me know, and when you re-flag or re-designate units, keep an eye on history. For example, the least you can do for the airborne guys is give them the flag for the 11th or 17th Airborne Divisions, as opposed to the 25th Infantry. As for Greene's crowd, and I'm sure he will enjoy the irony, designate them as 2nd SFOD-Delta. In the meantime, see if you can find out what the hell happened to the rest of the 1st SFOD-Delta personnel. I could use them right about now."

"Yes, sir!"

"Great, make it happen!" With that, General Gregg came to attention, saluted, and executed a perfect about-face on his way out the door. Jerry just stared at me and asked me one question, "Sir, what the hell are you smoking?"

"Nothing, Jerry, at least until you can scrounge us something from General Clark. I can't believe the bastard had the gall to brief me with a cigar in his mouth, and then not even offer me one." Jerry laughed and then headed out to "make stuff happen". As he left, I could only hope that we were starting on the right path. Now, it was time to figure out what to say to the Commanders and then, by extension, to the troops.

When the Staff reconvened, my briefing was short and to the point. I made it clear that my philosophy was not one of sitting on our hands, and it sure wasn't one for hiding forever. I explained to them our priorities. Then I briefed them on why I made staff changes, so that personnel were to be given jobs where they could excel and bring their individual and unique skills into play. After my brief was concluded, I opened the floor for questions and comments, and discovered some pretty bright talent was in the room. Several of the younger men were not bound by older thinking and, therefore, were far more resilient in their ideas. I noted with more than a little sense of relief that General Clark, the stodgy old G-4, was more than a little responsive and excited about the ideas that supported his notions that were briefed that morning.

I was equally pleased at the conclusion of this briefing when General Clark approached me with a carton of my brand of smoke. He handed them to me with a huge grin and said, "Thanks be to heaven, another smoker! Oh, and your wife told me your brand!" All I could do was laugh and thank him. He then said, "No need, more guys are smoking now than ever. I guess they aren't as worried about their health with this hanging over our heads." With that deep thought, he whirled around on his heels and headed back to the logistical world from where he'd just come.

I again ducked into my office to enjoy my first smoke and an actual cup of coffee in several days. I was convinced that I had reached a pretty good place when I finally started making notes about my briefing to the Commanders. After a few drafts, I gave up trying to do anything more than an outline. I think despite the sense of history, preparing anything formal that didn't come from the heart, would be just a waste of everyone's time.

When the knock came at my office door, I was so lost in thought; I think it startled me a little. I looked up and it was my Aide, Captain Simmons, who said, "Sir, they're ready for you." I got up, put out my cigarette, and we headed to the briefing room. Like before, as I walked in, it was the rousing command of, "ATTENTION!" that brought me back to the reality of the moment. I left them at attention until I had reached the podium, and as I stood there, I waited almost another full minute, looking each of them in the eye, before saying, "As you were." Then, to make sure they understood that this was serious, I let them know what a genuine old SOB looks like...

"Gentlemen, we are at war! There is no room for political correctness, there is no room for hurt feelings, and there is no room for personal advancement at the sake of others! We are the United States Army, and our sole function is to protect our people, our country, and now, for the first time in recorded history, the whole damn planet. We are now fighting an enemy that has demonstrated that there can be no quarter, no surrender, and nothing other than extinction. Ladies and gentlemen, I have no intention of allowing us to become extinct! Each and everyone who is in this room or can hear my voice, or later read my words, has an absolute duty. That duty is to each other, our men, our people, and our country. WE will fight, and WE will win! Whether it takes days, months, years, or a whole fecking millennium, giving up is not an option. Right now, we are working to get you the tools and information you need to kill these bastards. We expect you to keep us informed, and we expect you to do your absolute best to keep this the finest Army in the World. Now, when I say in the world, I'm including these friggin' Gomers that are circling our planet. We are better than them, and do you know how I know? I've killed one of those nasty faced bastards in my own home! They can be killed, and we are going to figure out how to send even more of these Gomers to the deepest pits of Hell! Let me make this perfectly clear, we will not waste lives nor will we engage the enemy until we are damn good and ready, but when that time comes, we're not going to hold anything back, either. This is why I'm telling each of you, personally, that it is my intention to kill as many of them as we can, and the sooner the better. Now, some of you are asking how? First, we're going to learn all we can about them, their tactics, their weapons, and their vulnerable spots. Second, once we know more, we're going to exploit what we know to make them hurt so badly they will leave us and slink back to whatever corner of Hell they came from. I also want them to leave thinking they've grabbed a very pissed off porcupine by the shorts and to never come back to our little corner of the universe. Lastly, we're going to do it by remaining disciplined, trained, and fit. Right now, we're in the beginning phases of our Phase I. Phase I is staying disciplined, trained, and fit. The stupid Gomers have given us the day, and we are not going to waste it. We are going to continue to train! We are going to wear our uniforms with Pride! We are going to maintain discipline to the nth degree, which means some of you scruffy assholes will have to shave on a regular basis. You will make sure everyone shaves and demonstrates military courtesy at all times. Most of all, you will remain fit. There will be PT, and working hard out in that sunlight and, when you get guidance as to intelligence or areas to train, you will approach it with all you have. We are going to reward the initiative. Initiative includes helping us learn about the bad guys, and feeding ourselves, and accepting change as a new way of life. Gentlemen, all of this is going to get us to Phase II and Phase III, and beyond! So, what are the next phases? Phase II is kicking those SOBs off our planet, and Phase III is getting our planet back to normal! What comes after that? Your future! Finally, and I can't emphasize this enough, as officers and commanders you set the example! Many of you are serving in positions that are way above the pay grade you had just a few days ago. Some of you will be asked to do things that you normally would not do until you had years of training and schools. Well, I'm sorry, but suck it up, and learn quickly. Read, Study, and Train! Remember General of the Army and former President, Dwight Eisenhower? Well, he started World War II as a Colonel, after spending almost 7 years as a First Lieutenant. If any of you really feel like you can't handle it, or you are too far over your head, say so now. You can and will be replaced without any recrimination! If we are required to replace you after people are killed by your incompetence or when the crap is running down your legs, then I'll promise you that there will be something worse than my recrimination coming your way. Instead, it will be an overwhelming guilt that you WILL live with for all eternity! So, Senior Commanders, watch everyone closely, just as I'll be watching you. If you can't get the job done then, rest assured, there will be no hesitation in replacing you. It is not my intent to scare you, but instead it is my intent to remind you that your responsibilities go much further than your own hide. Do not betray the trust of our people, your soldiers, and our Army!"

With those last words, I looked at my Aide, who immediately brought the room back to "Attention. I left the podium just as I entered, leaving them all standing. My message was sent, and now it was all about keeping these people focused.

Following the adage that there is no rest for the wicked, as I reached my office, there stood the newly promoted Colonel Greene, with a haircut, a shave, and for the first time, wearing a real and complete uniform. Now, it was time to give him his mission. As I stepped into my office, I called General Whitney and together we gave Greene his marching orders. His mission was simple in the statement, but a real bear in practical terms. He was to form his men into functioning teams, go out and collect scientists and their equipment, and also find out whatever he could about the bad guys, their habits, weaknesses, tactics, and operations. He was also to collect more captured equipment and, if possible, try to bring us a Gomer back as a prisoner. I knew these latter two things were probably a long shot, but there is no question it might be helpful to at least find one we could study. I think it truly excited Colonel

Greene because I just gave him a hunting license which meant, at the moment, he was the sum total of the Army's offensive.

Just as Colonel Greene and General Whitney walked out, in sauntered the "Green Giant". The look on his face was priceless, and he didn't even wait for the invitation. He flopped down in the chair across my desk and let out a long whistle before saying, "You know, Mouse, Marty was right. You really are a cross between Patton and MacArthur! Here, you got your own mountain like MacArthur on Corregidor, but your speech was right out of the damned movie, Patton! I swear I was waiting on that 'best friend's face and goo' line!" I was about to retort to that when he leaned towards me and said, "Your speech made a real impression. We didn't have anybody quit, but I heard at least four of the new Battalion Commanders telling their Brigade Commander about setting up a two-mile run for PT at sunup tomorrow. I heard another one talking about putting together a fire and maneuver course in the woods about a mile from here, and the Brigade Commanders are putting together local Officer Training Schools. Seems we have a couple of old farts who used to teach at the War College, and/or at the Command and General Staff College, who are going to help get some of the kids up to speed."

As I lit up a cigarette, I tossed one to Jerry, who also lit up. As we thoughtfully sat and smoked, Jerry said one last thing, "Mouse, we seem to have one other little issue you need to know about."

"Oh?"

"Yeah, it seems you are married to one of those egghead scientists, and she is volunteering to work with the other egghead scientists we've got coming in. Is that okay with you?"

"Hell, yes, I wondered how long it would take before she volunteered for something. Just tell the chief egghead not to let her get hurt or experiment with anything dangerous. Hell, the whole time we were coming here, she wanted to try and shoot that friggin' weapon. I had no idea if it would work or just explode on her, so I made her promise not to do it. So, seriously, she can't do anything that will get her hurt, but if she can help with the math or concepts, then, by all means, feel free to use her expertise. Of course, now that you've opened that can of worms, I want you to set my daughter, Christine, up as my secretary."

"What... more nepotism?"

"Nope, in the civilian world, she was my office manager, legal assistant, paralegal, and 'chief cook and bottle washer'. She knows me better than anyone other than my lovely bride. Besides, it will keep her from going insane hiding in a cave with her son, while wondering about what happened to her missing husband.

"Okay, anybody else you want me to hire?"

"No, but you maybe can sniff around and find out what happened to the rest of my kids? I've got a son, Robbie, who was in Afghanistan as an avionics technician with the 'Nasty Guard' unit deployed from South Carolina, and then there is my youngest daughter, Holly. She is an egghead in training as a college student, and according to Marty, she got pulled out of class by the FBI at about the same time we got the call to leave our house. So, it would be nice, and I'm sure comforting to Leah to know where the hell they might be right now."

"Sure, Mouse, I'll ask around. In the meantime, if you don't mind, my wife can watch your grandson if you want your daughter to work up here. She loves kids, and since we never had any, it might be fun for her."

"Gee, I don't know, he is three and a REAL handful! You should have seen him during the helicopter ride up here. Talk about a ball of fire. So, how is Maggie? My God, how long has it been?"

"She is great, maybe we can all get together later. She is in the room next to Leah. They met earlier today and seemed to really hit it off."

"That doesn't surprise me, I always thought they would. In fact, when I first met Leah, she reminded me of your Maggie. Same fun personality! Now, tell me, Green Giant, just where the hell are my quarters? I need a little sleep and maybe even a shower and a shave!"

"Sure, come on!"

As I dragged up and out of the chair, it really hit me how tired I was and how long the last several days had been. Cat naps are great, but that can only last so long and, right now, I know sleep might be my best weapon. When I was shown my "hole in the wall", I was very pleased. It might be a half mile or more underground, but it was like stepping into the Presidential Suite at the Waldorf Astoria. When I walked in, I was met by the happy 3-year-old and a very large hug from my bride. It wasn't home, but it sure would do for the duration. I ate a quick bacon sandwich and even though I was running on coffee and nerves, I was asleep within minutes of lying down.

When I awoke, it was with a start, and I could sense that my bride was awake and watching me. When my eyes finally popped open, she said, "Honey, I'm very sorry to wake you, but it has been almost 7 hours, and you said you wanted up at the latest in 6. You just looked so tired when you came in that I couldn't bring myself to drag you out of bed."

"Crap, that's okay, but I do need to get moving. Do we have coffee?"

"Sure, I got you a cup right here, and I've also been thinking about something. Here! Now, let me ask you, why do our wind-up watches work, but the electronic ones do not work? If it was an EMP burst, wouldn't even the wind-up watches be magnetized?"

"DAMN!" Now I was wide awake and staring at her. "You are absolutely right, even the old wind-up watches wouldn't work if it had been a real EMP burst! Baby, get me another cup and have my Aide tell Jerry and my G-2 to meet me in my office in 10, no, make that 20 minute." With that, I gave my bride a huge "bad breath" kiss on the cheek and headed to the bathroom to shave and get cleaned up. I think that little extra sleep and my wife's idea just struck a chord somewhere in the back of my mind. Now was the time to find out what song it was playing!

Chapter IV.

When I got into my office, I was pleased to discover that my daughter was already out front and keeping people at bay. I knew she was a great "gate keeper" and right now I needed one very badly. As I walked into the outer office, she looked at me and said, "Sir, Generals Whitney and Larkin are waiting to see you, but before you go in, I think you should know that there is somebody else they are calling the 'rofessor' with them."

"Thanks, Chris, I'll get with you later, but right now, see if you can get Captain Simmons to round up Colonel Greene for me, too." She nodded and immediately picked up the line to my Aide. When I stepped into the office, everyone jumped to their feet, except for the civilian, who looked more like a lost puppy than a professor. When I took my seat, General Larkin was the first to speak. "Okay, sir, we're here, and General Whitney brought along his civilian expert since from what your Aide said, you seemed to have a technical question in mind."

"I do, Jerry, and that was a good idea. Care to introduce him?"

"Sure, General, this is Doctor David Abramson, the former head of the science and technology department at Virginia Tech." As I looked at Dr. Abramson, the chubby little man finally showed some signs of life. He looked at me for the first time, and our eyes met as he extended his hand. You could see a kind of a cold intelligence behind his eyes and, even though his eyes were red-rimmed from lack of sleep, his grip showed that he was anything but a passive dishrag. As we stared at each other for that brief moment, I broke the silence with that traditional greeting, "Welcome aboard, Doctor. I hope General Whitney is making sure you have what you need."

"He is, General, or at least he is trying. I would like to test fire the weapon, though, and I was told that you had to approve the test."

"Well, that is true, Doctor. The last thing I want is for the damn thing to do something inside, so I told General Whitney that all testing of the operation of the weapon needed to be done a safe distance from here. Still, before you actually fire the damn thing, I've got a few questions that I would like to have answered."

"Okay, General, go ahead."

"Okay, Doctor, the first one is this; Shouldn't an EMP burst magnetize a watch and throw off a compass?"

"Yes, that is my understanding. Although I've never actually done research in that area, I do have an assistant that has some background in the field."

"Then tell me why, after Columbia, SC was hit and the electronic or battery-powered watches all stopped, that the wind-up variety watches we found all still worked?"

"Uh, I don't know."

"Doctor, let me pass on some information to you, and let's see if you can make some sense of it. First, the wind-up watches and apparently the old wind-up clocks at a pawn shop were all operational. In fact, I am still wearing a wind-up watch that was liberated for me before we left that area. Another thing you need to know is that on the flight from Columbia to Georgia, and then all along the route to here, I noticed that the Radio Magnetic Indicator or RMI was off. The flight crews were all using the old standby Magnetic Compass, which seemed to be far more accurate. I think it really hit me when my wife asked about the watches, regardless of whether I know that something here is off. Can you find out why?"

"General, I don't have a clue at this point, but it raises some very interesting questions. Let me get with my people, and we'll see if there is an answer. So, are you saying that you aren't sure it was EMP that took out our power grids?"

"Well, Doctor, what did it take to get the old Hueys flying again? The flight crew told me that it was just a matter of using an external power unit stored here to get them going and then, after starting the engines, the batteries recharged just fine. I would have thought that EMP would have disrupted that, even on the old non-solid-state stuff."

"General, the older aircraft have tube technology, and mechanical flight controls, which means that once the electrical systems were restored, then it was a matter of using equipment that was protected or hardened from EMP to get them going again."

"Doctor, did they have to change the 'exciter box' on the old T53-L-13B engines?" This question was met with complete silence, and then the Doctor met my eyes with an "oh crap" look. He slowly nodded his head and said, "No, we didn't have to, and I know this because I remember hearing the maintenance crews fussing that if they were going to have to change them, then they were going to be hard to find. It seems that one of the older airmen mentioned that there were some in an old, hardened storage facility near Fort Lee, in case they were needed after a nuclear exchange." You could almost see a light bulb go off over the Doctor's head, and he became rather anxious almost immediately.

"Sir, with your permission, I'd like to go check on some things and get back to you. I
have a feeling that we may have missed something pretty big here."

"Doctor, before you go, I want you to know that you have 24-hour direct access to me and General Whitney. Right now, you just might be the most important man in this mountain so, on the question of weapons testing, you can go ahead, but I want it done remotely or by someone other than you, and preferably outside this cave complex. Are we clear?"

"Yes, sir!" With that, Doctor Abramson literally bolted from the room. When I looked over at Jerry, he smiled and said, "Weird little duck, ain't he!" I had to agree, but said, "Weird duck or not, that guy could be part of our answer, so whatever you do, get him whatever he needs, when he needs it. As a matter of fact, I've already decided that I'm going to get Daniel Greene to assign him a team for security, and to test any theories that come out of that part of the cave."

Jerry nodded and said, "Good idea. Now, are you ready for the morning briefing? We've had a big night, and several of your staff guys are beside themselves wanting to get you informed."

"Yeah, let's get about it. I think we're in for a very big day." As I stood up and headed through the outer office, General Gregg stuck his head in the door and said, "Sir, you got a minute?" I asked if it could wait until after the briefing, and he nodded, "Yes, sir, but please, first thing afterwards. It is kind of a personal matter, and I've got another officer doing my part of the briefing. You might know her, a Colonel Miller."

"Lou Ann Miller?" Gregg nodded, and all I could say was, "You're kidding me, Lou Ann? I thought she retired years ago." Gregg smiled and said, "Yes, sir, but within several days after the first attacks, she showed up out of the clear blue ready to work." This was an interesting twist, and I immediately thought that my bride just may not like this one little bit. It wasn't that Lou Ann and I had a history that was relevant to today, but we did have one some years before I met my wife. She was almost the one that got away, and those are the ones that linger no matter what else happens in your life. We'd been engaged at one point, but she went her way with a reassignment in Human Resources or personnel, and I went mine into Special Operations and Aviation. There was no doubt that in those days, we both valued our careers over each other and, while it was dead for me, Leah might have an issue. Eventually, Lou Ann married, but it didn't work out any better for her than my first marriage did for me. What is certain, at least in my mind, is that any marriage between us would never have worked out any better. Leah knew about her, but there was never any reason to make it an issue, and I am sure as hell didn't need the issue now. I know that cave was huge, but I'm not sure the almost 25 miles and multiple levels would be quite big enough.

The morning briefing went a whole lot better than the day before. There was less rambling and far more useful information coming through, especially with regard to the array of our forces, their capabilities, and the initial training efforts. There was no question that putting General Davis in as my new Staff Director was the right choice. Even General Carter seemed far more confident and comfortable in his role in Civil Affairs. When we got to the G-1 or personnel portion of the briefing, there stood Colonel Lou Ann Miller. She smiled at me and then launched into an extremely thorough report on the status of the efforts to replenish our manpower shortages, promotions, and personnel related issues from non-judicial punishment, up to and including the status of a couple of court martial cases that had been pending. As she was wrapping up her portion of the briefing, she then addressed my plan for reorganization. While General Gregg might have been lukewarm to the idea, Colonel Miller was openly hostile to it. I wasn't surprised, since the newer "reorganization" into Stryker Brigades, and shifting the power to smaller, more modular units was, in large part, her brainchild. It was precisely this thinking that I had to change.

At the conclusion of her briefing, I took the podium to give my Command Decisions and guidance for the day. After dealing with operational and training details, I finally addressed my position on the new/old regimental reorganization. I explained that the current system was not going to work for the kind of warfare I could see coming, especially given our limitations in mobility. Then I dropped my bomb. We were going to the new system, and it was to happen as soon as possible. Her former Stryker Brigades were now going to be beefed up and become a Division under the older triangle system. My plan was that we were returning to the system where three Regiments of three Battalions each would be our new Divisions. The only difference was that now the special troops, artillery, armor, and aviation would round out the overall strength with what would require only another regiment in strength. They would be smaller than the traditional divisions that everyone in the room was used to seeing, but each would be easier to move, hide, and maintain at a fighting strength.

After making it clear what we were going to do, I wrapped it up by saying, "Ladies and gentlemen, I need everyone here to think outside the box, while remembering that there are some very good things still in the box. We have a new paradigm, and I want this staff to be prepared to adapt to it quickly. The last time we won a global war was in World War II. When that war started, we were forced against a wall, just as we are here, and they had to reshape the Army to fit that new paradigm. They came back from it and soundly whipped the bad guys, but we then immediately shifted to a new paradigm because of the Cold War. As we moved forward, we've tried to adapt to wars that were called conflicts, terrorism, and keep an eye on a global threat. The problem is that we're always fighting the last one and forgetting what worked before the last one or seeing what could work for the next one.

Right now, we are faced with a huge challenge of just such a new major shift in paradigm. We can do the same thing as before, but we need the inner strength to admit that it is a new day, a new world, and a very new enemy. I need units that can hide until it is time to fight. I need units we can maintain, retrain, and sustain with tighter command structures based on the skill levels of those commanders. Are there any questions?"

As I was leaving the room, Colonel Miller was hot on my heels and there was no question that she was pissed. As she reached me, she made a huge error, "General, I've got to speak with you right now because what you're doing is stupid!" At that moment, I'm not sure whether something just snapped or if it was her sense of location in front of the entire staff that was irritating to me at the moment, but I wheeled around on her and let her hold it. I never do this in front of others, but at this point, her actions, already with a large audience, demanded a response in kind.

"COLONEL! *I have made a decision*! The time for discussion is over, and YOU don't have to like it, YOU don't have to personally support it, but YOU, *BY GOD*, will make it happen! If not, I'll find someone who will, and your ass can go right back outside to whatever the hell you were doing before you got here! Do I make myself perfectly clear?" She turned white as a sheet and backed up a step. I went on, "Look around you. There is no more viable Joint Chiefs of Staff; instead, we are doing the job just like during World War II, with piecemeal guidance from above. The Chairman is now in Thunder Mountain and the former Chairman is now the Secretary of Defense. More to the point, the Secretary of Defense Blanchard is the Department of Defense, since the rest, along with most all of the Joint Staff, are now at the bottom of a HUGE smoking hole that used to be Washington, D.C. The paradigm has changed, Colonel, now... *Make It Happen*!" To his credit, General Gregg stepped up and took her by the arm. Almost as an afterthought, I looked over my shoulder at General Gregg and said, "I want both of you in my office, NOW!"

As I strode into my outer office, Chris looked at my face and knew instantly I was not a happy camper. I just confirmed it when she offered to bring me coffee, and I told her, "Later!" Then, when she saw General Gregg and Colonel Miller enter, she knew immediately that they were the source of my irritation and that I wasn't just pissed off, I was in her words "Four plus pissed off."

Now, I know Lou Ann, and I also know that, for her, an apology is not something she really had much experience with on any regular basis. In fact, the entire time we dated and later when we were engaged, I think I heard it once, and that was on the day we split up. As they came into my office, she stood before my desk at a very stiff position of attention and saluted me. General Gregg stood behind her and was watching the whole thing like a hawk. I returned her salute and she stared straight ahead, waiting.

"Colonel, do not ever challenge me like that again in front of the staff. These people are hanging on by a thread and if they start to waver, even just a little, then it could fall apart! I do not ever want to have to say something like that in public again. If you want to argue your point, then we can do it here, but never out there. Understand?"

"Yes, sir, and I'm sorry, I really am. I knew it was a mistake the second it came out of my mouth. It won't happen again, I promise."

"Lou Ann, you are bright. Hell, you are brilliant, but right now I'm holding the head of this goat we're roping. Work with me and I swear we'll get through this. You are dismissed. Now, General Gregg, you had something you wanted to discuss with me?" As General Gregg smiled at her, Colonel Miller started to leave my office like a puppy that had just peed on the new rug. As she reached the door, she turned and looked at me over her shoulder, giving me that exact same grin she did all those years ago when she walked out on our engagement.

General Gregg just smiled at me and looked at the door as it closed before he went on. "Yes, sir, I've got a request."

"Okay, let it rip."

"Sir, it isn't real common knowledge, but I have a Master's Degree in Engineering from MIT, and I'm a dissertation away from my Doctorate in Engineering. I was hoping to get that so I could get a retirement job as a professor somewhere. I guess what I really wanted to ask is for a chance to get out of this job and work with the folks down in the science area on those alien weapons."

This revelation was perfect, and General Gregg had no a clue of his timing. The reason I wanted him to come into the office was to get him or his people to start digging through the piles of records to find me a science guy or three to send down with Doctor

93

Abramson. I disclosed this to him, and then told him, "Gregg, I was hoping to find maybe a Major or Lieutenant Colonel to send down as a liaison, and I definitely wasn't considering a brand-new Lieutenant General for the job. Then again, the Manhattan Project had a General... what was his name?"

General Gregg wasted no time with a response, "Sir, that was Lieutenant General Leslie Richard Groves, Jr., who was a Brigadier General at the time of the project's inception. He was an Engineer officer like me who helped design and build the original Pentagon. He was my hero, my inspiration, and the reason I want this job! I am a lousy G-1 and have been since you gave me the job. I would be delighted to take off two of these stars, hell, I would take off all of them if it would help you make the decision!"

"Well, General, you don't have to remove your stars. I think having three of them down there might be just the signal to the rest of our Army about just how important this is to all of us. Now, before you run down the hallway towards a new assignment, I need your recommendation for a replacement, as if I didn't already know who you had in mind."

"Sir, I know she has been gone awhile, I know you two have a personal history, and I know she just peed in your cornflakes this morning, but, yeah, I was thinking Colonel Miller."

"General Gregg, let me say if you want to make her the Deputy G-1, and even hang a star on her, then I'm all for it. Right now, I would like to sleep on my choice for the actual G-1 position, just like I am waiting to make the right choice for a new G-3. Get me a list of your three best choices for both of those positions, and I'll convene a board to make a recommendation as to that choice. While we're at it, I need you to either find me the Sergeant Major of the Army or get me a list for us to consider for promotion from the available pool. You know, there is a reason that an Army Board selected you for your original job at the Pentagon, and it might be high time we got back into the board business or at least gave it a shot for these upper-level positions. The last thing I want is someone to claim favoritism."

"Sir, is it just because of your personal background with Colonel Miller that you want someone else to make a recommendation?"

"Nope, it is primarily because someone stuck me with a General Carter as Staff Director, and a Colonel Rhymes as G-3 on the first day. This shooting from the hip is mighty dangerous when it puts square pegs into round holes. As for Lou Ann, I have no doubt she would make a great G-1, but if you think jumping her over other general officers is a good idea, then you don't know some of these guys."

"I understand, sir, and it makes sense."

"Oh, and by the way, General Gregg? I will need you to cut orders by appointing Generals Larkin, Davis, Whitney, and yourself to the selection board. They are to consider three of the open senior positions; the first is a replacement for Rhymes at G-3. The deputy did a good job this morning, but I don't know if it was Davis covering it, or if it was that kid that had his act together. Still, I need a senior man, who Davis can work with closely. The second will be for the G-1 Position, the Colonel doing it this morning did a great job, right up until she stepped on her own tongue." With that remark, I looked at General Gregg, who dropped his gaze and smiled. "Finally, I do want a new Sergeant Major and he needs to truly have his stuff squared away. Hopefully, this newly appointed board can get me some recommendations no later than tomorrow."

"Yes, Sir, I'll take care of it."

"Now, on a more pragmatic point, I'll need a list of Units off the reflagging list and orders cut to bring some of our old units back out of retirement. I would say at this point to leave the deployed guys alone, which means if half of the 82nd is in Afghanistan, then leave them as the 82nd. Reassign the local boys first and don't forget to give them the histories and a shot of pride when you have given them their new divisional flags."

"Sir, you do know that their flags are in museums and not in this cave, don't you?"

"Sure, I do, and I also know where these museums are located or at least where there are some official flags just lying around. I guess we'll see who has guts and is savvy enough to scout around or scrounge around on a recon to bring back their new colors! Now, get out of here and make it happen. OH, and tell Colonel Rhymes that being a division commander with a star will take study. If he needs advice, he just needs to ask." General Gregg stood up, saluted, and was walking out when I personally realized that, deep down, I really was hoping that the board came up with someone else for the job of G-1. I could only guess what Leah's reaction would be about it all. After all, the one time they met before it was oil and water, which don't mix worth a darn!

No sooner when General Gregg walked out, then came in Chris with Jerry Larkin. She had coffee and he had a message. I must admit that neither was particularly palatable. As I sipped the heinous witches brew, I read about how the Russians had tried to attack one of the larger objects with some pretty horrid results. I wasn't sure whether it was the coffee or the message, but I had an awful feeling in the pit of my stomach. Once the missiles cleared their silos, they were attacked by the smaller objects. None of the missiles got through to the target and, to make it worse, the smaller objects were able to track most of the missiles back to their source with the same results we had seen around Columbia in South Carolina. More craters of various depths, and more dead or more to the point, more missing. The exceptions to the rule were those missiles fired from silos near mountains. For some reason, the smaller objects broke off their attacks and continued with their decimation of anything in a built up or open area. After reading it, I looked at Jerry and said, "Well, what do you think? Did General Bozeman or Admiral Morton sees this report?" Jerry nodded, and explained, "We got this report from Bozeman's people and Morton's folks confirmed it. I was also briefed about the situation at Marty's new home."

I responded, "And? How are things in new Washington?"

"According to Marty, things are worse than confused. Apparently, when the President heard about the Russian's attempted attack and failure, he just went back into his quarters, and now he won't come out at all." The only response I could even think to utter was "Jesus, Mary, and Joseph!"

"Okay, Jerry, do I need to talk with Marty, maybe give him something to cheer him up? I think we've got a few things going for us, and I think we might even be on the verge of finding some answers. Should I tell him now or wait until we know a little more for sure?"

"Mouse, I'd leave it alone. From the sound of things, I'm more afraid that the despair at the top could be contagious, and if we try to cheer them up, they could say 'no' to what we're trying to do here. Hell, when General Bozeman heard about the Russians, his deputy swore he saw the old man physically crying. I think they had the same plan in the works, and now they're kind of frozen in place. From what I can tell, only the Navy and this bunch of vagabond soldiers are still really trying to stay in the game."

"Okay, Giant, here is what we're going to do. Keep most of Washington and the Air Force off my ass, I'll talk to Marty personally, but for now, keep Bozeman out of my hair. In the meantime, I think maybe the Admiral and I might need to have a little chat."

"Consider it done, Mighty Mouse! I'll have him on the horn in a few minutes. Now, what is this garbage about a board of officers?"

"Yeah, we need a new G-3 and G-1. It seems that our old friend, General Gregg, is a bona fide egghead type scientist, and we need to get him down with the other egghead scientists to figure out what is going on. The sooner they get us useful information, the sooner we... WHAT THE HELL JUST HAPPENED?" As we were speaking, the lights within the entire complex dropped down to barely a glow, almost as if a dimmer switch had been turned down. Then they surged to half again their normal brightness before returning to normal.

As we sat in my office trying to find out what happened, there was much running back and forth outside in the corridor. Then within a few minutes of the power fluctuation, Colonel Greene burst into the office with a look of absolute dismay. "Sir, are you okay?" After being assured that I was fine, he ran down the hallway towards the depths of the cave, checking on each of the rooms as he went. Within a minute, General Whitney appeared at my door. He was sheepish and more than a little perturbed. "Sir, I've got some news for you, and I'm not sure you're going to like it very much."

"General, this is the day for it, go ahead. Do you know what just happened?"

"Yes, sir. Despite you telling Dr. Abramson not to test fire the weapon himself, and not to do it inside the facility, he did both just a few minutes ago. Unfortunately, we are probably going to need to find a new science and technology director, but the good news is that his team has discovered something that I think we can use to help us and to use against the Gomers."

"Whitney, what do you mean 'probably'? Is Dr. Abramson dead or alive?"

"Sir, he is alive, but barely, and two members of his team are completely gone off the face of the earth. Apparently, when the weapon fired, it evaporated two of the team and seemed to drain Dr. Abramson, almost like draining a battery. The Doctor was the one firing and his team members were actually beside him, as opposed to being behind him or down range."

"So, what does this tell us, Whitney?"

"Well, it tells us that your hunch was right. It wasn't EMP, it was an energy drain. Which is why recharging batteries on our old technology is all it takes to get them up and running again. The solid-state equipment, on the other hand, has enough capacitor usage that replacing all the circuit boards could take a while. Still, it might be worth a shot. As Dr. Abramson went limp, he apparently was telling anyone that would listen that you were right."

"Whitney, get him to the Docs and back on his feet as soon as possible. In the meantime, get his deputy or assistant, or whatever the hell you call them, moving forward with proper testing in a more controlled environment. We need to know why the hardened stuff here wasn't drained. Is it our shielding or something else, and now you can add a new factor to the equation, why didn't the Gomers attack stuff in the mountains of Russia and why haven't they bothered to hit us here yet?"

"Yes, sir, I'm on it. Oh, and I heard a rumor that General Gregg is a bona fide scientist, is that true?"

"It is true, and so I want you to get him briefed and down there now. His original orders were to clean up things here first, but obviously we can't wait to get adult supervision in place immediately."

"Yes, sir."

"Jerry, would you get Greene in here, and while you're at it, get me Admiral Morton on the line."

"Yes, sir."

As everyone headed out, I tasted my coffee again, and realized why it not only sucked, it stunk, literally. "Chris? Where did you get this coffee?" She smiled and pointed to an older coffee pot in the corner. "Okay, well, where did you get the water?" This time she went over and opened up an access panel in the wall that revealed a small spring well that formed a pool in a little basin. She said, "The facilities engineer came by this morning and showed me that trick. He said I could use the water for coffee but to be aware that it did have some Sulphur in it, so it might have a little weird taste. He assured me that it would be something we'd get used to tasting and it shouldn't kill us."

"I'll be damned. So, sweetie, do me a favor. Get him in here, too. I think it might be time to find out what these hills are made of. And by the way, please see if you can find some better water. This coffee is beyond horrible!" As I was finishing my thought, the phone rang, and it was Admiral Morton.

"Admiral Morton, good morning, sir. I hear you confirmed that attack by Russia?"

"One of my boats saw most of it and they monitored the attack initiated by the Russians. It got ugly quick."

"Admiral, is it true that the bad guys avoided the mountains?"

"Yep, apparently, they go within a few miles of the ridges, and then immediately turn or fly straight up to almost space, and then over the top, without pressing any of their attacks. Why do you ask?"

"Not sure yet, Admiral, but it looks like we might be onto something, and we'll keep you posted as we go along. Do you have any science types that love things like geology?"

"Of course, we do, the nuclear navy is chocked full of 'science guys'. Hell, I've got a degree in nuclear physics."

"Excellent, Admiral, since I'm just a simple ground pounder, I'll defer to your knowledge, but what we are seeing is that what took place was not EMP, but instead an energy drains of some type. We've got our older UH-1 Hueys up and flying and we even have a couple of our M-1A1 Abrams tanks starting to get their legs under them."

"NO KIDDING? How are you pulling that one off?"

"Admiral, I need to get my eggheads on the line with your guys. You open to a little cross-service collaboration?"

"Hell, yes, we just need to get Bozeman on board."

"Okay, if you say so, but I've heard that he isn't really in the mood now and neither is Marty. What if we kept it amongst us girls, at least until our science guys can figure it out a little more. You still game?"

"Sure, it isn't like we can do much else than watch right now. I've been wondering why they haven't attacked my submarines; maybe it is the shielding of the water. Perhaps a factor of density of the water?"

"Or minerals..." I interrupted. "Listen, we've got one or two of their hand-held weapons we managed to capture, and we had a very interesting event a little while ago. Once we get that data together, all our respective experts need to be talking. Maybe collectively we can figure it out, but let's keep it quiet until we can give the powers that be something to be hopeful about."

"Sounds like a done deal. I'll get my Deputy CNO to talk to your guy, and we'll set it up. Right now, I've got a couple of

Aircraft Carriers that are still around, but useless. Maybe any idea would be better than what we have now."

"Excellent, Admiral, I'll pass it off and my guy will be in touch. Oh, and for your Deputy's information, my Senior Science guru is a General Gregg. He will talk with your Deputy within the hour. Have a good one, Admiral!"

"You too, General."

I broke the connection and had my Aide gather the key staff in the briefing room. This time, the room only contained Generals Larkin, Davis, Whitney, and Gregg. Colonel Greene came in with what was left of the science staff, and an extremely pale and weakened Dr. Abramson was helped into the room in a wheelchair by my senior staff physician. Finally, the Facilities Engineer, an older officer aptly named Colonel Farmer, came into the room with the plans and specifications for our "new Pentagon".

"Gentlemen, we are here to discuss science, cooperation, and hope. Dr. Abramson, you or one of your people need to tell us about your rather ill-advised weapon experiment and what you have found." With that, Dr. Abramson pointed to a younger man, who explained to everyone in the room what they had discovered and what they thought would work to get our equipment up and running. I then got Jerry to explain the Russian attack and what we had discussed earlier. Finally, I got Colonel Farmer to talk about our mountain home. Specifically, I wanted him to discuss the geology, the minerals present, and the chemicals, which were all items that not only surrounded us, but probably surrounded our

Russian neighbors that survived an onslaught from the Gomers. I then gave them their marching orders.

"General Gregg, take this bull by the horns. We need to know about the shielding properties provided to us here, and the Navy's experiences with their submarines, salinity of the water, mineral contents, and the whole shebang. We also need to get our key equipment back up and running and provide the Navy whatever you can on how to get some of their aircraft back in an operational status. According to Admiral Morton, his deputy CNO is waiting to hear from you about what you had found, what you know, and what you can collaborate on in the future. General Gregg, you, sir, are now my General Groves, and we're all counting on you and Dr. Abramson to make this happen. Keep us in the loop; let us know what you know and what we can do to help. Okay, thank you, gentlemen." I signaled to Jerry and Colonel Greene, and we left the rest of them behind to work out details about moving forward. Once we were clear, I advised Colonel Greene to grab a map of the local area and meet me in my office.

Chapter V.

As I stepped into the office, my daughter was on the phone, and she had the look of someone who had seen a ghost. She was completely pale and her eyes were full of tears. My knowing that something was very wrong did not require an advanced degree since her look of horror was obvious and very genuine. She motioned for me to take the phone, and I did. It was my old friend, Marty, our new Secretary of Defense. After a fairly short discussion, I, too, felt the horror creeping over me that was so clear on my daughter's face. As I hung up, she fell into my arms and just sobbed. This is how General Larkin and Colonel Greene found us, when they walked in discussing the new science of our situation. I guess it was the look on our faces that made them stop because the news I had to give them was beyond the pale. I told them both to give me a minute and I asked General Larkin to get the primary staff and my personal staff together in my office, and NOT the briefing room.

Five minutes was all it took to get everyone together, and now I was standing behind my desk, looking at all the key members of my General Staff. As the staff stood around the office, I asked Captain Simmons and Colonel Greene to come in and for everyone to get comfortable. What I had to say was going to make them uneasy, and frankly, made me just a little sick to my stomach.

"Gentlemen, approximately 30 minutes ago, it was discovered that the President and his family are all dead. It seems that he snatched a weapon from his Secret Service detail and then locked himself in his quarters. There is only supposition as to how things progressed from there, but the results are very clear. His wife and young daughter were both shot and the President died from an apparent self-inflicted gunshot wound." I looked around the room and there was nothing but dismay registering on everyone's faces. Like my daughter and me, the first reaction was one of shock, which then turned to anger. Once everyone had a minute to assimilate this information, I continued. "We need to be careful how we disseminate this information. I think at the present we only need to release that he is dead, without reference to the reason for his death. The last thing we need is for despair or hopelessness to pervade the troops. Dammit, there is hope, and I fecking KNOW we can beat these guys. Everyone in this room knows that we've found out more in the last 24 hours and, who knows, by tomorrow we could have the answer. Regardless, this news is a real problem if not handled properly. Normally, I would never advocate downplaying something like this, but these are not normal times. Are there any comments or arguments to the contrary? If so, I'd love to hear them."

This was met with complete silence and a few nodding heads. With that acquiescence from the group, I continued. "Here is our immediate problem, aside from the 'how to tell people' question, and that is the official line of succession. From the President, it goes to the Vice President, who we know was killed in Washington, along with the Speaker of the House and the President Pro Tem. This gets us down to the Secretary of State, the Secretary of the Treasury, and then to the Secretary of Defense. Of these last three positions, we have the Secretary of State who went missing, and is presumed dead, when all of this started in Korea. The Secretary of the Treasury was in Chicago on a visit when we were hit, so he is the highest man left on the food chain that might still be at large and alive. This leaves us the Secretary of Defense, who was the only temporary appointee to the Cabinet made after the fur flew. So, in a nutshell, we need to send a team to Chicago to see if our next president is going to be Secretary Markus or the Secretary of Defense, Martin Blanchard. Right now, Marty is holding onto the head, but we need to know the deal about Markus, and we need to know very quickly. Anyone have any ideas?"

After some silence, Colonel Greene offered, "I guess I can get a team to Chicago if we haul ass first thing with the sunrise and then hole up there for the night, we can try to pull it off. Do we have a clue where to start looking?"

"Daniel, I got nothing, other than a last known address at the hotel where he was supposed to be staying. General Whitney, do we have anything about that part of the country?"

General Whitney pulled up some notes, and then said, "Sir, oddly enough, the areas of Michigan and around the Great Lake shoreline appear to have spared some of the bad guy's attention."

"Really, I wonder why? Just as an aside, get our science guys to look at what geologically significant stuff is going on around there, and do we have any secure nodes and/or personnel nearby?"

General Carter actually roused up and said, "Yeah, actually, we do, since I've been trying to get a National Guard Unit that is operating in and around Chicago to assist with the local population.

I believe it is the 33rd Infantry, out of the Illinois National Guard, and they have been establishing food centers, and guidance to the locals about how to shelter at night."

"Excellent! Get them on the horn right now and get them the address that my daughter has out on her desk. Captain Simmons, go with him and get him whatever assistance he needs to get through to them so they can determine if he is still alive and what is it going to take to get him here. The sooner we know, the sooner this whole country can take a breath. I think before the news about the President gets out, it might be damned important to know that his replacement is in place and in charge."

I admonished them all, including my daughter, to keep the story under wraps as long as we could, and then I sent General Gregg off to ponder the notion that certain parts of our country were not being hit as hard by the bad guys. 'What the hell do these places have in common?', was the recurring theme in my mind. Not to put too fine a point on it, but the commonalty was a far more important matter than the President flipping out and quitting on his people. The more I thought about the President, the madder I got, and the more determined I was to make sure we held on and won, no matter what it took. Another thing that made me mad about it all was that we needed to keep our troops' morale up, and this kind of desperate behavior was the last thing they needed to hear, especially since this brand of stupid has a nasty habit of being contagious.

Then, for the first time, I thought about how every Commanding General also had a more complete personal staff.

This was one of those very rare times that I could have used one, since I had managed quite well without it in the past. Usually, such a staff consists of a chaplain, judge advocate general, inspector general, and maybe even a public affairs officer. While I didn't need most of them under the current circumstance, right now a JAG or a Chaplain could come in handy for these burning questions. As I turned to ask about whether we even had anyone that remotely qualified for either position, Jerry stuck his head in my office. "Sir, I know what you're thinking, and I found a Methodist Chaplain in our midst, who just might be what you need right now."

"Jerry, you're a scary guy. Okay, brief him up, and put him on standby for anyone that was in here earlier that wants a little time with the 'holy joe'. While you're at it, you might even want to scare me up a JAG officer for the legal ramifications, and a PAO to spread the word when we are ready."

"Yes, sir, I'll get Colonel Miller on it, and we'll let you know. Is there anything else?"

"Nope, I've got some reading to do, so keep me in the loop!" With his departure, I began reading more of the reports out of Korea and Japan, and of the Russians' recent encounter. I was deeply engrossed when General Carter came in shaking his head. "Sir, we've got people out searching, but they have no idea of where he might be or even if he is still alive. All they know for sure is that the hotel where he was staying no longer exists. I did take the liberty to do a little homework on him though, and for whatever it is worth, you do know that Markus was born in

Germany and wasn't naturalized as a citizen here until sometime in the late '90s?"

"I'll be damned. Are you serious? I mean, I hadn't thought about it, but you're right. Now that I think about it, there was some discussion about him not being a natural citizen, yet he was now in charge of the treasury. The supporters were all pointing to Kissinger and the detractors were screaming that a foreigner should not oversee our money. General Carter, you are a genius. Congratulations, you just earned a Legion of Merit for using your damned head!"

"Thank you, sir. I was afraid I was in the doghouse with you."

"General Carter, you were never in the doghouse. You were stuck in a job that you weren't ready to do yet. It is not your fault, and I hope to hell you never think it was your fault. I will admit to being irritated at first, but please know that my irritation was more about having to shake things up to get people's attention and our overall situation than it was anything directed at you personally. I apologize for any misunderstanding about it, and please know, you're a key part of this staff right now. Good job for using your head!"

"Thank you, sir, I'll keep that in mind."

"In fact, General, it was my intention all along to kick you into play, so hold what you've got. Keep contacting these Guard Units, and keep in mind that once we go on the offensive,

I'm going to need people to lead them. It might be a good idea to wander down to the library and study up on what Division and Corp Commanders do and how they handle things when the fur flies."

"Yes, sir!"

The moment General Carter cleared the door; I asked Chris to get the Secretary on the line. I had something that was going to either make his day or make him the most miserable SOB alive on our planet, or maybe even both. Within minutes, I was on the phone with the Secretary of Defense and this time it was my turn to do the talking.

"Mr. Secretary, it is my duty to inform you that you are the ranking member of the presidential cabinet who is still alive and eligible to serve as the president. We have run down the list and the only person senior to you that might be alive is not a natural born citizen as required by the United States Constitution. As you will recall, Secretary Markus was born in Germany, which means I am now addressing the nominal President of the United States. Upon taking your oath of office, I will be delighted to serve under you as our new Commander in Chief."

The audible sigh that followed was not very reassuring, but after a moment of silence, Marty said, "Thank you, Mike. I really do not want this job... especially now, and under these circumstances."

"Sir, with all due respect, Truman didn't want it either, but he was one of the best Presidents we ever had in the history of the entire country. Rest assured, if you will get them straight in Washington, I'll do my best to keep it going here. Besides, I've got some possibly good news for you."

"I could use some good news. What do you have for me?"

"Sir, we think we've found some anomalies and some commonalities that will help us kick their asses off our planet. I've got my scientists working with Admiral Morton's scientists and we are starting to find out that they just might have some weaknesses. We are away from getting all the details straight, but our camel now has his nose under the tent."

"General, you need to keep me informed, and I'll go take that oath. Once I'm on board, the first thing I want is a full briefing. Can you guys handle it?"

"Yes, Mr. President, I do believe we can. If you'll give us about 12 hours, we'll lay it all out for you. Would you care to visit us in our humble hole?"

"Yes, General, I believe I would, and if you have a stiff single malt scotch lurking somewhere around there, I'll be happy to share it with you."

"That is a done deal, sir! We will look forward to seeing you tomorrow." With that, I hung up and told my Aide to gather the key staff together one more time.

This time when I looked around the room, there was a look of grim determination, and in General Gregg's case, a look of slight irritation. I know he was getting upset that he kept getting dragged into my office, but I didn't know what else to do. Right now, he was about to become a star and I could only let him know what was coming in person. Besides, I planned not to bother him again until the new boss got here. I began by praising General Carter and his revelation about the line of succession. Then I explained that we had a new President, who was now going to be visiting us in our little paradise. So, news of the President's death had to be given out, but only without any mention of details such as how he died or the death of his family. If they could leave the troops with the impression that it was a heart attack or some other natural cause, then so much the better. I advised them not to lie, but the actual cause of death was, for now, classified, so omission of details was going to be the order of the day. Finally, I told them that we now had a Chaplain, and if they wanted to meet with him, General Larkin would be happy to set it up.

Finally, I advised them that, "Tomorrow's dog and pony show needs to include everything we have on the bad guys. What we know, what we think we know, and what we still need to find out. Then we need to start our planning for what we are going to do to rid our planet of these pests. In other words, you're briefing the President tomorrow, so please comb your hair, and maybe even break down and shave. OH, and General Clark, this time if you show up with a damn cigar in our mouth, you'd better offer one you haven't gnawed on to the President."

As the staff broke up, their entire demeanor was different. They were, to a man or woman, almost buoyant. I stopped General Clark and asked him if he had any decent single malt scotch in his endless storehouse of goodies. He smiled and asked what brand. I laughed and gave him the list of Marty's favorite stuff. I also made arrangements for Marty to bunk in my suite with Leah and me for the evening. Then I cornered Jerry and pushed him on the Promotion Board issue. We needed to get the G-1 and G-3 items worked out immediately, and so I wanted names in about three hours. I also took Gregg off the hook, since he had better things to do with his time. I had a clue about the outcome, but it needed to happen with enough time for them to brief our new President.

Precisely two hours later, General Larkin came into my office with the results of the Board, and they were exactly what I expected. My new G-3 was going to be that young Colonel that briefed that morning, Colonel Roberts. Even though he was young, he was extremely sharp and, apparently, a solid planner. My G-1 was now going to be Colonel Miller and, regardless of my own personal misgivings, I co-signed them both and told Jerry to give them to the new G-1 to be processed for orders. Within an hour, the new officers were assigned to their respective posts, and their real work continued since neither of them really had a new job from what they were already doing; they just now had the Brigadier General stars to go with it. For now, all focus was on getting answers and getting ready for the next briefing.

The question of the Sergeant Major of the Army was still an open one and while I wasn't happy about it, they did provide me a couple of names. As I perused the list, one name jumped right off the page at me. Sergeant Major Clagmore, who was, without a doubt, the meanest SOB I'd ever met in a uniform. He was a legend in the Airborne, Ranger, and Special Operations communities. I had even served with him years before and, frankly, he still scared the crap out of me. He was also about as subtle as a grenade and about as politically correct as a gorilla on steroids. Now, I could see why Jerry was having problems. When I got to the third name, I decided that his qualifications were almost as impeccable as Clagmore's, and I gave Jerry the nod. We now had a Sergeant Major of the Army, a veteran of three conflicts/wars; Sergeant Major Laird seemed like a good choice for this one. I told Jerry, "Get him the orders cut and get him on board by tomorrow at the latest."

With that decision, I took the opportunity to head to my quarters and give Leah all the news. Most of it she wouldn't like, but then there was little in the way of news we were enjoying right now. We'd come a long way from watching CNN or FOX before heading to bed. When I got to my quarters to grab a meal and be with my bride for a few minutes, she had a surprise of her own. My grandson wasn't the only child running around in this cavern, and my bride was now fully engaged in a different war of her own. She was getting a school established and finding wives, husbands or significant others that could teach these kids. It made my day to see that these things were going to continue and I made a note to make sure that Marty heard all about it. Then I told her about the President and Lou Ann. Neither nugget of information made her very happy, although she took them both in stride. Her only comment on Lou Ann was to say, "Honey, I truly believe in you, trust you, and love you. Her, on the other hand, maybe not so much." With that, we ate and then it took some time to just be together. It didn't last long, but we savored it, and with my batteries recharged, it was back to the salt mines. Literally!

Once I left, I wandered with my security detail down to visit with General Gregg in his new habitat. I also took the chance to wander the cave with Colonel Farmer as my guide. It was a real eye-opener, to see that we had, virtually, the largest military installation in the world, all underground. There was housing for at least two divisions, and I mean the old divisions with their four swollen brigades and special troops, which means I could put one of my new Corps in here with room to spare. It was a real ant hill, and the more we toured it, the more I got a weird feeling in the pit of my stomach. Oh, we had plenty of room, and we even had absorbed some of the civilian populace who came to us through the efforts of General Carter. I did not spend long looking over the civilians, but from what I saw, they were being fed, housed, and provided with what little amenities a cave can offer. Leah was correct, as this place was literally crawling with kids of all ages. Some, I noted, were of military age, and even a few were approaching my detail asking where they could join up. I made a note to make sure that my new G-1 earned her pay be getting a basic training program up and running and assisting Leah in setting up some DOD type schools. Kids need something and wandering around bored and exploring not only the cave but each other, struck me as being a lousy way to spend their time.

As the "tour" continued, Colonel Farmer was delighted to point out that the warehouse facilities were massive, and the repair shops were running full time working on both ideas and equipment. He was like a car salesman pointing out all the features of our new Lexus, "We have multiple entrances, and even a few that operate like massive garage doors to allow for the movement of tanks and aircraft with ground handling wheels. Sir, we even have fuel in an adjacent facility, carved out of the ridge line next to ours!" Sure enough, this fuel depot was full of all types of fuel, running the gamut from aviation to regular gasoline and loads of diesel. I know it wasn't Colonel Farmer's intent, but the more I saw, the more I felt that we were really in a rat hole that was way too vulnerable. The bad guys don't seem to like mountains, but why? More importantly, how long would this last? They know their weaknesses, which means they are working just as hard to cover them, as we should be at covering ours. I know historically that neither caves nor reliance on terrain alone has ever really worked to keep out the bad guys. Ask the guys on Bataan or Corregidor, or even Singapore, for that matter. In each of those cases, the leadership thought that holding up in a cave or using what they thought was impassable terrain would keep them and their armies safe. That latter thought sent a chill through me because none of those cases had a happy ending.

When we got back topside, I decided that my new G-3 needed to get to work on a better defense plan and an evacuation plan to fall-back positions somewhere. We would also need to figure a way to direct attention away from us and make it part of either a solid deception plan, or at the very least, we would need to disperse our resources before we lost everything in one attack. There would be no way to launch an offensive if all we had were starving troops using clubs for weapons. For some reason, deep down, I knew that time was working against us. I filed this away and decided that once the new President had a moment, I was going to see what he thought about this posture, after all, he was a real General and a tanker before he got all the serious responsibility. Tankers, like aviators, think in terms of mobility, and I figured his perspective might confirm my suspicions.

I finally reached my office, and waiting patiently were Generals Larkin and Davis, my Staff Director. I passed on my notes to General Davis, and we had a brief discussion about my impressions and the civilian presence in the lower levels of our facility. As I was wrapping up, Captain Simmons knocked on the door with a message for us. "Sir, the weather is dropping outside, and I mean dropping. Seems we have an early "spring" seasonal weather pattern and the 'new Washington' cave system should be under 2 to 3 inches of snow by tomorrow morning." No sooner than he got that out, then our new G-3, Brigadier General Roberts, rushed up with a very grim look, "Sir, 'new Washington' is under attack from the air!"

I looked at Jerry and General Davis and said, "Okay, gentlemen, get everyone up on alert, get them dispersed as much as possible. Tell all the commanders to be prepared for the worst. If they are hitting new Washington, then I'm betting we're next. Get your butts moving, and I'll be in Operations. Get cracking!" As General Davis and General Roberts headed off to the staff, I grabbed Christine and told her to get back to our quarters and let Leah know to hunker down. Then it hit me, the thousands of civilians! When I walked into Operations, I immediately called for General Carter. His deputy said, "Sir, General Carter is in the civilian area, getting everyone back to their quarters and having them get down until told otherwise." I think I may have audibly sighed in relief because Jerry came up behind me and said, "Sir, we haven't been just sitting around, you know. Carter has this situation covered; you are selecting him for that position may have been one of your better moves so far."

"Gee! Thanks, Green Giant, you know how to make a girl blush!"

"Mouse, I always wondered about you!"

Now that we had traded our obligatory barbs, it was time to settle down and see just exactly what was going on in new Washington. As the reports came in, I was pleased to note that there was no actual breach into the heart of their stronghold. The two brigades of Marines charged with the outer ring of security did suffer some casualties, but the strength of the enemy's weapons was not doing any appreciable damage to their underground facilities. The thing that hurt them was that the vermin had used the weather system as a cover to advance some of their ships ahead of the twilight line. I also noted that their weapons did not appear to be quite as powerful as they would be at night. In the end, it was mainly a probing attack, which failed again because of their inability to close the mountain. Now, this was news we could use. With each tick of the clock, we waited and, as the weather closed in around our new Pentagon, the tension was palpable.

Still, nothing happened until darkness had set in around our mountain. Outside it was cold, wet, and windy. All reports indicated that the visibility had dropped to almost zero, and while we didn't have heavy snow like they did over new Washington, we did have darkness and heavy rain with sleet. The attack at new Washington was apparently over and people were starting to breathe again when the first loud explosions began along our outer defenses. The power beams were devastating the further out from the mountain you went, but as the foothills merged into the higher ridges, the weapons seemed to lose effectiveness. In fact, there was almost no impact at all over certain portions of the mountain, and the Gomers were nowhere near our fuel reserves. Naturally, this was filed away to research the composition of that portion of the mountain, since 'the why' it didn't work would be a key to unlocking their technology. As they pressed their attack, it seemed to build in intensity. Almost as if they'd brought in larger weaponry, which, of course, is exactly what they had done. Reports from our observers were that one of the large ships was directly to our east, between the Blue Ridge Mountains and our position. It was firing along the entire mountain range and after about 50 miles or so, it turned into a racetrack pattern and was repeating the process.

Other reports about damage were flowing in constantly, with the worst being the collapse of two lateral tunnels leading into the civilian areas. There was no word on civilian casualties, but we were making some losses in our military personnel. At this point, we considered the idea of how to return the fire without risking the positions or the personnel. It was then that I had an idea. We got Admiral Morton on the line, and I asked him if he still had any armed drones available. Fortunately, he did, thanks to our earlier discoveries, and he could get them in the air overhead us within an hour. I didn't ask where they were coming from nor did I care. I wanted them to bounce on that big bastard that was hitting us when he turned to make another run on our ridge. The little ones were not much of a threat, but that big one was making a dent, and I was truly concerned that the dent would eliminate our abilities later to ever attack them. This being on the defense was not working worth a damn.

I then told Jerry to get a hold of our air defense batteries to coordinate an attack from the Blue Ridge Mountain sites. My idea was that when it turned and was focused on us and our ridge line, then it might not notice the heavy stuff coming from the direction of the opposite mountain range outside of Wytheville, Virginia. "Tell those guys that once they have fired what they have, they are to do the 'shoot and scoot' and get their asses under cover. I have a feeling that once they let go, then the little guys will be all over them." Granted it was a long shot, but since the large enemy ship could stop our future abilities to fight back, it was now or never.

As the rocking of our cavern continued, there were other reports of minor collapses and the loss of more personnel. At this point, we were more alone for the ride than anything, but we had to do something. About 45 minutes later, during the fourth turn of the large ship, we got the green light from Admiral Morton that the drones were on station and ready to fire whenever we were ready. I explained to Admiral Morton that we were going to fire our batteries and give us a 10-second delay for his drones to fire. I was hoping that this might distract the bad guys long enough to let our guys in the batteries get a chance to get away. When General Larkin confirmed that our batteries were set and ready to move after firing, I gave the command. It didn't take long to unfold, but this time we got some results. The firing on our positions stopped immediately and it was clear that the large ship was now focused on the more immediate threat coming from the opposite mountain range. Fortunately for us, the stupid Gomer completely missed the stealth drones that now launched a half dozen of their "anti-ship" missiles right up his tail pipe.

While it was a small thing to the overall global conflict, we had just gotten our first major kill and it was spectacular, according to everyone who saw it. Unfortunately, it was truly a mixed bag for us. While we had taken out one of the big ones, the little ones carved a huge chunk from our air defense personnel and equipment strength. Out of 25 batteries located in the area, 8 fired their missiles, and the losses in men and material from those 8 were horrific. The attacks stopped, but losses on and around our ridge were telling. The civilian areas came out fine, and except for the two tunnel collapses, there was little to tell that we'd been hit with a pretty major attack. Most of our casualties came in the Air Defense batteries, but there were losses in almost all of the combat units. Still, it was a victory because it stopped the attack, and it allowed us a chance to see their technology in action. I know that Dr. Abramson and his people poured through every after-action report, photograph, and written weather analysis they could get their hands on. Colonel Greene had teams headed out to the crash site almost before the thing had hit the ground. What they would bring back would tell us a lot.

As the staff were enjoying their victory, another report came in that was almost as chilling as the original attack. Shouting to get everyone's attention, I made it clear that we had another problem, "Gentlemen, we now need to fan out to every nook and cranny in this tomb. We have Gomers in our midst, and as of now, they are being reported in the upper levels. Get our security personnel on high alert and search this cave from the lower levels all the way to the outer perimeters." With the new threat, I wondered if new Washington was having the same experience. As I stepped out of operations, I motioned Jerry to follow me and I told my Aide to get Admiral Morton, General Bozeman, and the President on a conference call. We needed to advise them of our experience, and we needed to let them know what else might be coming.

Back in my office, the phone lines were crackling like mad, but they were at least usable. Once the President was on the line, I began, "Mr. President, we have Gomers inside the wire and the line is probably not secure." This was a signal that Marty would pick up on immediately. As for General Bozeman and Admiral Morton, I was not sure they would get the code I was about to send to Marty, but there was no question that the President would know exactly what I was telling him. "Sir, the squid and the mouse gave the elephant an enema, and it is no longer with us. Once the roads are clear, we'll get you the medical report. Unfortunately, all of this may have allowed some of the roaches to come into the pantry. So, everyone needs to be careful, and check real close for roaches in their areas."

Everyone should carefully inspect their areas for roaches.

The President responded immediately with a chuckle and said, "I love mice and squids, good job, and yeah, we've had a roach problem around here for the last few hours. We are working on it, and I have the Terminex number on speed dial." Admiral Morton got it, and he responded, "I think calamari is great, so long as it isn't fried. We solved the roach problem but will keep an eye out." General Bozeman simply responded with, "I have no damned idea what you're saying, but when someone decides to let me in on the joke, I'll be happy to listen." This time you could tell that the President was no longer chuckling when he said in his cold voice, "Bozeman, ask a Ranger or one of your forward air controllers to translate this for you immediately. Okay, let's go get our roads cleared up and our pantries cleaned. Out!" When the line went dead, I was wondering what the weather over Thunder Mountain was going to be like for his sundown. I just hoped for Bozeman's sake that it wasn't like ours; otherwise, he was going to have a damn long night.

As the night wore on, it almost became a game for our younger airborne troopers providing security. They would corner a Gomer, shine a light on him and pop a flash bang, collect his equipment when he disintegrated, and send it all back to the science section, along with the residual pile of material that once was the Gomer. I even ran across one young private with a dustpan and a flash bang, who told me that 'he ain't never been a-huntin' like this afore, but damned if it ain't as much fun as spot-lightin' a raccoon'. I just smiled and patted his shoulder, and as I walked back to my corner of the cave, I somehow knew that we might be turning a corner. Morale was the highest it had been since we crawled into this hole and despite having some of them come inside the house, there was no sense of defeatism anywhere.

Fortunately, no Gomers were found in the middle or lower sections of our complex, but a long and thorough search was done into every section and space in the caves. Naturally, this took a great deal of time and manpower, and it would be noon the next day before the threat was completely eliminated inside the cave. The reestablishing of secure communications was a slightly easier process and we were back up and able to communicate freely by midnight. It was at this point that I spoke with the President again and made it clear that he did not need to come to us. Instead, I was sending a team of briefing officers up to him, headed by General Davis, along with the science data we'd collected so far, and once the sun was up, they would be on their way. I told Marty that maybe his eggheads on staff could look over the data we were collecting and confirm some of what our people were finding.

It was mid-morning when we heard from Colonel Greene's people. It was a short and simple report, but their excitement on the communications channel bled through and attached itself to everyone in the room. "Operations! There is a veritable ass ton of stuff out here, to include a lot of dead Gomers. They don't look like the ones that came at us and these didn't disintegrate on impact. We're going to snag one or two and bring them back. We also have what looks like communications equipment, and we're taking pictures of the crap we can't carry. Get us some trucks and maybe some air cover for some aerial shots, and we'll get back as much as we can scavenge. This looks like the damn mother lode. We even have one smaller object that appears to be just stuck in the side of the mountain below what is left of one of the air defense batteries."

I looked around me. The staff was beside themselves with excitement and Dr. Abramson was bouncing up and down like my grandson on the helicopter. I think I might have been the only one that was waiting on the other shoe to drop which, thank GOD, didn't happen, at least not right away. With more questions than answers, I decided that maybe sleep is a weapon and I turned things over to General Larkin, and headed to my quarters for at least a cat nap.

I opened the door to my quarters and realized that sleep just wasn't something that apparently was ever meant to happen. My grandson ran up and grabbed my leg in a huge hug the minute I stepped into the room. "Grandpa! We gots lotsa company." Sure enough, we had a packed house, and as I took it all in, I realized that I was in the middle of a real family reunion. When the attack started, my mother had been on a visit with family in West Virginia. While I'd been worried about her, just I was worried about our missing kids, Holly and Robbie; I knew there was little I could do about it. In some ways, if she had been with us, the journey we had to take to get this far would have been even worse for her. Still, here she was, along with my aunt and uncle, and several of my cousins and their children. In short, the place was packed, and the noise was continuous. Over the din, here was my bride, Leah, explaining to me what happened.

Right before the attack hit us in the mountain, my bride had been in the civilian areas recruiting anyone that could teach. Flyers and notes had traveled the area, and it seems that one of the teachers to step up to the organizational meeting was my mother. I have to give her credit, because with her failing eyesight and the years that had passed since she retired, she was still quite willing to help. I guess old teachers are a little like old soldiers and fire horses, they hear the bell and come running. When my mother saw Leah walk in to the meeting, she reacted with more than your usual surprise. She couldn't believe that Leah made it this far north or that I had anything to do with this underground city. In fact, she had given up on us, thinking that we must have been lost in all that had transpired over the last week. When she discovered that we were alive and actually in the same place, she couldn't wait to get to Leah. There was apparently much hugging and crying when we were sounding the alert.

At about the same time, my oldest, Christine, and my grandson, Michael, were hitting the door to our quarters, so was my bride along with my mother and the rest of the family. The entire time we were getting pounded, they were riding it out and catching up on all of the travails of the last week. With everyone talking at once, I hit overload almost instantaneously. With a sheepish grin, I said I had work to get done and would be back later. I gave my mother a huge hug and said, "I was just checking in to grab a shave and clean uniform. You know how it is, no rest for the wicked." With that, I smiled, shaved, changed, and hauled it back to my office. Once there, I sent my Aide to find me a cot, where I promptly fell asleep behind my desk.

Chapter VI.

After about a four-hour nap, I was awakened by the smell of that nasty brew my daughter was forced to pass off as coffee. She was looking down at me and smiling. "Now, why did I just KNOW you were going to be hiding here on a cot?"

"Well, the reunion was getting just a little loud and I had to get some sleep, so what have I missed?"

"Nothing on the home front, but somehow I have a feeling that isn't what you're asking."

"You know me too well, little girl! Now, get Captain Simmons in here and find out where Jerry is hiding. I need an update."

With that, the roiling bag of butcher knives I call a daughter handed me my coffee and headed for the door. Within minutes, I was back in business, and when Jerry came in, you could tell he was as wiped out tired as I had been a few hours before. I let him get me up to speed and then I shipped him off to his quarters for a nap. Before he had even cleared the doorway, General Gregg and Dr. Abramson came bounding into my inner sanctum like two kids who had just found the Christmas tree full of goodies. The look on General Gregg's face stopped Jerry dead in his tracks, and he wheeled around to come in with them. I handed Jerry my coffee and told Chris to get a couple more cups for our guests. As we sat down in my office, you could tell that General Gregg was about to burst.

"Okay, Gregg, whatcha got?"

"Sir, we have learned a shit ton about the Gomers. For example, we now have two classes of them. The first is what we call the dusty Gomer'. They are the ones that you encountered, and what we've had all over the upper levels. We call them dusty because they disintegrate with noise waves. The second is what we call the 'meaty Gomers' because they have real substance and appear to be the aliens that are running the show. You can kill them, but they take a little more than a flash bang to do it. We can tell that a gunshot would do it because all of the ones we saw died of blunt force trauma when they crashed."

"Excellent! Go on... what else?"

"Well, two of the 'meaty Gomers' survived the crash and we have them as prisoners down in a seclusion area. Oddly enough, we found out by accident that if you put them too close to the walls of the cave, they get violently ill and their skin begins to sluff off like a lizard or snake shedding, only these guys emit a lot of heat and steam depending on the amount of sulphur they are exposed to at any given time. If they get close enough to the walls of the cave, they can even send off a toxic smoke. Oh, we also found out during the autopsy of one of them that the water we have here is like acid to them. Distilled water wasn't a problem, but the high sulphur content of the crap we're using for this nasty coffee does a real number on their skin tissue."

"Really? We clearly have enough sulphur in this water to kill them with this coffee, hell, it is killing me. Maybe we should invite them in for a cup. Okay, so what else have you got?"

"Well, sir, the mineral deposits here are high in sulphur, lead, iron, and dolomite. We think that the lead, iron, and/or the sulphur are what prevent them from flying too close to the mountains. It must also mess with their navigational equipment and it is clearly toxic to the 'meaty Gomers'. Sunlight also screws them up, and we think we have the answer to that one now, too."

"Good, so….?

"Oh, well, Dr. Abramson here has a theory, so I'll let him explain it."

"Okay, Doctor, but please do it so a simple old soldier can understand."

With that, Dr. Abramson reached into his notebook and pulled out a spreadsheet of numbers and began his dissertation. As I looked at Jerry, it was obvious that this was a perfect sleep aid, but the doctor finally got to his point.

"So, with that, we were able to determine that what we thought was EMP was actually their 'sucking' all the energy from the various power sources and power grids."

"Wait a minute, you mean to say that all that has happened to the infrastructure is that it was just completely drained of all energy?"

"Yes, sir, that is exactly what I'm saying. For example, we replaced the batteries in the electronic watches and they work like new ones. No change, no difference, no problem. Your question about the exciter boxes on the helicopter engines and some work with capacitors demonstrated to our satisfaction that with some minor repairs in the electronics, we can get most anything up and working or flying, in no time."

"Well, I'll be damned as a Son of a Gun! Have we passed this 'theory' on to Admiral Morton yet?"

General Gregg cut in, "Yes, sir, we have, and the Navy already has some of their aircraft fleet back up and running. We even passed our data on to the President's staff and the folks at Thunder Mountain."

"I'll be damned. I wonder how Bozeman took the news that the Army and Navy cracked the nut before his own whiz kids." With that last statement, Jerry broke out laughing and then looked at me very seriously. "Sir, you don't suppose that the President should have a word with Bozeman before he goes off half cocked before we're ready?"

I thought about that one for a minute and then told Jerry to get an encrypted message to the President with just those concerns along with our autopsy results for his science advisors under my signature. As we wrapped up the briefing, I asked General Gregg to tell me a little more about the 'dusty Gomers'. "Just exactly what are they? Holograms? I mean what is their composition?"

"Vanadium Oxide, Fluorine, and Sodium Chloride are all elements we've found in both the 'meaty' and 'dusty' Gomers. The dusty ones seem to have more Sodium Chloride in them than the 'meaty' ones, but none of them do well inside these leaded, sulphur-encrusted cave walls. Our best guess is that instead of being Carbon-based, they all seem to be Fluorine-based, while the 'dusty Gomers' are 'saltier' and simply held together by some electrical charge. Their hand-held weapon is used to help keep them together by pulling the electrical charge from within our bodies to help hold their own bodies together. That is why the noise or anything that disrupts that process makes them just fall apart. They don't need to eat anything other than energy yet when the sunlight hits them directly, it is almost like they can't deal with the surge of energy, which means there are limits in their absorption capacity. Needless to say, we're still working on that one, but that is at least our best theory for the moment."

"Doctor, how did they travel across space without having a surge stop them before they got here? I mean, why wouldn't a star along with way have stopped them before they got here?"

"Sir, if you will recall, these jokers came at us from a part of our sky that isn't loaded with stars. It is our best guess, and again it is only a guess, that they plotted a course that permitted them to get only the energy they needed to get here. This is why they work the night and keep their main ship on the dark side of the moon which is away from the sun."

"So, do we have any ideas on how to stop these jokers?"

"Yes, sir, we think that a pretty simple solution could be the answer. It seems that they can't see through anything with lead around it or on it."

"You mean to say that all we need is the lead-based paint that is now outlawed as being harmful to the environment to do the job?"

"Yes, sir, although the good news is that some shipyards may still have lots of it since they used a lead-based paint on ship bottoms, the bad news is that they only used it a lot until fairly recently. I think it is banned now because of the damage it was doing to the sea water. So, we hope we can lay our hands on it from several known sources that aren't that far from here."

"You are kidding me, right? I can get a toy from China covered in lead paint, but I can't easily find a bucket of lead paint somewhere in the United States? Hell, even our gas is unleaded, wouldn't you know it."

"Sir, we'll find it, we just need to get out and start looking. The good news is that we might be able to make it or at least a lead coating that we can put on our weapons."

"General Gregg, make it happen. I want our weapons retrofitted with lead, our armor coated in lead, and while you're at it, let's start using the distilled water for our coffee and this nasty stuff in the walls for weapons. Can do?"

"Yes, sir, we're on it." With that, my brain trust left the office, and Jerry and I were left to our thoughts. After a minute or two, I looked over at my old friend and said, "Jerry, get some rest, and in about 4 hours, I want to see nothing but assholes and elbows around here. We have an offensive to plan, new weapons to distribute, and an Army to get back up and running." Jerry nodded, and then I added, "Jerry, I think the Gomers really screwed up badly last night. They pulled the switch too soon, and now they have tipped their hand. What they have wanted all along is our energy. Man-made or natural, it is their staff of life, and now it is going to be the club we use to beat them in the head."

As soon as General Larkin headed to his quarters, I gathered the rest of the Staff. General Davis and some of the key briefing officers were still at new Washington with the president, but we sent them the encrypted message, so our latest information was being briefed even as I was gathering the remaining staff. My new G-3, General Roberts, and G-2, General Whitney, began the slow process of trying to piece together our operations plan. Meanwhile, Colonel Greene was passing on the newest information about the Gomers, their locations, habits, and tactics. It was all enlightening, and with each new discovery, the latest information was being passed on to those who needed it.

When the UH-1 Huey helicopter from new Washington arrived, I was out on the pad to greet General Davis and get him moving on to the latest information that came in while they were still in the air. The sun was about an hour from setting, and it was the first time I had stepped outside in the fresh air in days. The damage around the top of the mountain was obvious, and while it looked a lot worse than it had been inside, it was still a little unsettling. The first aircraft had landed and I was talking to General Davis as the second bird touched down. We were headed back towards the entrance when I heard a scream that pierced the air even over the sounds of the rotor systems and aircraft as they wound down through their shut down sequences. It was a simple scream, but one that completely froze me in my tracks. "D-A-A-A-A-A-D!" When I turned around towards the scream, my youngest daughter was running straight for me with a look of sheer joy. Her leap was almost a little short, but she wound up in my arms, hugging and crying, as she held on for dear life. I'm not sure who was happier, her or me, but at least now we had Holly home. After we hugged some more, I motioned for my Aide to get her down to her Mom. While I would have given my right arm to head down for the big reunion, there was no way I could go with her. I gave her one last hug and watched as she walked into the tunnels to her new home.

General Davis had been watching all this and just smiled at me as she was walking inside. He wiped a tear from his eye and said, "Oh, yeah, I forgot to mention… the President sent you a little surprise. I'd say from this angle, your surprise was about 5'8" tall!" I was so choked up that I really couldn't say much of anything, except muttered, "Thanks, man, I… Thanks!"

Unfortunately, that brief moment of joy passed, and as we walked back into operations, it was clear that we were an Army about to shift over to the offensive. I was getting hourly updates on the strategic and tactical situations as the planning process ground its way forward. The only thing holding us back was the acquisition of the materials we needed to do the offensive work. Of course, then there were other things that we found to be almost equally problematic.

Our Chairman of the Joint Chiefs was an interesting study, and while now it was more of a ceremonial position with little real meaning under the new paradigm, you still had to respect the position. General Bozeman was a bomber pilot, with plenty of experience in the air, but not much experience with anything nearer the ground, like real human type people. He was a champion of missiles but apparently was having staff problems over in his part of the world. Unlike my original staff that needed work, training, and tweaking, his staff knew their business. No, his staff problems were apparently created by his own hand, and more closely resembled those issues that existed between Captain Bligh and Mr. Christian. It would be precisely this type of conflict that would lead our President to the painful decision of having to relieve his most senior military Commander. In fact, General Bozeman's relief could best be characterized as just plain ugly.

When I got this message, it was during one of the tactical updates and our endless readjustments to the defenses around our current home and of new Washington. The Gomers were not messing with us at all and in fact, there had been no overflight or appearances of Gomers in our area in almost 24 hours.

Instead, they were now all passing to the south of our mountains and leaving their western travel clear of all our mountains and northwest around the Great Lakes. Still, we wanted to keep our air defenses mobile, and undercover enough, to make sure that the Gomers couldn't pinpoint their exact locations. We made maximum use of the lead and sulphur filled geography, and we even found a mountain formation that the locals called the "iron gate." We shifted frequently to keep the Gomers guessing, so when I got the "Bozeman" message, it came as a surprise that wasn't a really a surprise.

I read with some interest that he was relieved, but I was even more interested in his replacement in the Air Force, a Major General Thayer. From what I was told by General Davis, he knew this guy from their days at the Pentagon on the Joint Staff, and that this guy was a "Good Egg." Shortly afterwards, I was summoned from operations by Christine. "Dad, the President is on the line, and he really needs to talk with you!"

With this summons, I jogged into my office and picked up the line. Sure enough, it was the President and, boy, was he pissed. "Mike, I've got a real fricking problem! I had to dump Bozeman. That man was crazier than an outhouse rat, and his staff was falling apart. In fact, right now he is under arrest, just to keep him from doing something else stupid."

"Mr. President, if you don't mind my asking, what happened?"

"Aside from being a pompous jerk, he just decided that the warning about the Gomers and all of the other data from you and Morton, were just useless scraps of information. So, he was literally infested with what you are calling...what is it? . . . . 'Dry Gomers?' No.... 'Dusty' Gomers."

"Not good, what was the outcome?"

"Stupid bastard lost almost 500 men, and a third of his strategic missile capability, all in one fell swoop. You know why?"

"No sir."

"Because he said that none of us knew what we were talking about, and that he was untouchable inside his damn mountain. Well, he wasn't, and now his ass is unemployed. Hell, he wasn't even taking the steps you passed on to get his C-130 and C-17 fleet operational again."

"Wow, I'm sorry, sir."

"Don't be sorry, you and Morton are all I've really got right now. The new guy should be a good one, although he is relatively green. He was a Major General on my Joint Staff when I was Chairman, and his area of expertise isn't strategic, but at least he knows how to fight and keep his head out of his ass. Right now, that is a real plus!"

"So, what can we do to help him?"

"As soon as they get their C-130s back up, can you help them with some personnel to root out Gomers and set up security?"

"Yes sir, I'll alert my 101ˢᵗ Airborne guys to be prepared to head there as soon as transport can be sent to them. I can guess it will be tomorrow at the soonest since we're not too far from nightfall today."

"That works, and, by the way, when I was briefed on your new structure, I was somewhat skeptical. Your G-1 did a good job explaining it, and right now, you're telling me that you're sending a Division is extremely comforting. I know it is about the size of our old brigades, but darned if it doesn't sound better to me. I've even just told the Marines to adopt the same set up. So, now instead of a couple of brigades, I'll have two divisions covering me here."

"Glad I can help, and before I forget, thanks for finding Holly for me. I truly appreciate it and so does Leah."

"Not a problem, besides, I owed you one. The civilians you're protecting in your basement contain my two kids and all of my grandchildren."

"I did not know that sir. Can we send them your way?"

"Hell, no, I'd never get anything done if I had them under foot. Instead, I might send Antoinette your way, this first lady crap is starting to go to her head. Last week she was Toni, and now she is getting way too formal for me playing the Antoinette card!"

I burst out laughing, thinking about my own quarters. Then I told Marty, "You got it, sir. We'll keep an eye on them and give Toni our best."

"Thanks, Mike, and for the record, Admiral Morton is the new Chairman. You'll be pleased to note that he not only didn't want the job, but said that when it comes to ground forces, you're the guy. Hell, he even wanted to assign the Marines to you, but then the Commandant started raising hell, and Morton backed off. I haven't appointed a new Secretary of Defense since I can't afford to lose either you or Morton. The COG guy that is acting in the position doesn't really have a clue, so you'll continue to answer directly to me. Is that a problem?"

"Thanks, Mr. President, but you know me and Marines, and NO, I'm more than happy to answer to you. At least I know you know your business."

"Hah, I wouldn't spread that one around if I were you, and as for Marines, last I looked you have a pot load of them in your mountain, so play nice."

"Aye, Aye, sir!"

"Damn, Mike, be careful, this line might be bugged by a jar head with an attitude!" With that, the President broke the connection with another very hearty laugh. I guess the rest of the world would never know, but Marty and I as young men would often engage our brethren in Marine Green in a friendly game of "break up the bar." It was never personal, but more about testing our individual combat skills. Of course, that was back before we had to worry about the 'Pepsi Generation' getting their knickers in a knot when soldiers acted a little rough around the edges.

Once I broke the connection, I briefed General Davis, and we got a warning order out to our 101st Airborne Division. Sure, it was smaller, but it still had as much punch as the original 101st of World War II fame, and they were every bit as motivated. The remnants of the rest of the unit were now the 17th Airborne, also famous for their exploits in southern Europe in the same war. As you went around the horn, we were seeing regiments and divisions spring out of the ashes, and each was starting to adhere to their "ancient" military histories. We even had an incident that drove that point home right in our own cave system, when members of the newly formed 11th Airborne Division and the 13th Airborne Division decided to mix it up in a friendly game of "rearranging noses." What made this remarkable is that just a day before, both units were brigades in the same 82d Airborne Division, and now they were fighting over their respective turf and histories. While I wasn't wild about the fight, these kinds of events meant that units were coming together with pride and a sense of purpose. Now all I needed to do was to point them and their excess energies towards the enemy.

As the day progressed into several days, the scientists were working their magic. Paint for weapons began to appear, as did other items that our scientists felt would blind the enemy, or at the very least, keep them off balance. Some genius even started fitting some of our 155- and 105-millimeter artillery shells to carry bursts of sulphur. Right under our noses, a civilian industry began to take shape among our population, and they were coming up with other creative items that were high in sulphur and lead content. I guess putting a community of miners in a cave wasn't such a bad idea after all. General Carter was running this show and was literally making mountains out of mole hills. The collapsed tunnels were all repaired, and tighter security was put in place to make sure that the Gomers stayed outside.

The civilians that weren't digging or making what we needed were out working for General Clark in his food program or teaching for my wife. I was especially delighted to see this happen, since it freed up a lot of our soldiers to get refocused on honing their combat skills again. Leah had her schools up and running and was even turning it into a first-class school system. With the help of my Mother's advice, and even the former superintendents of several of the local school districts, a complete education system was emerging, to include limited college classes. All this effort had one purpose and one purpose only: Winning against an enemy that had no business on our planet.

As with the quality of life, our plans were improving daily. With the addition of each innovation, we were getting closer to being able to strike back. Colonel Greene's unit was sending teams out gathering information, and when they could, they were testing some of the simpler things out on our Gomer enemies. One such test almost made me mad enough to consider relieving Colonel

Greene for going too far in his testing regimen. My guidance was to keep all our testing limited to our passive systems but, in this one case, Colonel Greene's curiosity almost let the cat out of the bag.

Colonel Greene, who was never a tanker, was headed from the mountains out into the flatter terrain in Virginia, driving an M-1A1, Abrams Main Battle Tank. This particular Tank was now coated in a nasty shade of pinkish-red lead-based paint. Using more guts than sense, Colonel Greene parked the beast in the middle of an intersection near a main interstate highway, turned on the lights, and then waited for a curious Gomer flying object to come check him out. Sure enough, right after twilight, along came an object moving up the highway in search of a source of energy to suck in with its weapon. When it clearly spotted him and was moving in his direction towards the FLIR and main lights, he killed all the lights and backed the tank up a few dozen yards. The object stopped and began a search pattern. It was not picking up the heat from the idling tank, and it continued to work the same pattern, right up until Greene pulled back right into the object's path. As it went over him, it still didn't see him so, being the curious soul, he decided to give the main gun a brief but violent work out.

As the object turned to come back over the road, Colonel Green, along with his running buddy, Sergeant Major Gamble, fired their main gun at point blank range into the object. The results were immediate, and quite favorable, assuming someone ordered the fried Gomer dinner special. The downside was that when it was hit, it flipped over and crashed inverted, almost taking out the tank with Greene and Gamble inside. When I heard about the incident, I honestly did not know whether I wanted to give him a medal or put my boot up his behind. Both ideas crossed my mind, but Jerry reminded me that it was precisely that kind of crazy stunt that got me a Bronze Star once. I had to agree, so Daniel Greene, Colonel, Special Forces, was given a Bronze Star, and so was his compatriot Sergeant Major Gamble.

This was our last active test, as we began getting everything, we owned ready for the next step. In these few remaining days, the Air Force was well on the way to getting a lot of our C-17 and C-130 fleets back in action. They were even making significant progress on some mainstays of our tactical air assets, like the F-15 and A-10 aircraft. I was particularly pleased with having the A-10 coming back online, since it was a low-tech tank buster that could be very helpful with any low-level attacks. The Navy was also responding with innovations arising from the data we developed. In short order, much of the Navy's weaponry was becoming modified to address the weaknesses of the Gomers, and it was clear that we were rapidly approaching the point where a counteroffensive was quite possible. We only hoped we would have enough time to make it all happen before the Gomers figured out how to hit us first.

After two weeks the initial planning was going well, and it was well into the middle of the night that second week when I finally got some more good news. Jerry came into my office with a huge grin and said, "Well, Mouse, you didn't make it easy, but we finally ran down your boy."

"What do you mean, I didn't make it easy? I gave you name, rank, and unit, how was that confusing?"

"We were looking for a young Sergeant working in avionics in Afghanistan. What we didn't know is that he is now a young Lieutenant in charge of a remote communications relay site somewhere near the Indian portion of the Himalaya Mountains. So, thanks to him, we're able to get messages from our forces in that part of the world."

"Giant, you have got to be kidding me. You mean he is fine?"

"Mouse, he not only is fine, but right now, unless a Yeti grabs him, he is about as safe as anyone on the planet."

"Leah needs to know; can we get her the word? Although, you might go easy on the Yeti talk, I wouldn't want her dreaming of abominable snowmen munching on her baby!"

"You got it, Mouse, I'll let Maggie break the news to her. Now while we're on the subject of that part of the world, what are we telling the Chinese and Russians about what we know?"

"Jerry, I've got nothing. I'm not talking to them, but then again, that isn't our job. That decision comes from the President and whatever passes for a State Department these days."

"So, what do you think? Should we share with our new global allies, or are we still thinking that they are up to no good."

"Seriously, Jerry, I mentioned all this to the civilian leadership, and now it is up to them to make that call. If it were up to me, I'd probably tell them, but it isn't our call. Nobody asked for my opinion on this subject, I just happened to volunteer it, and when I did, you'd have thought I had something fuzzy and meant growing out of my head. My belief is that we need to get rid of the Gomers and worry about the politics later. What the folks in new Washington think is a whole different matter."

"What about our former allies, like the UK and Germany?"

"We actually have shared information with them already through our military leadership in both Italy and in Spain. It isn't like we can hide stuff when we're collocated with them and needing to defend ourselves, so yes, they know and are acting on it just like us. Now whether there is a global offensive or not remains to be seen. Right now, do NOT plan on it. I think we're in this by ourselves. Most of our 'friends' are waiting to see if we can pull it off or not, before they leap into the abyss with us."

"Don't you love fair weather friends?"

"Well, fair weather or not, if you're down to your last four divisions I can almost see them being skittish about things. I guess I would be too, except right now, I'm too pissed off to wait much longer. I hate having someone else fight my battles for me, but then again, I'd make a rotten Frenchman."

"Ouch! I'll try not to quote you for posterity, especially since the French gave us such wonderful things as French bread, French fries, and white flags."

"Get the hell out of here, Giant! I've got stuff to do before I pass away from old age. By the way . . . don't worry; I'll tweak the new Washington again. I'm like you, since I really would like to know what we should tell the Chinese and Russians, especially because I would love to have their assets on board with us for a more coordinated global attack. Then again, if they're not going to help, then to hell with them, and we'll stick to the local campaign we've been planning." On that note, General Larkin headed out to start putting the final touches to our rather simple plan.

A common element to all serious military operations, whether it is a D-Day or the invasion of an Inchon, as the clock ticks down and the assets are brought online for the attack; there will be a huge mix of both excitement and trepidation, along with copious amounts of excrement. This operation merely typified this concept. Sadly, as with most things involving politicians, the final plan came together as something that we would have to pursue without any other global assistance. I think the world was waiting to see if we could make it stick before they stuck their necks out. As the time ticked away towards our final H hour, I was beginning to wish it WAS someone else sticking their necks out. Our initial assault was planned for the passage of the "twilight line" into the mid-section of the Continental United States, almost right along the Mississippi River basin; however, this left us with too much area, and not enough forces to pull it off. What we needed was a smaller box, where the combined arms attack would not overtax our limited Air and Ground resources. I could only hope that the technological adjustments, our deception plans, and the sheer guts of our individual forces would make the final version work.

The overall concept of the attack plan was simple: We would allow the twilight line to bring the Gomers over the battle zone of our own choosing. We would have our air forces arrayed in front, and ground forces throughout their anticipated route of advance, based on what had become their rather routine, routes of passage. Finally, there would be the Navy, waiting silently under the waves, to stuff some serious fire power into their rear after they had passed overhead and were preparing to engage our land forces. If we were lucky, we could at least reclaim a large portion of the Eastern Continental area. If not, then we were rolling the dice with all we had available. No pressure there, I guess. The only bright spot was that we could limit ourselves to the middle and southern parts of the country and still achieve many of our initial goals. We never really lost the Northern latitudes, thanks to the time of year and the 'midnight' sun, but what we wanted back was our breadbasket and our living space. Having said this, personally, I wanted to hurt them like they'd hurt us. Maybe if we hurt them enough, they would call it quits and get the hell away from our planet.

Chapter VII.

With the call of "Attention" I entered the Staff briefing room and took my seat at the front. General Larkin followed me into the room, and we were both seated before I advised the staff that, "Ladies and Gentlemen, you may begin." I knew this was a moment for history, so my newly appointed Public Affairs Officer was taking photographs from the corner. I was just hoping that this historical moment was being recorded for future generations, not because of my ego, but because I truly hoped we would see future generations.

I was pondering this uncertain future when General Davis took the podium and began the briefing by stating the intentions, I had provided him as guidance over the entire planning process. It was simple, "Kill Gomers, Kill more Gomers, and whenever possible, Kill even MORE Gomers." Granted, it wasn't a new line exactly, and frankly I stole it and paraphrased it from Admiral William Bill "Bull" Halsey, but it got the message across just as his line had worked in early 1943, during World War II in the Pacific. Being far more eloquent, he managed to rephrase things for the benefit of the audience, but this was more about the dog, the pony, and to keep us focused than it was about getting the information to the staff. Call it a rehearsal maybe, because the result of this briefing would be the final version of the Operations Order that was going to go out to all our Commanders from the Corps to the Division, and eventually down to the lowest Private, who had to make it work.

General Davis wrapped up, and then handed it over to General Whitney, who began by explaining the situation by telling us about the Enemy Forces. He made constant reference to a world map and began by outlining what we learned about the Gomers, and their capabilities and tactics. With each new piece of the pie, the room would lean further forward in their seats. There was a complete hush and General Whitney addressed me by saying, "General, in short, they have worked the twilight to dawn lines as their area of operations. They are sweeping the world in a very methodical manner, and they love to repeat patterns where they scored sources of energy before. The most blatant example is their fascination with Japan, and the site of the nuclear facilities that were destroyed a couple years ago in the earthquake and resultant tidal wave. As we all know, it is still a hot area, and every night, until the dawn line chases them off, they position at least two to three of the large ships over the site, drawing as much energy as possible from the ruins. Russian sources state that Chernobyl is seeing similar activity, and the Savannah River Site is another location that garners a lot of attention. As to their passage over our potential battle area, it seems that they prefer to come over our coast and then bypass our eastern Appalachian Mountains to the south. They will leave a couple of ships over the Savannah River Site, and then continue moving around to the south, before moving back north to cover the middle of the country. So far, they have avoided most areas around the Great Lakes, and it is our belief that this is based on the amount of Iron deposits contained in those surrounding areas. When they begin to approach the Rockies, they move back to the south through Nevada, New Mexico, and Arizona until they enter Mexican airspace. It is our belief that this pattern is to maximize the amount of energy they can collect, while completely avoiding the mountains to the west and into the Rockies. We seem to have three naturally occurring bottle necks where the majority of the Gomers' Fleet will travel on any given night."

With a glance around the room, General Whitney pointed to the Map of the United States, and said, "Specifically, the first real bottle neck is a line that runs parallel to the James River in Virginia. As they cross the coast, they usually enter in a line abreast type formation around the New York area, and once the line contacts the mountains, they 'wheel' south to run down the coastal plain to Washington, DC. This takes them down towards Richmond, Virginia, where they are kind of bunched up until they cross into North Carolina near Raleigh. From there, their lines appear to expand back to just short of the Blue Ridge Mountains, and they continue their sweep until they reach the next choke point, which is just south of Atlanta, Georgia. This second area is much wider, but they still must consolidate themselves before turning to 'wheel' around the Mountains, to begin their sweeps through the heartlands of the country. The third choke point is further to the southwest, and it is here that they make their turn to leave the country and head southward over our border into Mexico. Frankly, it is at this third choke point where they get their sloppiest, but then again it is a huge area, and it is much harder to avoid the Rockies, so as they spread out, there isn't quite as much 'bunching' up as you see at the other two points."

Taking a sip of water, General Whitney then explained that "The Gomers' movement throughout the rest of the countryside is carefully choreographed to allow for the main force to move around the mountains, then to the north and then back south, within the nighttime hours. Their careful avoidance of the Northern latitudes coincides with the amount of sunlight in those areas. The converse is apparently true as well. Naval observers noted that in the Southern Hemisphere, the Gomers have made themselves at home in the Antarctic region. Specifically, we believe, based on the amount of traffic, that the Gomers may well have a base in that region; however, no hard evidence is yet available, since communications from the area are often disrupted or garbled at best. As of today, we can assume they are there, and we will make every effort to confirm this prior to H hour. Finally, the technical information we have gathered has been compiled in a new Field Manual for Official Use Only, which has now been provided to the commands in the field to permit the training required to educate the individual service members at the unit level. Unless there are additional questions, General Roberts will brief you on the availability and disposition of our friendly forces."

Without hesitation, General Roberts began by setting out the forces we had available for the offensive and their various commanding relationships to one another. It was the culmination of a lot of reorganization, and considerable movement and hiding of some forces from more remote locations into what we thought would be the target box for the attack. Going back to the World War II manpower model allowed for more flexibility for our attacking forces and permitted us to organize our units in various Corps and Army structures to maximize the effectiveness of our limited assets, along with permitting the most efficient command and control. I now had two new Army Commanders assigned in the continental United States, now referred to as either the CONUS Theater or Battle Area. These Army Commands were now organized as the First and Third Armies, and each of these Armies had three Corps at their disposal. These brand-new Corps Commands were to be prepared to establish their portion of the initial box around the trap we were going to set, and they were to do it with at least three Infantry Divisions and one Armored Division apiece. The Armor was there to round out their combat power, but each of these Divisions had what we hoped would be sufficient artillery to make a real dent in the Gomers.

Our total strength of our new "old style" Army Combat Divisions for use in the CONUS Theater, now ran at four (4) Airborne Divisions; twenty-two (22) Infantry Divisions; and seven (7) Armored Divisions (including two (2) Armored Cavalry Divisions). This allowed us to have almost another Army size element to operate as a strategic reserve if it became necessary. In addition to our two numbered Armies, my Headquarters was to retain direct control over the Airborne Divisions, who were to be staged at dispersed locations and be ready to move as necessary, either by helicopter or C-17 aircraft, to support the forward Armies. This left us with four of the Infantry Divisions, and one Armored Division that could also provide reinforcement as the battle might require. Finally, we also retained control over the equivalent strength of two more Marine Divisions, the regiment of Rangers, and all the Special Forces elements, to wage a special operation or two that might surprise the Gomers when they weren't looking.

When General Roberts finished briefing the various missions, attachments, assignments, and structure of all the units, both higher and adjacent, he then began to reinforce the concept of the lines of command and control, by making it quite clear exactly who was holding which head, where that head was now, and where it would be tomorrow. All in all, it was an excellent briefing, and when he finished, he introduced General Davis back to the podium.

General Davis did not waste time, either. "Folks, we are here to build a box, put the trap in the center, and then kill as many of them as we can. In other words, we are making a better mouse trap. Here is how we are going to get it done......" With that, he delivered the meat of the briefing where he explained how we were going to use choke points and set the bait. The Concept of Operation, the scheme of maneuver, the formations to be used, the routes, the tactical missions of the smaller units, were covered in detail, right on down to the Regimental level within the Divisions. I am not a fan of this kind of micromanagement but given the skill and experience of some of the senior leadership, we had decided that it might need to be spoon fed to the lower echelons. We felt confident about our Regimental commanders and their staff, but some of our more senior leaders were Battalion Commanders only a few weeks ago and now they were trying to run a Division. As General Davis got through all the coordinating instructions, General Clark stood up and began giving every logistical detail that would be required from beans, to bullets, to the new sulphur-based artillery shells. It was, without a doubt, the most monumental task anyone could put together with only three weeks' notice.

The point that the wheels fell off the wagon was in our discussions about the Command and Signal issues. I guess more to the point, I yanked the wheels off. As I was being briefed, I had what I hoped would not be the last of my epiphanies to prevent a fatal error. As we were looking at the encryption and radio issues, the briefing officer was setting out a great plan for communications, codes, and various keys to keep the various chains of command connected and operating. Then that one thought that had been bugging the hell out of me finally came to the forefront, or as my wife used to call it, it was just "on the tip of my brain and found its way to the mouth." With that I said, "Excuse me, I hate to interrupt, but there are a couple of things that we need to look at before we lock this operation down. The first is that this plan looks very good on paper, but I'm troubled about the Gomers' ability to pinpoint our key leadership. We have never addressed this question, and I think this is a good time to figure it out. So, just how did they know to hit our key leadership? It is the one thing that has eluded me and believe me, it has been bugging me since the first day this all started. Does anyone have a clue?"

As I looked around the room, there was some mumbling and glancing back and forth, and then a lone voice came from the side of the room from a young Assistant G-2. "Sir, Major Powers here, and I have been bothered too. So, I did some checking, and I do have a theory."

"Major, now is the time to share. What is your theory?"

"Well, sir, most of our leadership used encryption equipment for their cell phones, phone lines, and all of their radio communications. I think that it was the patterns, or lack of them, that differentiated leaders' communications from the millions of other transmissions crowding the airwaves. It was the random that attracted the Gomers, and it allowed them to pinpoint exactly which GPS signals went to exactly what locations for the people who were talking through devices that were meant to hide the meanings from prying ears. I started thinking about that lack of pattern idea and so, after we got hit a few weeks ago, I took the liberty of checking the amount of encrypted radio traffic that may have come out of our relays in and around the mountains. I cross referenced it with the stuff out of new Washington, and we were almost triple the amount of traffic as what they were sending."

"Major, you just might be onto something. Let me ask this, since you obviously did the research, is there anywhere else emitting radio waves or traffic aside from us?"

"Actually, there is some local radio AM traffic from the one or two commercial stations that remained on the air, but most of it is just a recording that says Emergency Broadcast, with the alert tones. Right now, it is just the military and new Washington that will use the FM, VHF, UHF, and HF airwaves. Plus, all our stuff is encrypted now, even the routine traffic."

"So, according to your theory, it wouldn't matter whether we were encrypted or not, since they have to know that the only people on the radio are the folks that gave them a black eye."

"Yessir, that just about sums it up."

"I noticed that you didn't mention the .... ULF is it? You know the ultra low frequency stuff the Navy uses to talk to their submarines. Isn't that system still up and running, and if so, how have the Gomers reacted to it?"

"Sir, it is up and running and the Gomers have not seemed to pay it any attention, since that is how we've been able to talk to our guys around the world. We've been relaying it all using the Submarines."

"General Whitney, please have General Gregg and the other guys in the basement work on this theory, and let's see if we can get some answers. Oh, and while you're at it, find out how and why these radio stations can stay on the air, and remain unmolested by the Gomers. Maybe it matters and maybe it doesn't, but it bothers me that they are there and remaining online and transmitting without getting anyone's attention."

Turning to look directly at the young Major, I said, "Excellent job, Major! That, sir, is worthy of a Legion of Merit!" As I turned back to the front, I noticed a huge grin on the young Major's face and, even though he was reaching for a phone line, General Whitney was smiling as well. Personally, I was quite pleased with both of them, because the young man felt comfortable enough to speak up. This meant that the command climate, and the climate within that staff section, were both working just fine.

General Whitney was already on the line to General Gregg, who was at that very minute working on a couple of back up plans we had in the works. As Whitney was moving the machinery to find out how to solve our communications issues, I asked General Roberts another question that made the room gasp. "General Roberts, have we developed a plan for what to do if that big monster behind the Moon decides to come and play, and have we a contingency for what to do about the Gomers at the South Pole?"

"Uh...... No, sir, we haven't."

"Is our current plan working with the Moon cycle as a variant?"

"Uh . . . . . . No, sir, it isn't."

"Should we add that into the mix in establishing H hour or D Night?" With that, General Davis immediately stepped in the discussion with a firm statement that, "Sir, these latest points could be critical, and I would ask that we postpone our operation, at least until we can address these concerns."

"General Davis, I wholeheartedly agree, but it is only postponed until we can get the Moon working for us. Once we have the Moon information, along with a rough idea as to how to deal with the big one, then I want to set a timetable. I think we can have those answers in no more than three to four hours, am I wrong, General?"

"No, sir, we'll get it and get back to you."

"Excellent. I will be in my office. In the meantime, General Larkin, I need to talk to you and Colonel Greene about a small idea I've got." On that note, the briefing broke up, but this time when I walked out, I had a much better feeling for what we were going to be able to accomplish. I was especially happy with the resilience of the staff, and the guts of the young Major to speak up.

As I got back into my office, I told Chris to get the President on the horn. I also told her to use the secure hard line, and I then briefed the President about my plans for Colonel Greene's series of special operations. This time I HAD to have a release from the President, and it had to be before other things moved forward. It wasn't easy to obtain his okay, but after much discussion and soul searching, the President authorized what I had in mind. It was audacious, and perhaps too risky, but if things turned into the worst-case scenario, I wanted the option of acting quickly. Once you were standing knee deep in the bucket of manure wasn't the time to start wondering if you had the ability to hose off your feet.

After obtaining the necessary approval from the President, I turned and gave Colonel Greene the handwritten and sealed orders he would need to put this part of the plan into operation. I passed on the codes and key words that would get him what he needed, and then we said our Goodbyes. Neither of us knew if we'd ever see the other again, but we accepted it, and knew that we simply had no choice. I couldn't help but feel a sense of sadness watching him walk out. It was almost like watching a son go off to battle, which is never an easy thing to watch, no matter how patriotic you might feel about your country and the greater good.

It was exactly twenty minutes after Colonel Greene left my office that General Davis entered with both the information related to the Moon, and another idea that might be a game changer. We got on the phone with our counterparts at the Air Force facilities at Thunder Mountain and learned that "yes, we still control Vandenberg, AFB, and yes, we can probably get some stuff up there, if you can find someone to design what you have in mind." I was told they also could probably get at least 6 or 7 rockets up and, on the pads, but it was going to take at least a week of that many successive nights to launch each one. It would be a very small launch window to get stuff up in the sky before the twilight line got to them, and that assumed that the weather would cooperate. As before, I left General Davis to work out the details with the Air Force and Navy, and then we sat down to work out a timetable for the attack. Despite our being ready, willing, and wanting, we simply couldn't pull it off for another two weeks.

Crestfallen, to say the least, we went back to the boards and modified, briefed, modified some more, before coming up with the final version of our attack plan. This time, the briefings went without a hitch and everyone, from the Staff down to the last private in our deploying Infantry Divisions, knew exactly what they were to do, when they were to do it, and how they were to get it done. Our deception plans, and a couple of surprises, were set to go and we were ready. The Air Force was on board and had been launching rockets every night for that last week. The Navy, with their invaluable assistance, had baited the trap and provided another targeting system to add to our plan. It seemed that we were ready, with even a primeval rudimentary fix to our communications issues. Simply put, we had done all we could to get ready, and now it was time to act.

Of course, I've always known the adage that "no plan survives first contact with the enemy," not even the one we had so carefully crafted to use against the Gomers. Still, history also has taught us that the winner of any conflict is the one who can adjust, adapt, and, more to the point, make the fewest mistakes. In our case, I knew even before the first shot was fired that our plan would not survive first contact with the enemy. I also knew deep down that our execution of the plan against our enemy, and how well we adapted to the changing situation, could only really be judged by whoever was left to write the history. Regardless of my mixture of both misgivings and grim confidence, it was now our turn to start taking back the night.

SECTION 2:

THE AMERICAN CAMPAIGN

Chapter VIII.

Somewhere along the James River Phase Line:

"Hey, Sarge, have you read this stuff? It says here in this FM that the Gomers don't like the woods, because the trees 'absorb carbon dioxide and produce oxygen.' Then they tell us not to cut trees for camouflage, because the dead stuff doesn't work as well for 'concealing our movement or positions.'"

"Yeah, I've read it! Where the hell you been?"

"Aw, Sarge, you know I hate to read."

"Ski, were you just born stupid? We have heard all this crap for weeks, we have briefed this crap for weeks, and you are just now getting it? What the hell, are you using your butt cheeks as earmuffs?"

"No, Sarge, I was just wondering is all. We've been sitting here staring at the James River, hidin' in these here bushes, and watching Gomers go by for the last two days. I still can't believe they can't see us or them their tanks o'varr."

"Well, hang on to your hat there, Ski, since I just heard the 'old man' tell the L-T that the crap is hittin' the fan starting tonight. We got the rest of today to get our final act together, rest, eat a hot meal, and then, by tonight, you're going to be up to your ass in Gomers and bad dreams."

"Damn, Sarge, you don't need to scare me like that, it has been bad enough watching them things go by, just knowing they had to see us."

"Well, Ski, again, this is why you're still a friggin' private. If they had seen us, they'd have already killed us. Now get your head out of your ass, and work through what YOU need to do tonight when it matters."

"Yeah, gotcha, Sarge. We've done rehearsed this pretty much to death, but we'll do it again. I just don't understand the strategy behind it."

"Private, I'm sure that the General is crushed that you don't understand his strategy. I'll be sure to pass it up the chain, that this all needs to stop because YOU don't get the strategy behind it."

"Awwww, Sarge. Why do you pick on me like this?"

"Because, Ski, just because! Now get your act together and try not to shoot off your foot with that freaking rocket launcher."

As the day wore on, Private Raymond J. Kowalski went from nervous, to terrified, to hungry, back to just plain scared. No matter how hard he tried, food was not really going down, and sleep just wouldn't come to him. Like millions of men in arms before him, he was having a hard time shaking that feeling of dread that falls on a man who is waiting for what he knows will be coming. The fight or flight issue has plagued man before every battle, since it is hard wired into all of us, and it is just one of those things that you can only counteract with lots of training. Ski was no exception, and there were thousands more like him scattered along the southern bank of the James River. Each soldier dealt with their personal uncertainty in their own ways. The Sergeants, Lieutenants, and Captains, all checked on their men, and then rechecked on them, and continued to pace and check on their positions. Nothing was ever quite enough, and they would continue this process until the fight was joined. The Majors, and above, were just as anxious, but they worked a little harder not to show it. Sure, some with more recent combat experience were perhaps a little less openly nervous than the 'rookies,' but everyone felt it, and if they said they weren't scared, they clearly were lying through their teeth.

In the Regimental tactical operations center or TOC, Ski's Commander was following the deception plan and gauging in his mind what the Gomers would do in response. As a result, he spent much of the day adjusting his lines and coordinating with the guys from the Armored Division, who were dispersed with his men around and throughout their lines. When the initial lighting of the 'bait' took place, even though nobody announced it out loud, to a man, they all seemed to know it had started. As darkness approached, a grim determination settled in, and the men took their positions with a real resolve to make the bad guys pay for every inch of dirt that was to their front.

Within minutes, the Sergeant came behind their positions under the cover of the woods and said, "Ski, get out to your forward position, get ready to fire, and then once you do, don't look, just haul it back to your secondary position. Woody, you ready?"

Private James Sandalwood just nodded his head, and Ski looked at his partner to make sure he was still with him. Woody had the ammo and, if he cheesed or bailed, then Ski would be highly pissed. With that as his only lingering thought, he grabbed Woody, and they took up their positions out about 50 yards ahead of the rusty red-looking tank. That tank had been parked in the middle of their field for the last three days and had even had Gomers passing overhead at night with no reaction to it. Ski didn't have time to ponder this anymore because, as he took their initial position, a very loud sound echoed from behind him. Diving to the ground he looked over at Woody who was lying on his back and laughing as he pointed upwards. Following his finger, Ski was delighted to see a flight of six A-10 Warthogs, hauling it straight towards Washington. For some reason, knowing they were there made him feel better. As they roared overhead, Ski noticed that parallel to their position was another flight of aircraft. They were higher, and there were missile trails with the fading sunlight flickering off their smoke as they flew away from the aircraft. As he watched them heading northeastward, he grabbed Woody and they got into their first position.

They dove into their holes none too soon because there were plenty of explosions to the north. The sounds were getting louder and, as the explosions got closer, the cacophony grew into a crescendo that even made his teeth hurt. The ground was shaking and, as he lay in the prepared firing position, he was being pushed away from the ground with each loud boom. He thought it felt a lot like when he was a kid, and his brother would jump on the trampoline to screw with him while he was trying to take a nap. Only here it wasn't just the bounce, it was the concussion he could feel inside that made him most uncomfortable. As each explosion got louder, he thought there would be no end, but then it got quiet. Almost deathly quiet, and then he saw it.

Near the distant trees, along the highway that ran through their position, were three of the Gomer objects. As they advanced, it was obvious that they were on their guard. They moved slowly and appeared to be covering each other as they inched forward. With a flash of light, a beam shot out of the lead object and went in the direction of the sky. It now seemed as if they were suspicious of anything around them in the air, but they did not change their pattern from what he'd seen the nights they had sat in the woods. They continued to sweep the ground and move forward, sticking to the open areas. As he was marveling at their inaction, he saw someone in a far position, rise up out of the ground, and fire at the lead object. The impact was quick, and the object began to almost wobble in place. It was still moving, but now it was using the light to search the ground where the shot came from. As it seemed to lock on the running figure, another shot hit the object. This time it went down to the ground and stopped. This didn't stop the second object from taking the lead, but within seconds all three were under fire. Seeing his opening, Ski rose, took aim, and unleashed his DRAGON at the only object that was still flying. The explosion was fantastic, but he missed it. He was too busy running like hell to the back-up position 20 yards away.

As he dove to the ground, he could feel something brush past him. It was Woody, diving just to the other side of the position. As they both rolled over to get another view of the initial kill zone, they sensed that something was different. Peering into the twilight as it changed to full darkness, they saw something huge approaching from the same direction where the smaller objects had just come. Ski and Woody both broke from their position and headed into their fall-back locations well inside the trees. There was no question that they didn't have a thing that would stop this monster, and neither of them was looking like a pointless statistic. As they watched, the large flying machine began to unleash several highly directed shots that seemed to take out chunks of the woods around them. "Now that is a game changer, ain't it." When he looked around at Woody, he realized that his statement was pointless. Where Woody had been, there was now nothing more than a very large hole in the ground. Ski wondered if this was it and, as he laid lower in his position in the woods, he began mentally ticking off the things he was going to miss in life. The noise and the monster overhead got closer to his position, and all he could do was pray.

Then, as quickly as it started, it ended with a real bang. The tanks that were left out in the middle of the field over the last few nights all opened fire almost simultaneously. This time the concussion not only lifted him from the ground, but it actually moved him a couple of feet to the left. He looked up to the sky just in time to watch the large flying craft start breaking apart. Tons of metal appeared to fall from the sky, and he was damn glad that his hole had covered over it. Unfortunately for Ski, the cover could have been just a little thicker. A large piece of something fell just near enough to his position to knock him completely unconscious, and it would be morning before he would wake up and shake it off.

The dense fog in his head took a while to clear out enough for him to even begin to remember where he was, and what had gone on around him. He was starting to remember Woody and the final hit that made Woody just disappear when he glanced over and saw a very familiar face. "Sarge? Sarge, is that you?"

"Yeah, Ski? Damn, Ski, you look like hell!"

"Hey, Sarge, what is going on?"

"Well, Ski, I think we gave them a real bloody nose."

"Sarge, Woody is gone!"

"Yeah, I saw it happen. The Captain is gone, too. He was talking to the Colonel, and that damn big thing lit them both up. The L-T is the new Company Commander, and the Major now has the Battalion."

"So, we won?"

"Not yet, Ski, but it is a start. Now we have got orders to pull out and move back to the mountains. I think we're supposed to be moving south, but right now, I got nothin'. Get your shit in one sock and mount up. Transportation is right behind that hill waiting to get our asses back to the cover of the mountains. "

"Roger that, Sarge! I'm up and moving!" With that Ski took two steps, staggered a little, and then got his bearings as he headed to the trucks. The Sergeant continued to police up men around their immediate area, and within an hour they were moving towards the nearby mountains. The Sergeant wasn't happy, since they'd lost men, but he was more than a little pleased that they had only lost about 15 out of the 200 or so that had been around that field. When he heard from the new Commander that their losses were typical, he thought that it could be a whole lot worse. Then he asked the more burning question. "L-T? What have we done to the Gomers?" The Lieutenant looked at him with a grin, and said, "Well, I don't know about anybody else, but we got all of the ones that came by us, AND the tanker boys, with a little help from some M-109 Howitzer Paladins, took out the big one." This time as the trucks bounced up the highway and back to the Mountains, none of them had any trouble at all in falling sound asleep.

The New Pentagon:

The view at the top at Headquarters was a mixed bag of emotions. The day preceding the main battle was as nerve racking as anything. On the morning of 'D-Night,' with the first streak of dawn as the sun was beginning to rise over what was left of Washington, DC., every electrical system that could be regenerated was switched on and lit up for the entire urban area. What was left of the city literally glowed for miles, and while a few trailing small objects reacted, it was clear that there was nothing they could do about it. The deception plan continued when a burst of encrypted traffic was sent from a point near Richmond, Virginia. The heavy traffic of encrypted radio traffic was nothing more than a pattern simulation of official traffic. Only this time, the text of these messages was nothing more than the transmission of "Old Testament" passages. As night approached, the messages continued, utilizing the same tape system that was allowing the old AM stations to broadcast the Emergency Broadcast signals. As the Gomers got near, they were about to attack a recording machine.

Throughout the day, information coming in via the Navy and their VLF/ELF transmissions, (Very Low Frequency and Extremely Low Frequency), showed that the Gomers were massing a large amount of their ships prior to the twilight line passing over our coast. While we were pleased that they were going to come into our target box, we got very concerned that they were about to overwhelm us with sheer numbers and volume. We had the First Army positioned in a curved shaped line along the James River in Virginia, with Richmond located at the open end of the curve and the ends of the line anchored against Norfolk, Virginia all the way to the Mountains in the west. The Third Army was moving into position at a more southern location, and we allowed them to remain hidden throughout the first night. I had already decided that if we needed reserves for the first night, they would come from my Strategic Reserve. Something told me to hold the Third Army in reserve the first night and so I did, despite more than a few calls to cut them loose.

Throughout the first night of our offensive, my Staff followed the battle as closely as they could from their distant positions. Parts of the plan were working perfectly, while other parts were falling to ruin shortly after the initial contact. The first shots were fired by the Air Force assets, and their impact was superb. They were mostly operating from the light side of the Twilight line, so they had the sun on their backs as they were able to get their licks in on the Gomers. We lost very few aircraft but, at the same time, we could have used their air support on the dark side of the line as the night moved on. The A-10s were the real stars, since they stayed longer over the battle area, and were down in the weeds with the smaller objects. One A-10 jockey had the honor of being the first "ace" of the war, as he made pass after pass over several objects that were being distracted by the initial ground fire. Sadly, the Air Force had to clear the area before they lost their advantage of the sunset and, once the tactical air support was clear of the battle zone, several of the ground units were pounded mercilessly by the Gomers when they added their large ships to their line of advance.

When the Gomers started running into the ground resistance, they lost a significant portion of their smaller object fleet. As their losses mounted, either through our anti-aircraft/anti-tank efforts or those of our ground troops, the larger objects would advance to begin a process of trying to clear the ground in front of the smaller ones. For the first time, the Gomers made an effort to attack the woods and trees around the fallen smaller objects. It was this part of the attack we didn't fully prepare to counter in our original plan. While predictable, based on our experience during the assault on our Mountain, we simply did not believe that the larger objects would be so protective of the smaller ones. Consequently, when the large objects descended to a much lower altitude, the losses of ground forces in the woods were significant. From the initial reports, we lost upwards of 7% men and about 5% in equipment. The good news was that, as the large ones came down to engage our ground troops, they were now at an altitude where tank and direct artillery fire could be leveled against them. It would be this latter fire, along with Colonel Greene's research from his 'test' a few weeks ago, that would start making a dent in the large object fleet.

Thankfully, at the end of our first night of assaulting the Gomers, we were able to destroy at least 35 of the large ones, and several hundred of the smaller ones. The Navy went even further, launching several Cruise Missile attacks from several attack submarines, when the Gomers started to move back to sea to bypass or flank our forces that were deployed along the James River line. Their efforts resulted in another 28 of the larger ships going down. If my G-2 was correct, this only left another 437 of the big ones lurking out there. Still, we did cause them to lose roughly 12% of their large objects, which had to hurt a force that had their strength capped by the distance of space.

Our score with the small objects was a lot sketchier. Because the numbers were a little more approximate on their total strength, we were confident that their percentage of losses would have to be a lot higher. General Whitney estimated that we had cleared the skies of at least 25% of their available strength, which had to make the Gomers hurt, and, when coupled with the losses in the number of actual Gomers, it was a pretty good first effort. Now would be the time, in the words of General George S. Patton, Jr., for us "to hold 'em by the nose, and kick 'em in the ass!" The only thing holding us back was moving men and equipment from the James River line to our next planned location. We also had to adjust our tactics from the lessons learned from the first night, so we could hit them again the second night. While it is amazing how resilient a fighting man can be, with so little time the hardest part is getting those hard-won lessons to the right people.

Chapter IX.

Near the Savannah River Site, South Carolina:

Just prior to sunset on the first night of the offensive, several men were positioned at the Crackerneck Wildlife Management Area, south of the town of Jackson, South Carolina, and at Patterson Mill, South Carolina. These men were joining several similar teams that were positioned both around and, in a few instances, inside the same site. All these quiet professionals had an extensive array of passive night vision equipment and other weapons for personal self defense. The last two teams were flown into those remote locations before sundown, after making a detour to a weapons storage area near Charleston, South Carolina. The nuclear weapons storage area had remained unmolested, manned, and defended since the first day of the war and, thanks to the Seals who immediately arrived there before the Gomers had struck Washington; it was as quiet as a tomb.

While the battle was raging to their north, these shadowy professionals took the Savannah River Site in South Carolina under observation, and the teams stood quiet but ready. Their observations through the night revealed that the Gomers were still "feeding" or "refueling" at the Savannah River Site (SRS), and that they were all staged around one general location on the site. With the new dawn of the second day of battle, these silent but deadly operators began to make their move into the interior of the site with one aim, get to the Gomers' "fuel pump."

As they moved closer to the main facility, they discovered more than a few 'dusty' Gomers were 'guarding' several of the structures. The man in charge of this operation, Colonel Greene, was quite aware of what a 'dusty' Gomer could do, and how they could wander around during the daytime, but only so long as they stuck to the shadows. Thinking it through, the special operators, who are far more comfortable under the cover of darkness, found themselves in the counterintuitive world of working in the bright sunshine. They were able to slip into the area, make their requisite "deposits" in key locations, and then move out again without being confronted by any Gomers. Unsure if they had been seen or not, they watched to see if an alarm of any kind was sounded. Seeing nothing, they made every effort to clear out as far and as quickly as possible.

Near Roanoke, Virginia:

Private Kowalski was delighted to be awakened and fed. It was his first semi-hot meal in two days because, the previous day, whatever he ate was immediately expelled again. Now that he was no longer standing in the middle of a battle zone, he was savoring every bite of the warm soup and sandwich provided to him by the Battalion's chow truck. As he looked around, he noticed that the sun was almost over his head, and it was getting damned hot. "Spring, my ass" he muttered as he took another huge bite of his sandwich. When he heard someone calling his name, he turned to look and was greeted by his new best friend. "Sarge," he said, "right here, whatcha need?"

"Ski, I have a new job for you."

"What's that, Sarge?"

"You're now the new Commander's runner. After watching the Captain and Colonel getting zapped for talking on the radio, he is finally adopting the system that they were all told to use before all this crap started."

"Huh?"

"Yeah, the Captain and Colonel both were told to stay off the damn radio, but they got careless. The Battalion S-2 figured that is how they both got targeted so accurately, because they were using the encrypted radio equipment. The L-T has made it clear he ain't makin' that mistake, so now you're his runner."

"Geez, Sarge, I was hoping to get another crack at the Gomers, since I figured I owed them one for Woody!"

"Not to worry, slick, I have a feeling there are enough Gomers around for all of us to get a crack, probably sooner than later. Now hurry up and finish eating, then get your sorry ass to the Lieutenant."

"Okay, Sarge, I'm on it. Besides, what idiot gives you soup on a hot day like this?"

"Christ, Ski, do you do anything besides bitch and complain? Yesterday you were griping about the fact that you had to eat eggs with only bacon! What do you think this is anyway, the friggin' Waffle House?"

When he finished his food, Kowalski headed over to the CP to check in with his new commander. When he got there, he was surprised to see that they were packing up and moving again. When the Lieutenant saw him, he said "Ski, get your gear, and let's go. We're headed south, and we've got 15 minutes to get over to the airfield. Sundown is in about 3 to 4 hours, and we've got to be ready."

Thinking this is how the Army always works, Ski asked his new commander a question, "Sir, how far are we going?"

"Dammit, Ski, just MOVE!"

With that admonition still ringing in his ears, Ski collected his pack and weapon and jumped in the back of the truck headed to the local Airport. After a relatively short flight in a C-130, Ski was convinced that the "middle of nowhere" was standard Army issue. This time when they finally stopped moving for the day, they were deep in the Blue Ridge Mountains and assigned to some place called the new Pentagon. So much for moving south, he thought. What Private Kowalski couldn't know is that he was officially part of the next adjustment that had to be made in the war.

The New Pentagon:

Both I and my Staff realized that there was no way to reposition the First Army personnel to the next phase line, so we bolstered the strength of the Third Army by using the strategic reserves. I would then take the First Army personnel, and put them in Reserve, until the Third Day. On the third day, the line to hold would be set at a location before the Gomers were to turn the corner near the second choke point near Atlanta. Today, on the other hand, the line to hold was along the Georgia side of the Savannah River, from Savannah, Georgia to the mountains of the Sumter National Forest west of Walhalla and Greenville, South Carolina. Now it was the Third Army that would be facing the Gomers. One other major difference between this and the previous night's operation was that, along with the larger area to cover, there were more units. Northwest of the Savannah River site, in a line roughly from Augusta, Georgia to the mountain end of the line, was the bulk of the Third Army. Southeast of the Savannah River Site were two Marine Divisions, two Airborne Divisions, and a Cavalry Division, all under the command of the First Army command and staff. I had this command element flown south the second the sun rose to control this second line of defense.

There was a wide gap between these two Armies, and there was a great deal of trepidation expressed by both my staff and the First Army staff about how this could ever work to keep the Gomers off balance. After all, once they encountered resistance, they'd just move to the center, and then ultimately in between our two groups of forces. When General Davis approached me to express his concerns, he was rather adamant that this would allow them to attack us from the rear once they had simply flown through our resistance.

I agreed with General Davis and his assessment, but still really couldn't tell him any details about why I wasn't that concerned about the Gap. General Larkin intimated it, but Davis never picked up on it. What we couldn't do was tip anyone off with any specific information, since security would be compromised if anyone made even a slip that might tip off the Gomers. I had no idea how much of our mail or radio traffic the Gomers were reading, and so silence was the word. Only at the last second would we tell our guys to get low in their holes, but it could only be the last second. Nope, all we could do is make sure there was one very large gap in our lines, and to keep it that way throughout this part of the battle. If it didn't work, then we might have some bigger problems. If it did work, then we could be looking at some decent gains. Balancing risk is all part of a commander's job, and this one was a huge gamble.

The day wore on, and General Davis kept trying to plug that hole. Finally, with only a few hours to go, I pulled him to the side and told him to stand down the rest of the airborne units he was going to try and put along the Savannah River directly across from the Savannah River Site. I needed them for something else and, besides, "right now we have a classified mission in that area that would be compromised if we added personnel." He looked at me in disbelief, and I told General Larkin to "go ahead and brief him, but him only, and if I hear one more word about sending anyone within 75 miles of that damn place, I'll have their head." It was the last we were to hear about "plugging the gap." Later when the cat was out of the bag, General Davis just looked at Jerry and me and shook his head.

My selection of forces was another source of ongoing discussion. When I had chosen the 1st and 2d Marine Divisions to move into the low country of South Carolina and Georgia, with the 11th and 17th Airborne Divisions more towards the Savannah River Site, I was told by one officer in the G-3 section that I just sticking the Marines in the swamps while my Airborne guys were sitting on high and dry land with their toes in the river. When he said it, I don't think he honestly thought I could hear him, but I looked at him with my best General face and said, "Colonel, the Marines all trained in that area at Parris Island, they know it, and they've lived in it. Now, who would you put there?" I didn't wait for a reply but just turned on my heel and walked away. As Jerry put it, "It was fun to watch that 6' tall guy shrink to the size of a piss ant."

As we moved through the next period of daylight making our preparations for the night's action, more critical information was rolling in from our Naval observers. The force coming around at us was again massing. The numbers were like the night before except, according to our seagoing friends, they had employed a little different formation. This time, while we could still expect them to hit the coast in force, the enemy Armada was deployed with the larger ships taking the lead, while most of the small objects were positioned at the rear of the formation. Noting this change of tactics, we notified both Army and all Corps Commanders to expect that the woods would catch more hell, and to expect to keep the infantry under wraps until the big stuff was already beyond them. Whatever you do, keep eyes on the large stuff, because we know damn well, they can turn on you.

Passing on the latest changes, we started the logistical effort to get our returning forces from the "Battle of the James River" ready to start another deployment phase at first light. Noting that there was little else I could do, I went to my office and contacted the President on our hard line.

"Sir, were you briefed on the first night numbers?"

"Yeah, Mike. Helluva job, you are making a dent in them. I was briefed earlier by your liaison and my staff was delighted. Now then, give me the rest of the story."

"Well, sir, there really isn't anything other than what we briefed already. You saw how we've set up tonight's line. Do you have any questions?"

"Only one."

"Go ahead, sir."

"I noticed that gap between your Armies in the area around the SRS. Is that for the reason I think, or have you lost your mind?"

"I've probably lost my mind, but no, sir, it is for the reasons you think. Do you have any problems with it?"

"Nope, that is as good a place as any to test Dr. Abramson's and Dr. Clarkson's theories."

"Well, sir, we'll keep you posted."

"Great, now get a couple hours sleep. I'll bet you haven't been to bed in at least two days, have you?"

"I guess I haven't, but yeah, I'll grab a short nap. Talk to you later, Mr. President."

"Good night, General!" And with that, we broke the connection. Looking around at the pile of things that needed doing, and assessing the state of my mental energy, I realized that sleep was not only a necessity, but it was also becoming an imperative. I wandered out my door, kissed my daughter on her head, and told her to get to our quarters and "tell the rest of the family good night for me. Right now, I'm taking a nap!" I was asleep on my office cot almost the second my head hit the pillow.

It only seemed like seconds, but after a little less than three hours sleep, I was awakened by General Larkin with these words. "Mouse, get your ass up, we have ourselves a real old fashioned bar fight going on, and I don't think you'll want to miss it." I was wide awake in seconds, and with a cup of coffee and a rather scraggly appearance, I was back in the "war room." Looking around for a moment, I realized that Jerry was correct, we had ourselves a good old fashioned bar fight.

Near the James River Phase Line:

A few observers, well under cover and with as much scientific equipment as they could carry, had taken up positions around the previous evening's battlefield to observe the reaction of the Gomers as they passed overhead. They were there to assess the Gomers' reactions, behaviors, and to gather as much additional intelligence as possible. Among these intrepid soldiers was General Gregg, who had managed to slip away from the new Pentagon Mountain complex that had been his home over the last month or so. He had to get out. Aside from being an avid sportsman, he loved getting out and roaming the countryside. Now was his chance and, as he remained hunkered down at an observation post near Richmond, Virginia, he had no idea that this was ground that the night before had been occupied by Private Kowalski and his former partner, Woody. All he really knew was that it had been the scene of a pitched battle, and it was time to gather the data necessary to see what, if any, adjustments the Gomers were making to their tactics.

As he and another soldier remained hidden away under a lead painted poncho, they kept up their vigil as the twilight line approached. Maybe 100 yards away was the wreckage of a crashed and ruined smaller object. The holes in the side of it were obvious and almost peered at him like a shark's eyes. All around him were remnants of the larger ship, wreckage that, thanks to his earlier studies of the large one near the Blue Ridge Mountains, seemed almost familiar to him now. On the other side of the clearing, he even recognized the body of a dead Gomer that was almost turned black from the previous evening's carnage and post-crash destruction. The Gomer hung there, along with a piece of the large ship's wreckage, as if it were suspended and waiting on a flock of crows to be scared away from the field. The entire area reeked

185

of battle and, while he enjoyed being outside the caves, he was genuinely beginning to question his coming on this mission.

As the night began to grow around him, he and his fellow observers first saw the oncoming formations through their passive night vision devices. What he then saw made his heart almost fail. It was the large ships coming first, and they were expending almost all their weapons below them into the woods and trees. Cutting huge paths through the forest with their larger weapons, they were simply removing everything in their path. As he processed this in his mind, he noticed that a large ship was headed directly over their position in the woods. It would be his last conscious thought, as he and his fellow observer simply ceased to exist.

Nearby, several other observers watched this phenomenon and contacted their higher headquarters back in the mountains. Soon they, too, would be eliminated, as was every other living thing that was not dug in deeply along their path. The expenditure of weapons was massive and, when the large objects finally passed the area, there were only a handful of survivors to return with this new intelligence data.

New Pentagon:

The news of what was happening along the James River line was shocking to many of the Staff. Mostly it was anger, and more than a little disgust at the sheer number of casualties being taken among the intelligence personnel who had been sent out only to observe. In many minds, it was the fact that these people were science types, civilians, or non-combat soldiers that made them even angrier at the Gomers. The first reports came into the 'war room' and I immediately sent General Gregg to come up and join us. I wanted his thoughts on the subject, but after several minutes, I was informed that he could not be found anywhere in the new Pentagon. At that moment, I had a feeling I knew why, and I told Jerry to have "Dr. Abramson haul his ass to the 'war room' now!"

Dr. Abramson came into our corner of the operational world with a look of horror on his face. He was losing friends left and right, and there was not a thing we could do about it. He also had grown very close to General Gregg, and when he told me that General Gregg was out there with the observers, to see it all for himself, he completely lost his composure. General Davis, another close friend of General Gregg, only shook his head and went back to monitor the enemy's movements. After a moment, he turned to me, and said "Sir, what about our guys in Georgia? If they are killing everything in their path in the woods, then how the hell are we going to be able to hide ourselves from them in that flat terrain?"

"General Davis, send out this new intelligence, but do not give any orders just yet. They should be well dug in, and if they aren't, this will motivate them, I'm sure. Let's see what happens when they get out of the Virginia area without a shot fired by us, and if they are still hitting the woods, too, then we can panic. Right now, they are not quite to North Carolina yet, so we've got a little time to react." Frankly, I was just hoping they were expending their energy sufficiently to make them weaker when we hit them.

Thank goodness my hunch paid off. The huge expenditure of energy to carve their path through the previous night's battle area was slowing them down. It was also depleting their energy at a rapid rate. As they began to approach tonight's planned kill zone, they had stopped firing, slowed down, and were rapidly eating up the very stuff they were here to collect. Now was the time to kick some ass. As the ships began to bunch up and head for the SRS to replenish the energy expended in Virginia, they had allowed themselves to mass in a relatively small area to get in line for the "fuel pump" we knew to be at the SRS. As this bunch of larger objects lined up over the central part of South Carolina, I ordered that the Air attacks begin. Within seconds, tactical aircraft screamed in from the direction of the mountains and focused their armament on the large craft. Even though it was now darker than the previous evenings' attacks, this time the smaller objects were too far back to adequately intercede to protect the larger ones.

Just when the TacAir hit them from the direction of the Mountains, the Navy busted them with a fusillade of Cruise Missiles fired from offshore. As all this fire power came together on the large objects, the smaller objects began to swarm past the large objects and head directly towards our line along the Savannah River and towards our Tactical Air, now retreating and leading them right back over our concealed positions near the Georgia line. This was the kill box we wanted, and Jerry had been dead right. "This really is going to be one helluva bar fight!"

Near Savannah, Georgia:

Positioned with the same array of weaponry as the previous evening, a company of Marines had taken up residence at an old pre-Spanish American war era gun battery, along the northern shore of Georgia and immediately adjacent to the pre-civil war fortifications known as Fort Pulaski. Positioned on an island that borders both the north and south channel entrance to the Savannah River, they managed to man-handle their 105 mm guns and place them where the original cannon had been placed all those years before. They also had quite a few leads based shells ready to fire and the Captain in charge, Captain Randall Lee, was excited that his position gave him a pretty good view of the entire harbor entrance. He also appreciated the history since one of his ancestors, a Colonel Robert E. Lee, had been responsible for surveying the area for the Army when they built the original Fort Pulaski.

"Dude, do you hear that? It sounds like the whole world is shooting at something!"

"Dammit, Marine, shut and keep watching. The second something crosses that river, kill it!"

"Okay, Captain."

The young members of the gun crew only had a few minutes to wait. As they watched out to sea and over the river towards Turtle and Dafuskie Islands, they spotted three of the large objects as they entered the river basin from the sea. As they watched and began to train their guns, the large object closest to the ocean disintegrated before their very eyes as a submarine- fired

Cruise Missile found its mark. As the debris was blasted forward, the falling hulk rammed the object to its immediate front. As these events unfolded, the young battery commander entered the Marine Corps Hall of Fame with his simple command, "God Damn Navy! Okay, we'll kill the other two! FIRE!" In seconds, the mouth of the Savannah River would have three burning hunks of the large Gomer ships to add to their collection of war relics to put in the museum at Fort Pulaski. Sadly, for the Captain, nothing else wandered his way on this particular evening, and he was forced to just listen to the guns to his north. This young man anchored the line, and it would be a line that might bend but, as long as he was there, it would never break.

Near Blue Springs, Georgia:

Command Sergeant Major Clagmore was a legend who not only didn't know it, but he just didn't care. He also had no idea that he had ever been in the running for the new Sergeant Major of the Army job, again not that he gave a damn. He was old school, and all the old Army. As he sat in the Division Command Post, he was watching the young Major General as the battle to their east began to unfold. Noting that Rhymes might not be the brightest bulb, he was way better than the idiot who was now hiding in Afghanistan with the old 82d Airborne Division. As he watched his General, he was thinking that "nope, at first, I thought the idea of calling us the 11th Airborne Division was silly, but now, I love it. Now we'll get the credit, and those jerk wads that are taking up space away from the real war can kiss my ass."

Seeing little to keep him occupied, he wandered outside the TOC to watch the flashes of the guns in the attack. It was because this old soldier decided to depart the TOC that he would walk away from another war completely unscathed. As he wandered down through the swamp to the river, to see how the forward observation units were doing coming back over into Georgia from the town of Shirley, South Carolina, the TOC ceased to exist. General Rhymes, just like the young Kowalski's Battalion Commander the night before, forgot to keep off the encrypted radio. The second the TOC was nailed, CSM Clagmore knew exactly what had happened, and he was pretty sure he knew why. He thought about it for only a second and then began directing the survivors into secondary positions. The entire time he was thinking the same thing he'd been thinking since he was a private, "STUPID feckin' officers, don't matter whether they're lieutenants or generals, most are just too damn Stupid to live!"

Using the non-secure, low-tech wire telephone system, CSM Clagmore advised his higher headquarters, the Assistant Division Commander, and the three Regimental Commanders, that General Rhymes and the TOC were both "officially tits up!" Despite the loss of the Division Commander, CSM Clagmore carried on with his usual efficiency and continued to direct the fight with what he had left out of the Headquarters personnel. He would have handled the whole division if given a chance and probably did until the Assistant Division Commander assumed command from his forward position at Solomons Crossroads, South Carolina. As the fight wore on, CSM Clagmore was constantly on the move. As several of the smaller objects came near their positions over the swamp, it was the Sergeant Major that ordered a nearby tank crew to "please take that asshole out, he seems to be blocking our view!" Then when one of the large objects hove to and was cutting a swath through the swamp towards his position, the CSM got down on one knee, picked up the phone and told the Division Artillery Commander that he would take it as a "personal favor if you would please shoot that son of a bitch!" Naturally, the artillery commander took care of it, since obviously it was probably safer to piss off the Gomers than it was to get CSM Clagmore even slightly irritated at you.

Near Elberton, Georgia:

The Third Army area had their hands full, too, and the southern part of their line was beginning to show some signs of cracking. Their southern-most units were being decimated as the large Gomer ships were doing their best to test how far south, they needed to go to get around this part of the defense line. Naval Fire was scarcer here, and the Third Army Commander was becoming more concerned with each new report coming out of the Augusta, Georgia, area. It would take a call from the Division Commander for the 3rd Armor Division to make it absolutely clear that something needed to be done and done fast. His guys were doing the 'shoot and scoot,' but they were about to hit a point where there was nowhere to 'scoot to as a viable position.' "Hell, General, I'm already backed up parallel to the old interstate, and we're swinging like a gate. The Gomers are pushing us back and then covering themselves as they turn back to the SRS! What are my orders?"

"Stand by, Henry, I'm getting on the line to the big man to find out if we can start pulling you guys back up the line towards the mountains. If we must, then we'll swing the whole line, and start to roll it back towards the Smoky Mountains."

New Pentagon:

I was just reading a message from Colonel Greene, when General Roberts turned to me and said, "Sir, I've got General Hampton on the line. He says the right side of his Third Army is getting hammered and they need to start thinking about rolling back to the mountains. He wants your okay to withdraw!"

I motioned for the receiver and got on the line. "General Hampton, I need you to hold just about another 10 minutes. Can your guys do that?"

"I don't know, sir, it is getting bad. It seems the Gomers are busting our asses to keep the area around the SRS clear."

"Okay listen, David, I need you to hold your position, is that clear? Don't worry, help is on the way, but you have to hold for another 10 minutes!"

"Sir, I'll try."

"No, dammit, don't try, do it." With that, I got off the line and told General Roberts to get me in contact directly with the southern-most division commander. It didn't take long, and I was talking to the Third Armored Division commander, Major General Henry Davidson.

"Henry, Patrick here, and this is what I want you to do. . . ."

Near the Savannah River Site:

As Colonel Greene peered through his night vision equipment and did a survey of the entire area. It was clear that just within his range of vision there were at least 35 of the large ships lined up over the facility, with another 35 to 40 about to pull out of the area, and another 35 or more still lined up waiting for their turn. Looking at his watch, he knew, this was as good a time as any. He sent out a micro-burst transmission with a one-word message via an old AM transmitter which immediately was picked up and passed into the new Pentagon.

Our reply was simple, and it went out to everyone along the entire front in clear plain language. "Get low in your holes!" With that simple response, Colonel Greene sent a short radio signal that immediately triggered an event that would leave the Gomers reeling, and our troops amazed at the light show that followed.

As the signal reached the various detonators, four small but powerful enhanced radiation weapons, better known as 'neutron bombs', began their fusion reaction that released a burst of neutrons with the help of their passing through X-ray mirrors made of chromium and nickel, as opposed to the more traditional lead casings found on the more basic nuclear devices. In that single instant, as Colonel Greene stepped back inside his lead-lined "hiding place", the Gomers had a brand-new problem to consider. The amount of nuclear energy far exceeded their abilities to absorb and, as Dr. Abramson and Dr. Clarkson had predicted, the surge of energy caused them to literally melt like an overloaded transformer.

In an instant, the Gomers lost over 140 of the large ships, and almost 4000 of the smaller ones. With the combined efforts of the Army and Marine Divisions, our Tactical Air Forces, and the Navy, our total score for the night was close to 210 large ships and almost 5200 of the smaller ones, all destroyed. Add this to the previous day's totals, and we felt confident that about half of the Gomers' larger objects were destroyed and, while it was a guess, it appeared to us that we had taken out at least a moderate portion of their strength in the smaller ones. We had finally made a dent in the bad guys' ability to wage war against us, but we were still a long way from solving our Gomer problem.

Chapter X.

New Pentagon:

The mood in the 'war room' was the most upbeat it had been since the start of the Gomer War. As I was pondering what our next move should be, given this change in situation, I had already decided to scrap the next part of the plan, because we simply couldn't move our forces into position in enough time to make things work. As I was debating the new course of action, I was handed a message from Colonel Greene from his "hide site" near the Savannah River Plant. After reading the short message, I looked over at General Whitney and saw that he was in deep conversation with Dr. Abramson.

"Dr. Abramson, I have some interesting news for you."

"Sir?" As I mentioned his name, he had turned, and along with General Whitney, they both approached me.

"Tell Dr. Clarkson that not only was he right, but the Gomers did exactly what we thought, and apparently his calculations with regard to residual radiation were right on the money."

"Do we have the actual readings in yet?"

"Not the full numbers, but Colonel Greene said that after the initial spike in radiation, it dissipated to nothing almost instantly. Dr. Clarkson's prediction was correct, the Gomers absorbed it all, when they opened their . . . . for lack of a better phrase, ... their 'gas cap.'"

"Yes sir, their energy intake system appears to be set up to take one constant flow that is regulated normally within that rather complex system. We found some interesting things in the wreck of the ship near here, but we couldn't find anything like what we would know as a regulator. When we found the remnants of what we thought was the power collector, we developed the theory that if you overload it, then whatever they are using to regulate the flow would take time to adjust, assuming they even have one, since it was not apparent to be a normal part of the collection system. The instantaneous burst of energy produced by the ERWs was just too much for them to handle and, without the adjustment, it was like a giant electrical and radiological surge into a computer. Sort of like what we know about them avoiding sunlight and the sun, it was hoped that too much of a good thing would be a bad one. We were hoping that we'd get lucky that their flow rate would also take in all the initial radiation, kind of as a side effect."

"Okay, Doctor, now that we have lots of wreckage to examine and a test of your theory that worked, I don't suppose you have any other ideas? Right now, I could really use one."

"We were just discussing that, sir." As he said that, General Whitney stepped up and said, "General, I'm concerned that they will change their tactics and, now that we have hit them hard, they have to be making adjustments. Like they did earlier with the slash and burn tactics over our intelligent people. Nobody, not even a Gomer, would be so stupid to do the same thing twice."

"General Whitney, I not only agree, but you're saying out loud the very reason that I'm scrapping the Atlanta to Florida defense plan. My only question now is where to send folks, and whatever we do, we will have to be quick. I don't have enough prime movers and air assets to send people very far, or with very much equipment."

"I understand and, frankly, sir, I'm at a loss." Turning to Dr. Abramson, General Whitney asked, "Doc, you were telling me about something I just didn't quite understand, and without Gregg here to translate, you may as well be speaking a foreign language. Can you dumb it down for me?"

"Yes sir." and turning towards me, Doctor Abramson said, "In short, General, I am not sure the ERW will work again. My guess is that they must be making the necessary adjustments to their collection system and while I predict it will greatly slow down their cross-country sweeps, it should also keep them from being surprised with that much energy being released into their collection system all at once."

"That makes complete sense to me, Doctor, so what would be a back-up plan?"

"Sir, right now we don't exactly have one. We've done some research into what the Gomers probably call their metallurgy, but we haven't really found anything we could use quite yet. The very structure of their ships appears to be made of something unknown to us, and we are undergoing some testing on it. As for the use of any more ERWs, you might get them with the blast effects, but I doubt we can do the same overload tactic, twice."

"Okay, well, keep plugging at it, Doctor. Let's hope you can find something in their metal structures that will help us. Thanks, gentlemen, now give me a minute, I've got some thinking to accomplish." With that, both men headed back to their corner of the 'war room' leaving me to my thoughts. The first of which was that nothing got past the Georgia line and for the first time in weeks, there was no sweep through the breadbasket of America. Instead, what was left of the Gomers' fleet for the Northern Hemisphere headed south, and then over Florida and directly to Mexico, as they followed the night sky around the globe. Is that the way they would return tonight? Would they bypass the East Coast, or would they slash and burn, like they did last night around the James River line? Either way, I had an Army to get moving. The problem was where to put them, and how to get them there. One other problem that was starting to rear its ugly head was refugees. With the combat, civilians were starting to surface from all around the map, and they were using the same roads into the mountains that we needed to use to move forces north and south.

Near Roanoke, Virginia:

The sun wasn't quite up yet, but the troops were standing by and preparing to move. As the sound of trucks starting in the first dawn light, and the movement of men, became unmistakable, Private Kowalski approached his commander to begin his runner duties. As he walked up and saluted, the Lieutenant turned and said, "Okay, Ski, we're moving out. I'll get you onto the first track behind me, and I want you to stick close to me whenever we stop. Clear?"

"Yes sir. I thought we were headed south, but these trucks are all lined up the other way. What's going on?"

"Ski, you ask more questions than any three people I know. Yeah, they're headed north and so are we! Now get your ass in the truck and remember, whenever we stop, find me."

Near Blue Springs, Georgia:

"Sergeant Major Clagmore, let's get this show on the road."

"Yes, but begging the General's pardon, where would you like me to take this fecking circus?"

"Sergeant Major, we have our marching orders. We are to move due east over the river and take positions on the east side of the I-95 corridor. We are to anchor the southern part of our line at a place called Yemassee. We are to link up our southern end with a line of Marines who will be along that end of the highway. Looks as though we're all swinging as far as the Interstate, all with orders to dig in and wait. Other than the movement, we've been ordered to stay in the woods, dig VERY deep, and stay quiet."

"Okay, sir, but this sounds an awful lot like a boondoggle to me."

"Sergeant Major, you're just Mary Sunshine, aren't you!"

"Yessir, that's my job!"

Near Elberton, Georgia:

General David Hampton, the Third Army Commander, was still basking in the victory of the previous evening when he was handed a message from those 'crazy bastards that think they are Gods on Mount Olympus.' He read it several times and finally called over his Chief of Staff, a young Brigadier General. "Okay, looks like we have our orders, and apparently the assholes in the Mountains don't think we need sleep."

"Yes sir, am I reading this right? They want us to redeploy north of interstate 85?"

"That, my boy, is correct. We are to abandon our positions and move north to occupy positions along the interstate in front of the mountains. We are then dig in deep and wait. Then it says, if pressed, we should be prepared to withdraw into the mountains where we will receive further orders."

"Sounds like someone has something up their sleeve again, at least I HOPE they have something, otherwise all we can do is sit on our thumbs. All right, we'll move. I just hope this time they warn us a little sooner before they light up the whole damn sky."

"Yeah, wouldn't that be nice. Now get on the horn to the Corps and Division Commanders and let them know we don't have much time to move. I want them in position and ready to dig in well before dark."

Near Savannah, Georgia:

The newest legend of the United States Marine Corps, the young Captain Lee, as the battery commander, was standing on top of the old concrete battery shaking his head. All he could think was that no good deed goes unpunished, and this was no exception. He and his men were to remain behind in their present positions, while the rest of his Division and the 2nd Marine Division were moving to positions running along the Interstate from Savannah up to somewhere in South Carolina. His mission was to sit tight, report movement, and remain under cover. Whatever they did, they were NOT to fire their weapons, unless ordered, and to remain down deep and quiet. After passing this information to his marines, he headed back into the fire control bunker and took a nap. He and his men were perhaps the only people in the country who got any sleep.

Savannah River Site, South Carolina:

With the dawn came a flight of three very large CH-53 helicopters, and a sizable team of Air Force personnel arrived on site. Within a few minutes of landing, an Air Force Colonel approached Colonel Greene and handed him another sealed envelope and additional handwritten orders. It took about an hour to have his men collected from their various positions around the site but, as each of the teams was collected, they were loaded into one of the CH-53 aircraft and immediately whisked away. It would be several more hours before the rest of the Air Force personnel were picked up from the site, but they didn't waste the time sitting around waiting on a ride. Instead, they were putting into place a different variation of the previous night's ERW. This time, if the Gomers made the mistake of returning to the SRS, they would find something new and far larger to ponder.

New Pentagon:

As the day wore on, finding time to cat nap was getting harder to accomplish. Aside from the tons of after-action reports pouring in, there were battle damage assessments, movement orders, and logistical snarls that would normally grind things to a halt. Now there just wasn't enough time to go around, so the snarls were either bypassed, or the plan altered to fit what was available. The 11th Airborne was a prime example. They made it to their new positions, but it took longer and required the troopers to be more resilient in finding alternate forms of transportation. In some instances, they used their feet, at least until they could find or steal other forms of transport. Apparently, even the Command Sergeant Major, CSM Clagmore, was forced to find and use an old nag plow horse. Still, they kept moving until they got where they needed to be within the time allowed.

All along the southern areas, soldiers and units dug in as deeply as possible, using the woods and natural terrain, they were able to hide until told otherwise. Most of them set minimal guards, fed their troops with what they could, and then bunked down until night fall. The northern soldiers, on the other hand, were having problems of their own. They had transport, but the weather coming out of the mountains was making it difficult to get them where we wanted them. Readjusting to the reality, we had them form a line along the mountainous terrain, from Harrisburg, Pennsylvania, to Allentown, Pennsylvania. Their orders, like the units in the south, were to dig in and watch. They were not to fire, nor were they to reveal their positions. The order of the day for the entire Army was to wait, dig in, and watch.

As the naval intelligence reports started to come in from the northern sea lanes used by the Gomers, it looked as though our plan just might have some efficacy. As the formation of Gomers appeared out of Europe, they took a slightly more southern path as they adjusted their formation. This time the smaller objects were back out front and, as they reached the middle of the Atlantic Ocean, they began to turn more to the south. When they were due east of our Mid-Atlantic States, they began the turn that would bring the bulk of their fleet over the coast at or near Savannah, Georgia. At the same time, a few of the smaller objects broke off and began a turn towards New York and New Jersey to follow their normal route.

Given the smaller size of the force coming in near New York, I advised the First Army Commander that he could go to 'weapons free' for his artillery units that were to the south of his line, but only to the south. Any unit positioned on the Allentown side was to remain hunkered down, so as not to give up the positions, and fire only, if necessary, to defend themselves. On the Southern front, it was a much simpler Order. Get down, stay down, and only fire if fired upon. Let them pass!

As the twilight turned to evening and then to night, there were absolutely no reports from the northern areas. The little formation of the smaller objects, probably doing a reconnaissance, came onshore and immediately turned to the south following the coast. As they continued south, it seems that they did a brief search around the James River line but, otherwise, there was no further inland incursion. It would be nearly dawn when the little formation moved inland to move just ahead of the dawn line.

The main formation was another story. It approached the coast from due east, right along the Savannah River basin, in a manner very reminiscent of a convoy of ships. The smaller objects moved out ahead and searched all the open areas and wood lines as they moved inland. The Marines on Pulaski, after taking their naps, decided that it would be a good idea to have holes to get small in. This was an excellent idea, since their area was well swept with the smaller light beams. The old Fort Pulaski itself attracted some detailed attention from the Gomers but, otherwise, the surrounding area was virtually unscathed. Thankfully, the Marines were not seen or found, and after the smaller objects passed, they were able to return to their positions and watch. Staying off the radios, they reported to their higher headquarters the method of movement, direction, and apparent speeds. The Marine Divisions up the river were well out of sight as the larger ships and their additional escorts crossed their I-95 positions.

Nearing the SRS, the smaller ships fanned out and formed a protective ring, while the larger ships began to take up positions to move into the SRS area. As this took place, we received one short report from the Air Force replacement for Colonel Greene. His words were chilling, but at this moment we knew we'd done the right thing. "Brass Hat! They are landing a butt load of Gomers. Request Weapons Free."

With his words I jumped to my feet and snatched the microphone away from General Roberts. "Brass Hat Actual! When they are massed you are Weapons Free!" It would only take a few seconds before the next phase of our war would begin. For the first time in the history of the United States, a Tactical Nuclear Warhead and not an ERW, was set off in anger on American soil. I wasn't happy about it, and I sure hated the fact that, in the process, I had probably rendered my old home, which is within 70 miles of the SRS, completely unlivable for generations to come. Still, it had to be done, since we had no other way of stopping them. The only good news was that we had selected one that had a variable yield set at a lower .3 kilotons. While an impressive blast, it was hoped that the shock waves might do things to destroy the ships themselves while limiting the blast zone's impact for the future.

Unlike the previous evening's release of neutrons that flooded the Gomers and then gave them their instant meltdowns, this one created an impressive radioactive smoking hole. We did destroy a lot of their ships, with no losses in personnel to ourselves. So, while the staff was delighted at this latest numerical success, I was not happy worth a damn. My concern was that all we really accomplished was to create a new feeding trough for the Gomers. At the same time, I was genuinely terrified that all we did was to make our next few days more than difficult, since there was nothing we could do to get back into the SRS, at least until the radiation dissipated in about 70 years. I just knew that if there was a major mistake to be made in this war, this was probably it, and it could be a real big one. The good news is that I was wrong!

Near the Savannah River Site:

As the shaking of the earth began to subside, and the blast force winds rushed back across their hidden bunker, the Air Force Colonel hollered to the man beside him, "GOOD GOD ALMIGHTY!" Once the wind was gone, there was absolutely nothing but a hushed silence. It was so quiet that the two men could hear each other breathing. After a moment of processing this dead quiet, the Colonel stood and peered into the periscope system that was built into the old Cold War bunker. He began his visual sweep while his partner started doing a radiological sweep of the same area, and they were both shocked by what they found.

"Christ, Boss, I got nothing. There is some residual stuff out there pinging off the monitors, but really, it is nothing compared to the normal radiation readings we get every day."

"Well, I have something. Aside from the smoking hole and an ass load of downed Gomer objects, there are a couple more Gomer ships lined up from the east. It looks like they are still feeding from the hole and, I swear, they might be putting even more Gomers down in the middle of it all. What did you say about the radiation readings?"

"I swear, Boss, either these instruments are busted, or there simply isn't enough out there to matter. I think you could get more radiation on a sunny day at the beach. The Gomers must be sucking it all in still!"

"I'll be damned. Okay, first light, we'll need to get the hell out of here before the Gomers find this place, and you need to get all that raw data back to the boys under the mountain!"

With that, the Colonel picked up a hard line and passed on his observations, which eventually wound up coming into the 'war room.'

New Pentagon:

General Larkin came up and said, "Sir, get some sleep!" I had been sitting there lost in thought and wondering how history would remember the asshole that 'nuked' his own country. When Jerry walked up, I really was in no mood to be 'mothered' and I just stared at him. I was formulating a 'smart ass' response when General Whitney appeared with another message. "Sir, I just got this from the boys at SRS!" As I read it, I did feel a small sense of relief that I hadn't left a legacy of radiation for future generations to clean up, and then I realized that I was also half right about what the Gomers were going to do about it. I had made their 'gas pump' even more attractive, and now it was going to be a nightly stop for them so long as I kept baiting the field. Talk about your double-edged sword. "Crap!"

I called my staff together and told them about my misgivings, and what I thought we would have to do to counter their moves. It was a short message, and with that, I felt exhaustion take me in waves. Handing it over to the staff and Generals Davis and Larkin to flesh out my thoughts, I headed off to grab a few hours sleep. As I entered my outer office, Chris smiled at me and said I had a surprise waiting on me. As I walked in, there stood Leah, with food, a hug, and after a few minutes of eating and chatting about nothing, she tucked me in. Those six hours were just what I needed and, apparently, it gave my staff a chance to get their feet back under them, too. At the same time, out on both the northern and southern troop lines, our Armies took a much-needed break as well. They were fed, replenished, and given a full day to consolidate and improve their positions. This was a break we all needed, even if it was because we just didn't have a clue on how to finish off the Gomers.

It would be two more nights before we were ready to move the offensive forward, but in the meantime, the stand down was helping each of our soldiers in the field to get more of everything he needed. It also allowed us to use the daylight to methodically move our forces around the battlefield. It was my hope that by repositioning the forces near the two main north- south interstates, that if we could get them the prime movers, then we'd be able to move them more quickly to where we needed them. It also helped that some of the straightaway sections were also usable as airfields for our C-130 and C-17 fleets. I should point out that this was originally by actual design.

The interstate highways, for the first time in US History, were fully being used for the purpose for which they were originally created. If General, and later President, Eisenhower were still alive, I believe I might have kissed him full on the mouth.

Bringing that idea back from Germany's autobahn system after World War II was the one legacy of his presidency that showed sheer genius. Sure, the various states forgot why the highway was constructed, and they forgot that the highway standards required certain reinforcement along the way. They even forgot that rest areas were required to allow for troop convoys to get off the road for rest periods. The fact that someone could take a leak on a long trip was a byproduct but, again, people forgot. Right up until now. Now they remembered, and now we were dealing with years of local neglect issues.

Still, we were way ahead of where we were before but, when this was over, I promised myself I was going to personally search out every state department of transportation director who was still alive and punch them right in the mouth. On the first day, we lost three C-130s and two C-17s, because sub-standard contracts had been allowed, and the aircraft simply broke through the pavement. With each incident, I made a note of which state and passed it on to the President's staff for future use. Right now, if I were the DOT director for either South Carolina or Georgia, I would probably put on a pair of steel shorts and a goalie mask. Working around these messes over the next two days, we were able to reposition most of our Army to move us into the next phases.

Each night, the Gomers returned, and each night we fed them another pill of nuclear food. We mixed it up with the same or similar results, using both the TNWs and ERWs. We killed a lot of their smaller ships and a few of the big ones each night, yet they kept coming back. Almost like a bug will circle a bug zapper on a summer evening, the Gomers would flock to the SRS, and feed or refuel. We would blow a few of them up, and then the rest would still return the very next night. After two nights of this pattern, especially since they weren't being molested along their path, they got just a little complacent. It was this complacency that led us to our next phase.

Over the last two nights, even though their numbers were smaller, the Gomers returned to their previous routes of sweeping in over central New Jersey and then turning to sweep south to the SRS. They didn't waste their energy weapons by carving up the woods much, although some of the smaller objects would take random flight paths to hit anything that drew their curiosity. The Gomers largely were returning to their original formations and pathways. Their only changes would come as they neared the SRS. General Whitney noted that the newer tactic was to get the little guys to sweep in low and set a perimeter, while the large ones would attempt to feed or recharge. They kept their spacing now and, at any one time, the Gomers only allowed a few of their larger ships into the refueling positions for actual charging or, as some would call it, their 'feeding.'

There was no question that the ground around the SRS was crawling now with dusty Gomers during the day, but this was becoming a small challenge for our special operators who had fun figuring out the best locations to stick our "Nuclear Exploding Radiological Devices", or "NERDS", as they were becoming known. I will credit some wag with the Air Force with the creation of this nomenclature, since it was simply embracing the young airman's inner geek. Regardless, these airmen and special operations personnel did a good job of mixing it up. With each night, they would try to base the locations for the placement of their "NERDS", based on their prior observations of the night before, with a focus on where the Gomer line was forming to get "fuel" and where they suspected the "tap" for the fuel was being located by the Gomers. They also made sure that the ERW weapons were placed nearer the tap, while the TNWs were further out along the 'queue' or boundaries to the north and east.

We were in a war of attrition, but we wanted things to become decisive. The only way to do that was to hit them where we were not expected, and before they got to the refueling point or the "trough", as it was now called by the Staff. With this in mind, we took our now replenished and relocated First Army, and portions of the Third Army, and built a box to deny them their most used route and their favorite local fuel source.

Near Cleveland, Georgia:

A patrol near the mountains in North Georgia was approached by yet another group of tired and hungry civilian refugees. This bedraggled lot appeared to be no different than those already encountered all along the mountains. Each of the civilians had the same look of being lost, hungry, exhausted, and traumatized. They also each had the exact same facial expressions as the thousands already encountered by the military patrols in this same area. Everyone knew little, other than what they had observed along their various tortured routes into the foothills or mountains, and each of them was approaching a point of despondency from which there seemed to be little hope of return. One thing they all knew instinctively was that the high ground was far safer than remaining along the coastal areas. As a result, after many days of running, hiding, and feeding off the land where they could, they all were making their way into the mountains. Men, women, children, and more than a few family pets would show up dragging their way into what they felt might be their last chance of any refuge from the Gomers, or in some cases, their fellow citizens.

In one specific case, it was more than instinct that drove him; it was a simple handwritten note. One that was co-signed by his beloved wife and a General, and one that he hoped would lead him back to his family. As the young man reached out and handed the note to one of the soldiers, he waited and hoped that this man in uniform would be able to point him in the direction he needed to go to find his family. When he looked at the soldier as he read the note, the young man, despite his exhaustion and hunger, was rather puzzled and amazed at the look that came over the soldier's face.

"Dude, do you know who signed this note?"

"Yeah, my wife and my father-in-law, and I was hoping that he might have told somebody in the Army where I could find them."

"This guy is your father-in-law? You gotta be kiddin' me!"

"No why? Where is he? He knows where my wife and son are, and I really need to find them. Can you help me?"

"Hang on." With that admonition, the young soldier ran off towards the main CP for his unit. As he walked in, he handed the note to his Commander who, on looking at it, immediately picked up the phone. John Loomis didn't know it, but he had stumbled into the camp for the same Ranger Battalion where the rest of his family had passed those weeks ago. What he also couldn't know was that as soon as the Colonel read the message, he made sure that the young man got food, water, and, more importantly, transportation. Instead of moving into a refugee settlement for the thousands of displaced civilians who were showing up daily, the following day the young chemist-turned-entrepreneur was reunited with his wife and son, Michael.

Chris was thrilled beyond words. It was finally the end of her personal pain of not knowing whether she was a widow or not, and while she thought it was a long shot, she was still praying that somehow, John was okay. For their son, it was a perfect present for his birthday, which fell only a few days later. The entire Patrick family was delighted at the homecoming of the prodigal son-in-law, John. With his finding his way back to the rest of the family, the population in and around the Patrick portion of the cave just got a little larger.

John's story was fascinating. It was pure good fortune that he had survived the initial attacks on the civilian populace in Columbia, South Carolina. The restaurant kitchen had run out of a staple for their patrons, and he had made a quick run into the basement of the adjacent building that was used for nothing but dry storage. He was there when the attacks came and, as the power and humanity were literally sucked out of the main building, he only knew that the lights had failed. When he returned to the restaurant's main dining room, there was nothing left. No staff, no customers, nothing. The Bar was also completely empty. He tried the phone, and there was nothing. Then he heard screams and could see an object right outside as it swept the bar located right across the street. Knowing immediately that this was something new and extremely menacing, he made his way back to the basement of the building where he had been when his own business was attacked. He remained there hiding for the rest of the night and well into the next day, wanting to make sure that whatever had hit them was now gone.

Unfortunately, while he was hiding in the basement, a new threat arose that had nothing to do with the invading Gomers. Shortly after dawn on that first day, the looters, and those who were more than willing to survive by taking advantage of the absence of any police authority, started to maraud through the city. While we were by the park waiting to be taken to the new Pentagon, John was still trying to get out of the city and work his way back to his own house. John was unarmed and moving very slowly, simply because he was forced to use empty buildings, sheds, or even the sewer as cover for his escape. During daylight he had to hold up and hide frequently, to avoid the pillaging crooks and, then at night, there were the Gomers who continued to sweep through the built-up areas. He had watched, without understanding the ramifications, our aircraft from a distance as we departed towards the airport from the park. Finally, two days later, John read Chris' note, when he arrived at their house after having to literally swim across the river that separated his home from the City of Columbia.

From there his journey remained on foot and always headed to the west towards the mountains. Having to forage for his food, he would often search through abandoned houses, cars, or closed convenience stores along his route. Many of these places also became temporary shelters, but oftentimes they were places that attracted more of the violent human element and therefore had to be avoided. All along his route, he was forced to hide often, again during the day from any roving looters, and at night from the roving Gomers. Towards the end of his long and perilous journey, he saw the first flash and then heard the bang off in the distance when the TNW was used at the SRS a few nights earlier. Grasping the implications instantly, he drove himself even harder to get to the mountains quickly. While there were others heading in the same direction, most remained very aloof and wary of their fellow humans. There were occasional acknowledgements from these travelers, but there was still a feeling that it was every "man" or family for themselves. After weeks of this misery, John, having not eaten regularly in days, staggered up to the patrol and handed over his note with dirty and shaking hands. This was the same note, along with a picture of his wife and son, which had kept him going through his journey.

Shortly after finding his way to the patrol, our scientists had him working again. Aside from being a stellar chef, he was a trained and highly skilled chemist. Within days, Chris had him working as a chemist again, only this time for Dr. Abramson where he was apparently doing a great job fitting in with our resident brain trust. While I described things like nepotism, there was no doubt that the entire family had committed to the cause of driving the Gomers off our planet. I also knew that having accountability on my family made us all a very rare group of people, and for that I would always be thankful.

Chapter XI

Our scrambling and movement of our larger units through the scores of migrant refugees, created some serious issues for our planning and execution. Finally, after much adjustment and readjustment to the plan, the First Army was now positioned along a line that stretched from Harrisburg, Pennsylvania, to Wilmington, Delaware. Down the coast, the Third Army was in a line running from just north of Richmond, Virginia, down to Hampton Roads, Virginia. Finally, our strategic reserve, now designated as Sixth Army and under the command of Lieutenant General Davis, my recent and now former Staff Director, was positioned from St. George, South Carolina to a little south of Savannah, Georgia.

The two days respite was perfect for rounding out General Davis' command. We now had almost a third full strength Marine Division to add to his mix, along with one more Armored Division that we were able to form from several National Guard units. This gave us a little extra punch, and the command group for this latter Armor force was composed of several experienced members of the main command group out of what used to be the III Corps staff out of Fort Hood, Texas. In other words, they knew their business, and they had more than ample quantities of lead paint to make their job just a little easier. General Davis knew what was expected of him, and he deployed his Army to make it work within its experience and limitations. His concentrations of artillery and Armor maximized his abilities to deny the Gomers their fuel and would be set up to protect himself and the rest of his new hodgepodge force.

This was also a combined operation of the highest order. The Air Force, who kept baiting the field, continued to plan on providing this support. This time, though, we were also getting an all-out effort of Tactical Air, and some B-2 Strategic assets were added to the mix to feed in their Cruise Missile payloads. Their attack was to extend the "linger" time for the Air Component of the operation for just a little longer after twilight arrived. Similarly, we were also bringing Army Aviation assets into full play to deny access to areas nearer the mountains where they could 'mask' and get off their shots. It was felt that they could unleash their weapons and then re-mask or hide behind the mountainous terrain for movement to other firing positions. This was a standard tactic in anti-tank warfare, and it was believed that a combination of this and A-10 support could be our ace in the hole to steer the Gomers where we wanted them to go.

Finally, the Navy had their game plan, too, and, if it worked, it could be a useful precursor to future operations in the Antarctic region. Standing off our coast, from New Jersey to Georgia, were several attack and missile submarines. They were all prepared to add their combat power to our onslaught and, at key points along the path of the Gomers to SRS, they could fire on command, if necessary, to keep the Gomers occupied as they tried to sweep down the coastal areas to make a turn back to SRS. Finally, as a third back up plan, several more attack submarines were prepared to fire TNWs at the formation off the coast of the US. They were there in case the Gomers decided to approach the SRS from the east as they had done on that first night after the original ERW explosion.

The largest difficulty at this point in the entire operation appeared to be that we were starting to run a little thin on lead-based paint. After our operations Orders were passed down to the Field Armies, a very tired Dr. Abramson approached with some good news. Motioning to General Whitney, they gathered around me and General Larkin, who was trying to cover the staff director position, recently vacated by General Davis when he took command of the Sixth Army.

"Okay, Doctor, let's hear it."

"General, you won't believe this, but I may literally have found a chink in their armor."

"You have my attention, so what is it?"

"Well, sir, it seems that their metallurgy actually breaks down when it contacts high concentrations of sulphur. Those shells we made and issued for use in case the Gomers were to make a ground attack, well, they will work on the metal of those ships!"

"You are kidding me! You mean just dry concentrated sulphur will break down what they call metal?"

"Yes, sir, it will. We found out kind of by accident when one of my guys . . . it was your son-in-law John, by the way . . . dropped a tiny piece of one of their ships into his coffee cup. When he poured out the coffee through a filter to get the piece back, there was nothing, but a film left in the filter. Once he saw that, he started messing with various forms of sulphur to see how it reacted on the 'metal', and each form caused the 'metal' to dissolve. Even the dry form, which took a little longer, basically caused corrosion at a pretty fantastic rate."

I immediately turned in my seat and said, "General Whitney, waste no time getting this out to all our commanders. Screw the standard protocol, let the higher-level commanders know, but get it out directly to every battery and company commander right now! This, my friends, could be the icing on the cake!" Turning towards Jerry, I noticed a huge grin, and I said, "Giant, you might want to send a message to the Air Force. I have a feeling this is something they can use, too."

With our last huge adjustment, we sat back and waited. We were two hours out from the twilight line, and the final movement of the Gomers was coming over the wire from the Navy. We were getting down to crunch time and I, for one, was damn glad to see it.

Near Savannah, Georgia:

The Marine Captain read the message, and then read it again. Turning to his message center sergeant he said, "You sure this was signed by the Chief of Staff of the whole stinkin' Army, himself?"

"Yes sir, it came out of his headquarters as a flash message, for distribution immediate to every level of the command."

"I've never seen a fire mission or change of ammo like this before, especially from the H-M-F-I-C, you know, the Head Mo-Fo in Charge!"

"Yes, sir and it is a clear message, too. It gives you the precise ammo choice and tells you what order to fire it in for maximum results."

"Okay, well, ours is not to reason why. At least tonight we get to shoot at the Gomers again. I was starting to get bored. What about you, Marine?"

"Hoorrahhhh sir!"

"Okay, get the gun captains in here, and let's get the firing order the way they want it. Clearly, they found something or know something we don't!" With that statement, there was much scurrying, and the loads were shifted around in the guns. The Marine Captain then said to no one in particular, "You know? I wondered why we had those funky ass shells in the first place. Someone said it was for anti-personnel use on the Gomers, but I guess now we're about to find out why." Almost as an afterthought, he told his Battery First Sergeant to double the perimeter guard and keep an eye out for any Gomers coming by land.

Outside Wilmington, Delaware:

"Captain, I have a message from Battalion for you."

"Okay, "Top", what is it?"

"Get this, it is from the 'old man' himself."

As the Captain took the message, and read it, he said, "You weren't kidding, were you, although when you said, 'old man', I thought you meant the Division Commander, not the damn CSA! Okay, make it happen and, in the meantime, get me the runner."

As Kowalski entered the tent, the newly promoted Captain handed him a message to take around to all the Platoon Leaders. "Ski, please do NOT screw this up! I want you to personally hand this to each Platoon Leader, let them read it, and then I want you to move on until you've got them all. I do not want any screw ups, so tell them after they've passed on the content to their platoon; I want to see them here in the TOC. Is that clear?"

"Yes sir!" With that, Kowalski was back out and moving between the platoon leaders. As each read the message, the look of surprise was obvious. Being the curious type, Ski stopped on his way back to the TOC and read it. After reading it, he just couldn't see the big deal. This is just another message from a General, so what? When he stepped back into the TOC near the Commander, he learned just what a deal it could be.

As all the platoon leaders came into the tent, the Captain began, "Okay, men, here is the deal. We are reloading our big stuff with Sulphur Shells and/or the Sulphur tipped Rockets. We were told on issue that those things were for anti-Gomers, so all I can tell you is that we need to be on the lookout for Gomers on the ground, as well as in the air. Make each shot count and, when in doubt, hit it with a Sulphur Shell first, and then the High Explosives second. Any questions?"

As the group broke up, Ski could not take it anymore and had to ask that one more question. "Sir, what's the big deal about this message?"

"Ski, did you look at who signed it?"

"Yeah, some General."

"Not SOME General... THE General. The Chief of Staff of the whole damned Army. They do not send messages directly to grunts in the field. They publish field manuals, but they don't send messages to grunts. That means that what he just gave us as information is not just important, it is RFI, you know... Really Fecking Important!"

Along the Southern Lines near Yemassee, South Carolina:

The message had the needed and desired impact throughout the entire three Armies, and it was met with the same reaction in every single location. Even CSM Clagmore with the 11th Airborne was impressed, which had only happened maybe twice in his entire thirty-year career. Standing next to the Division Commander as he read the message, he let out a low whistle and then said, "Shit, you mean this was sent to every swinging dick all the way DOWN to company level as a direct message?"

"That's right, Sergeant Major, to every company and battery commander in the entire US of Army!"

"Well, I'll be damned. I know this guy, too. He was one mean son of a bitch. I actually got along with him, but damn, he was mean. In fact, General, he might even be meaner than me if you get him cornered!"

"Really, how do you know him?"

"We were operators together in a past life. He was called Mighty Mouse in those days, and he was as mean as a damned rattlesnake in a bucket. He got the nickname because he was short but could whip his weight in bobcats and then ask for a beer. Saw him once in a firefight, he just went nuts and ran like a scalded dog, screaming like a banshee, right at the bad guys. They were so fucking surprised that, when he shot one between the eyes, the other two just gave up!"

"Damn, then what happened?"

"Well, they didn't give up fast enough, and that's all I'm sayin'."

"Okay, so if he is the man in charge, I guess you're okay with it."

"Yes sir, I guess I am. If anybody can stare down the devil and give him the bird, then it is General Patrick. And if he sent us that fucking message with his signature as the CSA, then you better believe every word. I'll get the boys ready at this end. I have a feeling what he is also telling us is that tonight is going to be a real bitch wolf."

Further up the Southern Line near
Walterboro, South Carolina:

General Davis had just finished the briefing with his staff when he was handed the message from General Patrick. Smiling, he immediately grasped the ramifications of the message, the addresses, and, more importantly, the content. After reading it the second time, he called his G-6, Command, Control, and Communications officer over and said, "Colonel, verify that all levels of this command got this message. If they don't, then make sure they do, because I want everyone on board with it. The Boss would not have sent it out under his signature if it wasn't a potential game changer. Now move, we only have two hours before it starts getting dark around here!"

New Pentagon:

As my message was making its way through the Armies, the Navy was giving us some real time information about the Gomers and their movements. We had worn down their forces some, but they were still coming back to refuel like clockwork. As the information arrived, General Whitney updated their positions and formations on our large map board. We did not have the advantage of the high-tech stuff anymore, since most of our Satellites were no longer sending us the useful real time information, but the old-fashioned grease pencil on a laminated map still worked just about as effectively. At least it did for an old dinosaur like me who learned the business with greased pencils and paper maps.

As we watched the map, it was clear that, while tonight was going to be different for us, the Gomers were treating it as their version of 'business as usual.' Their formations were the same as previous nights, and they were forming up to cross the coast over New York and New Jersey, just as we had hoped. We were now less than an hour from them crossing the coast, and all we could do was wait and pray that the men all knew what to do and that they got my message. My only regret was that I couldn't be in the field with them, but then I remembered General Gregg and thought, what a waste it was to lose such a brilliant mind. I wasn't that brilliant but, except for Jerry, I sure had a lot more experience than anyone in the room. GOD, isn't that sad? I am an old fart, and a former reservist to boot, geez what has this Army become?

As a last-minute precaution, I told Jerry to send out the 'weapons tight' guidance to the First Army and the northern line of forces. The last thing I wanted was some nervous type to kick it off too soon. Instead, they were to wait for our order, which would be based on the observations of the USS Providence, a Los Angeles Class Attack Submarine, hull number SSN - 719. The USS Providence was tracking the Gomers, and once the Gomers' fleet was all on land and roughly between the First and Third Army positions, we would hear a two-word transmission on the ELF. Minutes passed as the twilight line crossed our coast, and so did the Gomers. In about the same place where they'd crossed it over the last several nights. About 25 minutes later, we heard those two magic words on our ELF receiver. "SHOT OUT!" On hearing those words, Jerry hit the direct line to our three Field Army Headquarters, and simply said. "YOU ARE WEAPONS FREE!" Within moments, the battle was joined.

Near Wilmington, Delaware:

Private Kowalski was sitting behind the company commander in the bottom of their forward position. For some reason, even though it had been a hot day, tonight he was cold, damn cold. As he was sitting there, wishing he had something else to do, he started staring into the sky. As he looked up, he saw the unmistakable shadow of something large passing overhead. When it registered, he was on his feet and grabbing the sleeve of the Captain and pointing upwards. "Sir, they are right there, why the hell aren't we shooting?"

"Dammit, Ski, sit down and shut up. Be really quiet or I'll strangle you myself. Besides, they've been passing overhead for the last 15 minutes! So be quiet!"

Within another minute, the Captain heard something fly overhead and strike a large ship that had passed only moments before. With that, he raised his phone and said, "Okay, guys, that's our cue. Light these fuckers up!" What they didn't know was that they saw the punctuation to the extremely short two-word message sent by the USS Providence. That "Shot Out" turned into a direct hit on a large Gomer, and it was the signal for those who saw it to light up the bad guys.

Near Harrisburg, Pennsylvania:

Three Apache helicopters popped up above the ridge line and immediately spotted two of the smaller objects that were trailing a large ship to their front. As they unmasked, each aircraft let loose with two Hellfire missiles, then the formation ducked back behind the higher terrain as they turned to move to another location. Within seconds, their missiles hit their marks and both smaller crafts went down. As soon as the path was clear, an A-10 moved immediately behind the large ship, unleashing several of the new sulphur tipped missiles. As the missiles left the aircraft's rails, the A-10 also ducked behind the ridge and moved to an alternate firing position.

As the aircraft were attacking along the Gomers' western flank, the amount of artillery and tank fire from the northern line increased. All along the front, quite a few the Gomers were falling from the sky, and apparently, they were falling without the ships ahead of them taking any evasive action. In fact, there was little reaction from any of the leading ships as they approached the Third Army positions. All along both of their flanks the Gomer fleet of ships was taking fire from either the Air Force or the Navy, as they kept up their rate of fire. When the Cruise Missiles from the B-2 and Naval ships found their marks, the smaller ships began to finally react. As they moved away from the main fleet, the smaller guys made quite a few dashes searching for the sources of the missiles. In short, they began to blast with their energy weapons at almost everything on either side of their formation and, as they did, they completely neglected to patrol ahead to search for anything to their front.

Still working their flanks, the small ships would approach the mountains and then break off and begin their turns back to their fleet. Once the observing Combat Air Controllers reported that they had turned, the Army Aviation assets, in conjunction with their Air Force A-10 counterparts, would attack them from the rear and still maintain fire on the flanks of the larger ships. While the main body of the Gomer fleet continued the southern journey, their smaller 'protective' cover was drawn to the sides searching for the airplanes or naval ships that were attacking them. As a result, their eyes were no longer watching in front.

Without this forward cover or the use of their 'scouts,' the main fleet came under the guns of the Third Army. While the Air Force and Navy continued their attacks from the air and sea on the flanks, the Third Army opened fire with as much sulphur and lead as possible. The entire area was a classic ambush with a huge kill zone. As more and more of the large ships were going down, the Gomer losses were horrific. Some of the Gomers ships escaped out to sea, but the numbers that were able to get clear of the coast were a lot lower than we had anticipated. We were killing more than we had originally expected. As they turned out to sea, there were more surprises for the Gomers, and it was about to get even uglier for them.

The Gomers were still being tracked as they re-crossed the coast out into open water, and even though they thought they were safe by moving well out to sea before turning back towards the shore, they were mistaken. Instead of finding a quiet ocean, they ran head on into a barrage of conventional Cruise Missiles being fired from several attack submarines that were specifically positioned to catch any stragglers that might wander out of the kill zone. While their losses from this portion of the action were notable, the real impact of the attack was to turn the Gomers right back over the coast and into the waiting arms of the Sixth Army's guns and the B-2 Assets from the Air Force. When the remaining Gomer fleet entered the mouth of the Savannah River, the Marine detachment on Pulaski was waiting with their Sulphur tipped shells. As the Marines continued to pour on their fire, the Gomers could do little to react.

It seems that the impact of these new weapons was even quicker on the Gomers' metal than Dr. Abramson had initially predicted. It was also apparently completely blinding to some of the Gomer ships, with the result that their smaller objects were simply not up to anything, except running for their own lives. As each round burst and spread the sulphur, the gun crews said it was like the damn things just started melting. As the remnants of the Gomers' fleet continued up the Savannah River basin and further into the killing zone of massed armor and artillery, it was carved down to nothing but three larger ships and a handful of their smaller escorts. The Sixth Army did a fantastic job, and General Davis had positioned his larger weapons to take full advantage of the Gomers' bad habit of returning to the SRS for fuel.

Littering to the north, all the way up the continental coast, were thousands of both large and small Gomer ships. From our lines in Pennsylvania and Delaware, down to the Virginia-Maryland lines, there were hundreds of the smoking or melting ruins of the Gomer fleet. Then traveling south, out to sea, and throughout the Sixth Army kill zones, there were literally hundreds more of all sizes. As the small remnant of the Gomer fleet finally arrived over the SRS, it was the last time in this war that a nuclear weapon would have to be detonated over the site. It was quick, dirty, and to the point. With that last explosion of an ERW, the Gomer fleet in the Northern Hemisphere simply ceased to exist. Not a single ship of any size continued to sweep through the Mid-West, nor was there any traffic in the Mexican sky. What started with a little hope, and a huge amount of audacity, ended when that last Gomer ship at the SRS became a pile of melting dust particles. This time, the initial burst of Neutrons had to dissipate naturally, since there was nothing left that would absorb the residual radiation. I guess the best news was that we only used an ERW, which would dissipate far more rapidly than one of the more lingering TNWs.

The reports from the field were way beyond even our wildest hopes and imaginations. Consequently, the exhilaration that ran through the mountain and my staff was contagious. The casualties were minimal, with us having only lost a handful of aircraft, and virtually no forces on the ground. There was no question that the situation was cause for some celebration, but not much since this was only half of their fleet. Presumably, there were more hiding around the South Pole, and then there was that big bastard behind the Moon. How long was it going to wait before it decided to come out and play? As I left the 'war room' for the first time in almost 48 hours, I literally staggered into my office completely exhausted. My last conscious thought was to tell Jerry to start getting our forces back to the mountains as soon as possible. We still had a way to go, and I wanted them rested and protected before we had to make our next move.

I was awakened with my bride Leah standing over me, with a smile and a cup of decent coffee for a change. As I gathered my wits and shook off more than a few gallons of mental dust, Leah apologized for having to wake me, but "the President wants to speak to you." I looked around for Chris to see why Leah was telling me this, and not the staff. When I asked, "Where is Chris?" Leah responded, "Oh, she tried to wake you up, but you weren't cooperating. Besides, she and Jerry are tap dancing with the President until I can get you awake enough to talk."　　"Okay then, well I am as up as I'll ever be."

With that, I walked over to my desk and picked up the line, "Mr. President, Patrick here, I'm sorry to have kept you waiting."

"Hah, you old warhorse, you were sleeping on the job!"

"Yes sir, you caught me, now what can I do for you?"

"Well, when I heard how it all went, I thought maybe . . . just maybe I should call you and offer my congratulations."

"Thank you, sir, but we are a long way from being out of the woods. I'm still very concerned about their activities in the Southern Hemisphere, Antarctica, and then there is the beastie behind the Moon."

"Yeah, I know, and I need you to stay focused on that right now, but I've got some people here who need to hear it all from you. Some think that it is now all over, and they want to get us back to doing silly stuff like going home and returning to the way things were before all this happened."

"Sir, you know that can't happen yet. The minute we try that; we'll be inviting more problems when they move on us again."

"I know, Mike, but let's face it, with the average attention span in this day and age; you can expect some to start screaming about the peace well before it is over."

"Mr. President, you've had this job, you know the drill, and, most of all, you know better than anyone that we are a long way from finishing this war. We've only just pulled round two out of our ass, and I don't see Round three or four being in our grasp for some time yet."

"I know, so I want you here to explain that to the rest of the COG folks, who think they are going to be building a brave new world out of the ashes."

"Be delighted, sir, but just for the hell of it, would you mind if I got some sleep and let at least some of the Gomers' hulks cool off a little first?"

"Sure, Mike, I'll tell them you are coming sometime day after tomorrow. Oh, and bring some of your staff for the dog and pony show."

"Yes, Mr. President, be delighted." As I hung up, all I could think was that I lied. I wasn't delighted worth a damn.

We had just fought a pitched battle, and these bone heads in new Washington wanted a flipping briefing? What the hell was this all about? We don't have time for this, especially right now. That thought was still rolling around in my head when I kissed my wife and wandered back to my quarters to finally shave and shower for the first time in a couple of days. Then it was off to the 'war room' to find out what else was going on and start the Staff thinking about what our next move would entail. It dawned on me that we probably should have at least a rough plan for the next step and, right at that moment, I did not have a clue.

As the next evening progressed, it was quite apparent that the Gomers were not sending anything onto our part of the planet. There were rumors of a scout ship or two, mainly along the west coast, but the eastern half of the country was completely clear. There were also reports that there was no activity in Asia, Europe, or anywhere else north of the equator. Unfortunately, the same wasn't true for things south of the equator. There the reports continued as before, and the activities in and around Antarctica seemed to have picked up some. General Whitney was convinced that the Gomers were using the constant darkness as cover for building or repairing their equipment. As we prepared to head to new Washington, there were even some on my staff who were becoming a little concerned about the reports regarding our west coast. While I agreed with them, there was nothing to do but head to new Washington, and make sure we conveyed our concerns to the people that were making the policy for what would happen next. As I embarked onto the aircraft that would take me roughly 100 miles to my destination, my wife gave me something to give to Toni. It was a bundle of letters from the President's family and a bottle of good single malt Scotch for Marty. In retrospect, I should have hung onto the scotch myself.

Historically every war ever fought has ebbed and flowed. World War II is the classic reference for such things. It clearly ran in cycles and each theater, whether it was Europe or in the Pacific, had seen things take those turns. From the desperation that accompanied the Battle of Britain and the early days when England stood alone, through the humiliation of the early days in the Pacific, all the way up until we dropped the "big one" in Japan. Even in that war, where the goals were so clear, there were some who thought that peace could be obtained, and the killing could stop. Even at the beginning of the war, with the policy of appeasement between the Prime Minister of England, Lord Chamberlain, and Hitler, until the end, when the public was tired of the high casualties coming from the Pacific Island Campaigns, there was a belief that it could be concluded before it was actually finished. This fallacy of thinking has been repeated since then, with everyone thinking that "this war is different." For people who believe that bunk, I can only say "bull!" General George S. Patton Jr. was correct; we always finish too soon and leave ourselves another war to fight. In our case, we had only reached Winston Churchill's "end of the beginning."

I learned this same lesson on the micro level when I was 12 years old. A bully and I got into a fight one day behind my parent's garage. I would pin him down, after first pounding him to the pavement, and then, being the nice guy, I would let him up. He would hit me again, and we kept this up until I decided that this was not working and just knocked him out. With some people you just cannot be nice, and our Gomer enemies were no exception. Sure, we gave them a black eye, but not following up on it with a knock-out punch meant that they were just going to get back up and hit us again. I was right!

We did our dog and pony show for the mostly appointed government of the United States, and we even had some surviving Senators and House members who were originally elected to their office, as opposed to appointed, to give it all credibility. There were not enough of the "elected" survivors for a quorum, but enough to make it sound like a good show was taking place. Seeing their living arrangements, as compared to ours, was a real eye-opener too. While their facilities were far more appointed, they lived in a squalor like animals. The place was a filthy pig sty and, frankly, when we left, I had a burning need to take a shower. The long and short part of it was that, despite explaining the ongoing threat, I was still faced with their misguided belief that all was fine, and we had prevailed. In their minds it was just "game over" on a game console, and we could hit the reset button, and all go home.

There were a few in new Washington who understood what I was telling them, but many more actually believed that it was all over, and everyone could just go about their lives as if nothing happened. They sure didn't see the need to educate our former enemies, like Russia or China, or undertake any continued offensive action that would further upset the Gomers. It was the attitude of what is in the Southern Hemisphere or at the Moon, was someone else's problem. I think it was this deluded thinking that made what happened next so hard for them to believe. Despite our best efforts to educate and make it clear to them that there was still a huge threat, and that Gomers only wanted our energy, some of the new style politicians were back in their proverbial saddles running around and selling their snake oil to anyone who would listen.

When the Gomers hit again, I didn't know whether to be more pissed at them or at the damn fools that invited the fiasco through tying our hands. Either way, this time, despite those in new Washington that thought it was all done, we were getting ready to at least defend ourselves and take it to the bad guys. How? Well, because some of us simply ignored the carnival barkers, kept our eyes on the ball, and continued to plan and prepare. Thank GOD, the President was one of those who ignored the carnival side shows, and let us move forward with our planning, rearming, and re-equipping all our forces.

SECTION 3:

BUILDING A GLOBAL FORCE

Chapter XII.

Almost two weeks after we devastated their northern hemisphere fleet, the Gomers struck again. Shortly after the twilight line passed the Rocky Mountains in California, a moderate sized force of Gomers begins to sweep up the California Central Valley area, starting with Los Angeles, moving up to San Francisco, and then on through Sacramento, before turning around and returning south through the valley. What made this attack even worse was the civilian 'leadership' in that area. These people had been my loudest naysayers and, as a group, they were the exact same people that refused to believe that there was still a threat. They insisted that things were over, and that they could return to life as usual. Fortunately, they had not wrested the California National Guard back off active duty, but they were adamant that the lights could be turned on, and the people could return from their hiding places in the Rockies. They just knew that it was safe, and "besides, the only places hit before were on the other side of the country."

As a result, when the Gomers made their sweep, they were passing over real estate that was ripe for the pickings. All the lights were on, and night life was returning to some semblance of normal. There was even a baseball game going on between the Dodgers and the Padres when the attack came. Of the 25,000-plus spectators in Dodger Stadium, there were absolutely no survivors. Our mobilization of the greatest minds of science and the military personnel that were called to active duty out of that region were just about the only people left who were originally from Southern California. The fact that we still had these people was about the only thing that kept this from being a complete disaster. It was bad enough losing millions of people out of the urban areas. What made it truly criminal was that they had been warned and been led to believe that there was not a problem returning to 'normal.' If it was not for the fact that the people who led them down this path were now mostly among the dead and missing, then the cries for justice would have been more massive and continuous.

Once we learned of what was happening in California, we dispatched what assets we could to track the Gomers out of the area, and to try and put some combat power to bear on them. It was clear that this force came at us overland from the southern hemisphere, and it was equally clear that they departed in that direction as they retreated towards the South Pacific. As for our response, we did have a modicum of success in fighting the Gomers and were actually able to destroy a few more of the larger and smaller Gomer ships. Using the few Marines and remaining Navy assets remaining in California, we were able to do an excellent job against the Gomers with only a minimal loss to our combat forces. The best news from it all came from Vandenberg Air Force Base.

Once the attack force cleared the California Central Valley area, I was contacted by Colonel Greene. He advised me that the Commander of the 14th Air Force had done a stellar job of keeping his people and their strategic assets completely under wraps. With only a very little warning that the Gomers were headed north, he placed his personnel on full alert, and locked down the entire area. The result was the Gomers saw nothing except the beginning of the mountains, and lots of wilderness areas. The fact that the local command, the Air Force, and the Department of Defense have all been highly sensitive to the environmental areas around the facility paid dividends as the Gomers passed by. Not once, but twice, without the area drawing their attention. Colonel Greene's report was a huge relief, especially when he advised that his latest project was not molested or disturbed in the slightest.

Unfortunately, given the civilian leadership of the state insisting that we not upset the populace, there was no good news coming in about the rest of the central and coastal portions of the State. The State and Local Governments resisted most of our defense efforts by not allowing us to base any additional forces, or establish any of our special weapons, anywhere on their soil. Even though we were seeing an increase in the Gomers' using scouts to visit these areas, the local governments still refused to cooperate with us. Instead, we were faced with their openly stated concerns about the Sulphur and Lead being used in our weapons against the Gomers. In the short time since the East Coast campaign had concluded, an active protest sprang up in California against our tactics and weapons and, as a result, the Governor signed an executive order forbidding us to store or employ such weapons in the state because of their environmental impact. We knew the order could not stop us by law but, before the court fight could begin, they were pounded mostly into oblivion by the Gomers, and therefore the entire question became moot.

I was armed with this information, along with the details of the recent attack, when I returned with my staff to new Washington. We were to meet with the President, his cabinet, and the now even smaller contingent of Senators and Congressmen, to determine the course of a war that some of us had known wasn't over weeks ago. In much the same way as our leaders ushered us into our previous global conflicts, this one would take all we had, and maybe even more before it was done. It was now time to resume our full wartime production again, but this time we would have to do what was not necessary in previous wars. We were going to have to relocate our industrial capacity to safer locations; begin the process of conscription and training; start our own version of the 'Manhattan project; and mobilize everyone else for what would be a hard fight around the entire globe.

When we left new Washington, we left with a mandate and sufficient legislation to get things going in the direction we needed to eventually run the Gomers off. The wheels of bureaucracy, as opposed to democracy, were sadly now back in action. With this consideration in mind, I returned to the new Pentagon, ready to start the selection process to finally get my staff up and run in a new direction. For one thing, I needed someone who spoke 'bureaucrat' and we had to find the right people with "Gomer" fighting experience. Only then could we start creating a force that could take on the Gomers in their own new-found habitat. Now my concerns shifted to consider things like what would happen when the midnight sun ran out in the north and then turned on again in the south. I also pondered whether the Gomers knew this would happen, or if it would be a surprise to them. In one instance we could expect them to make a reasonable attack plan to achieve their objective, if it were the other, then their panic could make for a whole different response, and maybe create an opportunity for us.

Conscription and supplies were another headache that had to be overcome. Uniforms, for example, became a huge issue. As more personnel became available for training and equipping, we were having problems with finding the requisite weapons and uniforms for them to wear. Finally, out of disgust and desperation, we took another page from the World War II book. We went back to Khaki. The uniforms we were wearing, despite their versatility, were only camouflage if you were standing in front of a computer screen. In fact, service wide, there were eleven different types of camouflage, but none in sufficient quantities to fit all the forces that we were trying to get available. Moreover, we could not replace what we'd lost, since the manufacture, processing, and distribution of such things was eating up resources we needed elsewhere for higher priority items. Besides, the camouflage we had before was completely useless since our Gomer enemy was absolutely not fooled or impacted by it.

It was our collective experience that you could wear white, red, or purple and the impact on the Gomers was the same. The advantage to the khaki was that in every discount store in America, it was available as 'work clothing.' The Navy had a ton of it left, too, not to mention all the clothing warehouses in almost every city in the entire country. Finally, in our terrain and woods, it worked well in allowing people to at least blend into their scenery. As for personal weapons, initially they ran the gamut from hunting rifles to shotguns to the variations of other civilian weapons of all types. We kept the primary military weapons and equipment such as helmets in the hands of units that were subject to being deployed, while providing our "militia or reserve" home-based units with those weapons of varying calibers and types.

Over the next few weeks, we were also making personnel adjustments and moving key personnel to and from our far-flung locations. Most of these areas were previously cut off from us, especially those forces still in Europe, the Middle East, and portions of Asia, and we needed to adjust to the new reality now facing us. It was even time to empty the warehouses of things we could use, that were originally stocked overseas, in the event of a European war. This was no small task, since it required fast moving aircraft to follow the dawn line around the globe on a constant basis. While the Gomer threat was most certainly reduced in the northern hemisphere, it clearly was not eliminated. On a regular basis, the Gomers would still raid into the northern portions of the globe, just as they had in California. Russia, Japan, and China were now the Gomers' most frequent travel destinations in the northern hemisphere. India was being raided on a somewhat less frequent basis, but they could still expect at least two raids a week. The pattern for these Indian raids was as simple as the Gomers entering and passing through the more southern portions of the Indian countryside, before turning south and heading back into the lower portions of Africa.

In the southern hemisphere, the Continents of Africa, South America, and Australia, were the most commonly depleted areas. Brazil, Zimbabwe, and Angola were their common refueling destinations, but very few places were spared their marauding visits as the Gomers' "southern fleet" would transit their areas. There were only three areas that the Gomers avoided completely, and we took this as a good sign. The first such location was in the Islands of Hawaii along with many of the other islands in the

Pacific, because of their volcanic activity and release of sulphur into the air. The second was the nation of New Zealand, which was completely avoided by the Gomers. Thanks to the terrain and sulphur mining, New Zealand never had the Gomers attacking them directly; however, given their location near Antarctica, they were virtually cut off. The third was the region along the western coast of South America that was the Andes Mountains. The Gomers would go out of their way to fly either north or south, to avoid going over some of these mountains, which we discovered was again based on their aversion to sulphur.

Life for the Gomer southern fleet must have been difficult, or at least we were hoping it was difficult. General Whitney, along with the Air Force and Naval intelligence teams, agreed that the southern fleet was only roughly two thirds of the size of the original northern fleet and, for them; the amount of 'energized' land mass was a lot smaller. As our observations increased, because the amount of our intelligence assets had increased, we were seeing a different 'style' to the methods employed by the Gomers. This was the first real sign that the Gomers did have a chain of command, and that the Gomer in charge of their southern force was doing business just a little differently than his now deceased counterpart in the North.

The Gomers were not the only ones with command changes. We had a few of those, too, and with ours came both politics and attempts to rebuild diplomacy among the various nations. Trust is a hard thing to build or, in some cases, establish in the first place. The primary NATO countries were not a huge issue, but what remained hardly resembled a working government in the classic sense. Most of their efforts were nothing more than attempts to recover from their loss of key personnel, who were completely decimated, and to reestablish themselves in the most rudimentary ways. In short, with a few exceptions, our former allies were hardly in a position to offer any real useful support.

The United Kingdom had been hard hit with the loss of civilian and military leadership, but they had a plan for the continuity of government that put them ahead of the curve for functioning as a government. There was an heir to the throne who survived because of his forward visit into a then-existing war zone, and even though he was 28th in the line of succession, at least he was still alive to assume the position as King Alexander. With that framework, the UK was at least moving forward under their own COG type plan. They had both existing military formations, and some modicum of functionality for dealing with their surviving citizens. As we were fighting unassisted along our coast, they waited and watched, to see if there was a formula they could use to achieve any success. Their waiting would cost them credibility in the political struggle to form an 'allied force' among the surviving and functioning governments.

Similarly, Germany had a continuity of government plan and they, too, had lost a significant part of their civilian and military leadership. In response, rather than immediately recovering from their losses by filling or attempting to fill these positions, they opted to sit out the first part of the conflict without making any real effort at replacing their leadership or attempting to function as a government. Instead, the remaining ministers and military officers took steps to conceal their assets, while offering no resistance or assistance to anyone, including their own citizens. In short, they hid and watched the decimation of their population. They watched with great interest as the Russian strategic resources were used up in attack after attack against the Gomers. Finally, they watched as we engaged in our efforts to destroy the Gomers on our soil. It was only in this latter phase, after our first successful battles, that their submarines finally offered some minimal assistance by keeping us informed about Gomer movements.

Our other Allies within NATO were worn down. While some resisted, none were successful, and all were hiding when we finally took down the Gomers' northern fleet. Our losses in Europe were heavy at the top, but we had sufficient forces to reconstruct our Seventh Army command. Unfortunately, it was necessary to rely on the armored forces from our allies, since we had moved most of our last tanks out of Europe just a few months before the Gomers hit us. Following the standard NATO framework, the Seventh Army was now an Allied Command with divisions coming from the United Kingdom, France, and Germany. The Italian military, along with Belgium, the Netherlands, and Denmark, were only able to make small contributions. They were all welcome and were in far better shape than we expected. The greatest surprise, and perhaps the allies with the most to offer in rebuilding an allied force, came from Norway, Sweden, and Finland. Mostly above the Arctic Circle, these military forces were largely untouched. Unfortunately, these civilian governments, along with their military leadership, were all reduced to a point that was only barely above functioning.

On the first day of the Gomer attack, the United States Eighth Army was without doubt the hardest hit U.S. Army formation. Standing against a constant threat from North Korea, each side of the border was set to a hair trigger should the other side advance. When the Gomers first attacked the Korean Peninsula, each side of the DMZ erupted into gunfire, with each side thinking that the war had gone hot. As their firing at one another continued, the Gomers were systematically taking out the leadership on both sides of the border. As the conflagration grew towards epic proportions, the Gomers took full advantage, and it wasn't long before neither side had a fighting force capable of any resistance. Thereafter, with each succeeding passage of the Gomers' fleet, the populace of both North and South Korea were virtually wiped out. The only survivors were those soldiers who were in the mountains, and who were already dug in deeply against the onslaught of the initial artillery fire from the opposite side of the DMZ. As it became clear that the Gomers were the real source of the attacks, the survivors banded together, despite their political differences, and held on. When we were finally able to contact our forces in Korea, the Eighth Army was being nominally commanded by a Lieutenant Colonel, and the new leader of the forces for the DPRK was a Major, who was the highest-ranking survivor to be located within the North Korean Government.

It was against this global picture that President Marty Blanchard dispatched his Secretary of State, Timothy Case, to attempt to forge an alliance for the Campaign ahead. Conspicuously absent from the initial attempts were both the Chinese and Russians. Fortunately, this changed shortly after our discussions about the California attack. I had made it quite clear that we needed to operate in the Pacific and that we would need permission to do it. It was bad enough we had to fight the Gomers; we did not need anyone to get their feelings hurt and then stuff a nuke on our backsides while we were doing it. After serious soul searching within the new Washington inner circle, Secretary Case was finally sent to discuss an alliance with the Russians and Chinese. It was from these visits to Europe and Asia that we learned for the first time just how truly devastating the Gomers had been to each of these countries.

The Russians no longer had a viable military force, at least not beyond what they could now throw together from their former Army. In our terms, at most they could salvage less than one Field Army out of a total ground force that, before the Gomers attacked, consisted of about 10 full Field Armies. In short, even with Naval Infantry and other special units, the Russian Military could only field the rough equivalent of 6 total divisions. Their Air Force and Strategic Missile forces no longer existed in any usable form and their Navy was now minimal. Of the leadership that survived, many were too old to take an active role in operations, having retired from their services years before. One thing they had that did survive was a very large number of artillery pieces. Albeit in different calibers than our own, these extra tubes could prove to be handy if it came down to another slugfest over land.

The Chinese, on the other hand, took advantage of their terrain and sheer numbers to maintain a somewhat viable force. Unfortunately, while they still had personnel, there was little advanced equipment left that they could use for any offensive operations. Once the Gomers attacked, the Chinese military expended vast amounts of material and equipment in their initial operations against the Gomers. Their losses in equipment, such as tanks, artillery, and aircraft, were beyond high. Some would call it astronomical, even by Chinese standards, yet each night the Chinese fought on. Entire Chinese armored and air force formations simply ceased to exist, as each night they would attack, and each night the Gomers would use their power weapons to eviscerate these large formations. Finally, when they had nothing more to use in the fight, the Chinese continued by waging a simple war of attrition. The Chinese would attack from their mountain strongholds near the Himalaya Mountains, and they would gather information about the Gomers to pass on to anyone who would listen. Sadly, thanks to the limitations of communications in the earliest days of our battles, such information never reached us, not even through the relay stations we had on the Indian side of those very same mountains.

The rest of the Pacific Rim was a series of losses suffered by the various governments and their military forces throughout the entire Pacific. Australia was still within the main attack zone, and information received was minimal, at least until the Navy was able to establish a limited clandestine message service. Then we learned that the Australian situation was simple, they were there and hanging on, but barely, as they, too, were taking advantage of their mountain ranges.

The Japanese were equally hurt and, with a feeding area along their coast, they were having the same problems we faced in and around our SRS. The Japanese military forces hiding within their mountains were surviving, but their Naval and Air assets were completely devastated. With each pass of the Gomers, it only got worse and, even with the destruction of the Gomers' northern fleet; they were still seeing almost nightly sweeps by the Gomers' southern fleet. What truly complicated the Japanese situation was the fact that the entire civilian government of Japan was wiped out completely on the first night of the Gomers' attack. Tokyo appears to be the very first location on the planet that was attacked by the Gomers. It happened without warning, and it happened during a late evening session of the Diet. The real irony is that the attack occurred while the entire government was meeting to debate changes to their Constitution that would allow for a military that wasn't limited merely as a defense force.

This historical irony of the Gomers' surprise attack on Japan was one of those real oddities of any war. It was a Japanese military government that launched a surprise attack to lead us into World War II in the Pacific, a war that would eventually lead to the defeat of that military government, and then the creation of a civilian government that decried all things military. Now, thanks to an equally surprising attack on Japan, while that civilian government was debating on the question of whether they should allow for the use of their military forces beyond a purely defensive role, the military was all that was left. Never has a debate ended quite so abruptly, nor been rendered so completely moot, in such a short span of time. Now, regardless of the average Japanese citizen's political views on the question, reality just created a brand-new military government, and it was all they had left.

Information around the world continued to come into our 'war room,' and we continued to process what we were hearing.

We conducted as much analysis as the data from the various military forces would allow, and we studied the intelligence we gathered from all our sources about the various experiences of every military action fought by our allied and former enemies against the Gomers. Interestingly, and this is even more credit to the minds we had gathered in our own scientific community, we were the only nation in the world to discover the Gomers' weakness to both Sulphur and Lead.

While we were going through the After Action Reports of the worlds' other military forces and reviewing their actions against the Gomers, we were also trying to find the right people for the right jobs in our own Army. As our forces began to stick their collective heads up from their respective holes around the world, we were shifting personnel, where we could, to try and assemble a winning team. Concurrently, the President was also finding that he had positions to fill and, after a lot of discussions with the rest of his Cabinet, the President finally found someone to fill the position of the Secretary of Defense. He was another 'old guy' and someone with whom I had worked in my younger days. Richard Todd, our new Secretary of Defense, or SecDef, was a former operator himself, but with a different agency. His background was mostly CIA, but at least he spoke military, having himself served in the first Gulf War as a company commander in an armor unit. Frankly, I was darn glad to see him since this would allow Admiral Morton and me to get back to the business of war, and away from some of the functions we were required to perform in the areas of administration.

Within 6 weeks of our victory over the Gomers' northern fleet, from the ashes arose a new and improved Joint Staff in support of the Chairman of the Joint Chiefs of Staff. The President moved Admiral Morton officially to that position and appointed a 'submarine' man as the new Chief of Naval Operations. I was delighted, since Admiral Steadman was someone who had directed much of the Navy's work against the Gomers from the first day of the attack. He was stuck out in the Pacific near Pearl Harbor when the first attacks took place and, even though his bosses all the way up to the Commander of the Pacific were eliminated, he stepped up immediately as a junior Real Admiral (lower half) to handle the reconnaissance efforts of the Gomers throughout his areas.

A week after these changes took place; I was directed, along with the other Chiefs of Staff, and my Vice Chief, General Larkin, to appear at a meeting the next day in new Washington with the President. When I mentioned it to Leah, she told me that she already knew, because Toni had sent a message that she and Larkin's wife, Maggie, were to come along for a visit. Leah was excited because it meant that she could get the hell out of the mountain, and she had already collected some mail and pictures from the President's grandchildren to take to their 'Nana.' When we landed outside the entrance to new Washington, Toni was there to greet Leah and Maggie, and the three of them took off like delighted little kids at a birthday party. Jerry and I were met with the requisite security staff from the President and immediately escorted to the President's office. Expecting the other Chiefs to be in the room, we were a little surprised to see just the President and the new SecDef. As we entered, we were told to have a seat. The SecDef began by saying that the full meeting was going to be in half an hour, but they had something to cover with me first. It was then that I noticed the new Secretary of State seated in the corner of the office.

As I turned my attention back to the President, he was pushing himself out of his seat and as he stood up, he said, "General Patrick, it is my duty to advise you that you are being relieved of your duties as the Chief of Staff of the United States Army. You are to turn those duties over to General Larkin effective immediately. Do you understand?"

"Yes sir." On hearing those words, I felt a little sad, but I realized that it made sense. After all, it was nuts to give the job to an old reserve officer in the first place. Nope, it is high time to let the real professionals get back to their business, and time for me to put my life back together as a civilian who was just a part time reserve officer.

The President continued, "Mike, you've done a great job, and it was your 'out of the box' thinking that got us here. Hell, if it weren't for you, we'd still be in the bottom of the bucket of excrement, as opposed to standing in the upper part of the steaming pile!"

Laughing I replied, "Thank you, Mr. President. I do appreciate that very much."

"So, Mike, can I count on you to serve in whatever capacity I ask you to serve?"

"Yes sir. I'm just a tired old reservist who will serve at your pleasure in any capacity you need."

"Good. Effective immediately, you will assume command of all Allied forces, regardless of where they are located on this planet, and you will take whatever measures you think appropriate to defend our nation, our allies, and our planet. This is a job that has not been filled in about 70 years, and I need you to fill it. Now, there are limits, since you will have to keep the Russians and Chinese happy, while stroking the egos of God knows how many minor dignitaries from around the world. There are also the English, French, Germans, and on and on. You will need good people, and you will need a good staff, and you have a blank check to raid anyone you want from here. I would recommend that you raid other countries, too, and, if you feel the need, be creative and create whatever jobs you need to keep them happy. Never forget that your real job is to, as you put it . . . kill Gomers."

"Yes sir! And who is my chain of command?"

"Me! You answer only to me, but you still must be nice to the other leaders around the world, and I have asked the Secretary of State to brief you on the negotiations and personalities he encountered in setting this up. You might want to read these, too." As he said this, he tossed me two books, a copy of General MacArthur's memoirs and a copy of General Eisenhower's memoirs. "Mike, somewhere in these two books is what we need, except I will not tolerate any of Eisenhower's pandering, nor will I put up with MacArthur's 'Caesar' complex. Understand?"

"Yes sir."

"OH, and Mike, before you get out the door, you're out of uniform."

"How is that sir?"

"Well, for the first time since about 1947, the United States Army has another damn Five Star General of the Army. I'm kind of jealous actually, but whatever you do, be careful and don't foul this up!"

"Yes sir. I've been saying the old 'aviator's prayer' ever since I took the CSA job."

The Secretary of State looked at me, and then at the President, and asked, "Aviator's prayer? What is the aviator's prayer?"

The President and I both looked at him and said, almost in perfect unison, "Please, dear Lord, don't let me fuck this up!"

When we entered the President's cabinet room, the other Chiefs who were all gathered there immediately came to attention, and the President did the official ceremony taking my Four Stars off. After having done so, he motioned Leah forward and they replaced them with a brand-new set of Five Stars for the new rank. I personally was amazed, since I had no idea that such a thing could be found or created. I was even more amazed when I learned that Leah was the one responsible for having it made, and that she knew about this before we'd even left the New Pentagon. I guess that shows that, no matter what, the secret network of military wives can keep each other better informed than most of their husbands.

Once the congratulations were made, for me and Jerry, who was now the new CSA, we sat down and got busy. The other services briefed both the President and me since there was a lot of information that I would now need to know that I did not need before. A classic example was the status of the surface Navy and other elements of our strategic assets that were not items on my list of things to follow as the CSA. Oh, I followed them, but only in terms of what they could do to support my operations, as opposed to the grimy details. Now I had the added concerns of figuring out the best way to employ them around the world. As the brief was completed, I came to the painful realization that the staff I needed to create, and quickly, would have to be both multi-national and multi-service.

When we returned to the New Pentagon that evening, my wife was delighted and happy for me. At least she was delighted right up until I explained that, with this change, I was now going to need to leave this facility and create a new one that probably would not include any family. As that thought sank in, she lost some of her enthusiasm but, all in all, she took it well. Her only question was, "So, are you taking this staff or making a whole new one?"

"I might take one or two from this staff, but mostly the answer is no. I am seriously considering taking General Whitney,

General Clark, and maybe General Roberts, otherwise the rest will be staying here. Why?"

"Oh, there is no particular reason."

"Bullshit, I know you better than that, how long have we been married?"

"Okay, you caught me, but it isn't that I don't trust you, I just don't trust her, and honestly, neither does Maggie."

"Well, now SHE is officially Maggie's problem. I need someone from another service and maybe even another nation, to hold that position so, if she leaves here, it won't be on my staff. Fair enough?"

"Okay, fair enough!"

True to my word, as I started figuring out which square pegs were going to fit into which hexagon holes, I made General Whitney my Chief of Staff for my Supreme Allied Command, and then I appointed General Clark as my Chief of Allied Logistics. As for the rest of the CSA staff, I decided to leave them alone, at least for the moment. As I was putting together the rest of the staff, I had to rely on the format of the last major Allied Command. I reached into the US Air Force and grabbed the Commander of the 14th Air Force, General Anthony Stephenson, as my Chief of Allied Air Operations. My next choices came from our allies, General Sir William Fuller, UK, my Chief of Allied Ground Operations; and Admiral Stefan Lindemann, Germany, as the Chief of Allied

Naval Operations. I completed the staff with the Chief of Allied Intelligence, General Pavel Zhukov, Russia, and my new Chief of Pacific Planning, Admiral Zao Chan, of the Chinese Navy. I then relied on General Whitney to scrounge the rest of the staff from around the world, based on the recommendations of the State Department, or from the senior members of the respective participating nations.

With those selections, the rest of the staff and their personnel could be assigned, and the entire show could be moved to our initial Headquarters Location. General Whitney, now sporting the rank of General with the four stars that go with it, scouted three possible locations for our main headquarters. In typical style of dealing with all of the allies, we picked all three with my adding a fourth one that might be usable as the summer turned to winter. Sending out smaller caretaker staff personnel, we established a headquarters system that would allow for rapid movement as the future campaign might unfold. As it worked out, our first stop was the most hospitable terrain in Hawaii. Leaving the new Pentagon was damned hard, but Generals Whitney, and Clark, along with our aides, loaded up and headed out to stay just behind the Sunrise line. I followed with my aide three days later, after having reviewed the latest information from the State Department and the President about foreign staff members being provided to my new headquarters.

My first stop on my journey was at Vandenberg, AFB, in California. It was an overnight layover, but it gave me and the new Commander, General Randolph McDaniel, a chance to meet and personally discuss a couple of things we had rolling around with our special operations plans. It also gave me a chance to examine their facilities and get an idea of just what kind of rabbits they might be able to pull out of a hat, should push come to shove. With first light the following morning, we were back in the air. When we arrived at our final destination, it was great to see Colonel Greene waiting for me as I stepped off the C-17. The last time I saw him was when I handed him his first set of sealed Orders, with little expectation that we would ever see each other again. Now here we were together again and still on our feet. There was no question; we had both come a long way since that day in the park in Columbia, South Carolina. I am just thankful that I was able to steal him away from Jerry.

Chapter XIII.

I stepped off the tarmac and into a waiting vehicle, which literally flew down the road and away from the airfield at Barbers Point Naval Air Station. Colonel Greene was sitting next to me and Simmons, my Senior Aide, now a Lieutenant Colonel, sat beside the driver. Beyond the initial pleasantries, there was little being said between us. We drove through Pearl City on H1 and headed to the Fort Shafter area where my headquarters was to be located. We started up an incline near Halawa Heights, and Colonel Greene directed the driver to an area where we could overlook Pearl Harbor and Hickam AFB. "Sir, I've got something you are going to want to see!" We pulled to a stop along the highway, and then we stepped out of the car. As I walked up to the overlook, Colonel Greene handed me a pair of binoculars and, as I examined the area, Colonel Greene narrated.

I looked over the harbor and the surrounding military bases and, while I was no expert on this part of the world, it was obvious to me that some things were definitely missing. Most of the old Pacific Command Headquarters, the Hickam AFB Headquarters, and large portions of the surrounding areas were simply gone. In the same way we observed the perfectly round holes created by the weapons of the smaller Gomer objects, and then the larger holes created by the large Gomer ships, we were looking down on a harbor that had been hit by something even larger. It was clear that there was not any overlap in the circles, indicating the use of several weapons but, instead, we were looking at massive craters each created by one hit. Compared to what we had seen after the attack on our mountain, these craters were almost three times the size of the largest things we'd seen to date. Processing this sobering thought, I asked Colonel Greene,

"Daniel, any idea what happened here?"

"No, sir, and I have asked anyone who might have known, too. To one person, they all said that it came from nowhere, and then they were knocked senseless."

"Is it my imagination, or are we looking at something outside our previous experience with the Gomers?"

"No, sir, it isn't your imagination, I think this is definitely something quite new to us. I have been watching the Gomers ever since you got my ass out of jail, and we have seen some pretty weird stuff, but this is different. This is a damn sight bigger and a whole lot meaner. So, despite it being new to us, it sure as hell isn't new to the people around here."

"Then why didn't somebody tell us before we got here, so we could add something like this to the things to look for in dealing with the Gomers?"

"Nobody left that could, I guess. These guys had nothing to compare it with, and I guess they assumed we already knew. As a side note, the folks here haven't ever seen the smaller objects or the larger ones, they move at night, and don't really worry about the little guys showing up."

"Incredible. Then again, our science staff said that the sulphur in these volcanic rocks would keep them at a distance."

"Well, something ain't afraid to come here, even if it isn't the little guys."

"Okay, well, what are you really trying to tell me?"

"Sir, those massive hits are what happened on the night of the attack. As the twilight line came back here on that first night, something hit each of those locations. The best guess from the survivors who were in more remote locations, these hits were all within a time window of about 3 seconds. It took out the complete Pacific Command staff, and they even had several hours worth of warning that something was coming."

"You're right, they would have had at least 21 hours to get ready, and they still ate the big one."

"Yes, sir, which is why we are headed up here to show you the other thing."

"Okay, what is it?"

"Sir, the original high-tech headquarters was buried about 150 feet beneath Diamond Head, and that is where the USPACOM had set up before the attacks."

"So.................?"

"So, there were no survivors, and the new crater here is massive."

"Damn! So where are you taking me?"

"We are headed towards the World War II underground command post near the Aliamanu Crater. Same place where old General Short had moved his headquarters on the afternoon of December 7, 1941. You will love it. The place is full of bug spray and smells musty from about 60 years of being sealed off and out of use."

"Why do I feel like we're taking a trip down memory lane? Okay, why there?"

"Because the Gomers do not read US history, and because it was the only place we could find in a hurry that was secure. Don't worry though, General Whitney's folks have started a new location that is a damn sight deeper, and much further away from this harbor. It is over on the other side of the Island near Kaneohe and away from this mess."

"Still, I wonder...... What in the hell made those holes and didn't involve little objects?"

"I got nothing, at least not yet." We got back in the car to continue to our "new" Command Post, and Colonel Greene then said, "Sir, my theory is that they have something else down this way, and it is either a bigger weapon, a bigger ship or, my own personal belief, the answer is 'all the above'."

"You might be right, but damn, I hope you're wrong." Within a few minutes, we pulled up outside what looked like an old two-story ramshackle house. As we opened the door, I was surprised to see that it led into a long tunnel with several lateral tunnels leading off to either side. The stench of musty dark places, coupled with the smell of the pesticides that had flooded the place, was just short of overpowering. Frankly, the whole place reeked of Raid, wet cement, and someone's extremely dirty laundry.

As we turned a corner into a larger room off the main tunnel, I was greeted by General Edward Whitney, my new "Chief of Allied Staff." "Good morning, General Whitney, how are things here in the 'roach motel?'"

"Wonderful, sir ..." Then while looking at Colonel Greene, he continued, "Daniel, did you show the boss those big-ass holes?"

"I did, sir, and I mentioned our theory about them, too."

Turning back to me, General Whitney said, "Sir, can we have a word before you go in to meet the rest of the staff?"

"Sure, but first, let me ask you something. Do you prefer General, General Whitney, or Edward . . .?

"Uh, sir, we've worked together now for almost 12 weeks, and this is the first time you have even indicated that you knew my first name."

"Well, General Whitney, we are too far forward and, because this is now a fighting headquarters, I'm not inclined to keep it quite as formal as our previous circumstances. Besides, now if I were to say 'General' . . . well, over half the room would look up. Now if you prefer General, I'll do my best to keep that in mind."

"Oh, hell no, sir, please, I would be delighted if you called me 'Whit'."

"Seriously, you prefer 'Whit?'"

"Yessir, everyone else calls me that, even my mom. I hate Ed or Edward."

"In that case . . . 'Whit' it is, and when we are alone, please feel free to call me 'Mouse,' but only when we are alone. I'm pretty sure that the foreign officers on the staff wouldn't understand."

"Yes sir."

"Now, tell me about your take on this theory about a bigger, more powerful Gomer ship."

"Well, sir, I wanted to catch you before you went in there, but I've heard from both the Chinese and Russian representatives that they saw something much bigger than what we described to them. At first, I thought it was maybe an exaggeration, based on them having their asses handed to them, but they are pretty clear

267

that, while they recognize the stuff we have handled, they saw something else. Not often, but when they did, it was horrific. They also related that it was only reported from a distance, and never anywhere above the equator. Most of their observations were very brief, but they swear they saw it. Then I got the same thing from several survivors here on the island, so yeah, it causes me some concern. What if they DO have a larger ship?"

"I'm not sure, but one thing is for sure, we need to confirm it and then figure out what is different about it. Those impact holes, and what must have done to the USPACOM bunker system, really bugs the hell out of me. What are we doing to mask our presence here?"

"I took the liberty to set up an automated relay array, which sends all of our radio transmissions through the old bunker location just on the other side of Diamond Head, about 12 miles from here. In the meantime, we back up and send messages through hard lines and the transpacific cable system that runs back to the mainland."

"Let me guess, you're trying to bait a trap and see if the really large rat comes to visit."

"Yes sir, I'm hoping that they will think they need the big one to hit us, instead of their small or large ships, since it might be too deep to be hurt by a smaller one."

"Okay. Well, it sounds like a good first step. Now tell me, do we have anything to shoot back with?

"We are working on it, and your new Naval Chief is convinced that he has an asset or two that can provide whatever shows up a rude awakening."

"Okay, we'll let them move forward with their briefings, and I guess we'll see what comes crawling out of the Gomer woodwork. OH, let me ask one other question. Are we sure that this alleged larger animal is not the thing hiding behind the moon? If it were a new moon period, it might feel it could sneak out and do a hit and run for at least the one night."

"It might be, sir, but we doubt it. It was a half moon on the night of the first attacks here, and we know from that night that the large thing stayed behind the moon launching the larger ships. Then again, we will not know for sure what did this, until we see whatever it is in action."

"Alright, let's get down to business and start figuring out our next move. Oh, and Colonel Greene, I want you in this briefing, then we need to have a serious discussion about your future."

"Yes sir!" With that acknowledgment, the three of us stepped into the Operations Center, while my Aide moved our gear into our new quarters.

General Whit Whitney introduced me to the officers I did not know, and we began with all the formalities of military courtesy and decorum that foreign officers expected from such a meeting. I took my time meeting all my foreign staff, attempting to make them feel comfortable, at home, and part of the team. I found that, almost to a man, they were professionals and generally affable, at least towards myself and the American portion of the staff.

There was some initial friction between General Zhukov and Admiral Chan, but this was partially diffused by their Deputies, who were both Australian Navy Officers. I also took comfort in knowing that their respective staff sections would not have to be too intimate on a daily basis. Instead, I was quite pleased to see that Admiral Lindemann and Admiral Chan knew each other by reputation and seemed to have quite a bit in common. Admiral Lindemann's deputy was an American Rear Admiral, Carl Lynch and, since it would be primarily our Navy carrying the load, Admiral Lindemann was quite deferential in his approach by allowing Admiral Lynch to set the tone for our Allied Naval forces.

Once the "meet and greet" portion of our morning was completed, we settled down to establishing some general goals to get people moving in one direction. We discussed our lessons learned, our successes and failures, and the overall tactics that worked and had not worked around the globe. We gave everyone the status of our logistical and manpower situations, to include available weapons systems, and moved on through to discuss what we knew about the Gomers. Some of this was eye opening, but it was clear that our Russian and Chinese representatives did agree on one main point. There was something else out there that we had not seen yet in our part of the world. It was not the HUGE Gomer hiding behind the moon either, but instead, there was a consensus that this latest type of Gomer vessel or object was at least 1500 feet longer than their larger object and packed a weapons system several times more powerful than anything we'd seen previously in the northern hemisphere, at least outside the Pacific Rim area.

Our allies were also finding out for the first time that the Gomers do have a 'variety of Gomer' that will come out of their ships and attempt to act on the ground. They were also very surprised to find that we had, at one point, a few Gomer prisoners that survived the crash of the larger ship. Getting them up to speed on "dusty" and "meaty" Gomers was a fascinating process, especially since there are very few words in English to describe things in a way that would translate well into Russian or Chinese. Our insights into their weapons technology were then discussed, but in limited form. We did not disclose it all, simply because much of it was still an ongoing process of scientific study.

Finally, we made it clear that the tilt or axis of our planet, and polar light schedules were likely going to be a key to what would happen next. After a brief discussion, the group concluded, as I had before flying into Hawaii, that we would need some expert assistance available to us at our Allied Headquarters. At the very least, we needed a Polar Expert, someone who could provide us with information about the weather, light, and geology at each pole. We also needed an astrophysicist, an astronomer, and my old friends Dr. Abramson and Dr. Clarkson. I made a mental note to get Dr. Abramson to round up an expert who could give us a clue about the impact of chemicals, such as Lead and Sulphur, on things like ice and polar environments. The notion of putting an ERW or TNW at a pole concerned the hell out of me and, despite the temptation, I strongly suspected that it would be a bad move.

At one point in these latter discussions, a young Colonel piped up from the back and said, "We just need an old-style crop duster to fly over the South Pole and spray Sulphur on the Gomers." While it would have been tempting, I was not about to pass that idea along, since I already knew it would be disastrous for the environment, not to mention, where would you find an idiot to fly such a mission. No question, I needed my own scientists, and I needed to supplement them with some experts that could deal with questions and issues about our new potential battle zones.

This made it imperative that we not waste any time in getting the team of scientists either to our location or assembled somewhere that would allow for immediate communication. The other central imperative was to obtain more intelligence. What the hell was going on in Antarctica? What new equipment or tactics will they use here? What were our best approaches to them? Were there choke points we could exploit? As the list grew longer, we began to develop a plan for reconnaissance of our enemies and then set it into motion.

We also began the arduous process of trying to figure out what assets might be available globally and what we would need to recover as key equipment. At one point in the discussion, there was even consideration about the best weapons systems to employ, and we left nothing out of the mix for consideration. We knew we needed large caliber weapons and the lower the tech, the better. Russian Artillery assets would be rounded up and brought as far south as possible. Chinese raw materials and some products, such as lead-based paints, were being identified, stock-piled, and prepared for movement. Air cargo assets that had survived were being identified to move these stockpiles to the locations we would need them. Now came the hard part of the analysis. Where would we need them, and for what?

After our initial session, I sat down with Colonel Greene in my new quarters and laid out my plans for both him and his men.

"Colonel Greene, I have a couple things to go over with you, and I'm not sure where to start."

"The beginning is always a good place, sir."

"Okay, smart ass, first things first." With that I handed him a piece of paper containing the official seal of the President of the United States. As Colonel Greene read it, a huge smile ran over his face, and he looked at me with a grin and asked, "Sir, was this your idea?"

"Yes, it was, since I can't very well have one of my General Officers running around with a price on his head and outstanding warrants."

"Thank you, sir, I appreciate it, and with a pardon, at least I won't have to worry about that when this is........ Wait a minute. Did you say General Officer?"

"Yes, I did, and again, you're being a smart ass by not letting me finish."

"Sorry sir."

"Relax, General. Yes, I am promoting you to Brigadier General effective two days ago. You will be my 'Lord Mountbatten' in charge of special operations. The job title is Chief of Allied Special Operations, and you will officially be on my staff."

"Sir, I enjoy being in the field, and this will screw that up."

"Yes, it will, but the good news is that you will still be headed to dangerous places since, this time around, I am going to those places, too. Now, I need you to put together a couple of things for me."

"Yes, sir, whatever you need."

"Okay, first I want you to keep the Vandenberg project going, and I want you to personally supervise it all the way to completion. Second, I want you to pick your successor and get him to us as soon as possible. Third, I want you to get a team headed to the tip of South America to start doing what reconnaissance they can on the Gomers over in Antarctica. Fourth, beg, borrow, or steal whatever drone technology you can get your hands on from the CIA. I know the bastards are still out there because I can hear them frickin' breathing. Now do you have any questions?"

"No, sir, I'm on it."

"One last thing, General Greene, and I can NOT stress this enough. You are NOT going into the field without my express permission. Is that clear!"

"Yessir, I understand. I don't like it, but I understand."

"Listen, you remember what happened with General Gregg, and right now I could really use him, his skill set, and his intellect. I don't want the same thing to happen again, since you, my friend, are going to be doing some of what I needed him to do . . . you got it?"

"Yessir, I got it, and I won't go to the field without your express permission."

"Excellent, your read back is absolutely correct. Now start on my list and get back to me this evening." With that, the newly minted General Greene was out the door, and I was back to the next session with our command staff. As the afternoon wore on, we covered a lot of ground, and the list of things we needed to accomplish was horrendous. Each section, and each individual, had more things to do than the time would allow. The goal was to create a plan to use against the Gomers, and the sooner we go to that plan, the sooner we could go home.

As we were winding up our first full day, the surface guard was pulled into the bunker system, and passive systems were employed to monitor the sky in and around Oahu. Several of Admiral Lynch's submarines were patrolling around Peal Harbor and the Island of Oahu and they, too, were maintaining a watch on the sky. As the Twilight line approached, General Greene sent me a message that he was still at Schofield Barracks, and it would be much later in the evening before he could get back and brief me about our projects. I advised him to sit tight and get with me in the morning. With that, as my last official act for a while, Sir William, Whit, and I sat down to eat a quick meal. Within just a few moments of being seated, a young naval officer ran into my 'quarters.' "Sir, I hate to interrupt, but we just got a report from the USS Columbia. She is about 100 miles south on patrol, and she is getting a very strong reading of something really large headed our way!"

General Whitney immediately got up and headed towards the door, asking "How long do we have before it gets here?"

"Sir, the course and speed estimates put her about 50 or so miles away, and it should get here in about 15 minutes."

"Great, tell Admirals Lynch and Lindemann to meet us in operations, and then gather the rest of the staff."

"Yes, sir" and with that, the young Lieutenant turned just in time to be impaled by a large piece of steel rebar that came flying through the lateral tunnel door. The explosion was massive, and a portion of the bunker around us completely collapsed. As concrete and rebar flew about, Sir William, Whit, and I were knocked down and covered in falling debris. My last conscious thought was that they were supposed to be 15 minutes out. . . . .

The huge overpressure created by the explosion continued along the central tunnel of the underground headquarters. Anyone unlucky enough to be standing in the main tunnel was instantly killed by the massive pressure of the shockwave, while some in the lateral tunnels that were left open to the central tunnel were more likely killed by just the pressure. If the lateral tunnel was closed off with some sort of heavier door, then it was the flying or falling debris that would either kill or wound those inside. Further away, the impact of the blast was only slightly more tolerable. For anyone in the open, even as far away as Pearl City, death also came quickly. General Greene, who was then standing inside a bunker at Schofield Barracks, could feel the shock, and he instantly grasped the implications. As the shock waves passed, he assembled as many men as he could find and, despite the darkness, they moved as quickly as they could in the direction of the Aliamanu Crater.

The amount of destruction and debris hindered their passage, as did the obligatory stops to measure radiation levels along their route. General Greene was not too concerned about the radiation, since he knew there would be none; still it was a caution that was necessary. The real problem was getting through the portions of infrastructure that were now complete rubble. As luck would have it, most of the rubble appeared to be on top of the roads, and not the roads themselves. Once this was determined, General Greene knew what had happened. It would be just a few hours before dawn before he arrived at what used to be Supreme Allied Headquarters. Still, as dawn was breaking, the massive effort to clear the tunnels was well underway, and a few survivors were being pulled from the piles of concrete and steel.

Around noon, General Greene was able to get through to the portion of the tunnel complex where the main conference room and quarters for the senior staff was located. What he found was completely nauseating. Scattered around the main conference room were most of the senior Allied Staff. Some were simply dead in their seats, staring straight ahead at nothing, as if they were about to say something. The concussion had simply killed them where they sat, and there was no other evidence to reveal the violence of their passing. Still others, who were closer to the entrance to the main tunnel, were completely eviscerated. As General Greene continued his search and identification of the now quite dead staff, he was unable to find General Patrick, General Whitney, or General Fuller. General Clark was missing, too, as was General Zhukov and Admiral Lynch.

As the day wore on, General Greene was joined by General Clark, who had been on the other side of the island at Kaneohe, working with the construction of the new bunker facility, and Admiral Lynch, who was at Pearl Harbor at the temporary Naval Headquarters when the attack hit. The number of survivors they were finding within the tunnel complex was few, and their injuries were severe. It was almost dark again when they were able to finally uncover the entrance to the quarters of the Supreme Commander. As they began pulling the debris out of the entrance, they found the young Naval Officer, with the rebar embedded in his chest. Directly behind him was General Whitney, who was unconscious from shock, but quite alive and apparently not too seriously injured. As they continued into the room, they uncovered the body of Lieutenant Colonel Simmons, who also appears to have died when the steel from the walls impaled him to the floor.

They were about to clear the room, since there appeared to be little else that they could move, when they heard a small voice from behind one large piece of ceiling that had collapsed along the far corner of the room. As they chipped away and started removing the pieces, they were able to start talking to General Fuller. His voice was quite weak, but he was alive, and he advised them that he was behind this "bloody large rock" with General Patrick. "Would you kindly remove this damn thing? General Patrick just might need a doctor." It would be another three hours before the "bloody large rock" could be removed, and it would be almost dawn of the following day before Generals Patrick and Fuller could be recovered. It was obvious that they were both injured but, as General Greene bent over General Patrick to attempt to move him, it was clear that the "old man" had a little fight left in him. As he roused up, his first words were, "Did we at least get a picture of the bastard that hit us?"

Chapter XIV.

The next few hours were spent shaking some very significant cobwebs out of my head and assessing just how much I hurt, and how much the Allied Command was hurt. GOD knows, I hurt. My normal doctor, who had been on my personal staff since the first night of my arrival at the new Pentagon, was now among the many dead from my Allied Headquarters. I also lost my Aide, Lieutenant Colonel Simmons, and my newly appointed Junior Aide, a young Captain from Georgia, Lawrence Wilkerson. As we did a head count through the rest of the wounded and killed, it was staggering, the number of casualties we had taken. The Allied Senior Staff was decimated. The loss of almost all our Naval Command staff was almost crippling. Out of Admirals Chan, Lindemann, and Lynch, only Admiral Lynch remained. General Zhukov was still missing, and the Australian Officers who had kept Zhukov and Chan apart were both dead. The survivors who were in the tunnels with me were Generals Fuller, Whitney, and Stephenson. My Air Operations Chief, General Stephenson, had the most serious injuries. Aside from the concussion, he had both arms broken. General Whitney was next with a concussion and his left leg broken. General Sir William Fuller was perhaps the least injured. While dehydrated and sore in a dozen places, he was quite capable of flashing the typical British understatement to anyone who would listen. By quoting Monty Python he made it a point to tell us, "Ah, it's only a flesh wound."

My injuries were a little more complex, probably because of the myriads of old injuries I'd suffered through the years as a young airborne trooper. I did not think any of it was serious, but my old back injury was killing me. The worst of the new pains came from my four cracked ribs on the right side, and a piece of steel rebar that had imbedded itself in my left leg. The young doctor that was brought in to treat me could offer little more than a pain killer for the ribs, which I refused and a local anesthetic for the removal of the steel from my leg and the stitching of the wound. I was hurting loud and large when someone brought me a phone, saying "Sir, it is the President for you."

"Yessir, Mr. President, what can I do for you?"
"I just got briefed on the extent of the damage and your injuries, Dammit Mike, I want you and what is left of your headquarters out of there right now."

"I can't do it, sir."

"What the hell do you mean, you can't do it. I just told you to do it, what part of that don't you understand?"

"Right now, sir, we can't fight the Gomers unless we are here to fight them! If I move my headquarters, it will only be to get closer to the bastards."

"Dammit, General, I don't give a rat's ass about the number of stars you have, you still work for me, and I want you O-U-T. Is that clear?"

"Yessir, it is clear, but if we run away, what does that tell the rest of the world, besides, from what we learned from last night's attack, I can tell you that nowhere is going to be safe right now."

"What do you mean?"

"Sir, last night's attack is strong evidence of a HUGE new variable. What they unleashed came from a distance roughly 50 miles away. It was way bigger than what we saw throughout our East Coast campaign. Trust me, this damn thing can be fired from further away and, honestly, if they ever got a direct hit at your location, we would NOT be having this discussion."

After a lengthy silence, the President said, "Mike, what are you trying to tell me?"

"Sir, you had better rethink how we are going to build our shelters and shield them, because it seems to me that some of our old ideas just went out the window."

"Why didn't they unleash this before now?"

"Mr. President, they did unleash it. On the first night of the war, that is exactly what they used to hammer the hell out of the Pearl Harbor area. I've seen the evidence now firsthand and, trust me, if the night we got hit at new Washington and the new Pentagon had been this thing, we would not have survived it. So far, we have been lucky, because it has only ventured as far north as the equator, parts of Southern Asia, and Hawaii."

"Wonder why?"

"Beats the hell out of me, but when the polar days shift from the North to South Poles, we can expect this big bastard to make the trip, and then WE will have a real problem in our neck of the woods. I'm telling you, Mr. President, safety is merely an illusion, so there is no reason to locate anywhere new, unless it is closer to the enemy."

"What is your plan?"

"Sir, I need to rebuild my staff, get my headquarters up and running again, and keep up the pressure on finding out more information about these Gomers. We also have a project or two up our sleeves, of which you are already aware, and it is those things that need to keep happening."

"Okay, I'm with you. Is there anything else?"

"Actually sir, I've got one other request, and it is a naval request."

"Okay, what is it?"

"Sir, I need you to activate the Naval Reserve Fleet and, specifically, I need every big gun platform you can activate. Not to put too fine a point on it, I want every battleship and old cruiser you can find anywhere in the world that can be painted like our lead-based tanks. The bigger the caliber gun, the older the naval technology, and the simpler the overall weapons platform, the better it will be for usage moving forward."

"Jesus! Okay, so you're saying you need a damn big ass battleship. Isn't that just a little cliche?"

"Among other things, yessir. I realize that it sounds like a joke, but if we use them like General Greene did in Virginia with his lead painted tank, we might be able to hurt them a little. I know that they seem to pick up on anything we do with a high band radio emission and, let us face facts; the new stuff in the Navy doesn't have the ability to fire at anything without sending out some kind of signal! I still haven't figured out why they haven't slammed our submarines yet."

"Well, that dovetails with some rumors I'm hearing out of Dr. Abramson's crowd."

"Do they have anything we can use yet?"

"Not just yet, but I was assured that they had discovered something and were trying to make sense of it and put it into a package they could explain to us mere mortals. Once I get something, we will send it on to you there."

"Thank you, Mr. President. In the meantime, I told General Greene to round up any scientists that might be left around here to gather information about the impact of their weapon on us and then get that information back to Dr. Abramson."

"Make sure it gets here as soon as possible, and Mike...?"

"Yes sir?"

"Be careful! Leah isn't going to like hearing about what happened, and she would like it even less if you made her a widow."

"Don't worry sir, I have a feeling she already knows more than we do about my condition."

"Hah, I wouldn't doubt it a bit. Good night General, and dammit, be careful!" With that admonition, the President rang off the line. As I hung up, I realized that maybe a little something for the pain would be a good idea, so I told General Clark to bring me a scotch and a large bottle of aspirin. Then I picked up the phone and called my old friend, Jerry Larkin. As his line rang through, the voice on the other end kind of surprised me a little.

"Chief of Staff's Office, Christine speaking, how may I help you, sir?"

"Chris?"

"Yes, si............ DAD?"

"Yep, honey, 'tis me in the flesh. I am alive and well or at least working on that 'well' part. How is my grandson?"

"Dad, he is great, but we've all be scared to death since night before last. Are you okay?"

"I'm upright and able to take nourishment. In fact, General Clark is bringing me a bottle of nourishment and a bottle of aspirin even as we speak!"

"Dammit, Dad! Is this going to be like the time you came home from one of your stupid trips with a broken back?"

"No, Chris, I'm going to be okay, really. I do need you to do two things for me, though."

"Sure, Dad, what is it?'

"One, tell Leah I'm fine, and that I love her a lot!"

"Sure, what else?"

"Get me Jerry Larkin. I've got to hit him again for some bodies."

"Sure, hang on." It was about three minutes when General Larkin got on the line, and I could tell he was more than a little out of breath when he answered.

"Giant?"

"Yes, sir, I'm on the line. Glad to hear you made it out alive."

"Thanks, Giant, but now I'm going to need a couple of things from you, and I am so sorry to be asking them."

"Go ahead, sir, whatever you need, we'll get to you."

"Well, first thing, I need you to pass on my personal condolences to both Colonel Simmons and Captain Wilkerson's families. I know that the young Captain had a wife and two kids. I just want to make sure that we're in the process of taking care of them, and that we've broken the news as gently as possible."

"We have. In fact, Maggie and Leah are with her and their kids even as we speak. It won't be easy for them, but everyone knows the deal. Even the kids understand what is at stake here and, unlike some of our past experience with such things, everyone is prepared to do what has to be done."

"Doesn't make it easy though, and I still remember when we got back and had to talk to Daniel Greene's widow. Hell, I'd rather be shot at than tell a family that 'daddy' isn't coming back."

"No shit!"

"Now the other thing I need. I am going to need a new Aide, and this time, make him a bachelor who speaks Chinese. I am also going to need a second Aide, but I want him from the Navy. I need a translator there, too, so he needs to be able to speak both fluent 'squid' and maybe Russian. If you would, ask Admiral Steadman if he has someone, he can send me."

"Sure, is there anything else?"

"Yeah, dig your holes damn deep, Jerry. The bastard that hit us is about three times more powerful and has about three to four times the standoff range of anything we have ever seen before. I just told the President, and now I am telling you. This thing is huge, mean, and has a standoff range of at least 50 miles."

General Larkin let out a low whistle, and then asked, "How bad is it, really?"

"Jerry, do you remember Diamond Head?"

"Sure, beautiful mountain standing over the Harbor. It is one of the most beautiful views in the world."

"Jerry, it is completely gone. I mean, it was completely reduced to a pile of tiny gravel!"

"Seriously? You mean GONE?"

"Yes, gone. We were about 12 miles away and it collapsed our headquarters around our ears. Most of my senior staff are either dead or wounded. Whitney, Clark, and Greene are all fine, by the way, but with Whitney it was a very close thing. He is going to be on crutches for quite a while since the Docs had to plate and screw his leg back together."

"Gotcha. I do have to ask though, what should I be doing here to protect our position?"

"I would seriously consider making a new one somewhere in a deeper part of the Mountain. I would guess they know where to find you, they just have not sent the big one our way before. If that thing ever gets loose over that part of our world, then you would be a sitting duck."

"Did you pass that on to the President?"

"You know, I actually don't know if I said that specifically, so you might want to follow up. Right now, I hurt too damn bad to recall if I did or not."

"Hurt? Just how hurt are you?"

"Don't tell the family, but I've got a few cracked ribs, my back is killing me, and the place where they pulled that hunk of rebar out of my leg is throbbing like hell. Oh, and it seems that I may have a ruptured eardrum, too, in my left ear, but my wife will never notice that one. She has been accusing me of selective deafness for years."

"Christ, Mouse, what are you taking for it?"

"Thanks to General Clark, I'm on the 'Scotch and Aspirin' regimen for pain management. The stuff the Doctor wanted to give me would knock me out, and I cannot afford that at all. So, a little tape, a pillow for my chair, and we are back in business. Now all I need is a few new members for the staff. Fortunately for you, they won't all be coming out of your hide."

After hanging up with Giant, I got General Clark to contact the Secretary of State, to ask him to start calling in our allies to bring us some replacements for their now deceased staff members. At the end of the day, the only people that would be forthcoming were from China and the UK or Australia. The Russians said that they were out of people to send, but they did stand ready to get us the artillery pieces, assuming we could still use them.

My new Senior Aide was a Naval Commander by the name of Randy Bowen. He had submarine experience, working knowledge of Russian, and the added bonus of being available at Pearl Harbor. My new junior Aide was found in a brigade intelligence office over at Schofield Barracks. Highly recommended by both General Larkin and General Greene, Major David Cho spoke fluent Korean and Mandarin Chinese. If nothing else, I would now have the ability to directly communicate with some of the Russian and Chinese personnel who had survived the hit on Diamond Head.

I immediately dispatched Generals Fuller, Clark, and Greene to start putting the staff back together at our newer location near Kaneohe. I also sent my Naval Aide ahead to make arrangements for the movement of myself and General Whitney. Since I was slightly more ambulatory, Major Cho and I spent some time looking at the impact areas in each of the locations that were hit, both on the first night of the war, and then again when we got hit a few days ago. As I surveyed that damage, all I could do was shake my head and marvel at the sheer force that must have produced this kind of impact. There were several scientists from the University of Hawaii who were also quite fascinated by it and, although they had been sheltered in the mountains since the first night of the war, they simply could not resist coming down to assess what may have taken their landmark completely off the map. After countless hours of crawling through the remnants, they had gathered sufficient data to pass on to Dr. Abramson. Naturally, we facilitated this transmittal of information, and made sure it went via regular land line.

Another item, while it might seem minor, was that we needed to assign some classification for our various Gomer ships. So far, small, and large seemed to cover it, but now we had a third one and it was going to get confusing quickly, when these things were being reported. After some discussion, we finally decided to give them naval designations. The smaller or "small" ships were going to be referred to as "Fighters" while the large ones were now going to be called "Carriers". Finally, this new monster was now being referred to as a "Gomer Battleship." This only left the huge thing behind the Moon and, naturally, it was just referred to as the "Gomer Moon ship". One thing for sure, we had beaten the Fighters and the Carriers, but this Gomer Battleship was something else again.

Within two days, we were now reassembled at our new headquarters in the mountains overlooking Kaneohe Bay and the process of gathering intelligence and coming up with a plan were back on track. Far more guarded now, we made sure that emissions were eliminated at any frequency above AM and, even then that our antenna arrays were well beyond 25 miles away. We had been stupid the first time. We sure were not going to make that mistake again. Also, in the interim, General Greene had managed to get a team of special operators headed in the right direction down the South American coast. Now it was a matter of hearing from them and finding out what could be down there.

It was shortly after we set up shop in our new headquarters that I heard from Admiral Morton, who advised me that I was insane for wanting to drag the old stuff back in the Navy. Admiral Steadman, the new CNO, was all for it, but Morton was not. After going back and forth, he finally relented when I told him that if he wanted a surface navy in the fight, then I needed the "old" big guns with the most impact ability. When I told him that the Aircraft Carrier was now probably worse than useless, except as a source of casualties, he was anything but happy.

"General, with all due respect, you clearly are unaware of how a Navy is supposed to operate in today's world!"

"Admiral that is the second time you have pointed out my ignorance on all things Navy. Now, grant you, I am not a member of the US Navy, but I do happen to be a graduate of the Naval War College, and I am a Navy brat, so I'm not completely unfamiliar with how things *should* work."

"General, then I might think that you should know more about what you are asking me. Say, was your dad Captain Paul Patrick?"

"In fact, yes he was, but that doesn't have a damn thing to do with today's problem."

"General, your dad was one of the best skippers I ever had in my younger days, and I am pretty sure he would understand that this is not going to work."

"Jesus, Mary, and Joseph! Admiral! Let me clarify things for you. My dad was pretty fed up with the stupidity that gave the Navy a ship that could get outgunned by an 8-year-old kid with a damned BB gun! That Littoral Combat Ship is a joke, and we both know it. I need something with some firepower and armor that I can stick in the Gomers' asses!"

With each passing barb, my new Naval Aide would sink lower in his seat and, as we were nearing the climax of what was in essence a verbal war of epic proportions, he sat up and offered something that Morton had not fully considered. "Sirs, if I might interject?"

More than a little annoyed, Admiral Morton said, "Okay, Commander, but this better be the most stellar idea since the wheel."

"Well, sir, Tactical Air did work on the Gomer attacks on the East Coast, which means it isn't the aircraft that are the problem. The Aircraft carriers we've lost were all lost because of their electronic footprint, which we know we can mostly silence."

Morton snapped at Commander Bowen, "Commander, tell me something new here, please! Just remember that if we shut off everything, we have a harder time seeing ahead."

"Well, sir, we can use the standard formations for that, but we can also use the heavier guns and submarines out about 75 miles or so ahead of the main formations. Then we can use the remaining Carriers to draw out the Gomers. That might lure some of the big stuff out, and if we can take them out, then maybe we could launch a strike against whatever it is they might be doing in the south."

Morton said nothing. "Well, Admiral, the kid is making sense, and it dovetails with what I had in mind when I asked for the big guns. You remember my telling you about how one of their little ships got blasted when it could not see a tank painted up in red lead paint? Well, this is the same idea, only now we give them a headache with a 16" gun, as opposed to a 105 mm gun."

"So, you're saying that you'd use the carrier to draw them out and, given the ranges involved, you'd let the Gomer fly over the battleship, to get to the target they could see?"

"Well, over simplified, but in essence ...... something like that ..., yes."

"How will you know which direction they would approach them from?"

Commander Bowen answered, "We'd have to use the twilight line to at least limit it to a 180-degree relative approach heading, and if we used the available land masses, we might be able to pin it down more than that. For example, they hate the Andes Mountains, so if we used that terrain, and placement of the Battleships in the right position, we would know within a few degrees what direction they would have to use to approach the fleet."

"That assumes they come with the twilight line, Commander. What if they wait a while, and then come at you when it is darker all around you?"

Stepping back into the conversation, I said, "Admiral, the details are far from being worked out, because we don't have all the information we need. What I can tell you is that by the time we figure it out, we will not have much time to put it together. Now how long will it take to get me the big stuff up and moving? Can it be done in 48 hours?"

"Of course not, it would take weeks, and in some cases even months, to get that crap going again."

"Then you get my point, Admiral. Whether we use them or not, if we do not get the ball rolling now, then if we did need them out here in a hurry in a month or so, we'd be screwed."

"Fair enough, I'll get on it. We will do a search to find any of our guys or any veterans or civilians in the shipyards, who might know what they are doing to get this old crap running again. No promises though, since there are not many people around that even know how these damn things work, and then we must train a crew in gunnery. Geez, I was on the USS Iowa, but it was as an Ensign back in the late 1980s. I'm not sure even I could do it anymore."

"Then you know what we need, and I would truly appreciate your getting all your support behind Admiral Steadman to get this going as a viable project."

It had taken almost an hour of fighting on the phone, but we were about to create a new surface Navy out of the mothballed ashes. Another historical irony was that President Reagan, an old Army veteran, had insisted on the battleships coming out of retirement in the 1980s, and now here I was, another old Army guy, insisting on the same thing. Maybe we should just take them over, put Army sailors on them, and use our own artillery guys to run the guns. I have to admit, I've seen what a 16-inch gun can do to a grid square full of bad guys, and it was almost as impressive as seeing what the Gomers had done to Diamond Head.

The next group of people I was about to upset were the survivors of the CIA and the regular US Air Force. I wanted drones, and as many as I could get my hands on. I needed to start getting hard intelligence from Antarctica and, up to this point, everything we tried to send just disappeared. General Thayer and I spent another hour, not fighting as I had with Admiral Morton, but just discussing our problem. Any satellites we launched out of Vandenberg were being destroyed the nanosecond they started transmitting their information. Despite being coated in lead paint, they would explode or terminate transmission as the download sequence was initiated. Even when routed around the earth in a polar orbit, with the intent that they would download the images taken in the south at a location well north of the equator, they would terminate transmissions when the download sequence began.

Out of desperation, we considered sending in a submarine with a Seal team but quickly rejected the idea when we realized that with the ice pack surrounding the continent, it would be a suicide mission for anyone who would attempt to venture out for those distances required to observe anything. Our last hope would be to send a pre-programmed drone out, with just a camera taking pictures, that could be recovered the "old fashioned" way. We had tried it once, but the areas searched brought us nothing of any real value, and we lost three drones in the attempt, one through a programming error, but the rest under somewhat sinister circumstances. After learning on General Thayer, and the new director of the CIA, we were able to get enough drones to program for the flight path.

What we finally obtained was not perfect, but it was still damn scary. The Gomers were building something, and it was mammoth in proportions, and frightening in potential usage. There were four large structures that appeared to us to be like a solar collection device. Each of these structures was approximately 10 miles by 75 miles in size. They were also apparently networked into a different structure that resembled a satellite dish aimed back towards our moon. Tracing this to our moon, it was determined by our astronomers to be aimed directly at another structure that was rising at the edge of the penumbra, or shadow, cast by Earth on the moon during the new moon cycle.

Another development of note, when General Greene's reconnaissance teams got near the coast near Cape Horn, they encountered a perimeter that kept them from being able to move any further south to the coast. While they were not spotted, they were stymied by the fact that the area was clearly defended by the Gomers, and this time they appeared to be of a little more substance than their earlier 'dusty' Gomer types. The final item that got their attention, as well as the attention of the Drone operators, was the presence of the new kind of ship or object. The photographs taken by several drones revealed four massive new type ships that we had not seen before, at least before the Diamond Head strike. These appeared to be three thousand feet long, and approximately 500 feet wide, with several massive extrusions that appeared to be their main weapons systems. They were positioned strategically in a defensive posture around the continent and, while they did move to other positions from time to time, it was clear that they were there primarily for defense. Our men near Cape Horn also observed the Gomers' southern fleet with the Battleship, Carrier, and Fighter classes, as it would make the route following around the twilight line.

We were starting to discern the patterns, and we at least had a clue to positioning. What we did not have was any information about the Gomers. As we considered and rejected several plans for attacking them, we were hamstrung by what the impact might be on our world. Like removing cancer, we had to be careful that the cure wasn't worse than the disease. We knew we could kill them, but at what cost? Consequently, we took the position that we had to contain them, at least in their current areas of operations, and make sure that we continued to gather information so; hopefully, we could find a better solution. Sadly, the crop duster idea was starting to have a little merit. . . . .

Chapter XV.

Eighteen days after the Diamond Head attack, we were starting to see a glimmer of hope that a real plan would come together. We were told that there were some significant finds from the wreckage of the ships that were destroyed around the SRS, but Dr. Abramson and his crew of scientists were extremely closed mouthed about it. We were also being advised that several new weapons systems could be available for us to use in our assaults, and to expect either a full report or a briefing almost any day. In the interim, we were absorbing information from our eyes in the south near the Gomer perimeter area near Cape Horn. According to them, the Gomer "forces" were primarily engaged in defensive operations, and that it seemed that they were digging in to maintain a presence for much longer than just the period of polar night in the Antarctica region.

It was approximately 1800 hrs GMT, or Zulu time, and most of the staff was gathered in the main conference room engaged in a discussion about the ramifications of the Gomers' construction of defensive positions along Cape Horn. Did this mean that the Gomers were unaware of the polar daylight change that was forthcoming, or were they intending to maintain the defense posture to protect their array year-round, or both? Since General Zhukov had been missing since the Diamond Head attack, the position of the Allied Intelligence Chief was now held by an Australian Officer, General David Campbell. Given the repeated passages of the Gomer southern fleet over his country, he was intimately familiar with their current tactics.

General Campbell briefed, "Gentlemen, it is my belief, based on their tactics and methods to date, that the Gomers intend to . . .." Before he could complete his thought, General Campbell was interrupted when the senior Communications Officer burst into the room. Breathless, the Colonel said, "Sir, the Russians have just launched a major nuclear strategic missile strike, and General Thayer believes the target is the South Pole!" This pronouncement was immediately followed by the room erupting at once. I immediately called the room to silence and picked up the line in an attempt to speak with General Thayer at Thunder Mountain. As I was trying to contact him, Major Cho signaled me to pick up the other line. On the other end was Admiral Morton, who advised me that Thayer was blind and that it was our submarine force that was tracking the flight of the missiles from the northern to southern hemisphere.

I was stunned, "Damn, how many did they launch?"

"General, there are somewhere between 38 and 40 missiles, and they most likely contain their big stuff. I don't have a good count just yet but, given what they have left and can carry in their submarine force, we feel these are pretty good numbers."

"They were submarine launched?"

"As a matter of fact, they were, and they were launched from somewhere south of the Kuriles Islands."

"Don't those idiots realize that if this works, we still might have just killed the planet?"

"I know! That many nuclear explosions at the projected magnitude, and over that exact spot, could well throw the planet off its axis."

"I never thought I would see the day come where I would root for the damn Gomers! So how long do we have before either the world ends or . . . . I guess there is no "or" . . . . So, how long do we have?"

"Our guess is that we have about 18 minutes, give or take, and it will catastrophic when it happens. I'll contact you if I get more, but otherwise, let's hope we're all here to talk about it later."

"Thanks, Admiral." I hung up the phone and looked around the room at some extremely shocked faces. I made direct eye contact with the most senior Russian officer remaining on my staff, Colonel Vladimir Karnaukhov, and then I motioned both him and General Greene into my office. Colonel Karnaukhov came in and stood at attention, knowing that what had taken place was probably an insane act. He looked at both General Greene and me with tears running out of his eyes, and I asked him if there was any way to stop it.

"Nyet, uh, No, sir."

"Why not?"

"Sir, I did not know it was coming. I do not know who caused it or issued order."

"Can you find out?"

"I will see if I can reach my government."

"General Greene, escort him to the communications center and put him on the horn with his people. IF he is not telling us the truth, then I want him arrested, is that clear! If he is telling the truth, then do anything he needs done to get this lunacy stopped."

General Greene looked over the Colonel Karnaukhov, and said, "Okay, Vlad, let's go make a call. OH, and General, I think he is telling the truth."

"Excellent, so do I, but trust has to be earned and maintained, and let's face it, right now, it is a little hard to trust anyone from Russia given the circumstances." General Greene and Karnaukhov headed to the Communications Center, and I headed back to the Conference Room to wait it out and hopefully get the latest reports about what was happening. General Whitney was on the line with our people in Chile, near Cape Horn, and making it clear to them to get low in their holes, it was about to get ugly, and it wasn't us.

I took the receiver from Whit and asked who I was talking to right now. "Sir, this is Colonel "Deacon" Jones."

"Deacon?"

"Yessir, well my real name is Nathan, but . . .."

"Okay, I get it, Deacon; mine used to be Mighty Mouse. Now tell me what you can observe."

"Well, sir, the place is crawling, like someone kicked over an anthill."

"Gomers and Equipment, what is moving?"

"I've got close to 400 Gomers I can see from this position. They appear to be a mix of meaty and dusty, although there is something else moving around down there. It kind of looks like a crab. Geez, there are about a dozen of those ugly things, and I can't figure out if they are in charge, or if this is their idea of a horse."

"What else are you seeing?"

"Well, the crabby things are heading under cover, but the meaty guys appear to be aiming some of their weapons skyward towards the Pacific side. . . . . HOLY CRAP would you look at the size of that son of a bitch! General, right now I've got eyes on an object that is about the size of the US Capital Building, nope, make that bigger, anyway, it is about 10,000 feet and climbing. That thing is HUGE, which makes it a guess as to altitude, and I mean just that . . . . a wild ass guess. Right now it is passing from the Atlantic side to the Pacific side and is several miles to the south of our position."

"Okay, Deacon, I want you to get your guys under some serious cover. There is a world of hurt coming your way. We did NOT send it, but once the dust settles, give me a damage assessment, if you can."

"Roger that, sir. Deacon out!"

As I terminated the call with Colonel Jones, I noticed my Naval Aide, Commander Bowen, waving at me and pointing to the ELF teletype, which was now chattering away at almost 'warp' speed. I stepped over and began reading as it was coming off the machine. Two of our submarines were in position to observe events, and two more were relaying the information into our headquarters. Commander Bowen was also receiving reports from a listening and observation post on New Zealand, which was positioned to observe the ongoing event. I started passing the information to General Whitney and General Fuller, who were working on the grease pencil' magic on the maps. The picture that was beginning to form showed that the Gomers were setting up a defensive line in the path of the oncoming missiles and that ground based weapons were also prepared to unleash an 'air defense pattern' to intercept the incoming missiles.

We waited, tracked, watched, and, frankly, sweated out the next 10 minutes as the plotted courses from both forces came close to intersection. It was over within seconds. Fortunately, the hard line to New Zealand remained operational. In short, we were given the accounts from those who had a ring side seat to the show. As each missile came about 50 miles from the Gomer Battleships, they unleashed their weapon system. The results were immediate.

Each of the missiles simply disintegrated or perhaps shattered is a better word. The chunks fell into the sea, and it was over. When we realized that the Gomers had taken out the missiles, the entire headquarters gave a sigh of relief. It was one more irony in a war full of nothing but irony.

With mixed emotions, we then took the necessary steps to find out several things. The first was what lunatic would initiate such an attack and, more importantly, did any of these weapons use the "sulphur or lead" technology that had been discussed with our allies. Finally, we needed to determine what and how the Gomers were able to detect and then track the Russian incoming attack. If it was with the use of our "sulphur or lead" technology, then we might be screwed in our ability to successfully attack the Gomers where they sat in Antarctica. Another burning fact was that, in repelling the attack, the Gomers had pushed their huge ships to the very edge of the darkness available as cover. In fact, it appeared that in at least one case, the ship itself may have operated for a very brief time in an area that was on the border between light and dusk. As we wondered about these things, we were also struck with our need to get Dr. Abramson to get us what we needed as key information. If they did know something new, then we needed that information and in very short order.

Once the dust had settled from the attack, we got the answer to our first question about what lunatic ordered the strike. Colonel Karnaukhov was able to get a response from his government and, regardless of the truth of the explanation, it was our missing General Zhukov who was behind it all. Colonel Karnaukhov explained that "Sir, it would seem that on the night of the attack on this Island, General Zhukov was onboard the submarine K-277 down in Pearl Harbor. After the strike, General Zhukov ordered the Captain to depart and head back to Russia."

"You didn't know that your own submarine left the harbor?"

"Yes, I knew, but I did not think it was anything but precaution. Almost all ships, even American, left harbor right after attack."

"Okay, fair enough, so where is that bastard now?"

"He was on K-277. After the attack on South Pole, K-277 and K-189 were destroyed by Gomers."

"What can you tell us about that? Do you know what depth they were when they were hit?"

"No, but my guess is that American Submarine may know."

"Okay, we'll see if anyone has that information. Now tell me, does your government have any other information or instructions for us?"

"No instructions, just deep apology. I am told that Zhukov was acting without my government's knowledge or authority."

"Thank your government for being forthcoming, Colonel. You may return to your duties." Colonel Karnaukhov came to attention and saluted as he executed a perfect 'about face' and walked from my office. As he left, I looked at General Greene and asked, "Well, Danny, what do you think?"

"Sir, HE is telling the truth as he knows it. Otherwise, he is full of it, and so is his government. They knew about Zhukov, and they only sent him here to find out what we knew. If he was an ally, I'll kiss your butt in Macy's window during the friggin parade."

"That is my impression, too. Keep the Colonel honest, Danny, find him a relatively non-sensitive home, preferably in logistics, but don't trust him any further than you can see him."

"Roger that, sir!"

Once General Greene was clear of my office, I got the President and the Secretary of State on the line. We compared notes, and I advised them of the story I was given by the Russian Government. Secretary Case confirmed that Russia was taking this story as their official line, but he also questioned the veracity of it. He noted that it was funny how the government didn't have anyone to send after the attack on Diamond Head, but now suddenly, they were offering us a General named Delov, to replace Zhukov on our staff. I told the Secretary to stall them, but frankly, my slots were filled and besides, Colonel Karnaukhov "is providing invaluable service in representing their government in the war." After a brief discussion, it was decided to advise the Russian government that we did not have an opening, and

Colonel Karnaukhov could act as their official liaison to the Allied Command.

Once we resolved that issue, I then asked the President about the delay in getting us Abramson's report. He said he was on it, and that we would be hearing something very soon. We broke the connection, and it was back to the work at hand. Thanks to the Russians, we did learn a thing or two about the Gomers' defense plan, and it would be highly useful information when we shifted our offensive into their back yard. We also learned from "Deacon" that the Gomers at Cape Horn did not fire their weapons and, aside from their alerted status, once the danger of the Russian Attack was eliminated, things were now back to a state of 'Gomer normal.'

Several hours later, as we were winding up our day of planning, I got a very welcome call from Admiral Morton. As I picked up the phone, I was surprised to hear Admiral Morton in an almost giddy mood.

"Evening, Admiral."

"Good evening, General."

"Wow, you sound almost happy, what is going on?"

"I wanted to let you know that your plan for big guns is moving forward a lot faster than I even imagined. Would you like a short briefing on the project?"

"Absolutely!"

"We are about 15 days out from bringing the USS Iowa back up to speed, and probably 18 days from getting the USS Wisconsin ready to go. We are painting them both from the water lined up in black lead paint, and we have assembled roughly three crew members. Once we are ready, the Wisconsin, which is in Norfolk, will be ready to proceed south down the coast to either Panama or to South America, depending on how the plan finally comes together. The Iowa is going to head to your location with two crew members onboard. One crew will be training the other up to speed, so that they can take possession of the USS Missouri, which is at your location. It is my understanding that the yard there at Pearl is having a little harder time. Still, they think they can have her ready in another 25 days, which permits us to train up the third crew. The only thing else we can throw together is the USS New Jersey but, frankly, that one looks like a long shot right now. She is in Camden, New Jersey, and will take some real effort to get moving. Then we would have to find a crew for her, too, so she is a real 'long shot maybe.'"

"Admiral, that is excellent!"

"We dusted off the USS Kitty Hawk from the bone yard and have it just about ready; she was on twenty-day reserve. Our real issue is with deck qualification for the pilots, but it can be done. I also wanted to use the USS Enterprise, but they have already defueled her and started taking her reactor apart, so it would probably take too long to get her functional. Regardless, since our pilots will not be able to engage in flight operations before these ships deploy, they will just have to do it all during the daytime while they are en route to your area. As for our active assets, the USS Nimitz and the USS John C. Stennis survived so, along with the old Kitty Hawk, they will be available as part of the new Pacific fleet. On the Atlantic side, we still have the USS Truman and USS Roosevelt. The USS Roosevelt was coming out of a three-year complex overhaul and refueling when the Gomers hit, so they missed her completely. The USS Truman was just back from a deployment, so with minimal systems up and running, she did not attract the Gomers' attention either. Our aircraft strength is okay, not great, but okay, we can at least put most of the full complement of air wings together when we add our Marine Air Wings to the mix. Finally, I have several escort vessels; to include two old cruisers we were able to drag back out of the bone yard. They are not the big gun types, but they do have the ability to unleash some Cruise Missiles of the new type that Dr. Abramson's boys are putting together. Oh, and the airburst variety of the Sulphur and Lead tipped 16" shells are now being produced in quantity. We will have a basic load of these things, along with the new Sulphur Cruise Missiles on each of the big guys. Finally, I also have assurances that the new X-51A Waveriders will be available for our aircraft, and they are being modified to include Lead and Sulphur as well."

"X-51A Waverider?"

"Yep, a nasty little thing, it travels at a speed in excess of 3,000 mph."

"Jesus! How long before all this is ready to head out our way?"

"A lot of it will be ready for sea within the next two weeks, and we should be ready to fight as a fleet in about four or five at the most."

"Well, it sounds like a heck of a start. That is definitely good news, Admiral, and I know we will need every gun platform we can find, although I'm not sure we have five weeks."

"I figured, and after seeing the Russians screw it up, I now know exactly why. One final thing, General, I'm going to be hanging my flag back on the old USS Iowa."

"You're kidding; we can't have the Chairman of the Joint Chiefs running around at sea. How the hell are you going to pull that off with the President?"

"OH, I guess you haven't got the routine message yet. I got the President to finally agree that, since there were so few men with Battleship experience, I needed to get back to sea and let someone else run the Chairmanship."

"Wow, well, welcome aboard. Once you get here, I am making you the Chief of the Allied Naval Forces, and you can raise as much hell as you want with the Gomers. So, who IS going to be the Chairman? After all, I need to know my new sparring partner."

"Oh, some guy from the Army. You might know him. . . . Jerry Larkin?"

"You know, Admiral, one thing I have always admired about you is your ability to be a pain in the ass."

"Thanks, General, I'll see you in about three weeks. Oh, and do me a favor, tell those guys at Pearl to make the Mighty Mo look nice. Can't have your flagship looking rough, you know!"

"You got it, Admiral. See you when you get here!" Breaking the phone connection with Admiral Morton, I immediately got Commander Bowen into my office and told him the news. He was beyond excited and asked if he could brief Admiral Lynch on the newest development. I declined that offer, but did tell him to round up the Admiral, since I was the one who probably needed to break the news to him. Now that Admiral Morton was coming and would be our commander at sea, I was not sure how Admiral Lynch would feel at having to tell his old boss where to go. Of course, on further reflection, I have often wanted to tell several of my old bosses where to go.......

Admiral Lynch took it well and was happy to know that the Navy was about to get back in business above, on, and under the sea. Knowing the audience, he would be playing for a few weeks, he began putting to paper the plan already sketched out through countless skull sessions, usually over a bottle of scotch, over the preceding weeks. This plan would be a central part of our upcoming attack on Antarctica, and we all were quite vested in seeing it work. In the meantime, there was a ground offensive that would be required, and both General Fuller and General Whitney set about the process of identifying what forces would need to get where to make it work. The following day, the long-awaited report from Dr. Abramson came in via teletype.

For a scientific report, it was about what we all expected to see. While some of us understood the implications, there was something here for everyone. Some of the staff focused on certain parts, while others focused on different parts. Regardless, we finally were able to fill in the blanks about the Gomers, and what we read was invaluable.

SUMMARY OF FINDINGS

TO: *Supreme Allied Commander*

FROM: *Dr. Abramson*

In re: ***Scientific Findings from the recent
investigation of the Gomer wreckage found
in Georgia, USA***

Our military and scientific teams were able to recover a downed alien vessel and three bodies. We did not readily recognize the bodies as those of alien attackers, as they do not resemble the two life forms previously encountered. These bodies were also attached to the ships in such a way as to impair identifying them as discreet life forms until investigation of the wreckage was well under way.

Here follows a brief report of our findings. A complete report with detailed chemical and biological analysis is available for further study.

Alien Body Autopsy Report

Physiology

The bodies removed from the wreckage are larger than those of the previously encountered life forms. On first inspection, these appear to resemble a cross between a cockroach and a crab or lobster. The creatures possess an exoskeleton of small, pliable, overlapping scales on the anterior surface (see Figure 1). The posterior surface more closely resembles a lobster or armadillo with larger, harder, and wider overlapping scales (see Figure 2).

The creatures have two pairs of limbs extending from the sides of the body. The body is an elongated ovoid. One set of limbs is on a parallel with the eyes, approximately 1/3 the way down the body from the top of the body. The second set is on a parallel with the 'mouth', which is located at the horizontal midline of the creature. The supporting limbs consist of two main limbs with a third that seems to act as a tripod support when the creature is in a more up-right position. The upper limbs are jointed in four places. The first is analogous to our shoulder, forming a connection to the body. The second is analogous to an elbow, approximately half-way between the shoulder and the terminus of the limb. The third joint is half-way between the 'elbow' and the 'wrist'. Then there is the 'wrist' joint itself. These limbs are protected by two types of covering. The joints themselves are covered in a scaly, but extremely flexible, material not unlike certain lizards and iguanas. Between the joints, the covering is a hard substance more like a lobster or crab in appearance (Figures 3-6).

The two sets of upper limbs terminate in multi-digit appendages similar to hands. The 'palm' of the hand is a slight ovoid with three extensions/digits grouped on one side and a fourth digit in an opposing position. The spacing of the digits, as compared to the face of a clock, are roughly 12:00, 2:00, and 4:00 for the grouped digits and 8:00 for the opposed digit. The tip of each digit is almost flat, having only a slight rounding (Figure 7,8).

Each creature has a set of three dorsal 'ruffles'. The larger is located down the center of the posterior. Slightly smaller ruffles are aligned on either side of the main, larger center ruffle, equi-distant from the center ruffle and the limbs (Figure 9-11). These ruffles have a musculature than would allow them to be furled or flared, similar to the muscle structure of bats' ears. The internal nerve structures of the ruffles are extremely dense and converge to specific portions of what appear to be small satellite brains (Figure 12). These, in turn, are connected by dense neuropathways to a central brain located in the center of the body, posterior to the 'mouth' (Figure 13).

The creatures have what resemble tympanic membranes. There are two sets aligned vertically between the two sets of upper limbs on the sides of the creatures (Figure 14). There is also an array of 'eyes' (Figure 15), more complex that the tympanic membranes but joined by nerves to the same centers of what seems to be the main brain (Figure 15). Given the findings from our examination of the craft, it appears that the creatures can 'See' in the lower end of the energy spectrum.

The 'mouth' is a funnel-shaped aperture, the diameter of which seems to be able to be controlled by muscles, much as a human mouth (Figure 16). At the back of the funnel is an organ resembling a larynx, specifically that of a bat (Figure 16). There is an array of muscles (Figure 17) that functions like the rapid-movement muscles in bats, some fish and snakes. Applying an electrical charge produced rapid movement that suggests high frequency sound. The 'mouth' would act as a method to focus and direct these sound waves, like a bat uses echolocation.

The tympanic membranes, both on the sides and those of the anterior array, seems to function as receivers in that they react to vibrations in the $10 x8$ Hz to $10x10$ Hz, which would include all our radio and television ranges. These membranes did not react to visible light or to waves below $10X7$ Hz, which would include AM radio transmissions.

The chemical composition of these creatures is identical to the two previously encountered life forms, containing the same unique elements such as fluorine, high nitrogen content, etc... The major difference between the previous two and this new one is that these new creatures have a much higher content of silicon and calcium, which form the basis of their exoskeleton. The calcium also may form an important step in their communication. On Earth, calcium is an essential element in proteins that are involved in the rapid-movement muscles. The creatures may have developed much the same system in their own muscular evolution.

As noted in the first two life forms, the new creatures are highly reactive to sulfur and it should prove to be just as lethal to them.

Equipment

The ship appears to have no equipment sensitive to any energy levels much beyond 10X14 Hz, the infrared. Some of the screens seemed to have limited infrared capabilities but the images were of low resolution. Most equipment functioned optimally in the 10x 7 - 10x11 range. Higher frequencies produce a white-out effect, much like visible light does on night vision goggles.

The ship has flexible, extendible devices that fit directly into the creatures' mouths. We assume this is for communication. As one would assume, the machinery is tailored to fit the creatures' unique physiology.

The craft is still being investigated, but the team thinks we may have figured out the 'engine'. Located near the center of the ship is an object that appears to be an energy converter. After experimenting with various energy sources, it was found that electricity could be used immediately and 'as-is'. Other forms, such as low radioactivity and even steam from distilled water, seem to pass through a filtering or baffling system. This did not slow down the process significantly. The converter is connected to the ship itself and seems to pass the energy directly to the inner layer of the ship, almost like a continuous trickle charge. The creatures would be in constant contact with this surface and would, therefore, be in contact with the constant source of energy. We are still investigating this matter and how the creatures might function outside of their ship since we know that the other two previously encountered forms were able to function in the outside environment.

We have discussed the creatures' planet of origin and feel that, given our limited information, we are ready to make some educated guesses. We feel fairly confident that their planet would have had a greater gravity than Earth's, possibly up to 3 times our gravitational pull. The atmosphere would have been extremely dense, probably simple water vapor cloud cover, but deeper than our atmosphere. We also feel that their planet must have been a greater distance from their sun as we are from ours. This would explain the fact that these creatures do not seem to function at all in the ranges of visible light and the upper energy levels of visible light are mildly harmful to them. Direct Ultraviolet light quickly produces blistering and cellular damage. Humans would have a similar, but milder, reaction but our atmosphere protects us better, due in large part to our Ozone layer. This would also explain the exoskeleton as an evolutionary defense against radiation. We feel confident that theirs is a largely nitrogen-based atmosphere, quite similar to ours. We are also certain that their planet contains little or no sulfur since they have such a violent and deadly reaction to it. We cannot begin to explain how that can be, since Sulfur is one of the more common elements in our universe, but it is the only way we can explain why these creatures would come to a place full of and covered with something that is so deadly to them. We can only assume that they have had no previous direct contact with the element.

I finished the report, and immediately had it copied and distributed to the key members of the staff. From here, the discussions took on almost a tone of discovery, as we each were able to place things in immediate perspective. Colonel Deacon Jones was seeing the Crab like Gomers from his position, which was not put in complete perspective for us. As we read and re-read the report, we still had several questions that we wanted answered. For example, if they cannot "see" in our visual spectrum, then how did they know where the twilight line would be, and what would keep them from absorbing energy directly from sunlight? Their low IR capability would explain our ability to hide in wooded areas, and it would also help explain how lead shielding might keep them from seeing an energy source. What it did not tell us was how the Gomer weapons worked, or what made them come to a planet that is made up in large part of the very things that could kill them. Were they here to terraform the planet, or just steal energy? Where in the hell did they come from? What makes them tick? Most importantly, how can I blast them to hell without knocking the planet off its axis, or create a compound at the poles that would drown us in acid rain?

Despite my hating to pull Dr. Abramson from his work, it was time he and I had a chat. I asked my staff to come up with their specific questions, and we had those scrubbed to eliminate repetitions and irrelevant things. At the end of the day, I decided that the most important question for Dr. Abramson to answer was how we can hit them, without causing that ecological nightmare that would render our planet uninhabitable for those of us who might survive the Gomer invasion. In the presence of the staff, I picked up the phone and, after a considerable amount of time, was finally put into direct contact with Dr. Abramson.

"Doctor, I just read your initial report, and we need to ask you something."

"Sure, General, go ahead."

"Doctor, your findings about the Gomers make it clear that we can hit them with high doses of Sulphur, but they don't give us a method to do this without contaminating either of our Poles with something that, likely, would lead to the creation of Sulphur Dioxide and acid rain. Do you have anything in your 'trick bag' that might take us out of that arena? One of the guys here seems to think that maybe an attack on a cellular level might work, and he asked if there is such a thing as a radioactive Sulphur isotope that could be used in an airburst fashion over Antarctica or the North Pole?"

"We have been looking into the various possibilities. We think that our best bet might be to use Sulphur 35. This is one of the more stable isotopes with a half-life of 87 days. Its decay process yields Chlorine 35. This should hopefully give us the effect we need on the creatures initially, and then with continued effects from the Chlorine for any who survived the initial attack."

"What does this by-product, the Chlorine 35, do to the environment?"

"It should dissipate without any major adverse effect, at least none that we can discern at this point."

"Okay, Doctor, how long to produce a weapon that would use Sulphur 35?"

"We can make one in a week or so, by converting some of the existing warhead inventory, but they won't be stable, and they won't have a long shelf life before use."

"How long to get me several that I can use in, say, a month?"

"We can get you perhaps a dozen, maybe a few more, but we would have to work on the timing issue and get something going with the end users."

"Now a new twist, how many can be converted to work with the Cruise Missile system, and the heavier Polaris type missile systems?"

"I think once we get the conversion process down, we can get you several variants that will work with either or both delivery systems. General?"

"Yes?"

"One other thing I didn't mention in my report is that we have looked at the system in the South in those photographs, and most of us are convinced that this is a means of powering the thing behind the moon. We have no idea as to purpose, but clearly it won't be friendly."

"Then I need you to work with General Whitney to get the timing down and I will need you to deliver as many of the Cruise Missile types to Admiral Morton as soon as possible. Then I will need you to get at least 3 of the Polaris variety to Admiral Steadman, and maybe another 5 or 6 to General Thayer for use out of Vandenberg. Oh, and thanks to the Russians, we now know that we're going to need these systems coated with lead to keep them off the Gomers' radar. Can you do that, Doctor?"

"Yessir, I think we can, and I'll check with Dr. Clarkson on the process of conversion. If we can figure a faster way to do the conversions, we'll see what we can do about producing at least a dozen to two dozen of the Cruise Missile types."

"Thank you, Doctor, and good luck. If you need anything from us, or any of the service heads, just let us know."

"Will do, General, and good luck!"

"Thanks!" With that, I turned to the staff and said, "Okay, gentlemen, let us start this plan going in the right direction. Whit, get me General Larkin on the line. I think I have a job for the Sixth Army." General Whitney smiled, and simply said, "Yessir!"

SECTION 4:

TAKING BACK THE NIGHT:

THE GLOBAL CAMPAIGN

Chapter XVI.

The planning and movement phases were almost over, and we were on the cusp of the final operations phase in our war with the Gomers. The pieces, just as on a chess board, were now moving into place. Over the last 5 weeks, we had moved an entire Field Army with their equipment, and established support facilities along with the required supply depots. We had also trained naval personnel and started the final positioning of several major naval task forces. Each of these combat elements was now supplied with the appropriate numbers and types of new munitions for killing Gomers. The process of infiltrating our ground forces into Argentina and Chile was moving forward; but this was a painfully slower process. General Davis was working closely with the Navy but finding the tonnage of shipping that could move his men and equipment during the day, hide at night, and still get it all into the right ports along the coast was, at times, scary as hell. The fact that this task was completed in such a short period of time was nothing short of a miracle.

Our next miracle came from our scientists. Dr. Abramson and Dr. Clarkson had both done a stellar job and even discovered a method to convert existing nuclear warheads more rapidly into the very kind we needed to deliver the Sulphur Isotopes. We now had 24 of these special weapons in the Cruise Missile configuration, along with seven of the types needed for our people in the submarine fleet, and another 8 specifically modified for our personnel handling the Strategic Missile defense out of Vandenberg. Each of these new weapons was designed to generate or release massive doses of Sulphur 35 Isotopes to blanket our enemies when the time was right. Literally on the eve of battle, our tasks were now focused on bringing as much combat power, as quietly and unnoticed as possible, into the right zones for our offensive.

Aside from the Gomers, our biggest enemy was time. With each passing day, we were rapidly approaching that point where the summer period would virtually end in the north, and the summer would then begin in the south. We knew that two things were going to coincide with this event. The first was that the Gomers were going to shift their combat power back into our hemisphere. The second, which was far more ominous, the Gomers would be using their Antarctica-based power array for whatever sinister purpose it was originally designed. In our minds, the time was either now or never, since we would probably never again have a window that would allow us to take the offensive without even greater losses to ourselves and our planet.

We had done all we could to get ready. Planning was complete and the forces were either in place or were moving towards the enemy at sea. Now our efforts would consist of waiting on our first contacts with the enemy and adjusting the plan as necessary once we did meet them in battle. My staff and I were now relocated on the USS Columbia, an attack submarine, from which we could monitor the battle and maintain contact with our forces via the ELF radio. Once we got to the point where ground operations could begin, we would transfer to our "Flag Ship", the USS Missouri (TF-71). Right now, she was cruising down the coast of Chile, moving south 310 miles ahead of the USS Kitty Hawk and the balance of the invasion fleet (TF-74), and 110 miles south of the

USS John C. Stennis, Battle Group (TF-78). We all were waiting on that first contact with the enemy, and as it turns out, we did not have long to wait.

In position directly in line and equidistant between the USS Missouri and the USS John C. Stennis was the submarine, USS San Francisco. At the appointed time, she rose near the surface and began constant transmissions in the HF, UHF, and VHF bands. As the operator of the radio became more nervous, he began citing to verses from the Book of Psalms in his transmission. Within a few minutes the USS Helena, another attack submarine even further south near Antarctica itself, advised the ELF circuit that one of the Gomer Battleships had turned and was heading towards the position of the USS San Francisco. Other submarines also indicated the movement of this huge Gomer Battleship, as well as the other huge Gomer Battleships, in the various directions of three other transmitting submarines, who began transmissions just as the twilight line began approaching their positions.

Task Force 71, near the west coast of Chile:

Newly promoted Vice Admiral Becker was seated on the Admiral's bridge of the USS Missouri, waiting patiently as the reports came in from the USS Helena. Passing the word by light signals to the other members of the task force, he re-emphasized the obvious. "Make like a hole in the water. No radio to be used on any frequency. No ship to fire, unless fired upon, until I give the command." As they nervously waited, the gun crews, already at their battle stations, double checked that the Sulphur 16" shells were loaded, with the proper charges, and that the smaller 5" guns were set with proximity fuses for varying altitudes up to 20,000 feet. To quote a young gunlayer on the USS Missouri, "the silence was deafening." Within a few minutes, this would all change.

"Admiral, is that what I think it is, coming at us from broadside?"

"Yes, it is, Captain. Now pass the word to standby."

"Sir, the range is down to about 4,000 yards, and 8,000 feet."

"Standby! Keep the range count going."

"Sir. Range is 2,000 yards, and 8,000 feet."

"Standby. Waiting on the command from the Admiral."

"Range is 500 yards and closing, no change to altitude."

"Standby."

"Sir, she is passing overhead, still at 8,000 feet."

"Standby."

"Sir. Range is 500 yards, passing directly off the starboard side, still at 8,000 feet."

"Guns, at 1,000 yards, open fire broadside, starboard side, all guns. I say again, Target Starboard."

Within seconds the crew's entire world exploded as all twelve 16" guns erupted. The impact of the USS Missouri's gunnery appeared instantly, and with the secondary armament adding to the bark of the guns, the mammoth Gomer Battleship ceased to be a threat. With the crash of the Gomer's largest ship into the ocean, the USS Missouri headed due east at flank speed before becoming a hole in the water a few miles away. Slowly turning, she angled to a new position a few miles further south, where she moved quietly to wait until sunrise. After the destruction of the Gomer Battleship, a short ELF burst went out to the other large gun task forces, "Big Mo is one and done, splash one BF Gomer!"

The joy onboard the USS Columbia was beyond exuberant, but it was very short lived. Excited that the first crack of the bat was a home run, it was equally clear that there was still the rest of the game to be played, and everyone knew that the Gomers had one heck of a batting order.

Task Force 31, near the southern coast of Australia:

Here the conditions were different. The weather was a far greater factor, and the weapons would be more difficult to use as a result. The twilight line was another consideration, and there was concern that this time, the Gomers might be wiser to the game. Admiral Morton, along with an old friend who was now the USS Iowa's Captain, J. T. Elliot, were standing together on the Admiral's Bridge of the USS Iowa as they both searched the darkening sky.

"Thad, according to Admiral Becker's brief After Action on the ELF, the Missouri laid down a broadside by putting their port side towards the bad guys and letting them cross over to starboard. I'm concerned that we might not be able to play that game the same way."

"You're probably right, so let's screw with their planning curve."

"Whatcha thinkin'?"

"Well, why not wait until it is just short of us, maybe around 500 yards, and then fire with our forward guns and all secondary batteries. Once we fire the first salvo from the forward guns, then we will haul ass beneath it and follow up with the aft guns."

"Kind of goes against conventional naval tactics, doesn't it? You know all that 'crossing the T' stuff from the Academy?"

"Well, it is either that, or we could handle it like Becker did, and hope the Gomers haven't learned anything between that attack and ours."

"Thad, you're probably right, I guess we'll see in a few minutes. Darkness is almost here, and that damn submarine has been squawking for the last hour." As they slowly turned the ship to face the direction of the Gomer Battleship's approach, they double checked the weapons condition and took much the same steps throughout the task force, as did the crews of the Missouri task force. This time when the range dropped down to 500 yards, the command to fire was issued. Again, with the main guns' eruption, the secondary weapons began to fire to put Sulphur bursts above and around the Gomer's Battleship. As with the USS Missouri, the USS Iowa succeeded in downing the Gomer Battleship fairly rapidly.

Here the difference in the battle came when a sizable group of Gomer Fighters, along with their Carrier ships, attacked the USS Iowa in a style quite reminiscent of the attacks that took place over the East Coast. The secondary armament of the USS Iowa, along with her several escorts, were able to return fire and down a decent number of the attacking craft. Sadly though, the damage received from the Gomers was to prove fatal to the proud USS Iowa. While the good news was that another giant Gomer Battleship was gone, the very bad news was that, aside from the ship, we lost the Allied Naval Commander, Admiral Thad Morton. The Admiral, along with most of the ship's crew were lost in what would later be described as an epic explosion, reminiscent of the HMS Hood being sunk by the Bismarck in World War II. We were fortunate that the TF-31 Commander, Admiral Pollard, was onboard the Cruiser USS Mobile Bay and able to rescue at least some of the crew of the USS Iowa. Unfortunately, we lost Admiral Morton when, during the final attack on the USS Iowa, a small Gomer Fighter struck the bridge of the old battleship, which ultimately led to the massive explosion. Of note, it seemed that while the USS Iowa drew lots of attention from the attacking Gomers, the escorts themselves were oddly unmolested.

USS Columbia, near the coast of Chile:

The USS Mobile Bay, a Guided Missile Cruiser and Admiral Pollard's flag ship, sent a flash immediate signal via the ELF that advised us of the loss of the USS Iowa. With the initial reported information, we were not clear on the reason for the loss. Initially, we believed that the Gomers were now wise to the use of the battleships, and we were in the process of moving to the back-up plan of using some of our rather precious Cruise Missiles in the hope that they might get through to the targeted Gomer Battleship. As Admiral Pollard was able to assess the situation more closely from the USS Mobile Bay, we received more information about the circumstances of the sinking, and the attack by the smaller Gomer Fighter craft. Turning to Admiral Lynch, I asked him to go through the report and see if he could determine what the difference was between the two attacks. Why didn't the small stuff attack the Missouri? Why did they go after the Iowa? What was the difference?

In the interim, I ordered that the USS New Jersey stand down, and get really quiet. Her transmitting submarine, the USS Hartford, was ordered off the air, and to get as many miles between her and her transmission position as possible. My chief concern would be that this time the Gomer southern fleet might attack first, which would put the USS New Jersey in the same position as the USS Iowa. We had expected this as a potential adjustment by the Gomers, but we did not need to put the USS New Jersey at risk if we were going to have to use the back-up plan. The main reason for making this quick decision was the far more rapid passage of the twilight line at these lower latitudes. As these orders were issued, the staff was working to see what the difference in the two attacks could be, aside obviously from the timing. In the meantime, the battle group around the USS Wisconsin was told to maintain their present plan. We had known all along that this was the highest risk position, but we had no choice, since this was a position that would be needed for the ground assault to follow.

After almost an hour, and from the more detailed After-Action information making its way from the Australian area, an answer jumped up at us. The USS Iowa was almost 150 miles off the shore of Tasmania, while the Missouri was within 5 miles of the coast of Chile. Similarly, the USS New Jersey had been positioned almost 100 miles of the South African Coast, while the USS Wisconsin Battle Group was currently positioned roughly 6 miles from the coast of eastern Argentina. We believed the answer was now obvious, but completely overlooked in our initial planning. We could get lost in the ground clutter of small islands and islets, much the same as we had been able to hide in the woods near open areas in our earlier experiences with the Gomers. Making the adjustment and shutting down the USS New Jersey Battle Group left us with a hole, but not one we could not live with at the moment. Especially since she would still get her turn, just maybe not in the best order.

TF-20, USS New Jersey:

Vice Admiral Harper was not a happy camper. He wanted a crack at the Gomers, maybe even more than anyone else in the entire US Navy. He not only served on the USS Iowa as a Commander, but he was more than a little upset that she was not given to his command for this battle. He had been cursed by geography, and his being on the East Coast, when Admiral Morton put this crazy scheme together. Taking it in stride, he was less than impressed with having to bring the USS New Jersey back into commission, and then damn near halfway around the world. First passing through the Atlantic to the North African coast, and then moving down the west coast of Africa took forever, as did the need to clear the stench of museum off the ship. When he heard of the USS Iowa going down, he was more than upset, he was just plain pissed. When he got his orders to move positions and make like a hole in the water, he got even angrier. As a result, when this message came in from the USS Columbia, he was fit to be tied!

"Admiral, it appears we are to head directly for the Falkland Islands at all speed just behind the dawn line. If it is necessary to stop, we are directed to shut down and catch the sunrise again to continue moving. It seems that some genius wants us to a position that is within 1 to 2 miles of the coast of that island as soon as we can get to that position."

"Let me see that crap. Okay, Captain, signal the group and let's get as far as we can before we have to shut it down. Maybe they know something we don't."

"I think they might, Admiral. Admiral Lynch sent it directly, and it seems they learned something about the Gomers that might indicate why they got the Iowa."

"Bastards! Okay then, let's do it. I want some Gomer ass for breakfast." As the small task force turned west, the fleet came to the maximum of 30 knots, which is as fast as the older museum piece could travel. The Admiral ruminated on the fact that, in her day, the speed would have been somewhere between 32 and 35 knots, now it could take forever.

Task Force 40, within 5 miles of the coast of Argentina:

In a mirror image position as that of the USS Missouri, the USS Wisconsin was locked, loaded, and waiting along the eastern coast of Argentina. The submarine, USS Miami, was the radio 'bait,' and this time the radio operator was having a good time transmitting the complete contents of the New York City yellow pages for the benefit of the Gomers. As he was winding his way through the best plumbers in the city, the ELF message indicating that "their" Gomer was coming.

On the Admiral's bridge of the USS Wisconsin, Vice Admiral Harper was concerned about the message he had received about the USS Iowa and the position information. As he was talking with his Chief of Staff, the Captain of the "Whisky" was on the interphone with a question about how to "proceed" in the attack.

"Captain, I've read Pollard's message, and I have looked at Becker's plan of attack. I am convinced that part of the story is the proximity to the coast, and I am also equally convinced that it might have something to do with the 'bow on' attack employed by them. Otherwise, I can't explain why the escorts were untouched in both instances."

"Makes sense, Admiral, so what are you saying?"

"Captain, I want you to turn us broadside to the direction of travel, and I want the SOB to go over us before we open fire. Tell the escorts to hold fire until the damn thing is past us, and then they can open fire when we do. I think if we do it like Becker, we can make sure that the Gomer Battleship gets past the entire task force. I am thinking it might have something to do with his not being able to see anything in his baffles, and that this might make a difference in spotting for the rest of his fleet. Hell, we have nothing to lose."

"Yessir!" No sooner than the signal lights had conveyed the Admiral's intentions, the huge Gomer Battleship was spotted on a direct heading for their position. As everyone on board waited, the monster continued to approach with a steady heading, speed, and altitude. It was passing overhead without any indication that it may have detected anything hidden in the coastal ground cover. At the requisite range, the ships all opened fire and, as with the attack by the USS Missouri, the large Gomer Battleship collapsed into the sea. This time there was no follow-up attacks by any of the smaller Gomer Fighters or Carriers, who continued onward as if they had no indication that anything had struck their fleet or their largest ship from behind.

USS Columbia nearing the position of the USS Missouri:

"Dammit, General! I was wrong and Admiral Harper was dead on the money. It wasn't just proximity to the coast, it was about letting the damn thing go by, and then hitting them in the ass!" Admiral Lynch was beside himself, since it did make a lot of sense. The USS Iowa's escorts were all ahead of her, which meant that they were already underneath or behind the mammoth Gomer Battleship when it was hit by the direct fire from the Iowa's forward main guns.

"Admiral now isn't the time to beat yourself up. Now is the time to figure out what we are going to do about it. The Gomers are down to one huge battleship, and we are still at three and counting. We need to adapt, and Admiral Harper adapted. I want him to get a Navy Cross for having the brains to figure it out, and then the guts to stare the damn thing down when it crossed over his ship. Especially since he knew what happened to the USS Iowa and, with his own twist, did it anyway. He could just as easily have been wrong and just as easily dead. Now any suggestions?"

"Sir, we have the USS New Jersey moving to the Falklands, but it is a slow trip. The USS Wisconsin is closer, but we have her scheduled to perform the bombardment of the Tierra del Fuego area for the ground attack. My suggestion is to shift the Wisconsin to the Falklands, and let the USS New Jersey proceed south to the closest edge of the Ice Shelf, she could reach that in a much shorter amount of time. . . ."

"Okay. Tell the New Jersey to proceed to the Tierra del Fuego area, but right now, we will have to use someone else to send what we want into Antarctica. If the New Jersey gets a chance to hit the big bastard, fine, but right now, we will need to cover our forces on the ground. Tell the TacAir boys in all task forces that we are on schedule for the Ground Operation."

"What about the transfer to the USS Missouri, sir? We should probably hold off while that other Gomer Battleship is still at large."

"Nope. That stays on schedule too. I cannot ask the boys on the ground to do something I wouldn't do. I will say that I will take only my regular ground guys. I want you and General Whitney to stay on board and be prepared to take this to the Gomers if I am knocked out of the game. I am taking Generals Fuller and Greene with me, along with my Aides, but that is it. Understand?"

"Yessir."

"Oh, I just had an idea, what is that Peruvian Cruiser doing right now?"

"Sir, she is riding shotgun for the Kitty Hawk and TF-74."

"Great, in that case, maybe send her to the South with a small escort and let her do what the big guys have done so far. Become a hole in the water and wait for something big to come along she can use those guns on."

"Might work, she is no USS Iowa, but she is better than nothing."

"Okay, send her to the south of the USS Missouri, and she can protect us if we need it."

With the arrival of the dawn line, the bridge crew of the USS Missouri looked off her starboard side at the surfacing USS Columbia. Within about 30 minutes, Generals Fuller, Greene and I were aboard our new home in the southern-most reaches of the Pacific Ocean. I had to admit that, after being a little cramped up in the USS Columbia, the quarters I was given on the USS Missouri were absolutely palatial. Within a two-hour period, TF-74, with the III Amphibious Corps aboard the USS Boxer and USS Makin Island, hove into view. As the day wore on, the fleets amassed near the shoreline and prepared for the final run into the southern side of Tierra del Fuego. Vice Admiral Becker, Commander of TF- 71, Vice Admiral McIntosh, Commander of TF-74, and Major General Drew Sullivan, met on board the USS Missouri to iron out the last- minute details for the next phase of the operation. Our timing would be critical, and the ocean around our invasion area was especially treacherous. It was my hope that the plan would keep us from causing any more casualties than necessary, but it would be a long shot. The time had arrived for us to tip our hand, regardless of whether we had killed the last humongous Gomer Battleship or not.

As the daylight was rapidly diminishing, the Peruvian Cruiser, Almirante Grau, passed us heading south, and I bid farewell to General Fuller, General Sullivan, and Admiral McIntosh, as they returned to the USS Boxer and the USS Kitty Hawk. General Fuller was going to be camping out with Admiral McIntosh on board the USS Kitty Hawk throughout the invasion phase. As their respective Barges pulled away from the USS Missouri, I turned to Admiral Becker and advised him that our operation plan Bravo was in effect. Without so much as a wince, Admiral Becker headed off to his bridge, and I to my quarters to meet with General Greene and my Aides.

As we spoke, the USS Missouri, along with the destroyers assigned to TF-71, began a quick run to follow in the general direction of the Peruvian Cruiser to the south. As twilight approached, we dropped our speed, and eventually became that hole in the water again. TF-74 was tipping its hand, and the airstrikes from the Kitty Hawk were underway. Similarly, the Sixth Army unleashed their artillery and began the bombardment of Tierra del Fuego. Directly to our port side, and many miles on the other side of Cape Horn, the USS Wisconsin was also lying-in wait. Now the question became which of us would get the final Gomer Battleship, or would any of us get it?

With the firing of the Artillery barrage into the middle of their positions, the Gomers acted as though their anthill had been kicked over. Literally pouring forth and manning their perimeter. The Artillery fire was highly accurate, thanks to Colonel Deacon Jones' excellent intelligence work, observation, and later adjustment of fires. Over the course of the next few hours, many of the crab Gomers were finding that high explosives tipped with Sulphur can work quite well as a crab recipe. As the barrages continued, the smaller Gomer southern fleet was beginning to converge on the area. Still, we waited, following the battle from afar, and doing our best to resemble a hole in the sea. Our TacAir and Naval Air assets that were covering the invasion beaches were firing at the small Gomer Fighters with very decent results. They would hit their targets, and then immediately fly behind the Andes.

Our invasion fleet waited and, like us, were being silent as the dawn line was approaching.

Only then would they begin to move into the beaches and fire at the smaller Gomer Fighters operating in and around the area. It was not long before we got the message we wanted. The last Gomer Battleship was on its way and, as luck would have it, the beast was coming right towards us on the USS Missouri to avoid the dawn line that was rapidly approaching our position.

The Peruvian Cruiser Almirante Grau was roughly 10 miles to the south and west of our position. As the giant Gomer Battleship passed her by, she opened fire with her main guns. Unfortunately for the crew of the Cruiser, they fired while the Gomer Battleship was abeam their ship. The angle put the Peruvians in a parallel position as opposed to being astern. As they were making a turn to continue fire and hopefully escape their position, they were struck by the enemy main weapon. The power and intensity were the same as that which destroyed Diamond Head, so their end was swift and very final. Our temptation to fire in support must have been great as well, but Admiral Becker maintained position, and most importantly, silence. After the Gomer Battleship passed us flying towards Terra del Fuego, Admiral Becker unleashed a salvo that left our ears ringing for quite a while. The results were immediate, and the last known Gomer Battleship passed as a smoking wreck into the sea. Within seconds, I was on the radio to Admiral Lynch onboard the USS Columbia, and within a few minutes thereafter, a series of 10 specially outfitted Sulphur Isotope 35 Cruise missiles were racing to their targets in Antarctica.

Without anything that could protect their newly constructed facilities and their Energy Array, we hoped that the Gomers were now naked in their defense of the Antarctic base. It must have worked because the resulting explosions were impressive, even if they were not your typical nuclear impacts, and while the earth didn't move for us, we believed that it must have laid waste to the target areas. Within an hour we would know for sure, since we were going to attempt, for the first time in almost six months, to get real-time eyes on the targets. If we were successful, then our only threats now would be the giant Gomer 'Moon' ship that was still hiding behind the moon, the Gomers at Tierra del Fuego, and the remnants of the Gomer southern fleet. Except for the beastie behind the moon, the rest of the Gomer force was something we thought that the Six Army just might be able to handle, although it was anything but a foregone conclusion.

As we began racing the USS Missouri back towards the Chilean coastline, and the rest of the fight, it was clear that the ground game would be a tough nut for us to crack. Making it even more exciting was that we were getting reports that the big Gomer 'moon' ship, still lurking behind the Moon, might be making a move. If the latter was true, then General Greene's efforts, along with the efforts of our scientists and the 14th Air Force at Vandenberg AFB, will have our fates firmly and completely in the palm of their hands.

Within the hour we were confirming two things. The first was the complete destruction of the Gomers' Antarctic Power Array. The second was that the monster behind the moon was, in fact, now starting to move. As the combat raged around their perimeter, it wasn't long before our folks on the ground noticed that the larger Gomer Carriers were all departing the area around Tierra del Fuego and following the twilight line as they headed north. At the same time, many of the smaller Gomer Fighters were flying in support of the retreating Gomer southern fleet. We tracked them as they headed northward, just as we were tracking the movement of the monster as it was starting to visibly appear around the edge of the moon. Clearly, our war was about to enter a new and perhaps more dangerous phase than we had ever faced before.

Chapter XVII.

Tierra del Fuego:

Tierra del Fuego is an archipelago at the bottom of the world. Resting nearer Antarctica than any other point of the Globe, it sits at the very tip of South America. Argentina, prior to the Antarctic Treaty, laid a territorial claim on portions of Antarctica itself, based on their possession of the Tierra del Fuego archipelago and its associated islands. The explorer, Ferdinand Magellan, first named it "land of fire" in about 1520, and the northern body of water which separates the archipelago from the mainland is aptly named the Straits of Magellan. Territorial claims divide the main island, or Isla Grande Tierra del Fuego, between Chile and Argentina, with each having a provincial capital. This distant island consists of roughly 18,572 square miles, which ranks it in size as 29th in the world. Relatively mild in temperatures, most of the island during the winter months, April until October, may only have up to 7 hours of daylight a day. Now this part of the world was being claimed by the Gomers, and it was our mission to dislodge them and return this turf to its real rightful owners, the race of man.

The original plan for our invasion consisted of the Sixth Army placing the XIVth Corps, south of Cabo del Espiritu Santo, which is along the northeastern coast of the Grande Isle; the XXIVth Corps, just north of Rio Grande, which is the capital of the Argentine Province; and, XVIII Corps, in the central plain east of San Sebastian, Chile. Concurrently, the III Amphibious Corps. was to land the 1st and 2nd Marine Divisions along the south coast, on the Beagle Channel side, between Bahia Aguire and Bahia Valentin, while the 15th MEU was to land on the Isle de los Estados which lies off the coast towards Antarctica. My personal hope was that, with daylight periods getting longer, coupled with the destruction of the Gomers' Antarctic positions, their Battleships, and the balance of their southern fleet, the Gomer resistance would not be quite so stiff. In this, I was wrong, and it appeared that a significant ground fight was on our hands.

Shortly after the USS Missouri returned to the southwest coastline, the ship began a naval bombardment of suspected Gomer positions on the Isle de los Estados. At the same time, the USS Wisconsin began a similar barrage on the shoreline in and around the Rio Grande area, while Naval and Tactical air forces were used to keep the Gomers' heads down during our daylight landings. As the initial landings progressed, resistance began to develop in the three areas we suspected as Gomer strong points. Unfortunately for us, the Gomers had an uncanny ability to tunnel, and they had developed a system of tunnels that allowed them to be strongly entrenched on the reverse slopes of many of our initial objectives. This made it nearly impossible for our artillery, or even naval gunfire, to have much impact on the Gomers. Even our sulphur rounds seemed to be having little effect, since the rounds were not impacting close enough to spray them with the sulphur particles. There were also their much higher tech weapons, which may have limitations in the indirect fire mode, but as a direct fire weapon, they were quite devastating. It was this devastation to our men and equipment that forced us to consider a more viable method for clearing enemy positions.

At the end of the first day, we held the beachheads with some advances inland, but these gains were offset with considerable losses to some of our assaulting units. This was starting to resemble a trench fight that was going to go from hole to hole, and we would need the kind of weapons that hadn't been used in a while. The advance on the Isle de los Estados was far more successful, since it appeared that the Gomers only held minimal or observation positions. The fight was brutal, bloody, but relatively quick. The 15th MEU suffered heavy casualties, but at the end of the day, they had reached all the objectives and were expecting to accomplish their mission of controlling the entire island by the next day. As usual, this was perhaps a little optimistic.

Near the town of Rio Grande:

The young Captain was finding himself behind a berm overlooking what had to be a Gomer position. The hole was perfectly round and ran into the hillock at a 30-degree angle. As the Captain surveyed the hole, he looked around to find his runner. "Dammit, Corporal, keep up!" Hearing the tone of the Captain's voice, Corporal Kowalski turned and ran up the hill, dropping down next to his commander. "Okay, Ski, 'bout time you got here. See that hole?"

"Yessir."

"I want you to tell the first platoon to get their asses up here and tell them to bring the bug juice. I know damn well that is a Gomer hole, and somebody is going to have to go into the damn thing and get them out. Now move!"

"Yessir!" As Kowalski slid down the hill and began to run towards the first platoon positions behind the next hill, he heard the unmistakable sound of a Gomer weapon behind him. Turning to look, he saw the entire portion of the hill where the Captain had been lying was now gone. The perfect circle like that created by the Gomers in Virginia was now burned through the hill behind him. Instinctively he hit the ground, and felt the force pass above him and into the next hill.

Deafened by the Gomers' weapon, he jumped to his feet and started running. The entire time he repeated over and over, "GEEEZUS! The Captain is gone!" Clearing the next little hill, he slid in next to the platoon leader, who was just staring straight ahead, and quite dead. When he looked around, what he saw chilled him. That portion of the platoon sheltered by this second hill was gone, and in their place was more of the circle shaped impact area from the Gomer weapon. Ski thought to himself that the landing had gone too well, and now they were paying the price. Looking around and seeing that he was now the most senior man in the area, something in him snapped. Grabbing the ancient flame thrower, and three other men who were carrying Sulphur grenades, he moved around the flank of the two destroyed hills. When he eventually reached the upper side of the hole, he looked around and saw several more holes in the hills behind the one on which he was standing. Knowing that he was about to be a target from one of these other holes, he dove into the Gomer hole and unleashed the flame thrower. The results were quick and, once the Gomers were forced back from the entrance, the three soldiers with him threw their Sulphur grenades as deeply into the hole as they could. It would take a couple more hours but, working as a team, the hole was cleared of all the resident Gomers.

Near Bahia Valentin:

The Marines surrounding the Captain were shivering and waiting for the offloading of their equipment. As bitching goes, what the Captain was hearing was unusually creative, and becoming more strident with each passing phrase. "Dammit, Marines, shut the hell up! You bitched that it was getting hot outside Savannah, and now you are bitching because you're cold. Hell, make up your minds! Now, Sergeant, get these assholes broken up before a Gomer gets 'em, and get our guns unlimbered and on the lee of that hill!"

"Yessir, any particular Order you want them in?"

"Not really, just get 'em up and let's get this stuff ready to use. Nighttime is coming, and I want something to shoot with before it does!"

"Gotcha, Sir." The sergeant ran off to organize and complete the offloading of their ammunition and guns. In the meantime, the Captain was getting lines run to the Fire Direction Control Center, when he heard the distant gunfire. What had more puzzled him was the intensity of the sounds he was hearing in response. This was something he had never heard before, and it sounded almost like the sound itself was being directed or channeled through a tunnel. Little did he know at the time; he was the first to pick up on the idea that the Gomers were using a sound-based weapon system.

Over Antarctica at 4,000 feet:

The older P-3 Orion Aircraft from the United States Navy was conducting a flight over the former Gomer base. The intention of the flight was to gather data and to confirm that the site was destroyed completely and free of any Gomers. The Aircraft was conducting a grid pattern search and transmitting information via an ELF transmitter recently retrofitted to the aircraft. As he made this fourth turn back over the central part of the continent, the pilot pointed to his co-pilot and said, "Does that mountain look like it is moving to you?"

"Nah..... no, wait...yeah, I guess it does."

"Wonder if that is just our eyes playing tricks on us. Check with the guys in the back and get them to look close at it."

Within seconds it was determined that it was moving. Almost like a dog shaking off fleas, it began to rise out of the ice adjacent to the main dish position. The Pilot keyed his microphone and called to anyone who could hear him, "Alpha 66 to Operations, we have a Gomer Bogey, and it is massive."

"Say again, Alpha 66?"

"I say again, a really massive Gomer of a new type is coming up from the ice, it appears to be..........."

"Alpha 66, this is operations, you were cut off. ....
Alpha 66?"

After repeated calls with no response, the operations
personnel sent a Flash Message to all Allied Headquarters
containing this latest puzzle piece. In response, the USS Kitty
Hawk re-directed three fighters to the last known position of Alpha
66. Other than a quick transmission of "HOLY CHRIST LOOK
AT THE SIZE OF THAT THIN...," all contact was lost with this
patrol, and a second flash message was passed on to the Allied
Command onboard the USS Missouri.

Near the Shackleton Ice Shelf along Antarctica:

After firing her missiles into Antarctica, the attack
submarine USS Topeka continued to patrol the waters in her
quadrant around the continent. As she was turning back to a more
northerly course, she detected a huge magnetic anomaly passing
overhead. Turning to track it, the Captain was summoned to the
control room.

"Whatcha got, XO?"

"We're not sure, sir. We got some weird aircraft chatter via
ELF earlier, and now we have this spike in our readings. Whatever
we have, it is way larger than even the huge Gomer Battleships we
were tracking."

"How much larger?"

"At least twice to three times the size, sir, and it appears that she is starting to turn to port to sit right behind the twilight line."

"Get that off to Allied HQ via the ELF, and then let's do our best to keep a track on her."

"Aye, aye, sir!" Within a few minutes the message was transmitted, and, with that news, the already ominous picture was starting to become just a little clearer to the Allied Headquarters personnel onboard the USS Missouri.

Near the South Georgia Islands (South Atlantic):

The USS New Jersey, along with her escorts (TF-20), was nearing the South Georgia Islands in her passage from her original position near South Africa. The heavy seas were tossing her smaller escorts around like corks in a bottle and even making life onboard the large battleship pretty miserable. She had received orders earlier in the day to divert from the Falkland Islands and instead make all speed for the coast of Isle de los Estados. Vice Admiral Harper was again quite annoyed and was seated on the Admiral's Bridge when he was handed another message, this one was marked FLASH IMMEDIATE. As he read the text, he could feel a great deal of mixed emotions. On one hand, he was still pissed off that the USS Missouri had scored two Gomers, while he was coming up empty based on his first change of orders. On the other hand, this message did not bode well at all. In fact, it literally made him break into a sweat, despite the cold in the air. Calling

351

the Captain of the New Jersey to come to the Admiral's Bridge, he handed the message over to his Chief of Staff. As the Chief of Staff read the message, his eyes widened, and all he could do was shake his head. Admiral Harper did not say a word until the Captain arrived, and then he spoke. "Captain, we've got a major problem and, from what I've just read, it is a problem that we will not be able to avoid. Chief of Staff, how long before the twilight line catches us?"

"About two hours, sir."

"Good, it will take that long to figure out how we're going to crack this nut." With that, he handed the message to the Captain, who read:

FLASH IMMEDIATE
Commander, TF-20
Supreme Allied Commander

Submarine, USS Topeka, near the Shackleton Ice Shelf, 66 degrees 00' S. 100 degrees 00' E. has detected massive Gomer craft believed to be at least twice the size of the largest Gomer Battleship encountered to this point. Altitude unknown, but believed to be at approximately 9,000 feet AGL, traveling with the Twilight line. First detected by observation aircraft that was destroyed in the encounter. Additional aviation assets are also now missing in their attempt to intercept and engage. Proceed with caution to position at or near the South Georgia Islands. Air wing from the USS Truman, en route your position, should arrive at or near the twilight line, also be advised that the USS Boise and USS Scranton are near your position for additional support. You are to assume command of these forces, and to engage the enemy at your discretion. God speed and good luck.

> *Signed: //S//*
> *Michael Patrick,*
> *General of the Army*
> *Commanding Allied Forces*

The first to speak was the Chief of Staff, "Admiral, you said you wanted a bite of the bad guys, and it looks like you got your wish. What are your Orders?"

"You've read it, so let's start with what the General just told us. We can expect something 'massive.' I want to take the page from Becker's playbook. Get us close to the island, and we will assume that the Gomer ships, despite their size, will adopt the same or similar tactics. Advise the escorts to form a defensive ring around us, and we'll all become giant holes in the water."

"What about the aviation guys?"

"Signal via ELF for them to stay on the Sun side of the line and engage at preferably a maximum range. Hopefully, that will distract the Gomer long enough for us to stick one or two up its arse. What I don't want is for the airdales to tip the damn Gomer off that we're here and waiting. Now as for the USS Boise and the USS Scranton, please tell their Commanders to distance themselves from us by about 6 miles to the North and West of our position. They then need to be prepared to fire their Cruise Missiles if it looks as though we are in trouble, or if the big bastard gets by us in one piece. Finally, tell everyone to be prepared to move in a big damn hurry if it gets really dicey."

Turning to the Captain, the Admiral continued, "Captain, make sure that we are broadside to the bastard's approach course. We are going to do the same thing as the Missouri and Wisconsin. We are going to let the damn thing cross our path, and when the thing's stern is at about 1000 to 1500 yards, depending on the size, we'll hit it with all we have. Questions?"

"Do we know if this beast has any escorts of her own?"

"Not at this point but have every lookout in the task force on alert just in case they do have their own tactical air support. From what I hear, those little Gomers are hard to hit, and even harder to keep off your ass."

"Yessir!"

USS Charlotte 105 miles due east of the USS New Jersey:

"Captain, we just got the hand-off from the Topeka, and she is headed back to her station. The USS Boise is now joined on the USS New Jersey, and the Gomer will be passing us in about 3 minutes. We passed on the position to the boss on the USS New Jersey."

354

"Thanks, XO, once she is clear, bring us up to launch depth, just in case we need to move in quickly and help out. Those boys on the beaches at Tierra del Fuego have enough on their hands without this damn thing, too."

"Yes, sir. My brother is over there, with the 1st Marines, and well...."

"Yeah, I know how you feel. My cousin was on the Iowa and I've got a brother with the 11th Airborne Division."

"Sorry about the Iowa, sir."

"Yeah, me, too. Now get everyone up and to General Quarters. We are going to suck along on this bastard's trail for a while. Who knows, maybe we can take a poke at him, too, if it becomes necessary."

"Aye, Aye, Sir. Chief of the Boat, pass the word for general quarters......"

Aboard the USS New Jersey, near the South Georgia Islands:

"Admiral, we are getting a light signal from the USS Stout. They have the Gomer in sight at 6000 yards, approximately 9000 feet. All batteries are closed up, weapons tight, and on standby."

"Thanks, Captain. Hold her steady and maintain steerage way."

"Sir, our lookouts have the Gomer in sight on the starboard side, at 5000 yards from our position, no change in altitude, and she is friggin' massive."

"Thanks, Captain, hold what you've got." Hearing this, Admiral Harper picked up his own glasses and peered off into the approaching gloom. Turning to his Chief of Staff, he said, "That damn thing is really pushing the twilight line. We can actually see it and most of its features."

"Yessir, and despite what the scientists have said, I still feel mighty naked sitting here in the open in daylight."

"Yeah, no kidding, I don't like it either, but you......... what the hell is that?"

"I am not sure; it looks as though...." Before the Chief of Staff could get it out, the phone from the bridge rang, and it was the Captain. "Admiral, the Stout and Vicksburg both report that the Gomer is launching small Fighter ships."

"I see it, Captain, signal the task force to hold their fire."

"But sir..."

"No damn buts! HOLD your fucking fire!"

"Aye, Aye, sir." As they watched, the small Gomer Fighters continued to launch and began to deploy on either side of the Massive Gomer along the twilight line. The Massive Gomer began to drop off speed, but only a little, and allowed the smaller ships the chance to form up and follow the darkness towards the Task Force.

"Sir, Gomer fleet is now at 3000 yards and closing our position. Small objects are at 10,000 feet and the big one is at 9000 feet."

"Captain keep the ranges coming for the big one and signal our escorts to focus on the small ones. Remember to fire only on my command, and only after they have passed us. I say again, on my command and only AFTER they have passed us."

"Aye, Aye, sir." With each passing of the range information, it was obvious that the smaller Fighters were deploying for an attack, but their altitude appeared to be too high for a direct attack on his task force. Noting this, Admiral Harper held his breath, hoping that nobody would panic and fire on this growing armada that was rapidly approaching him.

"Sir, the range is down to 1000 yards and closing. Gomer Fighters are from 1000 to 1500 yards and descending to about 9000 feet."

"Keep the range coming and constant, Captain."

"Aye Sir, range is 800 yards, ...600 yards, ... 400 yards, ...200 yards. Sir the massive one is overhead and clearing the ship to Port."

"Keep the ranges coming!"

"Sir, Range is now 500 yards to port for the big one, and we still have fighters at 1000 yards to starboard."

"Sir, Range is widened to 1000 yards to Port for the Massive Gomer, last of the small Fighters are now at 500 yards to Starboard."

The Admiral, knowing that if he waited any longer, he would lose the chance for a more devastating hit on the Massive one, opted to go ahead and pull the trigger. He could only hope that his escorts could keep the little ones off his ass long enough to kill the big one. Allowing these thoughts to run through his mind, he made the call.

"Captain, Fire all main batteries to Port, secondary batteries at all targets of opportunity." With his command the USS New Jersey fired all her main guns at 1100 yards at the Massive Gomer. Unlike the attacks of the USS Missouri and the USS Wisconsin, his main battery fire was not quite as devastating on the Massive Gomer. Clearly it was wounded severely, but it would take a second salvo to complete the task. With the second round of 16" fire, the Massive Gomer began a slow roll to its port side and began to slide into the South Georgia Islands. The wreckage came to rest partially in the deeper water, with the forward section slamming into the rocky shallower water near the shoreline of the islands. With the destruction of the Massive Gomer Ship, the smaller ships began to swarm towards the USS New Jersey.

The secondary batteries of the USS New Jersey did a great job of keeping up, but it would be impossible to go completely without damage. Ultimately, it would be the guns of her escorts that would save her from more damage than she received. As the sea battle raged, the Air Wing from the USS Truman arrived and engaged many of the small Gomer Fighters as they broke off heading towards the forces near Tierra del Fuego. In what most would describe as a major dog fight, a huge number of smaller Gomer Fighters were destroyed, but not without some serious losses to our own aircraft from the USS Truman. As it was, approximately 40 of the smaller Gomer Fighters broke through, and were even now en route to the invasion fleet near Tierra del Fuego. The USS New Jersey acquitted herself quite well and, while one of her aft main batteries and several of her secondary batteries on the starboard side were no longer operational, she was full of fight, and now steaming towards Tierra del Fuego. The Captain of the USS Stout was even quoted later as saying that, "I swear, as we steamed behind her on the way to the invasion beaches, she was moving faster in the water, almost like she was holding her head up with pride, and boy was she pissed."

Near Bahia Valentin:

The sea battle that took place was completely unknown to the Marine Captain or anyone else on his beach. As he set up his batteries to support the advancing 2nd Marine Division, what he did hear about was that numerous Gomers were now up and out of their holes. With the approach of darkness, the Gomers were literally swarming out of their holes and headed south, directly towards the Marines who were scattered along their beachhead. As they approached the forward lines, the Marines opened fire with an intensity that appeared to drive the Gomers back. Still, some got through, and were infiltrating into various 'rear' positions throughout the Marine area.

"Captain, what the hell is that thing coming towards us?"

"Christ, Sarge, I haven't a clue. Looks like one of those Crab things they were telling us about."

"Sir, should we shoot it, or have Cookie boil it for chow?"

"Dammit, Sergeant, shoot the damn thing!" The Marines around the perimeter began to fire and as the first crab fell, several of the 'meaty' Gomers were up and advancing. It was to prove to be a long night with gunfire erupting almost constantly as multiple small waves of the Gomers were doing their best to break through the Marines' positions.

Near the town of Rio Grande:

The Marines in the south were not the only ones with a Gomer problem. Just as in the southern part of the archipelago, several waves of the meaty Gomers, along with a few of the Crab Gomers, made several intense attacks on the Army positions. As the night wore on, Corporal Kowalski was finding himself more exhausted than he had ever been in his life. He was also feeling more alive than he had ever felt before. With the ebb and flow of the events through the night, he was rapidly finding himself with more responsibility than he'd ever held in his life, and for the men around him, this was becoming a good thing.

"Hey, wake up, Ski, here they come again!"

"Thanks, dude!" Shaking away the sleep, Corporal Kowalski rolled over and peered into the darkness with the night vision goggles. "Okay, fire teams hold your fire until they get in the box, they are ahead of you to the right front. There are 6 meaty Gomers, and one each Crab about 25 yards to your front. I don't think they know we're here."

The Gomers got a little closer and were almost into their positions when Corporal Ski gave the order to fire. Just like the previous 4 groups that were trying to break out of the area, these too became short work for the ambush. Once the dust cleared, he shifted their positions to a different area. This would hopefully throw off any Gomers who might have been watching their friends get cut apart, and once in the new position, he set up a new ambush. Just like before, he then tried to take a short nap.

TF-40 and her escorts, off the coast of Rio Grande:

Vice Admiral Thomasville, on board the USS Wisconsin, had just finished reading Admiral Harper's initial report of the action to his east, and was quite aware of the oncoming flight of 40 small Gomer Fighters. Setting the appropriate Air Defense alert, his escorts deployed around his ship, while still in a position to cover the beachhead of the Sixth Army. In fact, even with the approach of the flight of Gomers, the USS Wisconsin maintained the firing of her main guns in support of the troops ashore. In this case, it would be his secondary batteries, along with the excellent gunnery from his escorts, that would decimate the flight of Gomers. The few that survived were then fired on by the escorts from TF-45, which completed the destruction of the smaller Gomer fighters before any of them ever reached the beach.

USS Missouri, outside the Beagle Channel:

My review of the various initial After Action Reports that were pouring into my staff was most enlightening. The threat from the Massive Gomer ship was immense, and I wanted to make sure that there were not any more of them hiding around the Antarctic. As a result, I ordered that, for the next 48 hours, we were to keep a constant 24-hour air patrol over the entire area around where the Gomers had their base. Their orders were simple, report anything, and get the hell out if it even remotely looked odd. Another thing of note was that the Gomers were originally pouring out of their holes, only to return after the destruction of their oncoming fleet by the USS New Jersey. This meant that they were in direct communications with a higher headquarters, and that at least on some level there was also local communications with local control over their operations. The days of a flash bang to disrupt the 'dusty' Gomer were gone, and in their place was a determined and fierce enemy with superior weapons. I was enjoying a smoke and one more of the many cups of coffee I had already had for the day, when General Whitney walked into my cabin.

His transfer from the USS Columbia, along with the last of the Staff, had now put most of our command eggs back in the same basket. I sincerely hoped that this was a sound plan, especially given our surprise earlier in the evening. Still, I personally was damn glad to see him again, since I had really come to lean on his insights into what we were facing. With the ground campaign starting to appear even uglier than we first thought, it would not be long before we would be back in the Army business and out of the Navy's hair. "Hey, Whit, glad to be off the Submarine?"

"Actually sir, I have been either underground or underwater for so long, I was getting used to the idea. Now, this surface stuff is a little unnerving."

"Hell, you should be here when they fire the really big stuff. Now that is impressive!"

"I know, Major Cho told me when he handed me these ear plugs as I climbed onboard."

"I guess now we have a new type of ship to identify for our list of Gomer ships. Since everyone keeps saying it is monstrous or mountain sized, how about Mountain class?"

"Sounds good, I'll send it out right away."

"Excellent, so what is the latest from our boys at Vandenberg?"

"The Gomer 'moon' ship has poked a little of its nose from behind the Moon, but it hasn't moved at all in the last 12 hours. Other than a serious case of nerves, the boys at Vandy are standing by with just the right amount of pressure on the trigger."

"Outstanding! At least that is one thing we don't have to worry too much about. Our plan will either work or it won't, and there is damn little we can do about it from here. I guess that one is on Thayer and his boys to accomplish. I just hope it doesn't become our problem here. That damn thing popping up today definitely causes some guys to leave streaks in their drawers."

"Well, it sure as hell left me with a few in mine."

"Ah, Whit, you can't be seen leaving shit stains, it looks bad when the person doing a General's laundry sees that."

"Thanks, General, I'll keep that in mind!"

"Okay, now on to the next phase. I've got constant air patrols keeping an eye on the former 'Gomer land', and so what is the status of their fleet that hauled ass north?"

"We are in luck. They worked the arc straight to the North Pole and are taking advantage of the shifting of the polar winters for darkness. They only move now in the small arc to keep themselves in the dark, and long enough to recharge their energy from a point up there near the Kuriles Islands. My guess is that it is another feeding point, although someone reported that they may be back on the coast of Japan, but this is a sporadic run right now. It is almost like they are waiting on something."

"I hope they aren't waiting on the big bastard by the moon, but it would make sense that they would. It is how they got here and may be their only way home. Makes me wonder if the 'Vandy plan' is the right course. Maybe we should let them leave. What do you think?"

"I'm not sure, that one could go either way, but given what they've done around here, I'd say fuck'em!'"

As we were wrapping up our conversation, the FLASH URGENT message arrived from Vandenberg. Reading through it, I told Whit to go round up General Greene. "Seems that the decision is out of our hands, and we are going to see Project Sky Hook before our very eyes." As Whit left my cabin, I poured another cup of coffee, lit another cigarette, and waited for their return. Clearly this was going to be either a damn long night, or a damn short death!

Chapter XVIII.

USS Missouri near the coast of Tierra del Fuego:

General Greene stepped into my cabin, and I showed him the FLASH URGENT message. As he read, his eye widened, and when he looked at me again, his look was extremely guarded. "Well, General Greene, it looks as though it is time to let the cat out of the bag. Gather the staff in the Senior Officers' Wardroom and be prepared to brief your operation Vandy and Project Skyhook in about 10 minutes." With that General Greene gave me his finest parade ground salute, did an about face, and literally double timed out through the hatch as he left my cabin. Before I could even leave my seat to head towards the Wardroom, I was handed another message by General Whitney.

"Sir, General Davis is raising all kinds of hell right now about having to cough up the 11th Airborne from the XVIIIth Airborne Corps. He says that with his manpower losses, he needs every trooper he can get his hands on right now."

"Whit tell him I know that and will replace them with the 101st Airborne from our Strategic Reserve. You can also tell him that I have decided to commit the Argentine and Chilean Divisions on their respective sides of their borders. They do not have any experience with killing Gomers, but Deacon says his guys have been trying to teach them. Right now, Deacon has split his force into three groups. One will continue observation for artillery support, while the other two will be assigned to the foreign troops as advisors."

"That isn't going to make him very happy, but I'll pass it on to him."

"Whit, while you're at it, look at the casualties and staff the question of sending in the rest of II Corps, out of the first Army. In the meantime, I still want the 11th Airborne to supplement the Marine Divisions in the south. They're getting their asses kicked, and the 15th MEU is pretty tied down and almost on the verge of not being combat effective based on their losses."

"Yessir, I'll pass it on."

"Oh, and Whit, you know about Skyhook and Vandy, so keep your nose to the grindstone. I'll head down to the Wardroom and listen to Greene advise the rest of the staff. It should be one helluva show."

"Yessir!" As we broke company, I started down the companionway to the Wardroom, while Whit headed in the opposite direction to the Comm Center. As was typical of my days now, I got all of 10 feet before I was handed yet another message. This one was a little different though, it simply said "CALL ME." When I looked at the origination address, it was the President, Marty Blanchard, in new Washington. Turning on my heels, I told my Aide, Commander Bowen, to head to the Wardroom, give them my compliments, and tell General Greene to start the briefing without me. The entire time I was thinking, why would the President call now? It just is not like him to interfere when we are in the middle of this much serious excrement. When I entered the

Comm Center, I looked at the Commander in charge and told him to get me the President on the secure ELF line.

"Yes, Sir, Mr. President, Patrick here, what can I do for you, sir?"

"Mike, listen, aside from all your other troubles, I have a new one for you."

"Okay, sir, lay it on me."

"Secretary Case just advised me that you're about to get some unwanted help."

"Really, right now I'm not sure that any help would be unwanted, but I'm listening."

"Okay, here is the short version. The Russians are coming, and they want to join the fight."

"Sir, I just committed our Argentinean and Chilean Divisions to the fight, and I'm putting at least one unit, maybe more, from our Strategic Reserve into the mix. What do the Russians want in exchange for joining the fight?"

"Simple, they want a piece of the pie, at the last minute, and they want Gomer technology. Their force is only a little better than token, and probably would consist of only a couple of ships."

"Sir, that isn't help, that is just getting in the way."

"My thoughts exactly. I need you to refuse their offer and send them packing. Can do?"

"Sure, I can do, and I get the point. This is the same garbage they pulled at the end of World War II, by finally jumping in on the Japanese within two days of the end of the war."

"Exactly! Now take whatever action you deem necessary to keep them from your zone and out of this one. I do NOT even give a shit if you sink one of the bastards in the process, and feel free to scare the piss out of them too. The days of putting up with their horseshit ended the second the Gomers arrived."

"No problem, sir, and I'll send word back through their 'liaison officer' that we're not interested. Does Secretary Case want me to put his ass back on a Russian ship when they get here?"

"Sounds like a good idea, get him out of there for all the damn good they've done us, especially after the Zhukov incident. Is he worth a shit?"

"Not really, sir, but he is a good spy for them, and a fairly accomplished liar."

"Good. Humiliate his ass then, and make sure he leaves without taking anything useful with him."

"Yessir, I'm on board with your plan, and we WILL make it happen." We terminated the conversation, and I finally was able to head to the wardroom where General Greene was wrapping up his descriptions of both operations. The look around the room was a complete mix that ranged from grins to a few looks of abject horror.

As the questions began, it was clear that General Greene was handling it just fine, and though there were a few questions that General Greene could not answer in front of our Allied officers for security reasons, he did his best to keep the explanation in lay terms. In short, Project Skyhook was the "mining of the channel" using lead covered ERW-type satellites in an extremely high orbit around the earth. It was based on what we knew as the approach point to Earth of the Gomer 'Moon' ship, and where it began to launch the initial assault wave of Gomer ships. It also considered several other variables that would influence a second approach of that ship if it were going to either launch or retrieve any additional Gomer ships. The details of Operation Vandy were a little more secretive, but this portion of the plan was brutally simple. Special tipped or Sulphur 35 Isotope weapons, along with more conventional strategic nuclear warheads, were now aimed to converge on the Gomer 'moon' ship the moment it was encountering the mine field. I had to admit the plan was simple and quite naval in the concept. Admiral Morton would have been proud, if he had lived to see it, especially since an Army officer conceived it, and the Air Force was going to execute it.

General Greene concluded his briefing, and I took the reins of the meeting. I then cleared the room of everyone except the top staff. The only remaining foreign officers in the room were my Allied Chief of Ground Operations, General Sir William Fuller, from the UK, and my Chief Allied Planner, General David

Campbell, from Australia. I wasn't sure how to broach a couple of tough subjects that had arisen in the last few hours, but I decided to bring the elephant on into the room. "Gentlemen, I just had an interesting conversation with my President." I then briefed everyone present about the conversation we'd had regarding the approaching 'Russian' assistance. Every single person in the room was of one mind, but Sir William probably had the best answer. "Tell the Russians to go to bloody hell and, once they get there, to have tea with that lying dodger Zhukov!"

The next political item was a little less palatable for me, and it was the subject of the Argentinean President's 'personal' request. As someone of not-so-distant Irish extraction, it was most certainly an understandable request, at least on one level, but it was also reprehensible on the professional one. At the height of the first day of our combat, I was contacted through Secretary Case about Argentina's 'official' protest over the use of a 'British Officer' in the command of the "invasion of Argentina's sovereign territory." I didn't want to tell Sir William, but I then decided that it was best to be forewarned should he try to visit one of the Argentinean units in the field. Responding in his typical English stoicism, he said, "That's okay, I would prefer to visit a Chilean unit instead, they have better food." Then he asked, "What did YOU tell them, General?"

"Well, Sir William, I told them that 'you were selected by Global consensus, that you were a professional and, if they were that unhappy with the choice, we could always just leave and let them deal with the Gomers as a local problem.'"

"Bloody excellent! Sir."

"Not to worry, but for your own security, I wanted you to be aware of the situation. So, just be careful if you start running around in the wrong places over in Argentina."

We broke up the briefing and it was none too soon, since even then the next crisis was only minutes away. I was hardly back to my office onboard the Missouri when a panicked call came in from General Sullivan with the III Amphibious Corps. A Gomer attack was now pushing his forces back, and he needed help soon, or his line was going to break. We increased our fire missions from the support ships, and then I got on the ELF to find out where the hell the 11th Airborne was in the mix. As luck would have it, the airframes to bring them south were now being used to drop the 13th Airborne west of Rio Grande, while the 17th Airborne was landing at the former Argentine Air Base near Rio Grande. Now that 66% of the XVIII Airborne Corps. was in play in support of General Davis, it should help him some, but it could be at the expense of the Marines who were getting their asses handed to them. I was livid! I had made it quite clear to General Davis that I wanted the 11th Airborne down south. I made up my mind that, even though I like the guy, he would have some serious explaining to do when we got a chance to dig through what happened.

I told General Whitney to increase our gunfire to a maximum tempo for the Marines, and for him to get as much TacAir into the Marine sector as possible. I realized that while this was not optimal, especially since we were used to the Gomers controlling the skies at night, it would have to do until we could get the 11th Airborne deployed. Fortunately, it was mere minutes before I heard from General Davis, who was extremely apologetic, and about as pissed as I was about the screw up with the 11th Airborne. He began by asking, "Sir, do I have your authority to relieve a senior commander in the field?"

"Talk to me, Dick. What the hell happened?"

"The Corps Commander is a box of damn rocks and decided that, instead of sending the 11th Airborne on south first, he would offload them and give the airframes to the 17th, which he is now 'air landing' into Rio Grande."

"Christ, really?"

"Really! I want his ass out of here. Do I have your authority to make that move?"

"Absolutely, but who are you going to assign in his place?"

"Not real sure, I guess the next senior guy is Major General Carterett, but he is Commanding the 13th Airborne."

"Okay, well shuffle whatever you need to shuffle, but get it done quickly. Wait, what about your deputy? He might make a good Corps. commander."

"True, sir, but he isn't Airborne qualified."

"I understand, but unless you expect that Corps. Headquarters to drop out of a perfectly good airplane in the next few days, I'm not sure that matters at the moment."

"I got you sir, okay, Major General Sturdivant it is, and I'll get his ass over there within the next few hours."

"Fine, but right now if you want to really impress my ass, get the feckin' 11th Airborne Division to General Sullivan! We clear?"

"Yes, sir. What do you want me to do with General Elliot?"

"I don't really know, but for now get his ass out of command."

"Yessir. I'll have him on the next plane headed north."

"No, keep him here, no sense in having him running around squawking with stars on his shoulders, that gives him credibility, even though he might be the guy responsible for a lot of other guys getting their teeth kicked in. Besides, if we take casualties at the senior grades, he might still have some value, assuming he learned something from all this. No, let him be your Deputy for a while, he might learn something...."

"Yessir. I don't like it, but yessir."

"Dick, I hate to see anyone get hammered for one screw up, especially since a few months ago before the Gomers showed up, he was a brand spanking new deputy Brigade Commander. I mean, how many guys do we have now at senior levels that were only experienced at the mid-level or lower command levels. Hell, from what I read this morning, you've even got a Corporal running a Company along the edges of the Rio Grande perimeter, and apparently he is doing one helluva job."

"That last thing about the Corporal is true. I just commissioned him as a second lieutenant, and you are probably going to read his recommendation for a Medal of Honor as it wanders its way up to you."

"Excellent, let's both hope the kid lives long enough to enjoy wearing the damn thing."

"Gotcha, sir, and I'll get the 11th Airborne where you need them." As we hung up, I was still pondering how our nation had gone from a well-trained professional Army to what we have now, all in about six months.

Near the Rio Grande Perimeter:

The brand-new Lieutenant was staring up at the sky, completely baffled by what he was seeing. "Hey, Sergeant, are those what I think they are?"

"Yep, those are C-17s, and... Hey, Ski, check it out, parachutes!"

"HOLY CRAP, don't they know they are jumping on a Gomer position? They'll have their asses handed to them! Sergeant get everybody up, and let's move in that direction. Single file, keep the spacing, and let's see what's going on."

"Yessir." It would only take a few minutes to get them up and moving, and like infantry the world over, the new Lieutenant and his men were now headed towards the sound of the guns. As they neared what was obviously the ground near the Gomer positions, they noticed that the Airborne troops were not only down, but they were not getting carved up. Instead, because the Gomers could fire laterally but apparently not above or vertically, when the Airborne guys landed on or above the Gomer holes, the troopers had the advantage of being able to attack the holes closest to them without having the bad guys shoot back. Amazed at what he was seeing, the new Lieutenant deployed his men back a safe distance and started digging in, just in case the Gomers decide to come out of their holes and start heading towards them.

Near Bahia Valentin:

The Marine Captain was tired, and so were his men. The last 36 hours straight had been a real bitch, and, at times, he and his men were locked in hand-to-hand combat with the damn Gomers. The Gomers would rush from the dark, straight at his gun positions, and he would give them a dose of sulphur rounds at almost point-blank range. Still the Gomers continued towards them, often dying from the Sulphur while they were still firing their weapons at the Marines in their dug-in positions. As he surveyed his positions, he realized that he was now down from six to just two operable gun batteries. "Damn, if this keeps up, we'll all be screwed by morning."

"What did you say, Captain?"

"Nothing, Sergeant. Just make sure everyone has the ammunition they need and get the gun crews without guns to supplement the perimeter. Get them all in their holes, and tell them to remember, 'a Marines' first job is to be an Infantryman!'"

"Aye, Aye, Sir! OH SHIT, here they come again!"

With this pronouncement, the Sergeant immediately began firing, and the pace of fire increased. It would be a few minutes before the Captain realized that the rate of fire was way beyond that which his men could ever produce. Looking behind him at the next small rise, he saw a unit of people he did not recognize, and they were firing over his position into the advancing Gomers. He swore then that it didn't matter who they were, so long as they were killing Gomers. The firing dropped off, and then a band of rather "tough looking hombres", as his Sergeant referred to them, passed through his position and continued off in the direction of the Gomers. One of them, a rough looking old Sergeant Major, stopped for just a second and told him, "Don't worry, sir, I am Sergeant Major Clagmore and I brought the whole damn 11th Airborne Division with me. Oh, and we really fucking hate Gomers!" As quickly as he arrived, the wiry Sergeant Major was then over the next berm and screaming like a Banshee in the night, as he and his men charged forward.

Vandenberg AFB, California:

"General, I just heard from Generals Thayer and Patrick. We are a green light for Operations Sky Hook and Vandy."

"Thanks, Colonel, keep me advised on the 'Moon' Gomer's movement." The Colonel saluted and headed back into the operations section. General Randolph McDaniel, at the start of the conflict, had been enjoying his retirement on a boat not far from the old AT&T or Oracle Park in San Francisco. Now here he was back doing the same stuff he had done before he retired. It was a wonder he had survived the Gomer attacks, both the one in the beginning and the one later in California. He was not one to ponder whether this was an act of God or just fate, since he was never religious, nor did he ever consider himself a philosopher. Instead, he thought of himself as a very old scientist. When he retired from the Air Force, it was because they made him leave, not because he was ready to sit on a boat and watch events happen from afar. He also thought Patrick was right after the East Coast campaign but, then again, maybe that was because dinosaurs all thought alike. When he was handed this egg to toss, he had jumped in with both feet, and relished every second now that he was back.

Stepping into the operations area and fire control center, General McDaniel was merely returning to his natural habitat, just like General Patrick had done in the Mountains of West Virginia. Now it was his turn to make a difference, and timing was everything. Looking at the Operations Chief, he said, "Colonel, keep me up to speed on position, course, and anticipated flight path. I want to know before it enters the 'mine field' and when it has entered. Keep me provided with the distance information as continuous as possible, and then wait on my firing order. Understand?"

"Yes, sir!"

"Okay, everybody, this is it. For all the marbles, and all the chips. Power us up to standby on the launching sequence!"

"Yes, sir!"

As the range information was sent, and the computer adjusted the firing sequence, General McDaniel bided his time. When the Gomer's 'Moon' ship was mere seconds from entering the 'mine field', the General turned to the launch control officer and simply said, "Okay, Slick, let's feed this bastard the sulphur." Within seconds the Gomer 'Moon' ship entered the mine field, and the explosive charges released the ERW weapons almost against the hull of the ship. It would only be another two seconds before the follow-on missiles, containing the special Sulphur Isotope 35 and conventional nuclear weapons, struck home. In all, it would be all 8 missiles that would hit the target and, with the final strike coming in a mere .3 seconds from the first, the Gomers' largest 'Moon' ship simply broke apart into nothing more than a debris field to hang in a very high earth orbit for several years to come. The good news was that Gomer 'Moon' ship was destroyed, while the bad news was that some points along the equator suffered some EMP-based power outages. Naturally, this meant very little in reality since the Gomers had already played havoc in these same areas with their weapons.

Once the results were confirmed by visual telescopes, General McDonald waved his communications officer over and said, "Colonel, send this message FLASH IMMEDIATE to General Patrick and the President. 'Results of the game are as follows, Vandy 1, Gomers 0.'"

"Yessir, uh, is that it?"

"Yes, it is for that message. Now then, I want a second message to go to General Patrick only, and it needs to say, 'Standing by for the kickoff for the next game.'"

"Uh, I don't understand sir, what is the next game?"

"Don't worry about it, Colonel, just send the messages."

"Yessir."

USS Missouri, off the coast of Tierra del Fuego:

When the FLASH IMMEDIATE came in, it was met with more than glee, we were thrilled. We were finally seeing the light at the end of the tunnel, and for once it was not an oncoming train. The word spread like wildfire throughout the entire command, and it was against this celebration that I was advised that our Russian friends were arriving.

"General, we have a Russian destroyer approaching flashing a signal that they are wanting a meeting with the 'Supreme Allied Commander.'"

"Thanks, Commander, please ask Colonel Karnaukhov, Admiral Lynch, and General Whitney to meet me on the Admiral's bridge." I made my way to the bridge, where I found Admiral Lynch waiting for me.

"Admiral, please advise your main gunners to load the High Explosive rounds, and discreetly turn their guns towards the approaching vessels."

"Okay, Sir, but you know if you're not careful what might happen here."

"Are you saying you can't take these guys?"

"Hell No! We can gut'em like a trout if you want, I was just wondering if the President really meant to go to war with these people."

"I don't know if he does or not, but orders are orders."

"Aye, Aye, Sir!" Admiral Lynch then picked up the phone and passed on my orders to the Captain of the Missouri, and at the same time the Order was passed on to the neighboring ships that were holding station near us. Colonel Karnaukhov and General Whitney arrived together, and I noticed that two of the Missouri's Marine security officers were following them at a discrete distance.

"Colonel, did you advise your government that we did not require their assistance in this theater of operations?"

"Yes, General. I pass on message."

"So, they sent me ships anyway?"

"Yes, General. My Government is here to assist you." With his statement I turned to him and gave him my best glare. "Colonel, your services are no longer needed, required, or wanted. You will be passed back to your government effective immediately, and you will take them this message. 'If I see so much as a Russian wolf hound in this part of the world again, I will skin it alive and eat its bones. Your help is not help. You almost killed the world with Zhukov's stunt, and now you want to get in my way again.' Look around you, Colonel, do you see space for another ship?'" I then turned and looked at the Marines who were discretely standing by the hatch, and said, "Sergeant, please escort Colonel Zhukov, excuse me, Colonel Karnaukhov, to gather his personal things, I say again, only his personal things and nothing in writing, and then get his ass off my ship."

"Aye, Aye, Sir." The Colonel turned and was leaving between the Marine escort when I stopped him. "Oh, and Colonel, one more thing."

"Da?"

"Look out towards the bow, and then towards your ships."

"Da? You point guns at our ships?"

"Da! You might want to pass on to the Captain of the destroyer that he will be escorted from the area by a squadron from the Kitty Hawk, and if he so much as twitches or even thinks of turning around, I will blow his ass so far out of the water, he will be standing on the planet Gomer. We clear?"

"Da, General, we are clear." As the Colonel left with his escort, General Whitney stood beside me and said, "Well, so much for diplomacy."

"No kidding, but I did what the President wanted and, frankly, I agree in that decision. We are under NO circumstances to allow the Russians any access to Gomer technology, and we are authorized to engage in whatever combat operations are required to keep that from happening."

"You mean the President gave you the green light to actually fire on the Russians?"

"Damn right he did, and trust me, after what Zhukov did with the full blessings of his government, shooting at them would only be slightly less pleasing than shooting at the Gomers. I hated making that point through Karnaukhov but, as General Greene pointed out, he had to know something about Zhukov."

"General, we'll watch them all the way, and make sure that the boys from the Kitty Hawk and the destroyers drive home the point that we're watching. Admiral Lynch has also notified some of our subs to watch them like a real hawk on their trip home."

"Excellent."

Later, after collecting Colonel Karnaukhov, the Russians pulled their ship away and, without any delay, turned to a heading taking them away from our position. It was later reported that at 30 miles out, they were starting to turn back in our direction, when a flight of 3 FA-18s, reminded them that it might not be a good idea. At approximately 100 nautical miles, the Russian problem was now exclusively in the hands of Secretary Case who, along with the rest of his State Department, made it equally clear that nobody was to enter our exclusion zone without prior permission. The Russians even later acquiesced in our making it clear that Antarctica was to remain closed for the foreseeable future. This latter decision was probably driven by the next series of events, and the desire of the Russians not to find the wrong things under that ice and snow.

With nighttime rapidly approaching our position, we received an ELF radio message from out sentinel flying cover over the Antarctic region. They had detected more movement and were moving in the opposite direction to the potential target. With that movement, a flight of two F-35 aircraft moved in to take over for the aged P-3, Orion. As this latest Gomer monstrosity or Mountain class ship, began to shake its way clear of the ice cover, it was struck by six X-51A Waveriders, traveling more than 3,000 m.p.h., and tipped with the special Sulphur based warheads. This was one Gomer that would not menace anyone. As it ceased to move and was wracked with a series of internal explosions, the P-3 was able to take a series of great photographs of the massive Gomer Mountain ship. It was also observed that at least one more such potential target might be lying in wait under the ice and snow. Based on this, our observation program continued, although now the air patrols were maintained and armed with the X-51A missile systems.

In assessing the success, from the day's ongoing combat operations, it was clear that we were now in the closing phases of the conflict. The Gomer's were left with a few ships in the North, possibly one massive Mountain ship still in the ice and snow in the South, and the remaining Gomers that were dug into the ground on Tierra del Fuego. Our Airborne elements had done a spectacular job of appearing where the Gomers did not expect them. It was a huge risk to land the troopers literally on top of their objectives but, as it turned out, it not only worked, but it also worked very well. As we started to hang on for the night, we all felt better knowing that we could now control the battle space a little better. Tomorrow, I was really hoping we were going to close the deal and take back the night for good.

When I headed to my cabin, an idea hit me like a thunderclap, and I immediately told my Aide, Major Cho, to have General Greene report to me. Once he arrived, I started quizzing him about our latest arctic gear, weapons, and tactics. It did not take long before General Greene came to the same idea that had been wandering in my mind. The following day, General Greene would be on it, and Deacon and his boys would be in for the treat of their lives. With sunlight returning to the Antarctic region, we just might be able to pull it off. Armed with this new idea that was right up his alley, General Greene was going to see if we could take that feckin' Gomer Mountain ship. We knew it was still hiding in the ice, intact, and just waiting for us to take it from them.

Chapter XIX.

Near the Town of Cameron, on the west coast of Tierra del Fuego:

Lieutenant Kowalski's Company, which was now almost replenished with personnel, had pushed their way into the small town of Cameron, which is located on the shores of the Bahia Intuit. They had been most of day and night moving cautiously over land but had encountered absolutely no Gomers.

"Hey, L-T?"

"Yeah, Sergeant."

"Ain't it kind of weird that we have yet to see the first damn Gomer today? I mean, we ain't been shot at all day, but we passed an assload of holes to get here."

"Don't look a gift horse in the mouth, Sarge, and while you're at it, get on the horn, and let Battalion know where we are."

"Yessir, but where the hell are we?"

"Geez, Sarge! Read the damned sign!"

"Oh, yeah… Cameron?"

"Yeah, Sarge, Cameron. Now send it!"

With their movement into the town, they had now completely cut off the northern portion of the Gomers' original positions on Tierra del Fuego. General Davis, having moved his headquarters in the Town of Rio Grande, now issued the Order for the XIV and XXIV Corps. units to begin their sweep down the archipelago, pushing the Gomers hopefully south, and into the waiting arms of the Marines and the 11th Airborne Division, who now comprised the III Amphibious Corps. As for the northern positions, the balance of the XVIII Airborne Corps was engaging in a "mop up" operation to clear out the few remaining Gomers who were unfortunate enough to have occupied those northern positions.

Near Lago Pagano:

CSM Clagmore was getting the headquarters set up when the Division Commander wandered into their new command post. "Sergeant Major, I haven't seen you look this happy since you ran past the Marines' artillery position two days ago. What's up, you never smile!"

"Sir, it would appear that the Gomers up north have taken the big powder. Nobody really knows where the fuck they went, and the boys up north are finding bupkis. This tells me that either they left in the night, which from my perspective sucks, or they are coming towards us."

"That makes you smile?"

"Hells yes, sir! That means we've got'em runnin' and if they are runnin', we can kill'em. Maybe even in our front yard. G-2 for Corps. says they are likely moving towards us, and we get to be the anvil to the boys' up north's hammer."

"Nah, I've known you a while, Sergeant Major, that is only part of the reason you're grinning, what is the rest of it?"

"Well, sir, I heard a rumor from a friend of mine, who got it from somebody on the USS Missouri. Seems that the Russians sent us some of their 'help,' and General Patrick told them to pound sand up their ass. Now I have no idea what he really said, but I know for a fact that if they wanted somebody to be nice to the damn Russians, General Mighty Mouse Patrick would be the last guy on the planet you'd pick. He hates the fucking Russians, always has, and probably always will. My buddy said that he even had the guns of the Mighty Mo aimed at the bastards when he ran 'em off!"

"You know, Sergeant Major, I believe you! Now back to the Gomers, you say there are a bunch headed our way?"

"Yes, sir, and we were told that they were hauling ass to get here."

Looking at his Chief of Staff, the Division Commander said, "We got about three hours until dark. Get the Regimental Commanders on the line, and make sure they know what is coming. Sergeant Major, do the Marines know what's coming their way?"

"Yessir, it was the Amphibious Corps' G-2 that passed on the word."

"Roger that, Sergeant Major. Chief of Staff, tell the Regimental Commanders also to make sure they have eyes on the guys to their right, and that includes the Marines. Got it?"

"Yessir, and we've also got preregistered fires laid on with both the Marines and the Naval assets offshore. TacAir is on the hook, too."

"Okay, then. I am going out to inspect what we've got. Sergeant Major, you wanna come with me?"

"Sure, General, might even get a chance to go Gomer huntin'. I don't think I've got my bag limit yet."

There had been a clear shift in the ground campaign. The once overwhelming odds of operating against weapons of much greater strength were finally drifting in the favor of the ground forces. Over the last day, the casualty rates had dropped enormously, the resistance of the Gomers had likewise dropped off significantly. Units throughout the archipelago were meeting their objectives virtually unmolested, although pockets of resistance did still exist and once fighting erupted, it was usually swift and brutal to both sides. As darkness began to fall, things were about to change.

Onboard the USS Missouri:

I was reading the reports of the day's ground operations and noting that things were going smoothly. Almost too smoothly, and I was becoming a little worried about what the Gomers might have up their sleeves. I called in General Whitney and General Fuller, and we discussed the overall situation. After examining the map and correlating the new lines of resistance, we realized that the Gomers had moved en masse almost completely southward and were now in their fall back holes. We weren't meeting resistance, but this was their choice. Someone in their command had decided to husband his resources, and in a new location. When our troops were engaging them, it was either an outpost to their new line, or they were there to be a rear guard to what was really their plan. Clearly, they were trapped between our northern and southern forces, and this could mean either we were about to reach a stalemate, or we could expect an all-out assault on our southern forces, as they tried to breakthrough to the South.

Then it hit me, the Gomers were trying to break through to the South and reach that last Mountain Ship we now knew was in the ice. This realization struck Generals Whitney and Fuller at about the same time. As we looked at each other, I simply said, "Whit, get Greene in here, and let's see what we can do about that ship. In the meantime, Sir William, get in touch with General Davis and tell him we are shifting forces from his area again. This time he's lost the 101st, too." They both leaped up and went to take care of my orders. In the few minutes I had to ruminate on the question, I realized that now we were trying to keep the bastards from leaving. Was that smart?

When General Greene entered my Cabin, which was more of a huge office and living room than a bedroom, I asked him to have a seat. "Daniel, here is the deal. The Gomers on the ground are trying to haul it south to that last ship. We are going to put an assload of troopers between them and their objective. Their mission will be to stop, or at the very least slow down, the Gomers from getting to their extraction point. This should buy us time to make an assault on that big sucker in the ice. So, where are you in the planning sequence?"

"Sir, I talked with Deacon, and we're on the fence about this one. We can hit it like a standard fortification, or we can try to do it like an airliner rescue."

"Well, my idea would be to do it like a short planning curve aircraft assault. Then again, I've been out of the business a while. The good news is that the bad guys don't have hostages, at least we're unaware of any, so when you go in you can take something bigger than a 9mm pistol."

"That was my idea too, and I also thought that, unlike an airliner, we could use sulphur to breach the hull. My one real problem is we've studied the photos from the P-3 on the one that went down, and Deacon even took a short trip to the South Georgia Islands to see if he could learn anything from that wreck in the water, but honestly, we don't have a clue how the damn thing is laid out on the inside."

"I know, and with airliner or building hostage scenarios, we always had at least a clue what the blueprints looked like on the target. I get that, but can it be done?"

"Hell, we think so, but we're not sure, it could go either way."

"Okay, how long before you can get people on the damn thing to give it a shot?"

"We figured by tomorrow morning, give us 24 hours, and we'll give it a shot."

"Wait, Daniel, there ain't no damn 'we'! Deacon and his boys can give it the shot, but NOT you. I still need you here, because we have at least one, maybe two other Ops that you need to run."

"Yessir, but this is a once in a lifetime kind of deal! Hell, anybody could run these last two operations, and I REALLY want a crack at this big bastard."

"Daniel, ... Oh hell. If your Dad were still here, he would kill me if anything happened to you. Then again, he was just as crazy as you, and would be standing here on my desk until I let him go. .... Okay, DO NOT make me regret this, Daniel. I want your ass here when it is over, you got that?"

"YES, SIR!"

**On the coast of Japan, near the remnants
of the Fukushima Daiichi Reactor:**

The CH-53 helicopters departed to the south, back towards what was left of the US Air Base at Yokota where they would wait in underground revetments and hopefully get a good solid decontamination. Twilight was approaching, along with the remaining Gomer southern fleet of ships. They began their refueling, or feeding as some would call it, and as the ships positioned themselves around what used to be a nuclear disaster, the SRS type campaign began. Surrounding the area were several new Sulphur Isotope 35 weapons, and one ERW that was strategically lowered by one of the CH-53s into position directly on top of the old reactor which was now the primary Gomer refueling point. Watching with night vision equipment and controlling the "trigger" was a detachment of Air Force special operations personnel who were watching at a great distance from high ground to the southeast.

Once the gathering of Gomers appeared to be at the maximum in and around the site, the explosives were set off. The more efficient, but safer, Sulphur Isotope 35 weapons were taking care of the ships that were further from the refueling point, while the brief but massive burst of radiation from the ERW overloaded the ships that were in the process of still taking on fuel or energy. Just like at the SRS, the Gomers lost a sizable portion of the fleet, all in one operation. The results were excellent and, as a sizable force, the Gomers were down to only one or two larger Carrier type ships and perhaps a dozen of the small Fighter craft. As this latter group departed, it was to head directly back north, and to the darkness of the northern polar regions. Naval assets and several Air Force ground stations monitored their progress along their route back to what the Gomers must have thought was now a safe haven in the north.

A submarine, the USS Virginia, was lying directly beneath the ice at the Gomers' final destination along the polar icecap. The USS Virginia was a new class of submarine to the US Navy, and she was quite capable of sustaining operations for long periods of time. Her crew had been sailing on her since before the Gomers showed up, and she was one of the finest Submarines the Navy could put to sea. Just a few weeks ago, she had sailed as part of the Strategic Reserve for the Allied fleet, and just prior to that mission, she was reequipped with the newest and latest in the Sulphur Isotope 35 technology and delivery systems during an UNREP or underway replenishment. As the USS Virginia now laid in wait under the ice, what the Gomers couldn't know is that she had already been studying their patterns and had determined the perfect location and timing to deliver her deadly cargo.

The USS Virginia waited for less than a half hour, and she started detecting multiple crashes into the ice above her present location. It was not long after that, a P-3 Orion aircraft, based on the USS Virginia's ELF reports, was confirming that the USS Virginia had indeed delivered the final blow against the Gomers' southern fleet. The delivery of the Sulphur Isotope 35 weapon took place while the Gomers were refueling in Japan, and when they returned to their lager area, they had flown into an area seeded with a lethal dose of Sulphur Isotope 35. The reports from the reconnaissance aircraft confirmed that the end was complete, and that the Gomers were now completely gone from the northern hemisphere. General Greene's two planned operations, acting in concert, had eliminated a large part of the remaining global Gomer threat. Now all that remained was his final operation, which would be every bit as important.

Aboard the USS Missouri, off the coast of Tierra del Fuego:

The news was extremely heartening about our operations in Japan and at the North Pole but, as it was coming through on our ELF, the Gomers were adopting a new tactic. I had to believe that the Gomers had just as efficient (if not more efficient), a communications system as we did, and that this latest shift in tactics was in direct reaction to hearing about the loss of their relocated southern fleet. I also now was convinced that they were no longer trying to exterminate us, but instead were attempting to get away to their ride still waiting in Antarctica.

As we were reveling in the news of the north, the local radio reports began to come into our operations personnel in the Communications Center. At first, they were a trickle, and then the message traffic started to become massive. All along the perimeter of the southern line, which now ran from Lago Pagano to north of San Pablo on the eastern coast, there was Gomer movement before the twilight line even arrived. Reports were that the meaty Gomers were almost in a state of panic and were rushing our lines looking for any spot to break through to the south. There were only a few reports that the Crab Gomers were on the line, but the meaty ones were pushing our forces with a ferocity we had not seen up to this point. After reading some of these reports, I was convinced that their actions were very reminiscent of what I had read about the Banzai Charges made by Japanese forces in the Pacific during World War II. If that was true, then we were looking at a desperation move.

Near Lago Pagano:

CSM Clagmore was in his element. The Gomers kept coming, and he was able to get his 'bag limit,' and then some. In fact, it was almost more than he could handle. As the Gomers plowed into the positions of the forward units, some even poured through any gaps they could find in the paratroopers' lines. As a result, it wasn't long before they had filtered back as far as the Division Command Post. Grabbing an M-16 rifle, and his old 12-gauge pump trench gun, CSM Clagmore rallied the headquarters personnel into a perimeter of their own. It would be a fight for the ages, and even the Division Commander himself was shooting Gomers at almost point-blank range. The battle raged for several hours, but when the dust settled, the 11th Airborne had held their place in the line. Still, it was a near thing and, as they assessed their wounded and dead, CSM Clagmore was madder than ever. He wasn't pissed about the Gomers nearly as much as he was the trooper who was now standing at the CP. Looking at the Division Commander, he said, "That son of a bitch is from the 101st, and now we'll never hear the end of their bullshit about having come to save us. Fuck that noise, they didn't save anything. We HAD this!!"

South of the Line below San Pablo on the eastern coastline:

The USS Bataan and USS Iwo Jima, two of the Navy's Landing Helicopter Dock, or LHD, ships, were putting the 101st Airborne Division and their associated aircraft on shore. The better description of the 101st Airborne Division today is that it is an Airmobile Division. With its large compliment of assigned aircraft, the division had more local mobility and striking power than your traditional concept of an Airborne unit. Thankfully, this mobility was precisely what we needed to stem the attack from the Gomers. General Davis at Sixth Army, and General Sullivan, the III Amphibious Corps Commander, made great use of the troopers from the 101st to shore up weak spots and plug holes along our lines. In several instances, their speed and mobility were critical to the mission of intercepting, and either killing or driving the Gomers to ground, before they could break through our lines in their efforts to head south.

It was a long day's work, which ran throughout the night. Literally thousands of meaty Gomers were either trapped or killed in their attempted exodus, and there were even reports that the Crab Gomers were either using the 'meaty guys' as distractions or had lost control over their 'forces' of meaty ones. One thing for sure, the Crab Gomers were not part of the panic, and were, instead, still quite entrenched in their positions still north of the southern line. I think the reports were right, they were either running them at us, in a desperate bid to buy time, or they just didn't have any control over the meaty Gomers who were even now running southward. My best guess was that they were buying time, and I believed that I knew why. The answer lay hidden in the ice and snow of Antarctica.

Near the Horlick Mountains, Antarctica:

The pilot of the C-17, that made the pass over the mountains, was always amazed at the bizarre things' humans would do willingly, and apparently with a certain level of joy. Over the last week of dropping airborne guys on top of known Gomer positions, he thought he had seen it all. Then these guys showed up, and they were even scruffier than the airborne troops. The jokers that just jumped out over this ungodly place had seemed as though they were completely unconcerned as they left the aircraft. One of them, a General no less, was even grinning. As he made a second pass back over the area, his crew chief released a pallet containing all kinds of odd equipment and, once it was clear and the chute was confirmed as open, he turned his course to head back north. He had no clue what they were all about, and he also knew he didn't want to know. Telling his co-pilot to take over, he poured himself a cup of coffee, and thanked the good Lord that it wasn't his ass landing on the ice under a parachute made by the lowest bidder.

Once on the ground, General Greene's men set about gathering their equipment and moving the quarter mile or so to what they believed was their primary objective. They had no idea what they would find, but they were excited for a chance to see the Gomers in their natural habitat. Nearing their objective, they each detected a slight humming noise emanating from the ground. You could feel it as much as actually hear it, but there was little doubt that something extremely massive was below them and in front. Using hand and arm signals, General Greene realized that Deacon had signaled him that they were standing on the hull of the thing, and that there was an open area with no ice on it. Taking a chance that it might be an open compartment on the other side, as opposed to their reactor room or whatever you might call it, they set a sulphur charge in place to hopefully breach the hull. Taking cover, and with a last-minute glance at Deacon, they set the charge off. When the snow settled, there was a significant breach, and fortunately there was an open space on the other side.

The first operator dropped through the hole, only to be immediately attacked by a Gomer who must have come to inspect whatever had made the hole. General Greene did not hesitate. Dropping through the hole himself, he shot the Gomer and pulled the first operator clear of the crab-like carnage. Taking as little time as possible, the last members of the team dropped into the ship, and they began to see if there was a pattern to the corridors they found. All they had were the photos from the P-3, and a quick inspection of the Mountain ship near the South Georgia Islands as a basis for their entry plan. At this juncture, they weren't even sure what part of the ship they were in, much less in which direction might be the bridge or command center.

Looking around him, General Greene decided to split his team and go in opposite directions. Deacon took the lead one way, while General Greene took the other. General Greene had only passed about 200 yards before he saw several Crab Gomers moving in his direction. Taking advantage of what he knew was their lack of any eyesight as we know it, General Greene waited and fired as they passed by on their way to the breach. The shots were loud, but there seemed to be little reaction by any of the Gomers, as he shot each one in turn from behind. Deacon was finding nothing along his route and said so with the code word on their radios, "nada." Two things happened with the transmission. The first is that it brought several Gomers skittering down the corridor from General Greene's direction of search. The second was that it gave General Greene a clue that he was headed towards the command center, or at least a point where more than a few Gomers might be located.

Sticking to General Greene's earlier methods, General Greene's team stayed to the side of the corridor, and simply waited until the Gomers passed them by moving towards Deacon and his men. Then they fired, killing each of the Gomers that had just passed their positions. This gunfire brought Deacon and his men running back forward, and it was decided that they could holler at one another, and that they would stay "the hell off that damn radio." Moving forward along the corridor, they came to a series of hatches that were like the holes on Tierra del Fuego. Perfectly rounded, with no apparent way of opening them, General Greene just shrugged at Deacon. Deploying on both sides of the hatches, one of the operators stepped back around to the side and, on order, keyed his microphone. His transmission was brief, but wonderfully stated, "BITE ME, GOMERS!"

Within seconds, the hatches sprung open, and 10 Crab Gomers poured through heading in the direction of the waiting operator. The resulting gun fire was brief but quite effective, as the Gomers were all shot from behind at point blank range with slug and .00 buck rounds from a half dozen shotguns. Moving on through the hatches, the team found itself in what had to be the control room. As they looked around the cavernous room, several

Gomers were seated and already connected to the ship, just as they had been when General Greene had gone through the wreckage of the large Gomer Carrier ships in West Virginia, and then later in Georgia near the SRS. Taking them as they found them, the team unleashed a fusillade of shotgun blasts and some automatic weapons fire, to eliminate any and every Gomer they could find. Taking a chance, General Greene, after positioning men at the hatches into the room, sent the code words back to General Patrick and the rest of the Allied Staff. "Now WE own the night!"

No sooner than the message went out than the corridors outside the control room were becoming flooded with Gomers of both the meaty and Crab types. This time there was no choice but to fire at the onslaught as they approached the control room. Taking turns at the hatches, the team kept up a steady stream of firing, as Gomer after Gomer folded up and fell to the deck. As the team was running dangerously low on ammunition, the radio in General Greene's ears crackled with the message that their 'back up' was on the way. The follow-up team was dropped shortly after General Greene's team had first blown their way into the ship, and that second team was now dropping in through another hole blown not far from their original entry point. As they came at the Gomer hordes from behind, the second team was able to eliminate the threat that was attempting to breach the control room. As the third team of special operators entered the ship, they began to move aft, systematically finding and killing every Gomer they could find. It took almost a full day and a half to completely clear the Mountain ship but, when it was over, the Allied Forces would have a treasure trove of alien technology in their possession. This would be extremely vital if or, as many of us believed, WHEN the Gomers ever decided to come back and try it again.

Onboard the USS Missouri near Tierra del Fuego:

The entire staff was electrified the moment they received General Greene's message, "Now WE own the night!" General Whitney even busted the hell out of himself on a "knee knocker" trying to get from the Communications Center to the Combat Information Center where I was monitoring the operations on the beach. When he limped through the door, he was completely crestfallen to know that I had heard the message as it was coming into the ship. As I sat in my seat, I could not help but grin as he was bent over rubbing both his shin and the ankle that had been busted since the Diamond Head attack. "Whit, what happened?"

"These damned knee knockers! Sir, I will be glad when we can get a real headquarters with doors for once. I just got off the crutches, too!"

"Oh, I don't know, this old girl is kind of growing on me."

"Easy for you to say, but with all due respect, General, when is the last time you had to run down the damn hallway?"

"Whit, you're on board a ship, it is a companionway here, not a hallway."

"I keep forgetting you were raised as a baby squid." With that last remark a young Chief Petty Officer turned and leveled

General Whitney with the most wonderful "stink eye" I had ever seen. I even say this after raising two daughters who had mastered the dirty look, just like their Mom, but none of them could hold a candle to this kid. Knowing he had been affronted, I told Whit that "I can only assume you meant that as a term of endearment, otherwise I'll have to have you keel hauled. I can do that, you know...."

"Okay, it was a loving term of endearment." Then he turned to the young Chief, and said, "Seriously, Chief, my uncle was Navy too, and we used to pick at each other all the time, I'm truly sorry if you were offended." The Chief looked at the General and cracked a huge smile, as he said, "That's okay, Sir, my Dad was a Ranger, and he used to pick at me the same way!"

I knew from this kind of banter between the Chief and General Whitney that we had finally won the game, at least for the present. For months, there had been little humor among my staff, and there was very little tolerance for anyone not focused solely on trying to kill Gomers. We had finally reached a point where we could start to breathe again, and maybe even think a little about the future. All that was left for us now was to ferret the last of the Gomers from their holes, and then we could hopefully be done with the whole mess. I was especially pleased that we didn't have to unleash our last trick from Vandenberg, since it would have been horrific for all involved. I was also pleased that we could save some of our punch until we might really need it, should the Gomers return.

It had taken right at seven months since their initial invasion until we were about to finally drive them off our world. As the ground reports continued to pour into the Combat Information Center, it was obvious that the Gomers knew they were beaten. Their supply of meaty Gomers was almost gone, and their dusty variety of Gomer was definitely a thing of the past. Now we were going from hole to hole, individually blasting the Crab Gomers into oblivion. Everyone, from me down to the private in the field, knew that it was only a short matter of time before this thing was going to be over, and the world could return to what we seem to think was a normal existence. I, for one, would be damn glad to see it, although I will promise you, my idea of the definition of normal would be changed forever.

In the meantime, we still had the more immediate job to handle, and it wasn't exactly going to be easy. I contacted General Davis to advise him of our "discovery" near the Amundsen- Scott research facilities in Antarctica and told him that I was going to be moving some of my strategic reserves to him. At first, he was thrilled, until I told him that I needed to relocate some of his forces to provide security for our find. While not happy, he understood, and my headquarters issued the warning orders for the XVIII Airborne Corps., along with their 13th and 17th Airborne Divisions, to be re-deployed southward. We also had to pull the rest of II Corps., minus the 4th Armored Division, from the First Army, to act as their replacements. We chose the II Corps. since the 101st Airborne was already operating in Theater.

Naturally, this required a huge reshuffle of forces, and General Clark would not be sleeping for days, especially since he had to find and equip these forces with gear that would allow them to survive on the ice for the next several months. Fortunately, it was going to be summer down there, but then again, summer can be a relative term in that part of the world. While we were jumping through hoops to protect our captured Gomer prize, Dr. Abramson and Dr. Clarkson were also scrambling to gather several scientific teams to get south as quickly as possible. There was no doubt that this was a colossal boon in technology and in giving them a better understanding of the Gomer. As a result, their efforts would soon be of more importance than anything my forces would be doing.

There were only two loose ends that really troubled me as we wound up operations. The first was that we had only encountered three of the Gomers' colossal Mountain ships, and the Gomers always seemed to do things in fours. The other was what had that monster by the Moon been doing all that time? Our observers at this point could only guess, since we did not have anything in place that could tell us with certainty. Yep, these things troubled me, and it would only be a matter of time before one of them would jump up at me.

Chapter XX.

It would take another 10 days before we felt relatively confident that the Gomers had been eliminated from Tierra del Fuego. We could not be completely sure since the amount of prepared Gomer positions was extensive, but there had been no Gomer activity, and we hadn't taken a single casualty in a little over a week. We felt we could start heading home, and I so advised the President. On his orders, we left the II Corps headquarters along with its two divisions in Tierra del Fuego, and one Regimental Combat Team on the Isle de los Estados. We also began a rotational deployment system for Antarctica, wherein we would rotate a light division, also under the II Corps, every three months in and out of the continent. A naval force was also being maintained in either the Southern Pacific or Southern Atlantic areas, consisting now of at least one battleship and one aircraft carrier battle group on station somewhere nearby. Their mission was simple, they were to respond to whatever threat, be it Gomer or man, should the need arise. It was hoped that once the scientists were done, we could withdraw these forces too, and the war would finally be over completely.

Now with thoughts of home, the remaining forces were headed back northward. Lieutenant Raymond J. Kowalski was given his Congressional Medal of Honor, along with a young Marine Captain, Randall Lee, for his actions at Fort Pulaski in Georgia; Command Sergeant Major Clagmore was also given one for his defense of the Division Headquarters near Lago Pagano. General Gregg received this honor, but his was posthumous, for his actions in Virginia near the James River line. There were other heroes of the Gomer wars. Some, like General Daniel Greene, could not be acknowledged in public, but his Medal of Honor was no less earned than anyone else. He was promoted to Major General and initially given command of the II Corps, as part of the first rotation of forces in the area. I figured it was his baby lying there in the ice, so he and his new deputy, now Brigadier General, Deacon Jones could see it through to completion. There is no doubt they would be upset if we made them go home, so much so that, when time for his first rotation ended, General Greene insisted that he be allowed to stay just a little longer. So much longer, that he was to remain in command until we finally withdrew the II Corps almost another six months later.

Admiral Lynch, General Whitney, and General Sir William Fuller, all received the Distinguished Service Medal for their services, and each was promoted accordingly. Admiral Lynch was delighted because he was made the first Battleship Division or "BatDiv" commander that the Navy had seen in years. It was in his hands to develop and promote the tactics to be employed by our current battleships, while remaining as my Allied Naval Commander, so his plate was full. There was even a movement afoot in congress to drag the plans for the aborted Montana Class Battleship back into existence with a few twists for the future. Along with Admiral Lynch, I supported this move, as did the President. There was no question in my mind that the Big Gun Navy needed to exist, and it needed to have as many tools available to it as possible to counter any threat, whether it is earth-based or not.

General Sir William Fuller would return to the UK a hero, and it was well deserved. His actions during the campaign with my Allied Command were beyond superlative. There were several instances where, at risk to himself, he would move forward to rally forces as they were being attacked. Within a few days of his return to London, he would assume the rank of Field Marshall in command of all the forces in the UK. This was no small challenge, since it would be all on him to lead his forces through their own rebuilding and reorganization. It was also thanks to his efforts that we were going to be allowing the UK units to assist us in the security of Antarctica, and in the retrieval of Gomer technology that was scattered throughout that region.

General "Whit" Whitney would remain as my Chief of Staff, after he turned down his chance to replace General Jerry Larkin as Chief of Staff of the Army. His reasoning is simple, he was madly in love for the first time in his adult life. In one of those weird twists of fate, it was not long after our return that he married Brigadier General Lou Ann Miller, who had been the G-1 for me when I was CSA. General Larkin and his wife Maggie remained at the new Pentagon, where he was to continue his service as the CSA, at least until more bad things happened. I was especially pleased with two of his decisions since he confirmed what I had started in the re-organization phase early in the war. He maintained the original World War II scheme of manning and unit structure, which as we'll see, was damned important for our future survival. His legacy is that he gave the Regiments more size in strength than we could before, but the numbers and types of units were fortunately maintained in the first "Gomer War" structure.

The other was the simple call about uniforms. Realizing how hard it was to get the camouflage patterns and how useless they all really were. Once things began to happen, General Larkin maintained my policy of using Khaki for the field and service uniforms. He did hang on to the dress blues, but that was all they were, dress uniforms. Like me, he thought that the Department of Defense was wasting time, money, and resources when, at one point before the war, they had a total of eleven different patterns of camouflage. There would be other wars and more visitors, but our unit structures and uniforms would all remain as our joint legacy throughout.

President Martin Blanchard was finally elected to the office in an overwhelming landslide. His concerns before the war, his efforts to move the government and activate the COG or continuity of government plan, were a major part of his popularity. Thanks to him, millions of Americans were saved and assisted back to their feet. The economy was starting to bloom, even better than before when the Gomers first invaded, and his handling of the Russians was met with overwhelming support from the population. His skill in office was exceptional, both at home and abroad. Perhaps his greatest skill was his ability to manage much of the worlds' issues with great compassion and with just the right touch of firmness when it was required. From my perspective as the Allied Commander and nominal Chairman of the Joint Chiefs of Staff, he was the perfect President. Even though he had held the position of chairman himself on the first day of the war, he did nothing to undermine my decisions or question my abilities. This remained true even in the face of what was to come.

On the diplomatic front, our Secretary of State did an excellent job of keeping some of our former "friends" at bay when it came to their moving back into either Tierra del Fuego or into their positions in Antarctica. In fact, Secretary Case was so successful in his efforts that the Russians and the Chinese remained away from the continent of Antarctica for years after this and after other wars were concluded. As for the Argentineans and Chileans, they maintained forces in their respective countries that share the archipelago, Tierra del Fuego, but they refrained from allowing their civilian populations back, instead maintaining the areas as "nature" preserves that were limited to scientific studies and military exercises. As a result, many of the II Corps soldiers were bored with no night life to share with anyone. Still, they remained alert, based on nothing else than the "Gomer Ghost" stories that spread through the ranks.

The Gomer Ghosts were becoming a pervasive story among the troops and were becoming a concern to General Larkin's Army staff as he tried to rotate soldiers through the short assignments process. The story was simple, late at night and only in the dark, the ghosts of the dead Crab Gomers would emerge from the ground and skitter around until they jumped into another hole. These stories led to an active patrol system, and numerous visits and minor "training" events to individual holes throughout the archipelago. Over the next year, this story would lead to almost 250 "hole clearing" exercises, and not once was any type of Gomer found or uncovered.

On my return to Washington, D.C., I found it re-occupied by the government and in the process of being rebuilt. When I stepped off the plane at Reagan National, I was greeted by my bride, the president, and several new foreign ambassadors that

411

were now finding their way back into the city. It was quite the celebration, but it meant little to me since what I really wanted was to be back in my wife's arms and away from all the publicity. I personally always felt that most of the media was only a half step above a Gomer for being a drain on society, but I did my best to tolerate my newfound celebrity status. Leah even joked that I had better be careful; otherwise, I might find myself on the cover of the National Enquirer, trying to take a whiz! Officially, I was placed in the now far more nominal position of Chairman of the Joint Chiefs of Staff, and I retained both the fifth star and my Supreme Allied Commander title. The thing that made me the proudest was that I was perhaps the only Reserve Office in US History to ever be considered for, much less hold, such a position. Needless to say, the press would not leave me alone, at least until they had other far bigger concerns arising a few years later.

It is at this point I have a small confession to make. I purposefully used the Supreme Allied Commander title as my excuse for getting the hell out of the city of Washington, D.C. Given my personal loathing for all things political, I knew that if I stayed, it would lead to my saying something that wasn't going to be received well by the political class. In short, I escaped! The new Pentagon was still in business in the Mountains and so, in part, was the underground complex known as new Washington. We originally left new Washington open for the use of the Government, just in case the Gomers returned, but we finally took over a lot of the official facilities as their office holders moved out and newer facilities were constructed elsewhere. One thing was sure, we knew that if something like the battleship or mountain class Gomer ships were to ever fire on some of these older facilities, then fighting back would become a moot point. Fortunately, we knew this, and newer deeper facilities were in the offing.

After a year, we had built, or in some cases rebuilt, an excellent place to raise a family and to coordinate the military's global rebuilding around the "old" new Washington. We expanded portions of the facility to accommodate more families and those units that were assigned full time to my command. My new headquarters was now in what used to be the underground war room for the President, and we maintained a thriving community both above and below ground in the mountains. Meanwhile, that new facility for the government was finally under construction in another undisclosed location. Face it; while the Gomers weren't here now, most of us knew they were coming back sooner or later.

Our personal quarter's situation was also something we had to deal with, whether we wanted to do it or not. We took over what had been the underground 'white house' as our living quarters, but every stick of furniture and our other personal items were still in the house near Columbia, South Carolina. While residual radiation was deemed not harmful from the SRS battleground close by, it was still a consideration when we were deciding if or when we would return home. In fact, we delayed our trip as long as possible, but we finally decided, after much soul searching, that it might be nice to retrieve our family's past treasures. I will freely admit that this trip home wasn't easy. We got my mother and the rest of the family, and headed south for a visit to pack up our household goods for shipment to new Washington, or as it is now called, Supreme Allied Headquarters.

I will always remember coming back into the old house, all those months after we had to beat our hasty retreat, after I shot the 'dusty' Gomer. It was eerie to come back into the house and discover the pile of dust and portions of 'dusty' Gomer that were still sitting in front of my file cabinets. It was also sad to see where some of the roving looters or perhaps the local refugees had helped themselves to some of our stuff. I guess when we left, neither Leah nor I really worried too much about locking the back door. Thanks to the scavengers, we did not have quite as much to pack, but we did manage to save more than we thought. We were all thankful that our extensive collection of books was largely undisturbed, since apparently neither the looters nor the refugees, were too concerned about reading. As we were identifying things for the packers, we were assisted in the process by my Aide, Major Cho. I have to say, he was invaluable in helping not only Leah and myself, but the rest of the family, as they all gathered their remaining personal items for our exodus back to the mountain.

Once we got settled and the pain of the move was completed, the mountain was becoming a real home. We were settled with the whole family in the same structure and we even had room left over for our frequent guests, like General Larkin, and Maggie. Christine, John, and Michael were all settled into their new home, and she continued to work as my 'gate keeper' and Senior Administrative Assistant. John was still in the lab, working with Dr. Clarkson in unleashing the mysteries we were discovering in the Gomer Technology coming back from Antarctica. Holly was settling in and finishing her education. By working with Dr. Abramson and his staff, she was learning more than if she were in a regular graduate school program. Always quite the science lover, Holly took to this lifestyle like a duck to water. My son, Robbie, also finally came home, and after a long leave, he went to several training schools we'd set up, to include a new Airborne School. After his training was finally completed, he was going to be sent to the 11th Airborne Division, where he would probably incur the ire of an old, grizzled Sergeant Major, who always thought that Lieutenants were useless. Honestly, the only thing that will probably save Robbie is that he came up from the ranks like me. Although, I remember CSM Clagmore would often opine, "L-T, with all due respect, you should have stayed a specialist! At least then you knew what you were doing." Before he left on his orders, I advised Robbie, "Don't do anything to piss him off, he knows what he is doing, and he is probably the meanest bastard on the planet!"

In the meantime, we were becoming quite settled in, and there were a lot of days where the highpoint would be playing with my grandson, Michael. The task of monitoring our scientific finds, incorporating new technology, and watching into space, made our allied headquarters a busy place. In fact, it would be here, almost two years to the day after their initial invasion, that I would learn of what, I sincerely but vainly hoped, would be the last chapter of this Gomer War saga.

Amundsen-Scott Station, Antarctica:

Dr. Clarkson had just returned from the Gomer site and was taking inventory of their latest finds and items removed from the hulk of the massive Gomer mountain class ship. He was especially pleased since there was darn little left that had not been removed and sent back to the United States. They were down now to removal of things that almost resembled toilet fixtures, and there was nothing left of the weapons systems that were now being reversed engineered or the navigational systems. Dr. Abramson had those latter devices and had already been working on the "backtrack" computations to determine exactly which solar system held the Gomer home planet. As Dr. Clarkson was going through the latest items, he felt a rumble off to the east of him. It felt almost like another earthquake, but there was a different, more ominous, feeling to it that made him very uncomfortable.

Troops providing the defense of the area were being rolled from their shelters by this latest rumble, and it was clear that there was something massive that was moving below the earth, ice, and snow. Yes, earthquakes were increasing here of late, but this was the largest one yet. The division commander immediately contacted II Corps to let them know that they were having another tumbler, and this one was literally shaking their fillings loose. In response, the Corps Commander put his men throughout II Corps on alert.

In a very short time, the Corps Command Post was getting a ton of "Gomer Ghost" reports, and the headquarters for the Regimental Combat Team was inundated with reports of Gomers headed past their positions to the southern tip of the Isle de los Estados. Grasping the significance of both reports immediately, the Corps Commander was on the ELF to my headquarters within seconds of his realization.

When I was summoned from my quarters, the events had taken a very odd course. Our fleet units were on the Pacific side of Tierra de Fuego, which was a lousy position for what might be coming. I advised them to become a hole in the water, follow standard tactics, and report back once in contact. I then told General Greene, who was now in charge of all Special Operators and of the forces still in the area, to have all his people get small in their holes. "I have a feeling something big is coming their way and the fleet can't stop it." Looking at the position of our available submarines in the area, they, too, seemed to be out of position for a kill shot, and from a quick check with Admiral Lynch, it was obvious that we might be able to track it, but not nail it like we had before. I told him to standby, and I contacted the President to give him an update on what was happening. Once we got past the update and movements, and discussed the alert required for the civilian population, I asked him the "$64,000.00 question".

"Mr. President, the Gomers moving to the southern end of the island are not engaging any of our forces. They are hell bent to get to the tip of the island, and I am telling you, this is an extraction operation. Do we let them go or do I use the really big stuff to try and stop them?"

"What do you recommend, General?"

"Sir, if we hit them, we can kill them. My only problem is that we have both our troops exposed and our scientific personnel still engaged in operations in Antarctica. If we hit the Gomers with what we have available then, while I can guarantee we can kill the Gomers, we stand a high likelihood of taking a bunch of our key people with them. Knowing this, I would also point out that if we let this last mountain ship escape, it just might go back to Gomerville, and tell the bastards that attacking us maybe isn't such a good idea."

"Yeah, but they might escape and tell the Gomer home planet about what it takes to kill us, too."

"Yes, sir, that is the risk, but I think they already have the answer to that question, and we've still kicked them in the ass all along. We've also discovered that they lost a little of their aggressiveness as they went along and the harder we hit 'em, the less fight we got back. So, I would prefer not to lose any more of our men, and especially the key scientific personnel, if I can help it."

"Okay, General. Keep them in your sights and if that bastard so much as twitches in any direction but to the tip of that island, and then the hell off into space, I want it brought down."

"Yes, sir, sounds like a plan, and I'll alert Vandenberg, AFB, just in case."

Getting back to General Greene, I passed on the order from the President, and told him to advise the Regimental Combat Team, to "stay low and let 'em go". Then I contacted General Randall McDaniel at Vandenberg.

"Randy, Patrick here."

"Yes, sir."

"We have a mountain ship that is going to be coming up from the ice and we believe is headed to the tip of Isle de los Estados. We think he is trying to extract survivors from that location. The President has authorized implementation of the final phase of Project Sky Hook, but I want to emphasize that this is ONLY to happen if the mountain ship moves in any direction except off-world."

"So, let me get this straight, if it does anything after picking up the Gomers but leaves, I'm to whack the bloody piss out of it?"

"That is correct!"

"Roger that! We will monitor and deal with it if necessary."

"Thanks, General McDaniel, I'll call you later when we're done."

With that, I hung up from Vandenberg and returned to my own monitoring of the situation. The entire extraction did not take very long for the Gomers, since they just didn't have that many Gomers left to retrieve. As the massive mountain class ship came over the Isle de los Estados, our troops sat in stunned silence as the enormous monster sent three smaller fighter type ships down to a point at the far end of the island. Within about three minutes, these smaller fighter ships returned to their massive home and the mountain ship turned almost due south. As it completed the turn, it almost seemed to waggle itself at our troops who were also on the island. Then with a short movement forward, it left the earth at a horrific rate of speed. It would be that final waggle side to side that many observers would hold onto as a sign of hope. I had a chance to observe the film footage with General Greene and we were both convinced that the Gomers were telling us that at least for now, "We give up." As we would learn as a painful lesson, that did not mean they were done, it just meant they were done *for now*. The only time the Gomers slowed at all in their departure from earth was as they passed through the debris field of their 'moon' ship and the surrounding 'mine field,' which General McDaniel did not need to detonate.

Man tends to be optimistic in life, but as a soldier, you learn that, while optimism is a fine thing, when it comes to planning, the sound practice is to err on the side of pessimism. We took what we learned from the Gomers, and their weapons, and are even now making sure that if they do come back, it will be a war we can hopefully win. Then again, we have felt that way before, and yet we still had wars. Ask anyone who remembers their history about World War I and the War to End All Wars. This one, as it turns out, was to be no different...

Appendix I
ALLIED NAVAL FORCES
(Admiral Thadeaus Morton)
PACIFIC FLEET

3rd Fleet, Battle Groups
Adm. Morton

7th Fleet, Battle Groups
Adm. Lynch

TF-31
Vice Adm. Pollard
BB USS Iowa+
CG USS Mobile Bay
DDG USS Howard
     USS Fitzgerald

TF-71
Vice Adm. Becker

BB USS Missouri*
CG USS Antietam
DDG USS McCampbell
     USS Stethem

TF-74
Vice Adm. McIntosh

CVN USS Kitty Hawk

CA Almirante Grau (Peru
vian Navy - Gun Cruiser)+
LHD USS Boxer
     USS Makin Island
CG USS Princeton
     USS Chosin
     USS Valley Forge
DDG USS Russell
     USS Benfold
     USS Cushing
     USS O'Brien

TF-38
Vice Adm. Mounts

CVN USS Nimitz
CG   USS Shiloh
USS Port Royal
DDG USS Shoup
USS Hopper
USS Higgins

TF-78
Vice Adm. Klein
CVN USS John C. Stennis
CG USS Lake Erie
     USS Vincennes
DDG USS John Paul Jones
     USS Decatur
     USS O'Kane

ATTACK SUBMARINES ASSIGNED TO THE PACIFIC FLEET:

SSN 688 Los Angeles
SSN 698 Bremerton
SSN 701 La Jolla
SSN 705 City of Corpus Christi
SSN 707 Portsmouth
SSN 711 San Francisco
SSN 713 Houston
SSN 715 Buffalo
SSN 716 Salt Lake City
SSN 717 Olympia
SSN 718 Honolulu
SSN 721 Chicago
SSN 722 Key West
SSN 724 Louisville
SSN 725 Helena
SSN 752 Pasadena
SSN 754 Topeka
SSN 758 Asheville
SSN 759 Jefferson City
SSN 762 Columbus
SSN 763 Santa Fe
SSN 770 Tucson
SSN 771 Columbia*
SSN 772 Greeneville
SSN 773 Cheyenne

*Indicates Flagship(s) for the Supreme Allied Command during the Final Polar Offensive of the Gomer War.

+Indicates ships lost in combat with the Gomers during the Final Polar Offensive of the Gomer War.

ATLANTIC FLEET
(Admiral Eric Showalter)

2nd Fleet Battle Groups, (TF-20)
Adm. Fraser

4th Fleet Battle Groups
Adm. Macklin

TF - 20
Vice Adm. Harper

BB   USS New Jersey
CG   USS San Jacinto
      USS Vicksburg
DDG USS Oscar Austin
      USS Stout

TF-40
Vice Adm. Thomasville

BB USS Wisconsin
CG USS Monterey
      USS Cape St. George
DDG USS Winston Churchill
      USS Mitscher

TF-45
Vice Adm. Williamson

LHD USS Wasp
      USS Bataan
      USS Iwo Jima
(6th Army, XXIV Corps)
CG   USS Gettysburg
      USS Vella Gulf
      USS Thomas S. Gates
DDG USS Bulkeley
      USS Laboon
      USS The Sullivans
      USS Porter
      USS Thorn

TF-27
Vice Adm. Bucklen
CVN USS Truman
CG   USS Hue City
      USS Ticonderoga
DDG USS Arleigh Burke
      USS Ramage
      USS Ross
      USS Spruance

TF-47
Vice Adm. Ellis

CVN USS Theodore Roosevelt
CG   USS Anzio
      USS Yorktown
DDG USS Barry
      USS Carney
      USS Mahan
      USS Briscoe
      USS O'Bannon

ATTACK SUBMARINES ASSIGNED TO THE ATLANTIC FLEET:

SSN 690 Philadelphia
SSN 699 Jacksonville
SSN 700 Dallas
SSN 706 Albuquerque
SSN 708 Minneapolis-Saint Paul
SSN 709 Hyman G. Rickover
SSN 710 Augusta
SSN 714 Norfolk
SSN 719 Providence
SSN 720 Pittsburgh
SSN 723 Oklahoma City
SSN 750 Newport News
SSN 751 San Juan
SSN 753 Albany
SSN 755 Miami
SSN 756 Scranton
SSN 757 Alexandria
SSN 760 Annapolis
SSN 761 Springfield
SSN 764 Boise
SSN 765 Montpelier
SSN 766 Charlotte
SSN 767 Hampton
SSN 768 Hartford

SSN 769 Toledo

ALLIED GROUND FORCES

6th Army - Lieutenant General Richard Davis

    III Amphibious Corps. - Major General Drew Sullivan, USMC

        1st Marine Division
        2nd Marine Division
        15th Marine Expeditionary Unit (MEU)

    XIVth Corps. - Major General Alvin Hendricks

        2nd Cavalry Division
        2nd Armored Division
        25th Infantry Division

    XVIII Airborne Corps. - Major General Gerald Elliot/ Major General James Sturdivant

        11th Airborne Division (Later attached to III Amphibious
Corps.)
        13th Airborne Division
        17th Airborne Division

    XXIV Corps. - Major General Sean Gregory

        1st Cavalry Division
        24th Infantry Division
        7th Infantry Division

ALLIED AIR FORCES

First Air Force	Lieutenant General L. L. West
Second Air Force	Lieutenant General C. Knapp
Eighth Air Force	Lieutenant General T. J. Lilly
Tenth Air Force	Lieutenant General H. Alexander
Eleventh Air Force	Lieutenant General C. C. Nowak
Twelfth Air Force	Lieutenant General R. Sumner
Eighteenth Air Force	Lieutenant General R. S. Young
United States Air Forces Southern Command	Lieutenant General F. R. Casner

STRATEGIC RESERVES

FIRST ARMY - Lieutenant General Stephen Richardson

    I Corps. - Major General Manuel "Manny" Ortiz

        4th Infantry Division
        7th Infantry Division
        3rd Armored Division

    II Corps. - Major General Daniel Mickelson

        5th Infantry Division
        101st Airborne Division
        36th Infantry Division
        4th Armored Division

    X Corps. - Major General Donald Thompson

        28th Infantry Division
        29th Infantry Division
        5th Armored Division

Naval Forces: (Adm. Charles Steadman)

Atlantic:	SSBN	USS West Virginia
		USS Louisiana
		USS Florida
		USS Georgia
Pacific:	SSBN	USS Pennsylvania
		USS Kentucky
		USS Ohio
		USS Michigan
10th Fleet		
	SSN	USS Virginia
		USS Texas
		USS Hawaii
		USS North Carolina

Air Forces: (General Quentin J. Thayer, Jr.)

    14th Air Force, Vandenberg, CA, General Randolph McDaniel

Appendix II
NATIONAL COMMAND AUTHORITY

President Martin "Marty" Blanchard
    National Science Advisors: Dr. Anthony Abramson and
                                       Dr. Walter J. Clarkson

Secretary of State Timothy Case
Secretary of Defense Richard Todd

SUPREME ALLIED COMMAND

Commander: General of the Army, Michael "Mighty Mouse" Patrick, USA

Aides: Lieutenant Colonel Paul Simmons, USA, (KIA); Captain Lawrence Wilkerson, USA, (KIA); Commander Randy Bowen, USN; Major David Cho, USA,

Chief of the Allied Staff: Lieutenant General Edward "Whit" Whitney, USA

Chief of Allied Air Ops: Lieutenant General Anthony Stephenson, USAF

Chief of Allied Ground Ops: General Sir William Fuller, UK, Army

Chief of Naval Ops;   Admiral Stefan Lindemann, German Navy (KIA)
                         Rear Admiral Carl Lynch, USN, Interim
                         Admiral Thadeaus Morton, USN (KIA)
                         Vice Admiral Carl Lynch, USN

Chief of Allied Intelligence: General Pavel Zhukov, Russian Army (MIA/KIA)
                         General David Campbell, AUS Army

Chief of Pacific Planning: Admiral Zao Chan, PLAN, China (KIA)

Chief of Allied Spec. Ops: Brigadier General Daniel Greene, Jr., USA

Peru Liaison Officer: Captain Pablo Martinez Escobar, Peruvian Navy (KIA)

Argentina Liaison Officer: Colonel Manuel Koffman, Army

Chile Liaison Officer: General Jorge Pizarro, Air Force

China Liaison Officer: Captain Li Dejiang, PLAN, China

Russian Liaison Officer: Colonel Vladimir Karnaukhov

Appendix III

JOINT CHIEFS OF STAFF*

CHAIRMAN: General John H. J. Bozeman, USAF (replaced for illness)**
Admiral Thadeaus Morton, USN (assumed allied position)(KIA)
General Gerald "Jerry" Larkin, USA, Interim
General of the Army, Michael Patrick, USA
Vice Chairman: General William C. Mahan, USAF

ARMY: General Michael "Mike" "Mighty Mouse" Patrick, USAR
(assumed Supreme Allied Command)
General Gerald "Jerry" "Green Giant" Larkin, USA
General David Hampton, USA, Interim
General Gerald "Jerry" "Green Giant" Larkin, USA

NAVY: Admiral Thadeaus Morton, USN, (assumed Chairman
position)(KIA)
Admiral Charles "Chuck" Steadman, USN

AIR FORCE: General John H. J. Bozeman, USAF (replaced for illness)**
General Quentin Thayer, USAF

MARINE Corps: General Albert C. Durham, USMC

*   The List includes only those personnel who accepted or were appointed to the positions after the initial attack of the invaders, and until the conclusion of the War. For many of those listed, their prior grades were significantly different, and in some cases, ranks were at the senior field grade levels at the time of the initial onslaught. The only Flag or General Officers at the time of the attack were, General Bozeman (GEN), General Patrick (LTG), General Larkin (MG), Admiral Morton (R. Adm.); General Mahan, (BG); Admiral Steadman (R. Adm. Lower Half). The remaining officers were either Captain (USN), or Colonels, at the time of the attack. All prior senior leadership had been either killed or were missing.

**   Served in the Chairman position while also serving as the Chief of Staff for the Air Force; however, this service was only during the period from the initial attack and early campaigns in the eastern United States. Prior to assuming the position, General Bozeman served as the Commander of NORAD. (At the time he relinquished the Chairman position and Chief of Staff positions, General Bozeman was suffering from severe fatigue and other health issues.)

Appendix IV
UNITED STATES ARMY COMMAND
STAFF DURING THE INITIAL EASTERN US CAMPAIGNS*

Army Chief of Staff: General Michael Patrick, USA (DSC, DSM, SS, PH)
    Aide: Major Daniel Greene, Jr. (promoted to Spec. Ops.
    Ofcr.)(MOH)
    Captain Paul Simmons, (KIA as a LTC) (SS and PH)

    Special Warfare/Project Officer: Colonel Daniel Greene, Jr. (MOH)

Vice Chief of Staff: General Gerald Larkin, USA (DSM)

Director of the Staff: Major General Hank Carter (interim) (DSM, LOM)
    Lieutenant General Richard Davis (left to assume
    command of Sixth Army) (DSC, DSM)
    General Gerald Larkin, USA, (acting in absence of
    LTG Davis)

G-1   Lieutenant General Gregg (Moved to R&D) (KIA) (MOH)
    Brigadier General Miller   (DMSM, MSM, ARCOM)

G-2   Brigadier General Whitney (DSC, DSM, SS, and PH)

G-3   Colonel Rhymes (Assumed Command of the 11th Airborne) (KIA)
(SS)
    Lieutenant General Davis (acting G-3 for initial planning phases)
    Brigadier General Roberts

G-4   Major General Clark (DSC, DSM, SS, LOM)

G-5   Vacant - functions by G-3 staff, coordinated by Generals Patrick and
Larkin
G-6   Vacant - functions by G-1 staff
G-7   Vacant - functions by G-2 staff
G-8   Vacant - functions by G-3 staff

G-9   Major General Hank Carter (DSM, LOM)

SMA   Vacant - Sergeant Major of the Army Marvin Laird (selected during the
    campaigns) (LOM, DMSM)

*   Staffing and strength were so severely depleted at all levels, that many normal staff functions were performed by the senior surviving leaders, to include the Chief of Staff of the Army or CSA. After the Eastern Campaigns, most of

the Staff was rounded out, and experienced personnel were advanced or returned to key positions. After the final battle of SRS, the new staff was put into place concurrent with the departure of General Patrick for the Allied Command position.